FEAR

A Ball & Chain Thriller

Book 2

By
John W. Mefford

FEAR

V1.0

This is a work of fiction. The events and characters described herein are imaginary and are not intended to refer to specific places or living persons. The opinions expressed in this manuscript are solely the opinions of the author and do not represent the opinions or thoughts of the publisher. The author has represented and warranted full ownership and/or legal right to publish all the materials in this book.

Sugar Hill Publishing

ISBN: 978-1-090191-66-3

Interior book design by
Bob Houston eBook Formatting

To stay updated on John's latest releases, visit:
JohnWMefford.com

One

One week ago

Gunmetal gray skies gave way to the last bit of sunlight as the enraged man jerked the car to a stop a block away from the park.

Take a deep breath, and then exhale slowly.

He repeated the exercise three times.

It didn't work a damn bit. The side of his neck pulsated as though some type of beetle-like alien was trying to punch its way through his skin—it had freaked out his wife the first time she saw it. But she'd never seen him in this kind of condition. No one had.

He glanced in the rearview and caught the edge of his right eye. He turned the mirror for a quick inspection. He almost didn't recognize himself. Blue and green veins outlined every stress mark—and there were too many to count—but it was his eyes that stole his gaze. He saw in his eyes exactly what he was feeling.

Pure. Fucking. Hate.

He picked up the Glock 19 G5 9mm pistol and let the weight rock his arm up and down a couple of seconds.

He slid out of the car, quietly shut the door, turned up the collar on his barn coat, and walked into the park. He spotted an old sign: *Opportunity Park, Built 1966.*

Someone will be receiving the ultimate opportunity in a matter of minutes.

The twenty-acre park had it all. Lots of grass, although it was a dormant brown right now, playgrounds, areas of thickly wooded trees, and…

He spotted the cage. It was the backstop to the softball field. The very same field on which Tasha had played her last game. She was only thirteen years old at the time. He was nine. He recalled her final game—she had two hits, including the game-winning RBI in the bottom of the seventh inning. They exchanged high-fives and Mom took them out for ice cream.

Two days later, Tasha was dead.

Died from a drug overdose. A goddamn drug overdose. Some fucker, whom they'd never caught, sold her the coke in a park just like this one. She'd snuck out of the house and met an older high school friend who said they needed to have real fun that night. Turned out her so-called friend was connected to some thugs who sold drugs to kids on the southeast side of Dallas.

Kids.

The man knew he was about to right a wrong that was thirty years old. He had two kids of his own. He would do anything to protect them, even if they didn't know it.

He circled around the softball field and stopped near the edge of the playground.

"Come out, come out, wherever you are," he sang to himself as his eyes scanned the darkness.

He'd been tipped off by a like-minded online friend who had given Rashad the scoop: he'd seen a group of guys selling drugs to kids at the park around this time of night near the edge of the woods. Three punks who wore saggy pants and red bandanas. Tattoos on the side of their necks: two dice and the words "Black Jack" etched just above the image. Some type of drug-dealing symbol, he was certain. Sitting in front of his computer at home,

Rashad didn't waste another minute. He thanked his online buddy, grabbed his pistol out of the safe, and drove over here.

It was time to right a wrong.

A hand touched his shoulder. He swung around while he pulled out his Glock in one rapid motion.

He gasped out a breath. It was just some older guy with his dog.

"Yeah?"

"I…" The older guy raised his arms, yanking the leash on his little poodle, and stared at the gun.

"Sorry," he said, putting the gun back in his waistband. The man, who wore an overcoat and fedora, didn't lower his arms. In fact, he wasn't blinking.

"Yo," he said, snapping fingers. "I'm no banger. You just scared me."

The older guy continued to stare at him.

"Seriously, put your arms down. I just carry the gun to, uh, you know…"

"Protect yourself."

"Yeah, that's it."

"I get it." The man patted his coat. "I carry a semi-automatic myself."

"Really?"

"I'm just joking. No one pays us much attention. Right, Barney?" he said to his pooch.

He swung around, looking for any sign of the dealers. Was that something moving over by the tree line?

"Hey, sorry to bother you," the man said.

That's exactly what you're doing, he thought. He looked over his shoulder. "What can I do for you?"

"Well, I'm kind of new to the area, but my daughter tells me there's a Waffle House less than a mile from this park. Do you know—"

"Yep," he interrupted. He'd do anything to get rid of this guy. The fewer people around, the better. He turned and pointed toward the street at the end of the park. "Basically, just take Pine Street right here down about a half mile, then turn left. You'll see the Waffle House sign just beyond the car wash on the left side of the street."

He felt a prick in his arm. As he whipped around, he lost his balance, stumbled off to the right. He looked at the older guy—there were two of him. No, three of him. The older guy smiled. Or were his own eyes blurred? He tripped, moving a step toward the man. "What did you…?"

And then his head bounced off the ground.

* * *

He lifted his head two inches off the ground, then let it drop. "Fuck!" That was concrete. It was so dark, he couldn't see where he was.

He tried to move his arm to scratch his head, but it was restrained by something metal. Some type of wrist lock. Both wrists were bolted to the floor. His ankles too. His heart leaped into the back of his throat, and he screamed, "Where am I?"

His voice bounced around, but there was no response. Panic gripped his insides as his mind worked through the sludge. He recalled giving the older man directions, and then…

He heard some movement. "Someone there?"

No response. He held his breath, hoping to pick up a clue as to where the sound had originated and maybe who or what it was.

But he heard nothing more. He blinked a few times, trying to adjust to the darkness. There might have been a wall nearby. Other than that, it was a blank screen.

A thought hit him. The older guy at the park with the dog must have been a setup. Those fucking gangbangers had paid off the man to distract him, and then someone had snuck up on him and stuck him with a needle. Who knew what kind of shit was in that syringe? Once he got ahold of them, he would put a bullet in their heads. No questions asked. No apologies. Fucking dead!

A spotlight flipped on. It was so intense and hot that it felt as though the sun had been placed five feet from his face.

A second later, a figure appeared. He or she was covered in some type of head-to-toe outfit, wearing a welding screen. "Who are you?" He broke out in a sweat, but at the same time, a tremble shook him from the inside out.

A blowtorch snapped on. The person held the lit blowtorch against his little finger.

He yelped and screamed until his voice cracked.

Then the flame went away, and the light turned off.

Writhing in pain, he struggled to hear through his own whimpers. A minute went by. Or was it an hour?

Then he heard a slight chuckle. A man or a woman? He couldn't tell, but it was a laugh just the same.

A door shut.

All was quiet.

He waited.

And waited.

And waited.

Two

Present Day

Cooper

The knock on the apartment door wasn't just loud, it vibrated my rib cage. It was an insistent rapping. My first thought: not a welcome visitor.

Could it be the Sack Brothers?

My pulse ticked faster as I swiveled my head to the front of the apartment.

It was quiet for a moment, although I could feel a silent, onerous energy on the other side. I hadn't gotten back to Milo and Elan Sachen yet, and two weeks had passed since I was given *the directive*. They hadn't given me a specific date for showing them proof that I had set up an illegal point-shaving scheme, but they knew my track record: cut and run. A few more seconds ticked by without another knock. Maybe it was a service technician, and he'd just given up. My eyes diverted back to the blinking cursor on my laptop. I'd just spent another two hours researching the topic of my first story for *The Wire*, a new sports blog, and I had actually started the opening paragraph. The oddity of the exercise was that I'd yet to speak to the person I was profiling, a former

NBA first-round pick who'd reportedly blown through millions of dollars over his career. While I was eager to interview him and those within his universe, I could already envision how I was going to approach the lead. It had to be a serious hook, and I was in the middle of writing it.

Which is why that pulsating cursor carried beats of creative verve. My zest to unleash all the ideas that had been floating in my mind the last week made my mouth water. I was slightly anxious—I hadn't written a story since my untimely fall from grace almost seven months earlier—but also excited. The thrashings I'd endured recently, both physical and mental, were (hopefully) behind me. This keyboard was my turf, my sanctuary.

I closed my eyes and released an audible breath to find my mojo.

Two more loud bangs.

"Dammit!" I pushed up from the chair, accidentally knocking the rickety card table. I paused, put a hand on the table as though it were a pet. Didn't need my laptop crashing to the floor.

I yanked the door open. "Yes?"

A finger and a nose. That's all I saw at first.

"Do you have any idea what you've done to this street?"

I looked curiously at a man who was easily twenty years my senior. I was thirty-nine. I guessed he was one of Mrs. Kowalski's neighbors, the nice woman from whom I rented her second-floor garage apartment.

"I'm sorry?"

"You're sorry, that's for sure. You're just another one of those mooching ne'er-do-wells," he said, looking at me down the slope of his nose, his eyes nothing more than dark slits.

Ne'er-do-wells? I'd last heard that term in a black-and-white 1950s Humphrey Bogart movie. "I'm not really following you."

"Then pay attention, you hippie."

I raked my fingers through my hair—something I'd instinctively been doing ever since I let my hair grow out a bit. (My mom thought I looked like Bradley Cooper. Go figure. Classic Mom.) Truthfully, my long hair was only a repercussion of not having much money.

"Hippie. Ne'er-do-well. Is this your strange way of coming on to me? I'm not really into that. But I can recommend an upscale S&M place on—"

"I heard you were a smartass. Goes with the look. You're all the same," he said with the kind of disdain that might normally be directed at someone who'd committed a felony. Hold on—I'd committed a felony.

I crossed my arms, leaned against the door frame. I was growing tired of his antics and eager to jump back into creating the ultimate hook for my story. "Is there a reason you knocked on my door?"

He walked right past me and into my apartment. Momentarily stunned, I didn't try to stop the man who had decent quickness for his age.

"Can I help you with something?" I said, turning around.

"Just looking for drugs. I'm sure you're into that kind of thing. You going to show me, or am I going to have to take this place apart?"

I waited a beat. My mind was trying to process what this guy had just said. Yep, he was being a complete asshole. "This isn't your place. You need to leave."

He glanced over his shoulder, snickered, then opened my lone closet door and started riffling through my things.

"Hey, dude, have you heard of personal property?" I walked over, put my hand on the door, but he still ignored me. So, I put my hand on his shoulder.

"Assault! Assault!" He jumped back, holding his shoulder as if he'd just been pounded into the ground by a Cowboys defensive tackle.

"What the fuck, dude?"

"You assaulted me," he barked, growling like an injured bear.

Was he really going there? "What's your name?"

"Myron Little, former Marine."

"So, because I touched your shoulder, a former Marine is claiming I hurt him? Give me a frickin' break."

"Doesn't matter what you think, punk," he said pointing both his finger and his nose in my face. "Your car downstairs is a disgrace."

"The Converta-beast?"

"Say what?" he snarled.

That was the nickname my buddy Ben had given my "classic" LeBaron, which was nothing more than a classic piece of shit. You see, I can admit my faults.

"My LeBaron is a little old, but I recently got it running. And Mrs. Kowalski has no issues with me parking it in front of the garage."

"She's not the only one who lives in this neighborhood." He swung around to the closet. "Where do you keep your stash?"

"Stash?"

"Your drugs. I've smelled things coming from this lot that I haven't smelled since 'Nam."

This guy was like a watchdog. Sounds like he was on patrol when my buddy Ben had dropped by a couple of times.

"You fought in Vietnam?" I asked.

He flipped his head to look over his supposed injured shoulder. "Got a problem with that?"

"None." I held up my hands. Being a former—well, I guess, now current—investigative sports journalist, I was naturally curious by people and their stories. Everyone had one. Some had more than one.

A second later, shoes were being tossed at me like they were being shot out of a cannon. "Too much crap in there to find your stash," the nosy neighbor growled.

"Can you stop looking through my stuff?" I swerved left and right to avoid the onslaught of sneakers. I felt like a boxer dodging punches. I probably had twenty pairs in the closet, most of which were gifts from athletes or coaches I'd interviewed in the past.

He stood upright, rubbed his shoulder again.

"Myron, this mission of yours has come to an end. I need you to leave. I've got stuff to do." I extended my hand to the front door.

"Ha! I'll stop when I find your stash."

Could this guy get any more paranoid? I still didn't understand his obsession with me being the next El Chapo. I moved a step closer. Bad idea. He swung his elbow back, clocking my chin. Momentarily stunned, I stumbled, falling over an old chest that served as my coffee table.

Now he'd pissed me off. I jumped to my feet, took hold of his arm, and started to pull him toward the door.

"Get your hands off me you drug-dealing buttmunch."

"Myron, you need to update your insult vernacular."

He hurled about thirty more lame insults at me while taking five steps. After that fifth step, he jammed his foot against the wall and did some kind of backflip.

A clip of *Teenage Mutant Ninja Turtles* flashed across my mind. A second later, he chopped his hand down across my forearm, just above my cast. (Long story on how I broke my arm.) As nimble as Myron was, the chop carried the power of a…turtle.

"Get out, Myron!" I yelled.

He went in for another chop, this one aimed at my neck. I juked left, and he swiped nothing but air. Still determined, he grabbed an empty bottle of Orange Crush off the floor that had never made its way into the trash and swung his arm across my space. The bottle brushed the whiskers on my chin.

"That's it!" I grabbed both of his shoulders, and we wrestled for control.

"Hold up!" a woman shouted.

Myron and I swung our heads to the doorway.

"Hey, Courtney."

"Detective Bouchard," she said, flashing her badge.

"It's the fuzz," Myron said.

"The fuzz?" She gave me a quizzical look as Myron and I released our grips on each other.

"Arrest this drug-dealing buttmunch," Myron said, pointing a finger at me.

She looked at me again. I just shook my head.

Five minutes later, Courtney and I watched from my second-floor landing as a sulking Myron Little plodded his way home.

"Man, I really know how to make friends, don't I?"

She turned and looked inside my apartment, which I knew was a catastrophe. Organization wasn't one of my strong suits. But my eyes stayed on her raven black hair that had the shine of a seal's wet fur.

"So," she said, turning to meet my eye. "You ready to give this dating thing a try?"

My eyes didn't blink. I'd forgotten all about it.

Three

Willow

The first swing of the blade ripped through the sleeve of my scrubs.

"He cut you?" Stacy yelled from the hallway just outside exam room 3.

"Not yet."

Ollie Randolph circled me like a drunk lion. He'd exploded into a fit of rage the moment he came out of his latest addiction slumber to realize I wasn't his dealer and couldn't give him what he coveted more than anything in the world: another fix of heroin.

"Ollie, put the scalpel down," I said, my knees bent, rotating to meet him straight on while scanning the room out of the corner of my eye for a way to protect myself.

"Not until you give me my fucking heroin!"

Blood snaked down Ollie's cheek. He'd already cut himself just to prove he was willing to do anything, including all forms of manipulation, to get his next fix. It wasn't necessary. I'd already seen his desperation. From the first time I saw Kelly open the door to the Community Health Clinic exam room, Ollie was trembling as though he were trapped on a glacier. His eyes were glassy and splintered with red lines. Without any input on his situation, I knew he was starting the process of heroin withdrawal. A new batch of the vicious drug had hit the streets of Dallas in recent weeks, and the rate of deaths had skyrocketed. And not just from the opioid itself. According to a cop friend of mine, violent crimes, including murder, had also ticked upward.

When I'd tried to take the blade from his hand, he lost it and came after me. I was pretty nimble on my feet, but that would only get me so far. Ollie had me trapped inside this small exam room and outweighed me by at least a hundred pounds.

"Have you called the cops?" I called out to Kelly. Thankfully, in Ollie's world, Kelly didn't exist. He was singularly focused on me. Lucky me.

She held up her phone. "Called twice in the last minute. Someone's on the way." A second later, she disappeared. Had she gotten scared and run off to find Dr. Alvarez, or was she letting the cops in?

I was alone with this guy—that's all I knew. My eyes were dry because I hadn't blinked in the last three minutes. They shifted between the scalpel and Ollie's enraged face, which sprayed spittle from his seething breaths.

"Ollie, you know you don't want to injure anyone, right?"

"I don't give a shit who I hurt. Get me a needle of the Black Pearl, do you hear me?"

"Ollie, you're not thinking straight. I'm a nurse, not your dealer. This is a health clinic. We don't have heroin here. But I think Dr. Alvarez has a methadone pill that will help with your withdrawal until we can get you to a detox center. That's what you need, Ollie."

"Fuck the detox centers! They don't help. They just lock you in a room until you go batshit crazy. I've done it, and look where I'm at."

Sadly, Ollie's case wasn't uncommon. Over ninety percent of the people who complete a detox program relapse. Ninety percent!

I'd been a nurse on and off for almost fifteen years, and I still found that number to be staggering.

"Ollie, I know you're in a lot of pain. I want to help. Let us give you that pill. It will help you, I promise. Then I'll personally drive you to the detox center."

"I told you that I'm not going to no detox center! Can't you fucking hear?" He swiped the blade horizontally. I hopped back—my sneakers squeaked hard off the linoleum—and watched the metal blade nearly rip through my torso.

"Hey, Willow. Catch," I heard Stacy say from behind Ollie.

A metal tray flew over Ollie's shoulder. I caught it with one hand and brought it up just as he hurled his whole body at me. His arm and the scalpel smashed into the tray, denting the middle. But he didn't stop.

"You're just like those fuckers at the detox center. I want to kill you!" He screamed at a falsetto pitch while banging the blade and his arm harder and harder against the metal tray. Each blow sent me lower, but I somehow kept the tray upright, protecting my face. My butt was nearly on the ground.

"Stacy!" I called out.

"They're on their way," she said, her voice fading down the hall. I didn't blame her for not jumping in. Only a crazy person would do that.

But a crazy person—actually, a very sick person—was about to slice me up like minced onions. His screams turned into wails. If he hadn't been about to kill me, I'd have tremendous empathy for the guy. But it was a game of survival right now.

The banging stopped. I opened my eyes, and from under the tray, I saw his legs back up three steps. He was preparing for a running start. If there was one thing in my favor, it was his current lack of dexterity. Almost like a bull stomping its hooves, Ollie stutter-stepped and came after me with an enraged yelp that could melt the polar ice cap. Just before he reached me, I swung the metal tray at his forehead. He threw up his arms while still moving, which is what I was hoping for. I kicked out my foot, which tripped his legs, and he dropped like an oak tree. On the way down, though, the blade tore through my sleeve and grazed my arm.

"Hold it! Police!"

Two cops paused at the door, then barreled into the exam room and pounced on poor Ollie, who dropped the scalpel as he grunted from the force of an officer's knee in his back. Kelly ran up and saw that I was bleeding. "Dear God, you're going to bleed out!"

Stacy was our main administrator and had worked at the clinic for years, but she wasn't a nurse.

"He grazed me, that's all. I'm just sweating a lot."

Her shoulders relaxed. "Well, I'm going to get Dr. Alvarez. That chicken shit was hiding out in his office. He'll treat your wound, or I'll cut off his dick."

The officers snickered. And so did I.

Four

Cooper

Courtney pushed the smoothie across the table.

"I'm supposed to drink that?" I asked, my eyes momentarily glued to her black-polished fingernails.

"It's good for you. Come on, give it a try. Kind of like you're doing with me." She smiled. "Wait, that didn't sound right."

I could have snapped off a string of one-liners that would have made some people laugh. But it would have made her uncomfortable. Who says a thirty-nine-year-old guy can't grow up…even if it came in small waves?

We both laughed, albeit a stiff laugh. This Courtney thing was new. We'd had coffee together one night, and from there, it was like we felt compelled to give dating a shot. We were both unattached and had a shared mutual experience. I'd survived being the next victim of a serial killer, and she had been the detective on the case, all during a period of time when so much of my past had caught up with me. Some of it could be classified as good (my old/new connection with Willow Ball), some bad (the Sack Brothers and their twisted boss Dr. V), and some quite ugly (did I mention Dr. V's teeth?).

"Do they have Orange Crush?" I looked across the expansive deli, a new place downtown at the corner of San Jacinto and North Akard, to try to see the menu above the chaos of the food line.

"You need glasses?" she asked with a giggle.

I shifted my eyes to her. "You're making fun of my age."

She gave me a mock pouty-mouth. "Little Cooper Chain doesn't like to be made fun of."

I chuckled. We were starting to relax around each other.

"Seriously, do you want my smoothie?" I started to stand.

She lifted a cup. "I have my own, thank you. It's quite good. And you can take a seat. There's no Orange Crush."

I plopped my butt back in the seat and ate my turkey and mushroom sandwich.

"How's the writing going?" she asked.

She'd caught me off guard. I didn't realize I'd told her about my new gig. In fact, there was a lot about me that Courtney didn't know. With her being a detective—and a very serious one at that—we were going to have to take this very slowly for her to learn the full truth of my past.

Who was I kidding? Me open up completely? No one knew the unfiltered story of Cooper Chain. Not even my new bestie, Willow Ball.

"Look what the cat dragged in."

It was Willow, standing next to our table with her hands on her hips. What's that saying about a Cheshire cat grin? Yeah, that was Willow's expression, like she'd caught me in the act or something. An act that she'd been pushing me to do ever since she decided to continue dating her ex-fiancé, Harvey.

Courtney and I both said hello.

"Pull up a chair and join us," Courtney said as I shook my head like a jackhammer. Why invite the inevitable ribbing? But she didn't notice my not-so-subtle gesture.

Willow gave me a quick wink, the kind that said, *There you go kid. You're finally riding your bicycle all on your own.* I wasn't jumping up to grab her a chair. Willow then turned to Courtney. "It's been a hell of a day so far."

"You're telling me," I said, slouching in my chair. "Some old neighbor of Mrs. Kowalksi basically did one of those home invasions on my apartment and my person." I twirled a finger clockwise next to my ear. "I think the guy's got a screw loose. He thinks I'm some kind of drug kingpin."

"You do have that look," Courtney said.

"What look?"

Courtney gave me a subtle wink. Two winks from two different women in one minute. But this one made my face flush. Time to switch gears. "So, Willow, you were saying that you stubbed your toe at the clinic?"

She looked confused.

"I'm kidding."

"Ignore Mr. Smartass," Courtney said.

Willow snickered. "I'm used to it. Mostly."

"Take off your coat and join us at least for a few minutes," Courtney insisted.

The moment Willow removed her coat, I saw a bandage wrapped around her arm, and her scrubs had been ripped in two places.

"Did you get in a fight with a cat?" I asked as she scooted up a chair.

"I wish."

She then started to tell us about trying to corral a heroin addict who'd jumped off the emotional cliff.

"So, the cops grabbed him before he tried to stab you?" Courtney asked. "I'm not following you."

Willow finished telling us what had happened, how she'd taken the guy down.

"What were you thinking? While you were practicing your jiu-jitsu skills, you could have been killed! You know that, right?" I sounded like I was scolding her, but really it was just because I cared. I wasn't always good about showing that side of me.

"Did he just say that?" Willow asked Courtney.

"Yep. He actually just said it."

They both glared at me until I finally raised my hands in the air. "Please stop. I can't take the heat of your death stares."

Courtney quizzed Willow more about the incident, like a cop would normally do. "We just can't get to the core of this new heroin ring that's hit town," she said, now speaking about the entire DPD.

"You wouldn't believe how many people are coming to the clinic suffering from withdrawal symptoms," Willow said. "There's almost nothing worse. I really feel helpless, to be honest."

Willow and her empathy for others. It was one of the reasons her heart seemed like a beacon. When we first met at TCU on the other side of the Metroplex, her gentle kindness to me and to others was one of the reasons I'd fallen in love with her. Even after an eighteen-year span of not seeing or speaking to each other, she still had it. One might say it was a genetic trait. Not so. If you met her mother, you'd swear they weren't related. As for her dad…

"Have you talked to Raymond recently?"

Her syrupy eyes got wide. I thought I'd asked an innocent question. Not that her father was innocent. Far from it. Which reminded me that I needed to have a private conversation with Willow about her dear old dad, who'd shown up after a thirty-year hiatus just days before her expected wedding that never happened. The man had thrown me a curveball at the wedding rehearsal, one that knocked me to the ground.

"Crap," Courtney said, stealing my attention. She pulled out her phone, typed a text, then rose to her feet and grabbed her coat. "Duty calls. I have to run."

"Can't you just hand it off to someone else?" I asked.

"Not this one. It's a murder." She leaned down and kissed my cheek. I touched it.

"Thanks."

She arched an eyebrow. "You're not supposed to thank me, silly. Anyway, I'll call you later."

She was out the door before I could return the kiss.

Willow rearranged the salt and pepper shakers so that they were symmetrically aligned on either side of the napkin container. Damn, she was anal. "Make you feel better?" I asked.

She grabbed my smoothie and took a slurp. "Not bad," she said, churning the straw in the cup. "So, are you sleeping with Courtney yet?"

I clearly wasn't prepared for this.

Five

Willow

I plucked a chip from Cooper's plate and ate it.

"You know you can order your own meal," he said.

"No need. I'll just have your smoothie. I'm assuming that Courtney ordered it for you?"

He shrugged.

"No Orange Crush?"

He frowned, then grabbed his cup. "But I have a water."

"Good boy."

"Thanks, Mom."

He looked around the deli, which was filling up with the lunch crowd.

"So, are you going to share the scoop on you and Courtney?" I asked while taking another pull on the straw.

"I thought you were kidding. Well, I hoped you were kidding."

"I was."

There was some silence between us. We were friends, but I couldn't help but feel a little more of a connection to Cooper than I wanted. It was a little complicated, but it was nice to have a male friend I could joke around with, although our renewed friendship had coincided with hunting down a serial killer.

"I can see you're stressed," I said, tapping my cheek.

"I'm not biting the inside of my cheek. But to answer your question, since I know you won't stop needling me, Courtney and I are not sleeping together."

"Damn, you move slow. What happened to the suave Cooper Chain moves?"

He shook his head. "I'm only doing this because you pushed me."

"What? Courtney is a nice woman. She's attractive, and she's got a strong career going."

"You're still pushing…"

"But, Cooper, she's really got her shit together. You need someone who's got their shit together."

He opened his mouth, then closed it.

Razzing Cooper at this age was more entertaining than when we were in college. "No snarky comebacks?"

He ate a bite of his sandwich, then sipped his water. "Enough about Courtney and me—not that there's anything to talk about. Have you spoken to your father since…you know?"

"Dear old Dad left town again last week," I said with a meaningless chuckle even as I felt my stomach twist into knots.

"Seriously? Did he just disappear again?"

"He sent me some lame text. Something about business. Said he'd be back soon. Wonder if 'soon' equates to three decades in his universe?"

"At least he communicated with you."

"You're taking up for him now?"

"Hardly. I'm not saying you should have amnesia about your past. I just know that he wanted to try to get past all the issues and be a regular dad to you again."

"How do you know that?" I shot back.

His head and shoulders moved in all sorts of directions. Uncertainty? Or was he holding something back? I grabbed the salt shaker and pounded it on the table. "How can you act like Raymond is a regular dad? He left his wife and three kids over thirty years ago. I was only seven. Seven! Mom worked more than one job just to put food on the table. I had to take care of Jennie and Kyle as though I were twenty-one years old. He's far from regular. I don't know if I'm ever going to forgive him or have any type of relationship with him."

I could feel eyes from nearby tables on me, but I really didn't care.

"Didn't mean to set you off," he said, squirming a bit in his chair.

"What's wrong with you?"

"Nothing."

"You're either about to pee your pants or you want to tell me something."

"Are you a fucking mind reader?" He sat up in his seat, glanced at my eyes, then turned away.

"Look, I know your life isn't perfect, Cooper." I leaned closer so I could keep my volume down. "The Sack Brothers and that crazy man they work for—"

"Dr. V."

"Yeah, him. They're holding this favor you owe them over your head, forcing you to be the ringleader of a point-shaving scam. You can tell all this to Courtney. I'm sure she'll bring in the FBI. And then your problem will go away."

"On paper, that should work. In the real world—my real world—it won't. Dr. V has eluded law enforcement for years. He even admitted to me that he had that DNA sample stolen or lost from the lab so they couldn't connect him or his two ogres to the murder of Ronnie Gutierrez."

I could feel the anxiety coming off him in waves. And it was making me more anxious by the second.

"Do you remember what they said would happen to you if I don't set up this illegal operation? They'd do to you what they did to Ronnie."

They'd allegedly dismembered Ronnie. "They're bluffing," I said.

"I can't take that chance." He put his hand on top of mine. I waited a second, then I gripped his hand. Even in the midst of our disturbing conversation, our bond was strangely comforting.

"Speaking of Dr. V, I'm assuming Harvey has disowned him as a client?" Cooper asked.

Harvey was a partner at an accounting firm, and they'd recently purchased another company, essentially inheriting their client base. One of those clients was Dr. Vijayakumar Khatri. He'd even attended a business function at Harvey's sizable home in Highland Park, Dallas's most affluent zip code.

"I assume so," I said, taking my hand back to hold the straw as I drank more smoothie.

"So you don't know for certain?"

I gave a reluctant shake of the head.

"It's not safe for Dr. V to be close to you or Harvey. Then again, Harvey is the one who asked him to take care of Ronnie."

"As I've noted at least once, Harvey told me that he never intended for Dr. V to kill Ronnie."

"So he says."

I held up a finger. "Stop cutting down Harvey, Cooper. It's just not fair."

"Okay, okay. I'm not saying Harvey has the scruples of some crime boss. But can you at least ask him?"

I gave him a single nod. Laughter erupted at a nearby table. Kids—well, maybe kids around twenty—were throwing napkins at each other.

"What are college kids doing in a deli full of people gainfully employed?" Cooper asked. "And remember, I still have my part-time job at Books and Spirits, so no talking shit to me."

"Who, me?" I fluttered my eyelashes while bringing a hand to my chest.

It worked. He chuckled.

"Speaking of college kids, what about favor number two that you owe Dr. V?"

Cooper rolled his eyes. "His brat nephew, Ishaan."

"You don't have to babysit him, Cooper. He only wants you to teach him the ropes of investigative sports journalism, right?"

"Yeah, that's all. Dr. V will probably threaten to stuff my gonads down my throat if his nephew isn't writing cover stories for *Sports Illustrated* by the time spring rolls around."

"Could be worse," I said.

"How's that?"

"He could cut off your gonads first, and then only give them back after you mentor his nephew." I snorted and almost spit up a mouthful of the smoothie.

"You're quite the riot, Will. Seriously, don't you think you're taking it a bit too far?"

"Pot calling kettle black."

"Maybe." He grabbed the smoothie from my side of the table and took a pull from the straw. "I've got a plan."

"To steal my drink?"

"You stole mine, remember?"

I didn't nod or shake my head.

"This isn't half bad. Still not close to an Orange Crush, though."

"Your plan?"

He looked around and then lowered his head like a giraffe begging for food. "I plan to use Ishaan as my point person to set up this point-shaving scam."

"You said 'point' twice in the same sentence. Doesn't that break some type of writer's code?"

"There's a written code, not a spoken code. Doesn't matter anyway."

"You're serious about using his nephew?"

"As a heart attack."

"I doubt Dr. V wants his nephew involved in the crime business."

"But I'd imagine that Ishaan is desperate to gain this knowledge and experience from me. So, I plan on making him an offer he can't refuse."

"And what if he goes to his uncle and tells him everything?"

"Then please ask if he'll put my gonads on ice so someday they can be reattached."

We promptly left the building.

Six

The man had no saliva left. He wanted to speak out loud in the deafening darkness, if for no other reason than to feel the rumble of his voice in his chest…to confirm he was still alive. As his mind dipped in and out of consciousness, his blurred state of mind had him questioning whether he'd already been pulled under. Maybe this mental moat was the first stage of death, his body's own way of completely shutting down.

Stop thinking that it's over. Blink once.

Now blink again.

There. He took in a breath. It sounded as if he were slurping on a straw through a tiny, dry hole. But he could hear it, at least. Unless it was another mental trick.

He opened his jaw and focused on pushing out a word. He closed his eyes and clenched his torso with what little energy he could muster. All that came out were a few cracks, as though his wife had just opened a can of soup.

His wife. Emotion scratched and clawed at the back of his throat, but there would be no tears. He'd cried for hours, if not days at a time, taking turns cursing whatever entity controlled his fate and begging for forgiveness for every sin he'd committed. He knew he'd been no saint.

But tears for his wife, his two kids, for himself had dried up long ago, just like the moisture in his mouth. His mind pictured tumbleweeds blowing across the space in front of him.

Another illusion. And there had been many.

His voice had been stolen. His hand had been scorched—three fingers and a thumb had been burned down to the first knuckle. And his mind was rupturing from the inside out.

How much could he endure?

How much did he *want* to endure?

After the first finger had been melted like a candle and he cried out in pain for hours and hours, the anticipation of what would happen next pummeled his mind. To occupy himself, he counted the beats of his heart, sometimes using his toes to direct the symphony. But after the next finger was burned, he knew he couldn't keep up the counting routine. It only made the buildup of the anxiety that much worse when the door from above finally creaked open.

Now, he let his mind drift. Sometimes, quite literally. He'd always been afraid of being lost at sea. But he had this recurring thought, where he was on board a two-hundred-year-old ship, maybe when the slaves were brought to the States, and he was put on a tiny wooden raft with no food or water or even an oar. His handlers pushed his little boat away from the hulking ship, and within hours, he was all alone on the rocking water that had no end. But as the reel played out this time, he wasn't frightful of being lost—he was ecstatic to be free.

Freedom. He, like most people, had taken his freedom for granted. Now, in his battered mind, he could take in the refreshing salty air out on the open sea. What would it take for him to actually live out this dream? Just as his thoughts fell deeper into this make-believe world, water sprayed on his face. It had come from a dolphin splashing next to his tiny boat.

The cool water—albeit another illusion—jarred him from his mental slumber, and his eyes opened wide, once again staring into the darkness around him. His wrists and ankles were bolted to a concrete floor. He felt as though steel rods had impaled his back and joints.

How long until the person showed up again? How long until the blowtorch would light up his space and sear another finger? Or would this person start working on another body part?

Panic rippled through his muddy bloodstream. The man started counting his heart beats once again. He couldn't stop himself. He made it up to one hundred and kept going. A few minutes later, he was up to one thousand.

Then he heard a creak. His throat clamped shut.

Seven

Cooper

It's funny what almost twenty years will do to you. As I walked the halls of the freshman dorm on the SMU campus, one might think I was some prehistoric mammal on display at the National Museum of American History in DC—one of the many places I called home during my nomadic younger life. None of the college kids said anything; their eyes said it all. They leered at me like I was an ancient relic.

I thought I saw a few gray whiskers in my stubble this morning prior to the home invasion. Oh well.

I meandered down a corridor, hooked a right at the T, and found room 317. There was a small whiteboard affixed to the door, and on it someone had drawn a red X. I understood that signal. Someone inside was a player. Was that Ishaan or his roommate?

I knocked on the door. I heard someone stirring, but no one came to the door. I was about to take a second round at the door when a kid walked behind me and popped his fist against his open palm while smiling. Again, no words. Only signals.

I knocked again. Now I heard a lot more stirring. A second later, a guy with a ponytail brushed my shoulder with his backpack. "Incoming. The cavalry is here." He inserted the key into the lock, opened the door, and walked right inside. I slowly followed.

A boy, who I'd bet was Ishaan, and a girl were scrambling to get their clothes on. The girl screeched as she wrapped a sheet around her and ran to the bathroom.

"Mo, what the fuck, man? You saw the sign," the boy said while searching for his shirt. He glanced at me, but kept his gaze on his roommate, who tossed his backpack on his bed.

Mo spun his key chain around his finger a few times. "Ishaan, this isn't a fucking pay-by-the-hour motel. I can't be locked out twenty hours a day. How many chicks have you had in the last week?"

Ishaan put a finger to his mouth. "Be respectful, Mo. She's just on the other side of the—"

"I heard that." The girl walked out of the bathroom, pulled her long mane of hair out of the back of her shirt, and plodded over clothes and shoes to get to the bedside table next to Ishaan. "I know I was pretty drunk, but you told me I was the one," she said, arching an eyebrow.

"My friend here is greatly mistaken. Mo drinks a lot, smokes even. He has me mixed up with someone else."

She glanced around. Her eyes stayed on me for a split second. "Unless he's referring to this old man here, I don't think so."

I lifted a hand. "I'm not his old man. In fact, I'm not old at all."

All three snickered. That wasn't meant to be funny.

"Just help me find my purse, and I'm out of here, out of your life, Mr. Playboy," the girl said.

Ishaan quickly tossed clothes up in the air until he found a small, black-sequined clutch. "Is this yours?" he asked.

Dumb move.

She snatched the bag from his hand ."Who else's would it be? Unless your roommate is into cross-dressing."

Mo stood up. "Ishaan asked me to be his bitch last Friday, but I refused."

I cracked a quiet chuckle. Well, it wasn't all that quiet. Ishaan looked at me, giving me the once-over, the kind that said he was superior to everyone in the room.

The girl walked to the door, then flipped her head around. "I'm not really into throwing shade at anyone. But since you're such a fucktard, I have one thing to share about our little experience." She held up her pinky and wiggled it.

Mo burst out in laughter. She winked and then left the room.

"Shut the fuck up, Mo. She's just… Well, it's all your fault anyway. The red X. That's our sign, dude. You broke the code."

"Whatever. Why don't you break open a book every once in a while? What was your GPA first semester?"

Ishaan slipped a T-shirt over his head. "I don't remember."

"Sure you do."

"I don't know, maybe a two point…"

Mo, who'd been pulling books out of his backpack, stopped and fell back with more laughter. "Dude, you mean a point two. You can't pull that shit by me. Another semester like that and you'll be working in the family business a lot sooner than you thought."

Ishaan flicked a hand at Mo while staring me down. His eyes were like dark caverns. "If you're not Mo's old man, who are you?"

"Cooper Chain. I'm your new mentor."

"A mentor!" Mo hollered. "Your uncle went off and hired you a personal lackey just to get you to go to class every once in a while? Dude, you're weak. Really weak."

"Ignore that asshole." Ishaan brought his hand to his mouth, studying me for an extra second. Then he walked over and stuck out his hand. "I'm honored to meet you, Mr. Chain. I've read a lot of your work, and it's outstanding journalism."

"The name is Cooper. Not Coop and certainly not Mr. Chain. And you don't need to kiss my ass. You just need to listen and watch and ask an occasional question."

"You got it." He clapped his hands and searched the room. "Mo, you seen my notepad?"

"The one you haven't used all year? Oh yeah, I used it to scoop up some nasty, molded pizza the other day."

"Seriously?" Ishaan said as his brow furrowed into an accordion.

Mo pulled a small notepad out of his backpack and tossed it to Ishaan. "Use that. You can pay me back later." Then he turned to me. "So, you're the famous sportswriter who crashed and burned."

"Huh?"

"Ishaan told me everything. Hasn't anyone told you there's all sorts of shit on the Internet?"

"Don't believe everything you read." I was curious as to what exactly he was referring to, but what would it change? Reading it wouldn't reestablish my reputation as a top-notch investigative sports journalist for the *New York Daily News*. "Grab your shoes. We need to talk about next steps."

"Anyway I can get my byline next to yours on this first story at *The Wire*?" he said all too eagerly.

"Honestly? No chance in hell."

"Oh, someone got dissed before he took his first baby step," Mo said with a chuckle.

"Mo, you better shut your trap."

"Or what? You going to put your little Roofie pill into my drink so I'll sleep with you?"

I swung my sights to Ishaan. He was drugging these girls to get them in bed? I could feel heat crawling up my neck. That prick definitely came from the same gene pool as his uncle. Part of me just wanted to walk out. Something told me this kid was too cocky to listen and learn, and that he expected the silver-spoon treatment in every setting he was in.

"Okay, Mr. Chain, I'm all ready to go." He was nearly standing at attention with a smile on his face and his notepad in his hand.

"Got a pen?"

He patted his pockets. "Crap. I knew I was missing something."

He found one on the floor, and we walked out of the dorm as I pondered how I wanted to approach my vision of this mentoring relationship. Ultimately, if the plan played out like I hoped, I'd get my story, and Dr. V and the Sack Brothers would finally get their just due: orange jumpsuits and a bar of soap in a prison cell.

Eight

Cooper

Ishaan and I walked three blocks without saying a word. He was either afraid or he'd read my serious mood. Probably the latter of the two.

"Let's find a place to talk," I said.

"Just up here," he said, pointing at a strip center I knew all too well. "I'm told that I need to buy a novel of some kind for my English class. Kill two birds with one stone, right?"

Hearing a Khatri talk about killing anything didn't go unnoticed by me, even in a clichéd comment. I tried not to let it rattle me. I looked up and saw Books and Spirits. My former full-time gig was now down to about twenty hours a week. I called it "retail hell." It was a great motivator to make *The Wire* the biggest sports sensation on the Internet.

The door dinged when we walked inside. "Good afternoon. Can I help you find anything?" my colleague said in a depressing monotone. He had his head down at a front table while sorting books—anything to look busy for our manager, Brandy. We were all required to recite that line of babble every time the door opened.

"What's going on, Slash?"

Ishaan gave me a curious look.

"That's what he goes by," I said with a shrug.

Slash looked up. "Hey, Mr. Cooper…I mean, Cooper. How's it hanging?"

"A little to the left today."

Slash chuckled, then looked at Ishaan.

"How did you know Brandy was looking to hire a new person?"

"Do what?" I followed his eyes to Ishaan, then finally caught on to what Slash was inferring.

"Excuse me, Mr. Slash." Ishaan moved a step forward and cleared this throat. Not that it needed clearing, I could see he was trying to ensure he'd captured our attention. Damn, he was condescending. "May I offer you a bit of advice?"

Slash glanced at me a second, a blank stare on his face. What little color he had on his peach-fuzzed cheeks was now turning ruddy. "Sure," he said as his voice cracked.

"Ishaan Khatri does not work for anyone, certainly not at a retail bookstore. The only time you might see Ishaan Khatri in a bookstore is at his first author book signing." He lifted his nose higher on the last phrase. I rolled my eyes and shook my head.

"That's cool," Slash said, not really understanding how Ishaan had just sliced him in two.

That was a metaphor. With the Khatris, one had to always be careful when making analogies.

"So, Cooper here is going to help you get to the promised land, right?" Slash nodded as though he were piecing together the whole puzzle. "I get it now. Cooper brought you here so you could envision your first book signing event."

"Something like that," I said, peering across the store for any sign of Brandy. I told Ishaan we could talk in the lounge by the bar and waved him on to follow me.

"Oh, one little helpful tip," Slash said to Ishaan.

"You have a tip for *me*?" Ishaan chuckled.

"Yeah. If you want to be a big-time writer and speak in front of crowds, you might not want to refer to yourself in the third person."

"Slash!"

That was a Brandy squawk from across the store.

"Damn, I might be in trouble. Gotta run." Slash motored away as Ishaan held up his hand, seemingly prepared to smack Slash with another condescending comment.

"Let it go and follow me." I led Ishaan back to the lounge area by the bar. No one was around, which was just the way I wanted it.

"Can I get you a water?" I asked, walking behind the counter.

He pointed at me. "You work here?"

I turned my palms to the ceiling. "Life of a big-time sports journalist. What can I say?"

"Uncle Vijay didn't mention that," he said more to himself than me.

"Water?" I asked again, while filling one glass with ice.

"What different brands to you carry?"

"One kind. Tap."

His shoulders sagged as though he'd just been dropped into a survivalist camp in the middle of the deep woods in East Texas. Water—the great humbler.

I poured two glasses, and we each grabbed a seat in one of the overstuffed chairs. He moved to the edge of the chair, opened his notebook, and rested his pen on paper. I was impressed. He actually looked like a student.

"So, let's talk about how this is going to work," I said.

He held up his pen hand. "I have several ideas for this first feature story that I'd like to share. These all came to me as we were walking over here. I think, over time, you'll be very impressed with how my brain functions."

There went my hope for him listening and not acting like he was the bomb. "Hold on, Ishaan. Having ideas is great. Write them down in your diary when you're alone, then spend some time doing some research and writing brief stories about your topics. Alone. Let me repeat that: alone. On your own time. This little arrangement isn't about how to take a toddler and make him an Olympic sprinter in a few weeks. It's about said toddler watching and listening, asking a few questions. It's called learning. You think you can handle that?"

He pulled in a slow breath while arching his neck. "Yes."

A one-word response. He was catching on.

I explained my idea for the first story: a profile on a former NBA number-one pick who'd made upwards of sixty million dollars over his spotty six-year career and then had supposedly lost it all.

"A riches-to-rags story," Ishaan said, nodding along.

"Yep. But I'm almost certain it will be more complex than how one guy blew through more cash than I'll see in a hundred lifetimes. Branches to the original story idea will come out of nowhere—from family members, so-called financial advisors, or even old coaches. You never know where you'll find a leech."

I paused a second, thinking about the irony. My leech was his frickin' uncle. Part of me wondered how much he actually knew about his uncle's plethora of illegal operations, especially how Dr. V exacted punishment on those he believed had done him wrong. Milo and Elan Sachen—whom I called "the Sack Brothers" for simplicity—were Dr. V's usual go-to muscle. The twin bodybuilders were born and bred in New Jersey, but they had Russian roots. Dr. V, on the other hand, was born in India, then somehow ended up in Russia. How long he stayed and what he did in Russia was a mystery, although I had a feeling he might have served an internship with the Russian mafia. Among his many rumored skills was pathology—thus, the "Dr." prefix before his name. Again, it wasn't confirmed.

Still, Dr. V had all but admitted to cutting up Ronnie Gutierrez—and enjoying every minute of it. Ronnie was slime, but who deserved to die that way?

"So, will you let me dig into one of these so-called branches?"

I had to throw the kid a bone of some kind. "Let's see how things unfold once I have my first sit-down with our poster boy."

"And you think he'll grant you an interview, just like that?" he said, snapping his fingers. "I bet he probably won't want to discuss such a difficult period of his life."

I picked up on one word in his argument: "bet." That's how I'd gotten into this babysitting assignment to begin with. I made one bet too many to the wrong person. With interest, I'd owed fifty thousand dollars. I'd already lost everything else in my life, so fifty K wasn't in the cards. I left the New York area hoping Dr. V and the Sack Brothers would move on to bigger fish. They didn't. They found me in Dallas. But after giving them their money, they said I owed them "favors."

Even worse, the payoff money that I'd found in the trunk of my car was no gift from the man upstairs. Raymond—yes, Willow's estranged father—told me he'd put it there, acted like he knew Dr. V and the Sack Brothers. He said he only wanted my help to nudge Willow into giving him a second chance at being a father to her. It sounded a little too noble for my tastes. I knew I needed to tell her about the money, but I first wanted to confront Raymond to find out how he knew about Dr. V and the Sack Brothers. But now I wondered, like Willow, if he'd left town for another three-decade hiatus.

"Maybe so, maybe not," I said to Ishaan. "It's all how you approach people. You have to give them a reason to want to talk to you."

He sipped his drink and set the glass on the side table, where it would surely leave a ring. Not that I was anal, and the table was already scarred and stained. But if Willow were here, she'd move the glass to a coaster. My drink was still in my hand. I downed a mouthful and saw Ishaan eyeballing me, as though he were trying to read my next move.

It wasn't possible.

"So, Ishaan, there is something you can do for me…for us. And it's important to how we work together, for this story and in future stories."

"I'm all in. You name it."

"You know many athletes at SMU?"

"A few, why?"

"Basketball players?"

He bit into his lower lip. "I met the backup center at a party. Cool cat. He's something like six-nine, so he's a foot taller than me."

A backup center. He would do us no good in setting up a point-shaving operation. "You think you could use him to get to know some other guys on the team? Key starters, maybe the leading scorer or the point guard?"

He had confusion written all over his face. This is where we'd see if my plan had any legs.

"How is this going to help get more information for our poster boy?"

I tilted my head left and then right. "It's a bit of a stretch, but there's a connection."

He wrote down a few notes, then went still. A couple of seconds clocked by, and then he slowly turned to me and said, "Hold on. Our poster boy was a point guard, who, for a while at least, led his team in scoring. You want me to get the perspective of a college star playing in this day and age, right?"

I thought more about my approach. Probably best to lead him along slowly. "Your mind never stops, Ishaan."

"Cool. So you want me to interview this person?"

"Not yet. Just get to know him. Become his new best buddy."

He gave me a slow nod while keeping his gaze on me. Was there something behind those dark eyes? I couldn't tell. Up to now, I figured he was just a silver-spooned kid with no real understanding of what his uncle did on a day-to-day basis. The reality could be far different.

A store patron walked through our space, which interrupted the stare-down.

We finished our waters and made our way to the front door. Once outside, I said, "Let me know once you've made contact with the top one or two players for the Mustangs."

"Yeah." He turned and faced me, lifting his chin in a cocky manner, as if he were trying to strike some type of defiant pose. "No worries on my end, Cooper."

That attitude was supposed to represent…what? Then, as he turned and walked off in the opposite direction, a red dually pickup rumbled through the parking lot. The glare of the sun blocked my vision, so I couldn't see who was in the front seat. But I'd seen that truck. That truck had pinned Willow and me in my Convert-beast in an alley a few weeks back. As the pickup drove past, I panned my sights to the right until the sun didn't block my vision.

When I locked eyes with one of the Sack Brothers—it was virtually impossible to differentiate between the twins—he gave me the one-finger salute. He had this blank stare on his face. But my sights focused on that finger and his Cro-Magnon forehead. A second later, he smacked his brother on the arm, lurching forward in laughter.

It was always nice to be the butt of someone's joke, even if their sheer presence sent a chill up my spine. The pickup spun its wheels, spitting up gravel and a heap of rubber-smelling smoke, and then tore out of the parking lot.

Three unrelated thoughts shot to the front of my mind: high school chicanery, steroid road rage, and Vin Diesel. Why Vin Diesel? In addition to the physical similarities between Diesel and the two ogres, he'd once starred in a movie where he was responsible for babysitting a bunch of kids. I think the Sack Brothers might be performing the same role with Ishaan.

The real question, though, was why? Was babysitting Ishaan just part of their normal duties for Dr. V? Or were they sending some type of message to me?

Usually, their warnings weren't very subtle. Yet, this little drive-by seemed different. A line of perspiration broke out along my spine. The Sack Brothers might have shit for brains, but I knew that Dr. V didn't see these favors I owed him as some little side game. If I didn't meet his expectations, someone would pay the ultimate price. Maybe more than one person. But he'd told me the *first* victim would be Willow.

I walked back to my car and pondered if I was putting her more at risk by trying to catch the snake rather than simply morphing into one myself.

Nine

Willow

While the recent surge of heroin addicts created the biggest stir at the clinic—this morning's violent outburst leading the way—the ailments that kept us busy almost nonstop were the flu and the common cold.

For starters, whoever came up with the term "common" to describe a cold, should be sued for lying to the public. For those of us in the medical field, we walked a thin line during the winter months when trying to determine if a patient had a cold or a flu. If a flu test came back positive, we could only hope that it was still early in the process. Otherwise, a prescription of Tamiflu to reduce the severity of the symptoms would do no good.

I stuck my head in the door of exam room 2. "Mrs. Burch, we should have the flu results back in a minute."

Resting on the exam table, her heavy eyes opened for a moment. "Thank you, dear. I'm not going anywhere."

A kind, peaceful woman. I wished all patients had her disposition. She was probably a good ten years older than my mom, but she was no Florence Ball. Born and raised in inner city Philadelphia, Ma had the temperament of a pit bull.

Mrs. Burch closed her eyes and pulled a blanket I'd given her up to her chin. All too often in nursing, the sense of helplessness outweighed the feeling of providing the care to truly make people better. The science of medicine, even in the modern era, was still wrought with so many unknowns. Let's start with finding a cure or, God forbid, a vaccination for the common cold.

Yet even vaccinations, especially flu vaccinations, seemed to be as reliable as playing the roulette wheel at a Vegas casino.

I was about to shut the door when Mrs. Burch's purse dropped to the floor. She stretched an arm off the exam table—crap, she was about to fall! "Look out!" I yelled, launching myself in her direction. I caught her body in midair, feeling the outline of her rib cage, and lifted her back to the table.

"Oh my, dear, I'm so sorry for causing all this trouble," she said, trying to situate herself on the table. I could feel her body radiating heat. I'd already given her ibuprofen.

"I thought I had better balance than that. I guess I'm not as young and agile as I used to be." She tried to smile, but her eyes were already closed.

Flu or a cold, she wasn't in good shape.

"No worries at all." I straightened out her blanket. "Did you say your daughter dropped you off?"

"Jada's a busy woman. Got a lot going on in her life. I worry about her. I truly do." Mrs. Burch smacked her lips.

"Let me get you some water." I poured her a cup, grabbed a straw, and supported her back while she leaned up and drank the water.

"Better. That helps." She exhaled a long breath, and she became more lucid. She reached out and took hold of my wrist. "I wonder if Jada is having a nervous breakdown. I'm not sure my precious daughter can hold up to the—"

The door burst open. "Momma, you okay?" A woman with a gaunt face and red nose shuffled up to her mother's side and rested the back of her hand to her mother's cheek. "You're still burning up. They treating you okay?" Her tone tried to be kind, like her mother, but it had an edge to it, as if she had serious doubts.

"We're just waiting on the results of her flu test," I said. "If it comes back positive, Dr. Mulligan will write a prescription for Tamiflu. Your mother is going to need someone caring for her regularly, a few times a day. Can you or a family member provide that?"

"Momma lives with…us. "Jada's breath hitched, then she rubbed the palm of her hand into her eye.

She was having a moment. Maybe she was coming down with the same thing, so I tried to give her some hope. "The pharmacies are running low on Tamiflu, but if you're taking care of your mother, I can probably convince the doctor to write scripts for you and your other family members in the same house."

Jada gasped out a breath, then braced her arms on the table.

"Are you okay?"

She stared into space as if she were being held captive inside of herself. The flu wouldn't do this to her. She held that frozen state for a good thirty seconds.

"Jada, tell the nurse what's going on. It might help you," Mrs. Burch said.

I looked at Mrs. Burch, then shifted my eyes to her daughter. "You can talk to me, Jada. What's wrong?"

Tears poured out of her eyes as though someone had turned on a spigot. She didn't try to stop the flow. She held her lifeless gaze for a few seconds, then turned to me. "It's my husband. I don't know where he is. I'm worried. Real worried about him."

I put a hand on her elbow, and she just about crumbled into my arms. She began to cry out loud while leaning against my chest. "I don't know what I'll do if something has happened to that man," she said through tears.

I rubbed her back for a moment, helping her to calm down. A minute passed, and she finally lifted her body upright. Her face was a mess, so I handed her a box of tissues. She plucked about five out of the box and used them accordingly.

"I'm sorry for creating such a scene. We all got drama, and I don't need to be putting my drama on you or anyone else. I saw the line of patients in the waiting room. And you've got to take care of Momma." She tried to laugh, but never quite got there.

"It's okay, Jada. Tell me what's going on?"

"My husband…about a week ago, he just got up and left the house. Hasn't been home since."

"He didn't tell you where he was going?"

She shook her head.

"What about his job? Could he be traveling for business?"

She swallowed, and a pained expression washed over her face. "Jobs have been hard to come by over the years. He's done his best…" Her eyes drifted away as her voice trailed off. Then she snapped back to it. "It's probably my fault. I've ridden him pretty hard at times. Frustrated that he can't really get his act together, at least not for long periods of time."

For some reason, I thought about my dad. Different situation, of course. But I'd never heard why he left in the first place. Was it because Ma was a pain in the ass? Or was Ma's disposition at least partially connected to the fact that her husband had walked out on her with no warning or communication? Of course, he could have been overwhelmed with having three kids and so much responsibility. Maybe I was the reason he'd left us. That thought chewed at the back of my mind as I tried to focus on helping someone and not wallowing in my pool of pity.

"Jada, all relationships are complicated. You can't blame yourself."

"You see?" her mother said. "I told you, Jada. Your husband's got a mind of his own, and no one is going to stop him from doing what he wants, what he thinks is right."

"It's not that simple, Momma, and you know it." Jada grabbed a new tissue and dabbed her eyes. She paused and released a jittery breath. I waited a moment. I could see she still had so much to share.

Finally, after her breathing cadence seemed to normalize, she looked at me. "He's had quite a life. Some incredible moments, and some horrific lows. And to get through it all, he turned to drugs. He's fought the good fight, but each time I thought he'd made it over the top of the mountain, he'd fall right back. And then he'd disappear. Sometimes only for a few hours; others times for days. I'm worried that he's done it again, fallen off the wagon, and…"

I glanced at her mother, who wiped a tear from her face. The emotion in the room was intense, but I tried to show a sense of calm, that there was hope. "Do you know what set him off this time?" I asked Jada.

She gripped her head and then began to shake. "I might be the reason. We've been fighting more than usual lately."

"You have?" her mother exclaimed. "You never told me that."

"Momma, it's my business."

"But I love you, Jada. I'm not judging you. I only want to help."

I could feel a lump in my throat. Was that empathy or jealousy? I'd always wanted a mom—hell, either parent—to show such compassion and kindness to me. Even at the age of thirty-eight, I still felt that void.

I said, "Jada, don't blame yourself. You're human and have had to deal with a lot. Addiction can really do a number on relationships."

She didn't respond. Her eyes were lost again. I wasn't sure she'd heard me. "Jada?"

"Something about this time feels different. He was agitated the last few days before he disappeared. Of course, I acted like an ass and pressed him even harder."

"I don't know your husband, but agitation can be a sign that they're struggling with their sobriety."

A quick shake of her head. "It's like something else was on his mind. I didn't see that same craving I've seen before. I saw…"

"What, Jada? What did you see?"

She locked her sights on me. "He looked pissed, like he wanted to kill somebody."

Her mother quickly chimed in. "Not literally, Jada, right?"

Jada moved her shoulders and shook her head. "I don't know, Momma. The last morning I saw him, he seemed really mad. I asked him about it, and he blew me off like always."

I could feel my radar go up, different from just my caregiving way. "Is there anyone in particular you think he wants to harm?"

Jada narrowed her red-rimmed eyes. "He's always got little beefs against people. Could be the pizza delivery guy one day, or the neighbor who lets his dog crap in our yard the next. When our daughter was in high school, he seemed to have a real problem with whichever guy she was dating. But she and her brother are in college now, doing their own thing, trying to make their own names."

I thought about some options for her. "Have you considered going to the cops? He's been missing for longer than a couple of days, right?"

"It's been a fucking week! But I can't. If he's sitting in some sewer getting high and he's picked up by the cops again, he'll never forgive me. Nope. Can't do the cops. I've been driving around town myself, though, hoping to find him or his car. No luck yet. For all I know, he could be dead in that sewer. Dear God, I just don't know what to do."

I told the two ladies to give me a minute, and I left the room.

Ten

Willow

I wasn't paying attention to where I was going, and I walked right into Dr. Mulligan.

"Excuse me," he said with his usual smug attitude. He had that God complex, but he also had no patience for the rest of the world. I guess we weren't smart enough for him.

"Sorry," I replied. I then explained to him about Mrs. Burch's condition and how I felt it was necessary to write Tamiflu prescriptions for their entire household.

"You know the rules, Willow. Can't do it. And I won't do it."

Damn, he was full of himself. I didn't want to tell him the details of what Jada had shared, but I was left with no choice. I kept it a pretty basic level, though. She was having marital issues, and her husband hadn't been home in days.

"And that's my problem?" he said, poking his chest. That's when I noticed a large bandage on the back of his hand. I could see red marks seeping out from the edges. It looked like a burn.

He saw me staring and put his hand in his pocket. "Are we done now? Can I go in and spend my two minutes with them?"

The Community Health Clinic didn't pay much to any of us, and the doctors only got a fraction of what they'd normally charge.

Most of us understood it was more about giving something back to the community. I felt certain that Joan, our director, was desperate to find doctors if she let this guy near our patients.

"Dr. Mulligan, if I may, the two ladies in that room are not well, physically, emotionally, mentally. They've been through a lot. We need to do something for them. Writing them extra prescriptions is a small thing to help."

"I'm sure there's a pathetic story there somewhere. Look, people need to learn how to stand on their own two feet."

"But you don't understand. Her husband—"

"What did he do? Knock her up and leave? Just like all the others." He blew out a breath. "Let me see the patient, please."

He walked past me and into the room. I wasn't going to let that vulture eat them alive, so I followed him.

Jada was in the chair, holding her stomach.

"What's wrong?" I asked.

"She's been in a lot of pain since you left," her mother said.

The doctor put his hand on Jada's head. "She's burning up." His eyes met mine, then he turned to Mrs. Burch. "Your test was positive for the flu. And I'm guessing your daughter has it as well. I'll write two prescriptions but no more."

The moment he left the room, I muttered, "Asshole."

Mrs. Burch snorted out a painful laugh. "You're saying what I was thinking."

I soon found out they had no car. Jada had been using Uber to get around. Apparently, her husband had their only car.

So, I clocked out and drove them to the pharmacy to pick up their prescriptions, as well as buy some chicken soup and crackers, and then drove them home. I got them settled in their respective beds and laid out their medicine routine.

"You're a gift from God, and I don't even know your name," Jada said.

"Willow Ball."

She nodded. "Maybe another angel will come down and find my husband," she said as her eyes started to shut.

I asked her for her contact information and what type of car her husband was driving. Before I could tell her my idea, she fell asleep.

Eleven

Cooper

A coffee shop in Deep Ellum wasn't your ordinary coffee shop. The requirements for employees and patrons alike were as follows: six visible piercings, hair had to be in some psychedelic pattern, and you wore a combination of clothes and accessories that literally came from Goodwill. The accessories, actually, could have originated in a local pet store. Lots of studded collars. One woman actually held a leash that was attached to the collar of her mate.

Clearly, they were making a statement. A statement that probably had something to do with a sexual fetish. Nothing else about the people or the establishment bothered me. To each his or her own. But all I ask is to not draw me a visual of your sex lives.

When I'd asked if they had Orange Crush, one young barista asked if that was a cousin to the Australian turtle in *Finding Nemo*. I kid you not. Talk about feeling ancient.

I received a few glares as I took a seat in the corner booth and sipped on a water. I wasn't exactly a clean-cut pretty boy. Besides my thick scruff and longish hair, I could use a shower. The appearance of the Sack Brothers had ignited a series of flashbacks. Probably a form of post-traumatic stress disorder. In other words, they'd beaten the shit out of me more than once, and my mind was projecting what could happen in the future. The cumulative effect of all that had made me breaking out in a mean sweat.

I pulled out my phone, itching to make contact with the person I was writing the feature story about for *The Wire*. After my meeting with Ishaan, I drove back to my apartment. Standing at the edge of Mrs. Kowalski's property was Myron Little. If looks could kill, I would have died a thousand times over. Fortunately, he didn't cross any line other than the creepy one, as he stared me down until I made my way up the white-painted steps to my apartment above the garage. Mrs. Kowalski called for me just before I shut the door. She was in the back yard and asked if I could help her rake some leaves.

Didn't she have a lawn company that did that kind of work? I couldn't say no to Mrs. Kowalski. So, I raked leaves for the next hour. Once I finished, she said she'd bake me some oatmeal-and-raisin cookies—one of my favorites. Feeling better about myself now that I'd helped out humanity, I was ready to dig into the story.

And then a text had come in from Courtney. She asked if I had time to talk. She didn't say much, other than the murder crime scene had done a number on her. She wasn't the needy type, so I quickly agreed to meet her at the coffee shop closest to the crime.

Then, just as I'd pulled into the coffee shop's parking lot, I received another text from my buddy Ben, who said he had an urgent need to meet with me about business. I thought I knew why, and I said he could join me at the coffee shop if he beat Courtney there.

Ben Dover and I had been friends in high school. We also both went to TCU, at least until I transferred to Canisius for my one shot at playing college basketball. Since I moved back to the area, apparently, Ben Dover decided he preferred the name "Benjamin" over "Ben." Willow gladly went with it, but I refused. I once told him he would always be Ben Dover to me. He said it created a stigma for him. My response? "Remember that TV show, *Growing Pains*? Mike had a best friend he always called Boner, and no one said a damn word. Don't you think Ben Dover is better than Boner?"

I'd laughed my ass off. He half-chuckled. Life moved on.

I spotted Ben sliding out of his shiny, silver Infiniti SUV. He paused as his eyes fixated on a couple making out while facing each other on a Harley. I wasn't sure if he was horrified or turned on.

He rolled up the sleeves of his purple button-down and strolled inside, hands tucked inside his pleated chinos. Shift the location of the coffee shop a mile to the west in the heart of Uptown, and it was like you entered a new universe. Ben's universe. But right now, he was out of his element.

He waved at me, put in his order, then brought over his warm drink that had steam pouring out through the middle of whipped cream.

"What happened to Ben Dover drinking black coffee?"

"Benjamin," he corrected me while scooping up the whipped cream. "This is Reva's favorite drink, so I gave it a try."

Reva was his new squeeze—literally. She'd put his entire life in a vice grip. "Meaning, she pretty much forced you to call it your favorite."

"She doesn't have that kind of control over me."

"Isn't purple her favorite color?"

His eyes shifted around. "How did you know that?"

"Because every time I've seen her and her triplet daughters, they're all wearing purple."

"I guess the cat's out of the bag." He waved a hand in front of his face. "Reva is Reva. Can't change her, but I can't live without her, either."

"Why not?"

He slowly arched an eyebrow as a teenage boy-like grin split his round, chubby face.

I held up a hand. "Don't go there. I don't need the play-by-play, thank you." I sipped some water, then looked through the window for Courtney. No sign of her yet.

"I'm meeting someone here in a few minutes, so…" I motioned with my hand for him to make it quick.

"Okay, well, if you haven't noticed, I've given you almost two full weeks, and not once did I pester you about making the final decision."

Ben thought he could leverage my contacts in the sports world to help launch his new sneaker company, GOAT, which stood for Greatest of All Time. It was a clever name. But I was no sales or marketing guru. And he knew that. Still, he insisted on offering me a job as executive VP of Marketing.

"I thought I gave you my final decision."

He wagged a finger at me. "Wow, Cooper, you never stop negotiating. Damn, I can't wait until you're out there cutting deals for GOAT. The sports world won't know what hit them."

Ben had always had selective hearing. Could he really be this clueless, or did he just not want to hear that this wasn't meant to be? "Hey, Ben…"

His gaze had wandered over to two women kissing by the jukebox. "Hubba, hubba," he said.

I snapped my fingers. "Earth to Ben Dover."

"Benjamin," he corrected me again. At least that had penetrated his one-track mind.

"Can you listen to me this time?"

"All ears."

"I don't think—"

"It's you and Willow. That's what you're trying to tell me."

"Huh?"

"BCDA."

I shook my head. "What's that?"

"Ball & Chain Detective Agency. The two of you have finally listened to my advice and decided to create your own PI firm. You're trying to tell me that you'll need to split your time between GOAT and BCDA. I told you that was the smart play while we get GOAT up and running. And because you're such a badass negotiator, for giving you guys the idea, I'll only take fifteen percent of the revenue for the first year."

"Ben, have you forgotten about *The Wire*? I'm back in the writing game again. Something you know I've wanted to do ever since I left the *Daily News*."

"*The Wire*." He said that like it almost made him puke. "I can just tell it's another dot.com bubble. Only a matter of time before that wad blows right in your face. Do you want that?" he asked while pointing at me. Then he pointed at himself. "I don't want that for you. That's what kind of friend I am."

He was exhausting me. A dark sedan pulled into a parking space near our window. Courtney walked toward the front door holding her purse as though it were a football, her eyes boring holes in the sidewalk.

"Hey, it's about time for you to leave," I said.

He snagged a glance at Courtney. "Gothic cop. You're doing Gothic cop *and* Willow? Damn, you are the king of ass."

"Who said I was *doing* Willow?"

"Can't hide it from me. I see it on your face and hers. But now you've got Gothic cop on the side. Epic," he said with a shake of the head.

"I'm not with Willow. We're just friends."

"Hell, you go after each other like you've been married ten years."

"It's all in fun."

"In bed."

"What?"

Courtney saw me and waved, then started walking over. I lowered my head so she couldn't see my mouth as I spoke to Ben. "Courtney and I are just starting to date. Don't say anything, okay?"

He winked. "Got your back, playboy." He lifted from his chair. "Here you go, my lady," he said, pulling out the chair for her.

"Thank you, I guess."

"I'll leave you two lovebirds alone."

My face started glowing red…out of embarrassment and anger. I could feel my jaw clenching as I envisioned clamping my teeth around Ben's neck.

"Is he smoking weed again?" she asked under her breath.

"Must be."

Ben stopped halfway to the door and flipped around. "One week, Cooper. Then it's finally time for you to grow a pair and come up with our marketing plan so we can both get rich."

Before I could tell him to go to hell, he looked over at the women in the corner and bit into a knuckle. Then he left the coffee shop without another word. Thank God.

"Help me," I said, running my hands through my hair.

"Help you?" She plopped herself into the booth seat across from me and braced her head in her hands. After a couple of seconds, she eyeballed me. "I just saw a dead boy who had two letters carved into his chest."

My jaw dropped open.

Twelve

Cooper

For a split second, I saw a quiver in Courtney's lip. I'd never seen a dent in her armor. Maybe she'd become really good at hiding it, considering her career choice.

"Are you okay?" I knew I'd asked a lame question, but I had to break the ice somehow.

"Honestly, I'm not sure."

I started to slip out of the booth. "Let me get you something to drink."

She let a hand drop to the table. "Not needed."

I slid back into my seat as her eyes slowly shifted to look out the window. I waited a few seconds, wondering what, if anything, I could say to help. "Do you want to talk about it?"

She released a heavy sigh. While she was a striking woman, the discomfort on her face made it difficult for me to look at her, which only made me feel guilty. She finally turned to face me. "I don't mean to be a bitch to you."

"What? You're fine," I said, pulling a foot up to cross over my knee. I couldn't sit still. This wasn't my area of expertise. Part of me just wanted to leave, but I couldn't do that to her.

She grabbed a white sugar packet and toyed with it. “Cooper, I’m not looking for you to fix me or have all the answers about how someone could do such a thing to a boy.”

I forced myself to take a breath and chill out. “You just want me to listen.”

She blinked rapidly for a few seconds, as if that helped process her thoughts, or how she was going to express them. Actually, I wasn’t sure what was going on in her brain. Would she just sit and stare for a while? Maybe that would slowly ease the pain. Or was she about to come unglued? Not knowing her that well, I prepared for the worst.

“Fucking crazy world we live in,” she said, more to herself than me directly.

Was I supposed to agree or just keep my mouth shut? I chose the second option.

The door to the coffee shop opened and happy teenage chatter filled the room. I counted five kids—three girls and two boys, maybe sixteen or seventeen years old. They were talking over each other while taking pictures and tapping their phones. I was certain the epic moment was being captured on TikTok and every other new and hip social media platform that existed.

Courtney glanced at the flock of noise and activity over her shoulder. “Dante will never have the opportunity to hang out with friends at a coffee shop.”

“That’s his name…Dante?”

“Was. He’s dead now, Cooper.”

Damn. I was not reading her very well.

“If you want to leave, feel free,” she said. “You didn’t sign up to be my shrink.”

“I didn’t sign up for anything. I chose to hang out with you.”

“Because I’m the life of the party,” she said in monotone.

“Hey, at times in my life, misery and defeat have been my closest confidants. Life isn’t about all those fake Facebook posts.”

"Don't I know it." She took hold of my water. "Do you mind if I have a sip?"

"No problem. You sure you want my cooties?"

The corner of her lip edged upward. Victory! She took more than a sip. She chugged like she'd just bounced a quarter into a cup from ten feet. College drinking games found their way into my mind at the oddest times.

"Ah!" She set the cup down, then used her sleeve to wipe her mouth. "Don't look so shocked," she said.

"What did I do?"

"Look shocked."

I didn't think I'd moved a muscle. "Okay."

"I've got to get it out, so here it goes…" She locked eyes on me as though she were giving me a chance to make a run for it. I didn't think about it.

"Ready when you are."

"His name was Dante Chilton. Just thirteen years old. He was found about four blocks from here, his body thrown in a dumpster."

I tried to swallow—I knew the worst had yet to be spoken—but my mouth was dry. And she'd already claimed the water.

She continued. "Blood was everywhere. Looked like a slaughterhouse."

I cleared my throat, searching for saliva.

"ME said he was raped before he was killed. Probably with a broom handle that was found in the dumpster."

"Jesus," I said reflexively.

"Sick. Fucking sick," she said with a shake of her head.

She started fidgeting with the sugar packet again. I wondered if she'd finished cleansing her mental palette.

Just as I turned my gaze to watch the teenagers interact—something on the happy side of the ledger—Courtney kept going.

"Dante was beaten. His entire face was bloated and bruised. Teeth were knocked out, blood seeping out of every orifice possible."

"Was that his official cause of death…the beating?"

"ME found ligature marks on the front and sides of the neck."

"He was strangled?"

"That's her initial thoughts." Courtney took in another deep breath, then grabbed the glass of water. "You want the rest?" she asked.

"Not thirsty. All yours."

She downed the water and finished with another sleeve wipe.

A clap of laughter came from the teenagers, briefly snagging our attention. They were really too loud for a coffee shop, but when you're young and hanging out with your friends, you mostly just live in the moment. You're not completely naïve to the world's fallacies, but it's pretty damn easy to ignore. So you do. As long as possible. And then something slaps you across the face, a reality that you can't dodge. It tears you up, and then you wonder if that's what being an adult is all about—taking on one trauma after another until you've gained forty pounds (or maybe lost forty, depending on your DNA), turned your hair gray, and squeezed your face until wrinkles show up.

"So, when you walked in, you said something about letters being carved into his chest. Was that to Dante or—"

"Dante. All of this happened to Dante."

"What…?" I wasn't sure what to ask really.

"Not sure what instrument was used, maybe just a piece of metal wire. But the killer etched two letters into his little chest. S and N."

"Was he black?"

She nodded.

"Someone was starting to write a word, maybe?"

"Don't know." She sighed and rubbed her temples.

"Might be some type of acronym."

"You think?"

"No clue. Just throwing ideas out there."

She pulled out her phone, typed in a message. "We'll look into that. See, I guess it was in the cards for us to talk."

"Glad I was more of assistance than that packet of sugar."

She tried to chuckle, and then she extended her hand. I took hold of it, and we just looked at each other for a few seconds.

"I'm guessing there were no witnesses," I said.

"None we can find so far. That part of Deep Ellum is a little seedy. We don't know much about Dante yet. But that will soon change."

"With you on the case, I'm sure this investigation will move as fast as humanly possible."

"We'll see. I can only do so much." She pulled back her hand. It was a little sweaty, but I kept myself from wiping my hand on my jeans.

"Thank you for listening to this horror story."

"Will you keep me updated on what you find out?"

"You sure? There's still time for you to bail."

"I'm not bailing. This is your job, your life. We all have crap to deal with."

"Like your broken arm," she said, eyeing my casted arm. That was an issue she knew about—I'd been attacked by a person who resembled Sasquatch. But there was so much more she didn't know, and I wasn't sure I could ever tell her.

"Yeah, my broken arm. It's fine. It will heal in a few weeks. Just don't be bashful about spilling your guts to me. A person can only take so much."

She put a hand to her chest. "Thanks, Cooper. That's really cool." She chewed a piece of ice, then said, "Besides these therapy sessions you're offering, maybe we can try for our second date soon."

"You're on."

Thirteen

A single thump ignited the first spark in his brain. A brain that felt like it had slept for a thousand years.

Just as quickly, the flame of mental light receded, and he began to fall back into his deep, peaceful slumber.

Another thump. This one pissed him off. He willed the gears in his mind to break free from their restraints and study the thump. It was directed at the middle of his forehead, and he couldn't help but think about that time in Helsinki when a private security team had finally caught up to him under a smelly bridge in the thick of the night. The leader, a square-headed man with spiked hair, was enraged because of what he had pulled off—killing the matriarch of the wealthy family that the leader's firm was responsible for safeguarding. Lego Head—that's what he called him—ordered his team to hold him down, including one who grabbed his head of curls and practically ripped his scalp off as he held his head still. Lego Head pressed a Glock against his forehead so hard he could feel the round imprint of the barrel deep within the confines of his skull. A bullet fired a second later, and Lego Head's brain matter sprayed all over his face. His backup had come through, allowing him to escape certain death.

But the thump from seconds ago wasn't nearly as defined as the barrel of a pistol. In fact, as more synapses fired, he ascertained that after the initial thumping, the object morphed into something resembling an amoeba.

Wait. His brain was waking up. Was that a drop of water that had landed on his forehead?

A third thump.

The man felt it slide off the slope of his head, but it didn't fall onto his nose or cheek. He felt it snaking through his scalp. How was that possible? Had this half-unconscious state warped his senses to where everything was turned upside down?

He felt something tight against his neck. That set up a domino effect of assessing his entire body as his eyes shot open to nothing but black. His ankles, arms, and wrists were restrained. Some type of steel cable wrapped his torso.

He heard a moan, and he tried to jerk his head in the direction of the noise. But his head couldn't turn. It, too, was restrained. And then he realized that he wasn't lying down on a flat surface. It was tilted ever so slightly back toward his head.

His pulse tripled in about a second as he finally put the pieces together, what was about to take place.

"Who's there?" he called out.

Another moan. It was a little louder this time, but it sounded as though the person's voice box had been removed.

"Can you speak?"

The moan pitched higher. The person in the room with him had become upset, which only made his heart race faster. A series of questions blurted out of his mouth.

"Who has us?"

"Where are we being held? Are we still in the States?"

"Why did you get taken hostage?"

"What have they done to you?"

He forced himself to be quiet for a moment, although the thud of his heart against his rib cage almost made it impossible to hear the whimpering moans from what sounded like a man.

He kept talking, hoping to convince his fellow hostage—hoping to convince himself—that they would live. "Someone must know we're here. They will come and find us. I've been in these situations before. If someone was targeting you and me, then someone important must be involved. They won't let us down. They'll rescue us."

He'd hoped to hear some type of affirmation, but the whimpers only faded into oblivion. And then there was silence. He held his breath for a few seconds, and during that time, a thought entered his mind.

Where had the water drops come from? Maybe there was a leak in the ceiling somewhere overhead. He could only hope.

A door creaked open, and then it shut. The moans of his fellow prisoner became more pronounced. Someone was inside the room now. He twisted and tugged his arms, legs, and torso, trying to loosen the grip of the restraints. He poured every bit of strength he could muster into his struggle to free himself until he was panting, his entire body coated with sweat.

"Who are you?" he asked in a voice that sounded like he'd already conceded.

No response.

"Tell me what the fuck I'm doing here!"

Still nothing.

A switch was flipped, and he was bathed in piercing spotlights. He quickly shut his eyes, but he could feel the heat against his eyelids. Now his brain was thinking in slow motion, thinking about what had just happened. Had he seen a spout of some kind about two feet above his face?

The table slowly tilted back, and his heart took off in another sprint. "No, no, no! You can't! It's a violation of every prisoner rule in the world."

The words sounded ridiculous to him even in his near-panic state of mind—he'd carried out far worse atrocities in his life.

Before he could ponder why he had ended up in this chamber, a wet cloth was draped over his face. And then water began to fall. A few drops at first. But it was enough to make his hands and feet start tingling. His blood was being directed elsewhere. He was in survival mode.

But he knew his fate was not in his hands.

The water began to hit his face in larger quantities. He held his breath, then blew out. He did this over and over again. But with every intake of air, no matter the speed, he choked water down his windpipe.

The waterboarding cycle had begun. And he knew he was going to die.

Fourteen

Cooper

I took a circuitous route back to my apartment. And it wasn't just to scope out the neighborhood for any signs of the resident pest, Myron Little.

A setting sun peeked through the evening clouds, as though it were giving a quick wink before retiring for the night. I punched my window down and let the last rays of light warm my face as cool air whipped through the front cabin of the Converta-beast.

The whole warm/cool thing was probably strange to some, but it both soothed me and made my blood churn. I supposed it had something to do with what was bouncing around in my mind.

My thoughts volleyed between the grisly playback of what Courtney had witnessed—of what Dante Chilton had experienced in the last few minutes before death—and what I felt for Courtney.

Dante was just a kid. Who could do what Courtney had described to a kid? To anyone? But to a kid? I wasn't sure how Courtney did this every day, walking up to a crime scene that she knew would rip her in two and make her question the humane piece of humanity. Did our world really understand what it meant to be humane? If not, was it lost forever, or could we capture it again?

Heady questions, for sure. But it was witnessing Courtney painfully conveying the details of what she'd seen that had left such an indelible mark on me. I got the feeling she didn't do that very often. I felt somewhat honored that she felt comfortable to open up to me, to let her guard down at least a little bit. But what did I really feel for her? Empathy, for certain. Beyond that, I really wasn't sure.

I parked my car in the same spot under my garage apartment and made my way up the stairs. Before opening my door, I glanced to the big house, wondering if Mrs. Kowalski might pop out of the back door and ask me to jump in and do a quick favor for her. I let a few seconds tick by, and then I went inside my apartment.

I immediately shut off my phone. I needed to have some uninterrupted time if I hoped to rediscover my writing zone, that magic wave that allowed the words to appear on my computer screen without realizing my fingers were tapping the keys. I'd started my opening paragraph earlier and was just starting to feel like I wasn't tripping over myself. But that was before the home invasion, before my conversations with Courtney, before she'd found a murdered child. At the same time, I knew I actually had to find the person I was profiling and convince him to talk to me. But for some reason, I first had to convince myself I hadn't lost my writing chops.

I saw my laptop sitting there, still purring. It was old, and I knew I was taking a chance of it not crashing while I wrote my stories, hoping that I could resurrect my career—my true passion—and that the money would follow.

Money. I logged into my computer and thought more about my decision to use the fifty K Raymond had left in the trunk of my car to pay off Dr. V. Of course, I didn't know that he'd left it there until he'd whispered those words into my ear at Willow's wedding rehearsal dinner—just a few hours before I was supposed to hand over the cash. But that was only his first zinger. The second had caused my blood to run cold. Colder.

How did Raymond know Dr. V and the Sack Brothers? Was it possible he knew of them but had no direct contact with them? I wrapped my knuckles against my head and wondered if the difference meant anything. If you're close enough to know of them, it probably means the people you're hanging around are not exactly choir boys.

So, what does that say about you, Cooper?

"Shut the fuck up!" I yelled as I clicked on about ten things on my computer.

"Not responding," I said, reading the error message in the ribbon of the browser. "Wonderful. Fucking wonderful." I huffed out a breath and folded my arms across my chest. After a few seconds, I shifted my eyes back to the screen. Same. Damn. Error message.

I walked into the kitchen—that's about a ten-foot excursion—and grabbed a can of Orange Crush from the fridge. I popped the top and took a few sips. My body tingled all over. I know, I'm strange.

Over at my workstation, the computer had shaken off the little demons, and the cursor was blinking. Eager to see what I'd written earlier, I clapped my hands, sat down, and read the words on the screen.

Money. We act like it doesn't shape who we are or how we act. But let's not fool ourselves. From our earliest moments of realizing what the world is all about, money is used as both the carrot and the stick. It's subtle, at times, like when your parents urge you to make good grades so you can go to a good college, so you can get a good job. Good job equals high-paying job, which is why your parents push you to get great grades. They crack the whip until you work your ass off, or figure out a way to lie or cheat and not get caught, and graduate high school in the top ten of your class.

From there, a perfect GPA in college—better known as under-grad for those who've been brainwashed into thinking that's just a step in the right direction—will land you a spot in graduate school. But it can't just be any graduate school. It has to be the best. Your parents won't say it's all about the money. But it is. And they only know that one path to push you to achieve your goal. To make as much money as possible.

But for a few people in this world, the path can be much different. The road to riches can be much quicker, the ascent to the top of the mountain attained in blinding speed. So fast that you can't possibly understand what it means to have seven digits sitting in your bank account while the rest of the world scrounges to have two, maybe three digits.

Enter the universe of a world-class athlete. The journey is something most of us can't fathom. It's unworldly, really. It can take the most humble person and inflate their ego until they are unrecognizable. And once their special talent is noticed by the right people, they latch on to the kid with their meat hooks and don't let go until it rips flesh from bone.

All in the name of money.

"Not bad," I said to myself. I knew the lead would change about twenty times over the course of talking to people and learning more information. Branches would sprout, and that could force me to do a one-eighty on my whole approach. But that was part of the creative challenge. And I reveled in it.

I cracked my knuckles, sipped more of my Orange Crush, and set my fingers on the keys. I blew out a slow breath, closed my eyes for a second, and allowed my mind to gravitate into the zone.

The pounding at the door literally made me flinch. "Jesus." I jumped out of my chair so fast, it toppled over. I was pissed. If this was Myron Little, then I was going to… Crap! I couldn't kick his ass. He was too old. That'd be considered inhumane. Maybe I could get Mrs. Kowalski to kick his ass. Now that would be funny.

I swung open the door.

"Willow?"

She turned her palms to the sky. "Do you ever answer your phone?"

"Oh," I said, glancing at my phone sitting on the card table. "I turned it off. I needed some quiet time to think."

"No time to think," she said, walking into the apartment. "It's time to act."

"Act? What are you talking about?"

"Did you have to do any community service when you were convicted of your drug felony?"

"Falsely convicted," I corrected her.

"Whatever. Did you?"

"I got out of that."

"Well, good for you. This is your time to do a service to your community."

I grabbed my Orange Crush and took a sip. "And what would that be?"

"We need to find a missing husband. Grab your phone and let's go."

I pinched the corners of my eyes. "Hold on a second. I'm just starting to write my first story for *The Wire*."

"You can write later. It's not like—" She stopped herself short.

"You were going to say it's not like a real job. I've heard it before," I said with an audible sigh.

"Don't be that way."

"Me?" I poked my chest.

She moved closer to my computer and leaned over. I stepped in front of her.

"You don't want me to read it?"

"It's just a draft. And I'm just getting started. I haven't even talked to the person I'm profiling yet."

She gave me a funny look. "Don't you have this backwards?"

"Now you're going to be my editor? A moment ago, you thought this was a throw-away job."

"Didn't say that. And don't be so sensitive. I just meant you probably had some flexibility in your schedule so you could help me out."

I *was* being sensitive. Kind of. I put my hand on my computer. "This means everything to me. When I think someone is trying to diminish its importance…"

She reached out and grabbed my hand and looked me in the eye. "I'm sorry." Never diverting her gaze, she gripped my hand harder, and I got the sense she wanted to say something more. I waited a moment, wondering what was at the edge of her lips…which, of course, momentarily drew my eyes to her lips. Her mouth opened, and I heard my breath hitch as I shifted my sights back to her eyes. I felt my head tilt to one side. We were drawing closer. But I didn't know how. It was all involuntary. I didn't want this to happen, did I?

Her hand touched my chest—she must have felt it racing—and blood zipped through my veins at a breakneck pace. Her big maple-syrup eyes were like magnets. I couldn't stop the pull, and right now, I wasn't sure I wanted to. I licked my lips just before impact, the heat of her breath pouring gasoline on the fire inside of me.

The moment we pressed together, a current of electricity sizzled throughout my extremities. All of them. I took her mouth in mine, and then she fought for dominance. Our tongues danced like they were possessed as our hands rubbed and gripped with a rawness I'd never experienced. While our kiss was full of wild fury, at the core of our connection was a soft, melodic passion, a warmth that gently cradled my heart as though we'd shared thousands of treasured memories over the eighteen years that we'd been apart.

Her mouth pulled back a couple of inches. "Did you hear that?" she asked.

I grabbed a handful of her curls and pushed her head back toward mine. We were lip-locked, once again lost in the zone where time stood still, where nothing else mattered.

Something cracked through my daze, and I pulled back this time. "Did you hear that?"

"Who cares?" She grabbed my shirt and ripped it open, spraying buttons all over the floor.

Was she for real?

Our bodies slammed into each other. We couldn't pull our mouths off each other long enough for me to start to pull her sweater up. My hands found her hips, though, and I didn't want to let go.

Then we both pulled back. "Someone's knocking on the door," we said in unison. We paused a second, then we both cracked up.

"Give me one more quick kiss," she said.

I didn't question it. I just did it. And it wasn't quick. My hands found her hair, and I think I moaned. It could have been her. It could have been both of us.

More knocking on the door. "Crap," I said, coming up for air. "I better get that." As I turned toward the door, I found my finger caught in a knot of Willow's hair.

"Ow, ow, ow!" she said, reaching up to grab my hand. "Are you wearing a ring?"

"Uh, yeah," I said, leading the shuffle to the door.

"What kind of ring?"

"Class ring."

"That would be your ring from Canisius, not TCU."

She was harping on the fact that I'd left eighteen years earlier without much of an explanation. I'd been offered a basketball scholarship at a tiny school in the north, and with little direction in my life, I knew I had to take it. I just wasn't solid on the communication part with her.

"That would be correct."

"Stop moving. You're hurting me."

I stopped. "Sorry." I tried to pry my ring from the endless bed of curls.

"Dammit, this isn't working," she said in a pissed-off singsong.

"Need to cut your hair?"

"I was thinking about your finger."

"Ha-ha."

More knocks on the door.

"I think I need to get that."

"Is it your booty call from your new girlfriend?"

It felt like a bucket of cold water was just dumped on my face. Courtney. *Damn.* "Whatever. You're frickin' dating an ex-fiancé you don't even love who ordered a hit from a crime boss."

"Cooper Chain, get your fucking finger out of my hair."

She was pissed. I'd crossed that line. "Uh, I might have crossed the line."

"You know Harvey didn't do that. You're just jealous."

"Of little Napoleon? Please."

"Oh yeah, I forgot about the estate you own over by the Perots and Cubans."

I could feel heat crawl up my neck. Or was my whole body already hot? "Sorry if I'm not elite enough for you. But you can go find your Sugar Daddy and live a happy fucking life."

"Just give me my hair back."

"Give me my finger back."

More knocks.

"The door," I said.

"Okay, okay."

She walked with me as if we were doing some type of dance.

We reached the door as the knocking became more insistent, but my finger was still stuck. "I've got to get this."

She kept trying to pry my finger loose, but was having no luck. "Get it, then."

I opened the door. Mrs. Kowalski yelped, and then she covered her mouth. That's when I realized my shirt was wide open, exposing my chest. She turned and saw Willow tugging on my hand, but her sweater was hiked up her torso, exposing the bottom part of her bra. I quickly pulled her sweater down.

"What's going on, Mrs. Kowalksi?" I tried to act nonchalant, even as my hand was still stuck to the back of Willow's head.

"Hi, Mrs. Kowalski." Willow waved. "Cooper accidentally got his hand stuck in my hair."

"An accident," she said with a single nod as her eyes inspected our scene.

"Can I help you with something?" I asked.

"Actually, I was just letting you know that you may not see my light on the next few nights."

"You going somewhere?"

She tried to hide her smile, but it was impossible. "Remember that gentleman I told you about?"

I queried my mind—it was still recovering from the influx of oxygen—and I came up empty.

"You know, the one I met in the Biography section at Books and Spirits."

Wait. Wasn't that the guy she was going to hook up with in his SUV in the parking lot? I tried not to look like I smelled something foul. "Oh, right. How is…?"

"Clark. And no, he's not a Hunt."

I wouldn't have gone there. "Of course not."

"Well, he's got a nice cabin on Lake Texoma, and he's asked me to tag along. He's picking me up in about ten minutes. Just wanted you to know."

"Thank you." I started to shut the door, but she put a hand on it and eyed Willow for a second.

"Treat her right, Mr. Chain. All women deserve that much."

Fifteen

Willow

I peered in the mirror and didn't like what I saw. It wasn't the smeared makeup or my wild hair that just couldn't be restrained. It was me. My conscience. I'd cheated on Harvey. Kind of. A hundred questions hit me so fast I couldn't answer one of them. I just knew that I felt guilt and shame, something I hadn't felt in years, not since I'd been humbled professionally and personally. Which took my thoughts full circle back to Harvey.

Already a partner at his CPA firm when we first met, Harvey had taken an interest in me, just a simple waitress. He soon learned that I was a former nurse who'd been disgraced for writing painkiller prescriptions for a so-called friend. I'd been naïve at best, and it cost me, big time. I had a felony on my record, was humiliated and forced to wait tables to make ends meet.

Harvey didn't focus on that. He saw me for the kind of person I was, not by the size of my paycheck or the name brands I wore or drove. He also knew that his elite group of friends and colleagues would find out. But Harvey took it all in stride. He saw something special in me. He didn't run away.

Are you saying that because he showed you loyalty, you owe him your life...to get married?

I knew I had unfinished business on that front, but it could wait. I huffed out a breath and walked out of the bathroom. I saw Cooper's back. He was sitting at his cheap card table tapping on his laptop. I walked over, and he quickly stood up. He'd put on another shirt, untucked, and as usual, his hair just kind of fell in the right places. We looked into each other's eyes, but we kept our hands to our sides.

"Hey, about our…" I wasn't sure what to say or how I should say it.

"I know. It was wrong. Shouldn't have done it. I'm not even sure where it came from." He tucked his non-cast hand in his jeans.

"Yeah, it wasn't wise for either one of us. A weak moment," I said.

"Very weak." He paused, glanced around his apartment that looked like it hadn't been cleaned in months. "You want an Orange Crush?"

"Why are you asking me that?"

'Because it's the most awesome drink on the planet."

"Cooper, you're too much." I tried to take in a breath. My chest felt constricted. "What about Courtney?"

"What about her?"

"You going to tell her about…this?" I said, volleying a hand back and forth between us.

"You going to tell Harvey?"

"Why do you have to twist my words back at me?"

He seemed to ponder that question. About time. "I don't know, Will. I'm not sure about any of this. About Courtney, about you and Harvey, about me and..."

"Me," I said, patting my chest. "Look, we just need to grow up and admit what happened. No big deal. Everyone slips up. It meant nothing, right?"

"Absolutely."

"And you think I'm an anal pain in the ass anyway."

"And you think I'm a no-good, underachieving slob."

Silence.

"Actually, you're pretty cool."

"You are too." He cracked a smile. "So, what's this community service you want me to do?

Of course, the reason that had spurred my visit.

"Grab your phone." I picked up my purse and was in my car seconds later.

Sixteen

Cooper

Willow had started backing out of Mrs. Kowalski's long driveway before I'd even reached her BMW. She jerked the car to a stop, and I slid in.

"What's the damn hurry?"

She punched the gas, ricocheting my door open and then shut before I could pull it closed myself.

"Willow, what's going on?"

She hit the brake again and looked at me.

"We were up there screwing around." She shook her head, and random locks of curls fell across her face. She tried to blow them out of her face. No luck. She pushed them to the side. "And there's a grieving, sick woman who I promised to help. That's what's going on."

"And you're pissed at me because I was part of this… By the way, we weren't exactly screwing."

She narrowed her eyes and then jabbed a finger at me. "Now you want to break down the words I'm using?"

"I'm just pointing out the difference between screwing and a simple kiss, that's all."

She looked through her windshield at my apartment, then she slowly turned back to me. "First of all, I'm pretty sure I know the difference between screwing and not screwing."

"I never said you didn't know how to screw." *Did I really just say that?*

We stared at each other for what seemed like an eternity. I braced myself for a punch to the shoulder socket. Suddenly, she exploded in laughter, and I couldn't help but follow suit. I think we laughed for a good minute. Finally, just as we both calmed down, our eyes met, and then she snorted out another burst of laughter. Again, it was like someone punched the laughing gas button, and we were both in tears. This went three rounds, until the point where I accidentally banged my cast off my head.

She laughed some more. I cussed and scratched my head.

"Jesus, we're a mess," I said.

"Speak for yourself."

"Okay, now that I finally know why the hell you came over, you're wanting me to help you with this sick woman."

"*Grieving* sick woman."

"Are we helping her with the sick part or the grieving part?"

"She's got the flu, both she and her mother. But Dr. Mulligan gave them prescriptions for Tamiflu. I got them home, made sure they had food and their first dose of medicine and—"

I reached over and touched her arm. "Hold on. You went to your patients' house?"

She gently pulled her arm back. I guess I had cooties—a few minutes ago, not so much. "It's no big deal. Anyway, the daughter's husband is missing. They've had some problems in their marriage, but he's also had drug issues in the past. She hasn't seen him in a week. She's really concerned."

"Didn't you tell her to call the cops? That's what they do, find missing people."

She shook her head. "Are you trying to get out of this? Because if you are, just get out now."

"What? Don't be that way. I'm just thinking that's the logical place to go."

She punched the front windows down.

"You want me to jump out the window?"

"Just give me a minute to clear my head, Cooper."

Wind blew through the front cabin. I looked out my window, scanning the area for Myron Little. Never know when a nut like that might jump out from behind a tree in camo gear with a hunting knife between his teeth. I felt some pellets of frozen rain against my face, and I slumped lower in my seat. "Hey, are we supposed to be getting any bad weather?"

She didn't answer, so I swiveled my head around. Her face was buried in her phone. "Sexting with Harvey again?"

Her sigh, accompanied by an eye roll that was something akin to a lunar eclipse, sounded like windshield wipers scraping a dry surface. I waved a hand in front of my face. "I'd rather you hit me in the shoulder than give me that audio-video one-two punch."

"Funny. I'm texting with Jada right now to get more information on where we might look for her husband."

"Sounds like a good idea. He's been gone a week, though. He could be in Tijuana by now."

"Hmm."

"Hmm what?"

"She's saying she doubts he left the area."

"Not sure how she'd know that, but okay."

"They've been married for over two decades. They have two kids in college."

"Are you saying that people don't change once they get married?"

She opened her mouth, but no words came out.

"Got you on that one, didn't I?

"Not really. I just don't want to have another great debate with you." Her phone lit up, and she looked at the screen.

"Anything noteworthy?" I asked.

"She said that if he took any extended trip, it would probably be to the East Coast. He grew up in the DC area. Apparently, he went to Maryland."

That piece of information stuck in my brain for some reason. "The University of Maryland?"

"I guess, why?"

Two kids in college would probably put this guy in his forties or fifties. I sat up in my seat. "Who did you say this guy was again?"

"I only said his wife's name, Jada."

"But who are we searching for?"

"Not sure it makes a difference, but his name is Rashad."

My body went numb. Then it felt like my face was being sprayed with gunshot. I realized it was the freezing rain blowing through the window.

"What is it, Cooper? You know something."

"Rashad Hatley. It's got to be him."

"How did you know his last name?"

"He's the guy I'm writing my story about."

Seventeen

Willow

Jada had stopped sending messages. She was probably wiped out.

"We've got to find this guy, Willow. This is huge." Cooper jostled in his seat like a little kid in church.

"I know, I know. But I don't know that we'll get much more from Jada tonight."

"Do you know how big this is?"

"I know a wife thinks her husband might be sitting in a sewer with a needle in his arm. Hell, he might be dead. So, yeah, I know how big this is."

"Right, I know that's important. That's part of this tragic story. He's a former number-one pick in the NBA draft. He made something close to sixty million dollars in his career, and then he lost it all."

I lifted my eyes from my phone. "Sixty million?"

He nodded. "I've heard about the drugs, about all the excess in his life. In fact, there's an old story: when the team would travel, he reportedly wouldn't pack any clothes. He would just buy new clothes in every city he went."

"What about the clothes he accumulated while on the trip?"

"He'd either just let one of the members of his posse have them or just leave them behind. We're talking about four-figure suits and shoes, always going for the latest fashion trends. He'd just blow through them like they were a box of tissues. He didn't care; the money kept flowing in, and he had no concept of self-control."

"You seem to know a lot about a guy you've never interviewed," I said.

"That's the surface-level stuff. The headlines with just a little bit of meat. The point of my story is to go deeper, to see what he thinks about all that excess now, how it has shaped his life, and to look back at what made him go down that path, who or what influenced him."

His words made me think. "You really know what you're doing. I'm pretty impressed."

"I'm just curious, that's all. But his disappearance could change everything, including the approach I take on my story."

"Hold on. Finding Rashad isn't about making sure your story is wrapped in a nice red bow. These are real people who are in real trouble."

"I know, I know. He's got two kids, right?"

"Yep."

He let his hand drop to his thighs. "I'm sure they've witnessed a lot. But for them, I hope we find their father. Where are we going first?"

I handed him my phone and started backing out of the driveway, heading toward the east side of 75. "There's a list of bars. Let's start there."

He studied my phone screen and didn't say much on my eastward trek. I hit Greenville Avenue and went south until I saw the lights for the first place.

"Ive Bar," Cooper said, nudging his head at the sign as we got out of the car.

"Should say Dive Bar. The light's out on the D."

"Yeah, I pretty much figured that out. I have that deductive-reasoning gene. My friends call me Sherlock Holmes."

I rolled my eyes, although I doubted he saw me in the muted light.

"I saw that."

"How?"

"You have large eyes."

"That sounds like you're describing a Martian."

We got to the door at the same time, our faces only inches away from each other. He said, "A beautiful Martian, maybe."

I tapped his cheek. "Such a charmer."

"You can't take a compliment?"

"You just want to get me in bed."

He stopped pulling the door open at the halfway mark and stared at me. I'd dinged his ego. "I'm just kidding, Cooper. Adding a little levity to our…situation."

"Okay. Didn't expect that, considering the conversation you're going to be having with Harvey. Do I need to hire a private security firm of my own?"

Harvey. I could feel my insides knotting up as I temporarily let my mind open the gates of everything I'd been feeling since my wedding day. All that had happened…or not happened. "You have nothing to worry about. Let's just focus on something where we can actually help a family."

He gave me a mock salute, and we walked inside. The smell of smoke hit me like I'd run into a wall. "I thought smoking in bars was illegal."

"It is."

I scrounged through my purse, pulled out an old bottle of fingernail polish, and sniffed the edge. Cooper was about to say something, but he just shook his head then did a quick survey of the place. "Apparently the people who go here don't care about the smoke…all five of them."

He was right. I only counted five patrons. A man with a bar towel slung over shoulder plodded past me. "Excuse me, do you work here?"

He gave me a side glance, but continued walking until he made his way around the bar and anchored his arms. "Yeah, who wants to know?" he said, giving me the once-over. I counted about five teeth, his few strands of gray hair swaying back and forth like a handful of wildflowers on a barren dirt lot.

Cooper casually strolled up to the bar. "I have this old college buddy I'm looking for…"

The man gave him a nod. "What are you and your lady friend drinking?"

"Oh, I don't think alcohol would be a good idea right now," I said, pulling up next to Cooper.

The guy snickered.

"Two shots of tequila," Cooper said.

"But—"

Cooper nudged me with his elbow as the man set two small glasses on the bar and poured two shots up to the rim. Cooper handed me one, then lifted his tiny glass.

"Here's to everyone who wishes us well, and those who don't can go straight to hell." He clinked my glass, then tipped his head back and downed the shot. "Your turn."

I paused a moment. "Here goes nothing." The moment the tequila slid down my throat, it felt as though I'd just devoured a flaming sword. "Water," I croaked.

Cooper and the man laughed, but a glass of water appeared in front of me, and I drank it. When I looked up, I saw my shot glass was full again.

"What's this?" I said.

The bartender was now holding up his own full glass.

"You're supposed to pick up the drink, Will," Cooper said.

I cleared my throat and lifted the glass as if I were holding a glass of fire. I kind of was.

The man said, "May neighbors respect you, trouble neglect you, angels protect you, and heaven accept you."

My jaw dropped. *Impressive.*

"You thought I had shit for brains, didn't ya?" The man chuckled, then drank the tequila like it was water. I hesitated for a second—long enough for Cooper to give me the eye—and then he and I drank our shots.

"Nice, good stuff," I said, my voice sounding like a boy going through puberty.

"Really?" the man said, anchoring his arms on the bar again. "That's the cheapest shit we got."

"Oh."

"So…" Cooper brought up his cast arm and rested it on the wooden surface. "My college buddy. Have you seen a guy here named Rashad Hatley?"

"You got a picture?"

Cooper turned to me. I gave him wide eyes; Jada hadn't sent me a picture, and I hadn't thought it through far enough to ask for one.

"Back at my place, I think I have some old photos from college days, but you'd never recognize him," Cooper said.

The man nodded once, but his eyes became more suspicious. "Like I asked the chick earlier, who are you?"

"I'm Cooper. That's Willow. We're just old friends of Rashad, that's all."

"Old friends," he said, running his tongue across the largest tooth in his mouth.

"You know him?" Cooper asked.

"Never heard of him." He started using his towel to wipe down the bar.

Cooper glanced at me. I wasn't sure if the guy was hiding something, or he wanted us to offer him some money, or what the hell was going on.

I tilted my head, unsure of our next move. Suddenly, the bar towel whipped against Cooper's cast. "Joe Hardy and Nancy Drew…I was just shittin' ya. Of course, I know 'Rocket' Hatley. He had a better shooting stroke than Pistol Pete, but he didn't get all the pub. Well, not all the positive pub."

"You saw him play?" Cooper asked.

"Highlights mostly, although I did catch a game in his last season. Didn't seem to be into it that much."

"But you've seen him in this bar?" I asked.

"Yeah. He has a beer, maybe two. With his history, he knows he can't push it. Crazy thing is he doesn't like to talk about the good old days. He'd rather just blend in with the crowd."

"Has he been in the bar recently?"

He tried to slick back his crazy hairs, but they popped right back up. "Come to think of it, I haven' t seen him in here since he got in that fight."

I looked at Cooper, but he stayed on the man.

"So, what's your name?" Cooper asked.

"Rocky."

"Like the boxer," I said.

"No, like the ballet dancer." He rolled his eyes, then turned to Cooper. We clearly weren't connecting very well.

"Tell us more about this fight," Cooper said.

"It was during our Tuesday night happy hour, and the place was rockin'."

I almost snorted out a laugh. He slowly turned and looked right through me. "Sorry. Go ahead," I said.

"Anyway, these two out-of-towners who don't know how to hold their liquor recognize Rocket. It happens on occasion, but people usually get the vibe that he doesn't want to talk about his glory days, and people eventually just walk away. Not these two clowns. They start yanking his chain about one of them losing a thousand bucks because Rocket went one-for-twenty in a playoff game in his last season in the league."

I tapped the bar. "That must have been over ten years ago, and these out-of-towners remember losing money on a bet?"

Rocky looked at my hand, then shifted his sights to my eyes. "You don't think you'd forget losing a thousand bucks?"

"Uh…"

He looked at Cooper, then stabbed a thumb in my direction. "She doesn't think she'd remember losing a thousand bucks?"

He was speaking like I wasn't there, like I was a nobody. It reminded me of my days as a waitress, my first job at Waffle House, where groping and verbal humiliation were just part of the daily job. Ever since then, I told myself I'd never take that kind of disrespect again. Somehow, I withheld the urge to snap back at this guy. I had to keep the big-picture goal in mind: find Jada's husband.

Before Cooper could respond, Rocky kept going. "Look, for all I know, they were just giving Rocket shit. I mean, some guys, when they meet athletes, they get all alpha. They think they gotta prove something. That might have been the case here. They crossed the line."

"Who started the actual fight?" Cooper said.

"The short one started it by pushing Rocket. But Rocket finished it by using one of my pool sticks. He paid me back, so I was cool."

"Anyone suffer major injuries?"

"A few bumps and bruises, but it was mainly ego. Those guys left, but they threatened Rocket like you've never heard before."

"As in…" I said, rolling my arm.

He lowered his profile and spoke in a hushed tone. "Said they were going to get a rope and find a tree with his name on it."

I gripped Cooper's shoulder while shaking my head. "The hatred of some people…I just can't understand it."

A few seconds of silence, then Rocky said, "I told those fuckers to never come back to the bar again."

"Did you call the cops?"

He looked at me like I was a Martian, maybe a one-eyed Martian at that. "If I called the cops every time there was an altercation, they'd start charging me for every visit."

"But this was different. This was—"

"An altercation. Yeah, the guys crossed the line. They're probably bigots. They're definitely assholes. If I had a nickel for every asshole who walked through that door, I'd be a rich motherfucker."

Cooper accidentally banged his cast off the bar. The thud got my attention, and Rocky's too. "Is it possible that these two guys hunted down Rashad and kidnapped him or…?"

"You mean, hung him from a tree?" I asked.

He shrugged.

"As morbid and disturbing as that is to think about, I feel like someone would notice a person hanging off a rope. I'm sure we can dismiss that theory."

"You're thinking about right around here, or even in the burbs. But you travel thirty, forty miles in any direction from where we're sitting and you're in the country. I'm just saying it's possible."

I looked at Rocky. "Did you see Rashad leave the bar?"

"Actually, I saw the two bozos get in an Uber and drive off. Didn't see Rocket get in his car. But he chilled here a while before he left, maybe an hour or so." He wiped a hand across his doughy face. "I'm sure he made it home safely."

He didn't sound very confident.

"How do you know, Rocky? Did you check on him?"

"What the fuck you talking about? I'm not his ball and chain."

Cooper and I looked at each other with blank stares.

"What?" Rocky said. "What did I say?"

"Nothing," Cooper said, raking his fingers through his hair. I could see the gears in his mind crunching through everything we'd learned and what our next steps might be. I was doing the same.

Cooper knocked his cast off the side of the bar again. "Names. That's what we need. Do you know the names of these two guys? Maybe one or both of them used a credit card."

"I'll check." Rocky walked to the other side of the bar where there was a computer hooked up to a register.

"Not bad, Joe Hardy," I said to Cooper.

"It's just logical. Slowly, my journalism mind is coming back to me."

I made a scoffing noise. "You act like an athlete trying to get back into shape after a career-threatening injury." I smiled. He didn't.

Rocky coughed as he made his way back over holding a slip of paper. Cooper held out his hand, but Rocky pulled back his arm. "You know what I'm doing isn't exactly kosher."

"Neither is hanging a guy from a tree," I said.

Rocky looked at Cooper. "The broad's got balls, I'll give her that much."

"At least one," Cooper said, giving me a quick wink.

"Huh?" Rocky tilted his head like a dog that had just heard a high-pitched whistle.

"Just an inside joke," Cooper said.

Rocky shook his head, as if he were trying to erase that statement from his memory. I would have laughed had our situation not been so serious. "So, what do we have Rocky?" I asked.

"Okay. I got a name, and—"

"How do you know it's the guy who picked the fight with Rashad?"

"'Cause I see what he ordered. He ordered two Russian mules. Haven't had that drink ordered in this bar in years. I'm a Cold War kind of guy. I don't trust no Russians."

"Does this guy have a Russian last name?" Cooper asked.

"Hell no."

Rocky's logic, of course, made no sense, but to each his own. "So…?"

"Name is Albert Mashburn. I've got a zip code, but nothing else. It's 78728." He gave Cooper the piece of paper.

"Thanks," I said as we started walking toward the door.

"Hey," Rocky called out. "It would be cool if you let me know when you find Rocket."

"Will do," I said.

As we opened the door, Cooper said, "I hope it's a when, not an if."

Eighteen

Cooper

I snagged a quick glance at Willow, who seemed to be having some difficulty using my phone.

"Want me to do it?" I asked.

She did a quick double take on me. "Get your hands on the steering wheel!"

I moved my wrist off the top of the steering wheel and put a hand on it. "Better?"

"Two hands, please."

Willow had asked if I could drive her BMW because of the patchy ice on the roads, saying I had more experience from my time finishing college and working in New York. The conditions really weren't that bad. A few slick spots on overpasses, but the regular streets were just wet.

My second hand hit the steering wheel with a thud. "Okay, Miss Anal America, are you cool now?"

The glow of the phone screen lit up her face. I'd never thought that any expression from Willow would alter her attractiveness. This prune face, though, was pushing it pretty damn close. "You don't have to look like you're trying to push out a baby."

She turned and gave me flat eyes. Maybe I should have used something other than a baby reference.

"Why do you have to use that word?"

"Baby?"

"Uh, no. The A word."

"Anal," I said with a chuckle.

She appeared to shudder as she turned her eyes back to the phone. "For all I know, you get into that sort of thing now."

"Where I'm the pitcher or catcher?"

She reached over and pinched the side of my neck.

"Ow, ow, ow," I uttered in rapid-fire succession.

She finally let go. "Don't be rude."

I started rubbing my neck.

"Hands."

I put both hands on the steering wheel again. "Okay, Mom. Is that good now?"

"Ten and two."

"Equals twelve," I said with a smile.

"Come on, Cooper. You're being a pain in the ass. I told you about how I spun out on ice years ago."

"Actually, you didn't tell me." I moved my hand to the clock position of ten and two. "Didn't mean to scare you. So, where is this mystery zip code for Albert Mashburn?"

She held up my phone like it had been purchased at the Dollar Store. "This is a piece of crap, you know that, right?"

"And where is your phone, Miss Ball?"

"You know mine ran out of charge."

"So, my piece of crap works pretty damn good in comparison."

She showed off her pearly whites.

"Do you want me to use the phone? I'll admit, it requires a little bit of a special touch." I reached for it, but she quickly pulled it away.

"Ten and two, mister!"

"Okay, okay."

"And who says I don't have that special touch."

"Oh, I'm sure you do," I said quietly while popping an eyebrow.

She grabbed more skin at my neck.

"Didn't mean for you to hear that."

She let go and went back to work on my phone as I pulled into the parking lot of the second bar on our list.

"Okay, I think I have it." She tapped the phone screen about ten times. "I thought I did. The touch screen on your piece-of-crap phone sucks."

I put the car in park and snatched the phone from her hands. Two taps later, I had the answer. "Round Rock. A suburb outside of Austin."

"I know where Round Rock is, silly. Home of the Astros' Triple A affiliate, the Round Rock Express."

I moved my hand to my chest in dramatic fashion. "Did Willow Ball just recite a sports fact?"

She took the phone from me and said, "You want me to test out your anal fixation by shoving this phone up your ass?"

I cracked up. "You just like talking dirty to me." I jumped out of the car before her robotic grip pinched off an artery.

We walked into Pure Vinyl Bar and Grill. Five minutes later—after a manager confirmed he didn't know a Rashad Hatley and had no credit card charges from him on record—Willow and I were walking back to the car. "Sometimes, bad news is actually good news," I said.

"Which means we're just narrowing down our list."

We got into the car, and I revved it up and blew warm air into my hands as my mind cranked through what we knew and what we feared.

"You have that glare in your eyes, which means either you somehow drank fifteen cups of trash-can punch or something about Pure Vinyl bugged you," Willow said.

"Neither. I can't help but think about the worst-case scenario."

"Which is…?"

"That these Round Rock bigots somehow caught up with Rashad and…"

"Hung him from a tree?"

"Yeah, maybe. Or something equally deadly."

"You think you should call Courtney and get her take on what we should do, or maybe there's something she could do?" Willow asked.

"You serious?"

"Oh, right. Our little innocent kiss."

"It's not that, not really. Heck, Courtney and I haven't even kissed."

"I saw her kiss you today on the cheek," Willow said with an eyebrow raised.

I shook my head. "It was weird. But doesn't Harvey kiss you on the cheek some of the time?"

"The truth? I hate it. It's a grandma kiss. Sometimes I just want to tell him to grow a pair and kiss me like a real man."

I blew a puff of air on my fingernails and rubbed them against my shirt.

"And no, that's not my subtle way of saying you're a real man."

"That's not what you thought earlier," I said in my worst singsong tone.

"Whatever. Okay, Courtney isn't a good option right now. How about we hit the last bar, then figure out our next steps?"

"Sure. Just point in the right direction."

Working our way through only modest traffic on the slush-filled streets, we cruised into Deep Ellum without Willow having a heart attack, although she jammed her feet against the floorboard twice. I think she needed another shot or two of tequila.

We walked inside The Place—yes, that was the actual name of the bar. Not a bad marketing ploy on the name, really. The décor, though, made me think it wasn't the place to be, at least not for Miss TCU Preppy and me. The owners looked like they'd raided a 1990s Denny's. There was a dart board on a side wall and a single pool table that wore a coat of dust. The patrons were your typical Deep Ellum types, piercings and tats, but everyone seemed cordial.

A bartender with blue hair and a ghost-like face approached us at our two stools.

"Can you get my friend here your stiffest drink?" I asked.

"I don't need a stiff anything." The moment Willow said the words, she dropped her head into her hand. Then she grabbed my knee and squeezed. "Don't say a damn word."

I tugged at her arm while laughing. It didn't budge. "Okay, Wonder Woman, you've made your point."

"Good."

She looked at the waitress, who wore this look of dismay. "I'll have a glass of chardonnay."

Behind Willow, I got the waitress's attention and shook my head, hoping she'd understand to bring a stiffer drink. Either that or some anti-anxiety pills.

"And what would you like?" the young lady asked me.

"Do you have any Orange Crush?"

Willow elbowed my ribs.

"Ow. Do you still not know your own strength?"

"Do you not understand that Orange Crush was popular about thirty years ago?"

"Actually, our manager loves that stuff. Is a bottle okay?" the waitress asked.

"Is it chilled?"

"Is it chilled?" Willow exclaimed. "And you think I'm anal?"

I looked past Willow to the waitress, who said, "It's in the fridge."

"Perfect. Thanks."

"I'm Bella, if you need anything."

Sounded appropriate, given her pale look.

Bella returned a minute later with my bottle of Orange Crush and a drink I could smell from five feet away. "What's this?" Willow asked.

"We call it The Bomb. It'll blow you up. You know, make you chill."

"I…"

"Thank you, Bella," I said.

"I'll check on you guys in a minute." She walked off as Willow turned and looked at me.

"She's a good waitress," I said, taking a swig of my Orange Crush, then setting it on the bar. Willow swapped drinks.

"Hey, you can't have that," I said.

"Watch me." She took a gulp of my Orange Crush. "Not bad for dyed piss water," she said with a giggle.

Once she set the bottle on the bar, I switched the drinks back. "You do want me to drive, right?"

She sighed. Loudly. We both turned in our barstools to face the crowd and were silent for a few seconds. I noticed that Willow had the drink in her hands and was starting to take a couple of pulls on the straw.

"Are you seeing something a little, I don't know…off in here?" Willow stirred her drink, then took another sip. "Not bad."

"Uh, yeah. And it has very little to do with the piercings and tats. Actually, if you look at that table by the bathroom, that guy kind of looks like—"

"Indiana Jones," she said.

"Okay, so I'm not hallucinating."

"I'm the one drinking The Bomb. If I down this entire thing, I might see if Indy has his whip on him." She nudged me while snorting out a laugh.

A schnockered Willow would be a nice change. Maybe.

Bella walked up and set her tray on the bar next to us. "It's pretty obvious you guys are new here."

"We were that obvious?" I deadpanned.

"It's a pretty open place. Usually, no one judges, just because it's a place—*The Place*—to be someone you can't always be in your everyday regular life."

I nodded, catching on. "So, most everyone here is dressed up as some type of character, like a Halloween party?"

She tilted her blue head left and then right. "Kind of. I mean, I know Bella from *Twilight* didn't have blue hair. It's just the way I roll. But my pale face, and these…" She opened her mouth and showed four incisors that looked like they could rip my arm off. She must have seen my reaction.

"Don't worry. I don't bite. Well, not unless you want me to," she said, popping an eyebrow. And yes, it was also blue.

A second later, Willow wrapped her arm around my shoulder and gave it a firm grip, while sucking on her straw. "So, you were saying?"

Bella gently chewed on a nail—blue, of course. I wasn't sure Bella knew what to make of Willow's claim of ownership. I sure as hell couldn't.

"Uh, anyway, the people who work here, the patrons, most of us are pretty tight."

Willow goosed one of my ribs, and I lurched. She gave me a side glance, still working the straw. She was indicating that I should take the lead, which I was about to do.

"So, Bella, we're looking for a friend of ours who we think visited here pretty regularly."

"Do you see him?" She extended her arm like a game-show host.

I thought about creating some elaborate story, but what was the point? Willow and I weren't hiding anything. "It's kind of complicated. His wife hasn't seen him in days, and she's pretty worried."

"Fucking panicked," Willow added with a slight slur.

"Man, I'm really sorry to hear that. You don't think anything happened here, do you? I mean, this is a pretty tame bar."

"No, but can you tell us if you know him? Name is Rashad Hatley."

Willow lifted her drink and appeared to swallow a hiccup. "Some people call him Rocket." She sounded like a little kid trying to learn how to not mix her R's with her W's.

"Rashad, Rocket…no, I don't recall that name. Like I said, most people go with character names when they're in here."

Willow and I turned to look at each other, then turned back to Bella. "Given what we know about the guy, I'd put that likelihood at about five percent."

"Credit card," Willow said in monotone while she sucked the bottom of her drink.

"Right," I said, giving her a quick double take before looking at Bella. "Can you guys check to see if you have any credit card charges from Rashad Hatley and on what date?"

"I'll check. Give me one minute."

Once she left our space, I put my hand on Willow's. "You can remove your claws now."

She pulled back her hand, then tipped the glass backward. Ice fell across her face. "Fuuuck," she said, snorting out a laugh.

It was official. I handed her a bar napkin. "You're drunk."

"You think, Sherlock?" She tapped the side of my face. I smiled, then she yanked on one of my longer whiskers.

"Ouch!"

"Actually, I got it wong." She shook her head like a dog with fleas. "Check that…wrong," she said, emphasizing the R sound. "You're Holmes. I'm the female Sherlock. Call me Sherlocka."

I just shook my head. "Damn, I wish I had this on video."

A man in a tuxedo walked past us.

"What up, Holmes?" Willow said with a giggle.

The man stopped, brought his hand to his bow tie. He had a square chin and was clean-shaven. He could have been a model.

"It's Bond, James Bond."

So *that* was his character.

Willow arched her back, tried to sweep back some of her loose curls. "Actually, I was talking to my friend here. Holmes is his nickname."

Bond just stared at her.

"Do you like it shaken or stirred?" Willow asked with a straight face. Well, a straight shit-face.

He reached out and rubbed his thumb on her cheek. She touched it as though she'd just been blessed with Holy Water. "It's really you," she said in a breathy tone.

He smirked. "You're cute, but I'm taken." He turned, and I followed his gaze over to a table where some guy with green hair and a wide painted smile waved at us.

"Willow, he plays for the other team, so you can stop flirting with him," I said, on the lookout for Bella.

"Would you like to join my partner and me?" Bond said.

It took a moment, but I realized he was speaking to me. I chuckled. "I'm kind of into women."

"Only kind of. Hmm. Maybe Bradley Cooper's mind could be changed."

Had my mom somehow fed him that name?

Willow put a hand to her head, then grabbed Bond's arm. "Holy crap, James. Do you know what kind of ego this guy has?

The last thing you need to do is stroke it." She looked at me and then James. "Oops. Poor choice of words."

"Just ignore her. She's drunk."

He winked at me and left. "Why does everyone flirt with you? First Bella, and then James Bond."

"This coming from the girl who draws the eye of every male—straight and otherwise—every time she enters a room."

"Yeah, yeah, whatever."

Bella returned, thankfully.

"I'll take another one of these Bomb drinks," Willow said, dropping the empty glass so hard on the bar I thought it was going to break.

"She's good," I said. "What did you find out?"

"You're right. He was here."

"When?" Willow and I said at the same time.

Bella pointed a finger at both of us as if she wasn't sure what to think. I was in agreement. Then, she pulled a sticky note from her apron as a thin man in a pirate outfit walked behind her. "According to our records, Rashad Hatley last paid with a credit card here ten days ago. Looks like he had two beers and left a two-dollar tip."

"Ten days. So, three days prior to his last outing at The Dive," Willow said.

In her current state, I was a bit surprised she could do the math. Unless she was just playing up her inebriation to get under my skin. Yeah, I could see her doing that. Some sort of retribution for all the times I'd razzed her. While I'd never admit it to her, it was probably warranted, drunk or not.

We thanked Bella for her help and paid our tab. She gave me her card on the way out and said to call if we have more questions.

"You saw that, right?" Willow's breath pumped out white fog as we walked to the car.

"Saw what?"

"The vampire."

"Bella? What did I apparently not see?"

"How she put the card in your hand and held it there for a second. I'm surprised she wasn't wiggling her middle finger against the palm of your hand."

I snapped off a laugh. "Are you jealous? I mean, you basically stuck a flag in me and acted as though it was an act of war if she touched me."

"Don't flatter yourself. Oh, I forgot… You'll do that when you get home with your bottle of lotion."

"Ha-ha," I said as I reached the driver's side door. "I get it. 'Flatter yourself' is supposed to be some type of obscure reference to masturbation. By the way, I found your dildo in the back seat."

"What?" She quickly cupped a hand against the back window. Then she looked up, and I winked.

"Gotcha!"

"Asswipe," she said as we got in the car.

"You'd like to perform what service for me?" I said, cracking myself up.

Before she could pinch my neck or something else more valuable, a flash of silver swung across my vision and slammed into the hood of the car.

Nineteen

Cooper

Willow threw open her car door and put a foot on the ground. "That's my car!"

I tried grabbing at her to sit down, but she smacked my hand away. I glanced out the window and saw the pirate from earlier in the bar, rage in his eyes.

He lifted his arm—there was a hook on the end, something I hadn't noticed while in the bar—and he slammed it into the hood again, shaking the entire car.

"Willow, get in the car!"

She ignored me and pulled around her door. "Oh, great," I said, fumbling with my door handle to get it open. Once I finally got out of the car, the pirate put his good hand on the hook and whirled it around like it was a sledgehammer, aiming for Willow's head. I dove across the hood, ramming my shoulder into his torso. It was bony. Hell, I might have cracked one of his ribs.

He released an agonizing yelp that sounded something like "Argh!"

I quickly rolled off him and got to my knees as he curled into a ball. "Hey, I didn't mean to hurt you, but you can't be—"

"Look out!" Willow yelled.

The man uncoiled himself, slinging a switchblade across my face. I dodged the blade and fell to the ground. I saw a blur whizzing overhead. Was that Willow?

She belted out a karate-like noise as her foot clocked the pirate's hand, sending the switchblade skidding across the wet pavement. The pirate cried out like a wounded animal as he tumbled backward, holding his hand against his chest. "You broke my fucking hand, bitch!"

I got to my feet, grabbed the guy by the collar, then pulled him up and held him against the side of the BMW. He probably didn't weigh more than a buck thirty.

"That's attempted assault, buddy. You're going to jail."

"You a cop?"

With my hand still gripping his pirate garb, I turned to give Willow my phone, but I stopped and looked at the guy. "Not possible. But they'll be here soon enough. Here, Willow, call the cops."

She took my phone.

"Stop! I beg you not to call them. I lost my temper. I can't afford another arrest. No way they'll let me out of this one."

"What the hell is wrong with you?" I re-gripped my hold on his pirate outfit, but he was so lightweight, it shook him and all the tassels and dangling earrings. It seemed a little over the top, so I stopped shaking him.

"Okay, I admit my method was a bit too violent."

Willow walked up holding the switchblade. "Is this real?" She reached over and sliced off the end of one of his dreadlocks.

"Hey, that took me a long time to grow out," he whined.

"That's your real hair?" I paused and took in his full outfit. A gold and purple vest, pirate boots that looked more suited for dancing than working a ship, a goatee, a tat of what looked like an anchor on his right cheek, and a red bandana with some type of carved wood hooked to the inside.

"It's all mine, more or less."

Bewildered, I looked at Willow. She pointed at his eyes. "Eyeliner. It's a dead giveaway."

"You think?" the guy said, sounding all-too-normal right now.

She closed up the switchblade and stuck it in her pocket. "Cooper, I bet you never thought you'd meet Captain Jack Sparrow."

I stared at the pirate, who gave me a cheesy smile.

"Are you for real?"

"No one can match the original Jack Sparrow," he said as I took my hands off him and he stood upright. He was probably six inches shorter than Willow. Then again, she was five-ten, quite lean, and still the same agile girl who'd been an all-state soccer player.

"Tell me why you attacked the car and then us," I said.

"Actually, I only attacked you because you came after me."

I thought the guy's portrayal of events was ludicrous, but it wouldn't help things to get into a debate. "So, why did you attack the car?"

"I was pissed, okay?"

"About?"

"I heard you two talking about Lando, and I knew he had a bounty on his head."

I couldn't get any more confused, and I slowly shifted my eyes to Willow. "Do you have any idea—"

"You're referring to Lando Calrissian from *Star Wars* fame."

"The original three, yes, ma'am," he said with a wink.

I huffed out a breath. "Lando? We weren't talking about Lando." I stopped myself and thought it through. "Wait. You think Lando is… I mean, you know Rashad Hatley?"

"He's a good man and a great bounty hunter. But sometimes the hunter can be the hunted."

Had this guy escaped from some institution? "You can drop all the drama crap. When's the last time you saw Rashad?"

He used his real hand to curl his finger around one of his threaded locks. "Probably nine, ten days ago."

"The last time he was at the bar?" Willow asked.

"Of course. That's the only time I see him."

"Why did you attack the car, though? And don't give me this crap about him having a bounty on his head."

"You're taking the fun out of it."

"You did that when you swung your hook at Willow."

"Willow," he said with a smile. "That's a pretty name."

"Cut the crap, Jack Sparrow!" I nudged his chest, which felt concave.

"Okay, you don't have to get rough. Lando…I mean, Rashad actually thought people were after him. I thought he had anxiety issues. But when you showed up asking questions, and then I realized it had been a while since I last saw him, I kind of jumped to his offense."

"You mean defense," Willow said, pulling out the top of the closed switchblade from her pocket.

"Tomayto, tomahto…what's the difference?" He started running his eyes up and down Willow.

I snapped my fingers. "Earth to Jack."

"Yeah, what? I'm right here for chrissakes."

"Did Rashad get into any arguments or fights with anyone at the bar?"

"Can't remember any," he said, scratching his head.

"You can't remember, or he didn't?"

"Are you a frickin' lawyer? I don't ever remember Lando, or Rashad, getting into fights. But that doesn't mean he was best friends with everyone. He had some attitude, and like I said, he thought people were after him."

"Did he give any hint as to who that might be?"

Jack Sparrow's eyes wandered across the sky for a second. "Uh, no. He's not the kind of person to open his soul and share everything. He's kind of an old-school guy."

"Who thinks someone was trying to hunt him down."

"Pretty much, yep. Can I go now?" he looked at me and then settled on Willow. "Are you single?"

"I was, until my ex cheated on me. I cut off his dick."

The guy split between us and ran off.

"By the way, Jack Sparrow doesn't use a hook!" she called out while laughing.

I saw a hook fly into the air just before he darted through the bar door.

Twenty

The person on the other side of the room gasped and cried as though his lungs were being punctured over and over again. The sounds of his searing pain were practically baked into the godforsaken concrete walls.

The man knew that Aquaman—his nickname for the guy who was being waterboarded every few hours—was experiencing a misery few people could comprehend. The man had read about it online, personal accounts from prisoners of war. But he hated to admit that his ears, his whole body, craved what was heard during the few seconds when Aquaman went quiet.

The lonely sound of dripping water.

The man had been denied water from his captor for days—he'd lost count of how many. He had no idea if it was day or night. His concept of time had been stolen, just like every other aspect that made him human. Time was of no real consequence, not in a normal way. The beats of his heart…that was the only way he could mark milestone events. Those events had been solely focused on his demise until Aquaman had arrived.

Whenever he'd heard that door from above open with a creak, it would take around five hundred heartbeats for the lights to pierce his eyes and the blowtorch to come alive. Five hundred heartbeats might mean eight minutes to a person sitting in a doctor's office waiting to be called back, or standing in line at the grocery, or sipping a beer at a favorite bar. But in this setting, under the most extreme stress, he could hardly count as fast as his heart moved.

He had friends. Well, a few. And if he were honest with himself, those friendships were surface level. Most of his acquaintances were more enamored with his checkered history, wanting a nonstop playback of his old career. The one that had shaped who he'd become. An addict. A bitter, resentful person who wallowed in shame. He'd never really thought much about the concept of shame, not until his mind had so much time to consider his humanity and if this was the time he would leave the world.

He'd run from his demons at every opportunity. That's what you do when you're full of shame and regret. You run. You hide. You try to put on a false front, but it only makes you feel more disgrace for covering up who you truly are.

But as he lay there on the concrete floor, with now six fingers and a thumb burned down to mere nubs, his body withering away, his organs barely functioning, he couldn't really recall ever feeling normal, having that sense of knowing his real self.

While growing up, he knew everyone in his sphere thought he was full of confidence. He had that swagger, and he certainly spoke as though he had gifts all others could only dream about. He would be the person who would go down in history as the greatest ever.

Eyes were on him almost all the time. It was something that gave him purpose, but it also made him self-conscious. Doubt would creep into his mind, and he'd start to wonder if there was something more to life than just putting a ball through a basket. But he'd wait, usually not long, and one of his so-called friends at the time would build him up, boost that ego, tell him how much better he was than anyone else in the world. Yep, cutting down others was a go-to remedy to make himself feel more capable and, ultimately, to feel invincible.

Imagine being called the best at anything. How many people walked the planet? Maybe seven billion? Just thinking it sounded foolish and stupid. But he'd soaked it up, allowing that praise to become the bricks—bricks made of balsa wood—that built who he was.

That praise had faded into oblivion, just after he'd snorted and shot up his body with substances strong enough to kill an ox. His wife might use a mule as a reference, because he was blatantly stubborn. He rarely listened to advice, even though inside he was crying out for help. Help to figure out a way to escape the confines of addiction, to determine if there was a real person buried under his resentment and disdain.

How the hell had his wife and kids put up with him all these years? There had been a few good times, small moments of joy that caught him and his anxiety by surprise. Once, after working a double shift at the plant, he'd fallen asleep on the couch. Like most times when he slept, it wasn't peaceful. So, when he felt the initial thump and shove, he almost lashed out. But what he found when he opened his eyes were his son and daughter giggling with unbridled enthusiasm as they tickled him and sang a happy birthday song. His daughter finished the song with her typical "Eat more chicken!"

Or that other time, when he was sitting at the dinner table brooding over how his supervisor had screwed him over on his holiday pay, his body on the verge of quaking from the anger that boiled inside. He recalled picking up his water, taking a sip, realizing he didn't hear the kids hollering and playing. And he didn't see his wife over at the stove cooking. But a moment later, he heard the velvety voice of Luther Vandross singing "Always and Forever." It was their song.

The lights were dimmed, and his wife appeared at the doorway holding a candle. She began to belt out the lyrics in a way that made his heart crack open, telling him that *every day you love me in your own special way, and that we'll share tomorrow and I'll always love you forever.* She finished the song, and they made love, his anxiety briefly evaporated.

But it wasn't long thereafter when he felt like he couldn't breathe, the weight of the world crushing his chest, the buildup of internal pressure creating so much hate that he wondered if he had any goodness to give the people he cared about.

Damn, how he'd wasted the opportunity to live in the moment, to take those special times and not just cherish them, but to fertilize them, to create a snowball effect of love and joy and happiness.

As he looked back now, those moments were the only times when he'd felt any ease in life. Sad, but true.

The truth. It was about fucking time that he was truthful about who he was to everyone around him. But first to himself.

A creak split his thoughts like a razor slicing flesh.

He knew Aquaman had suffered immeasurably from the waterboarding. But he had suffered too, just in a different way. In fact, part of him, a very demented, illogical side, hoped that his captor would trade the methods of torture. He'd finally have his drink of water—just before he drowned from it.

It made no sense, but his mind couldn't help but go there.

He heard shuffling footfalls. Would the man stop at Aquaman or come over to his corner and light up one of his fingers or some other appendage?

The steps drew closer.

Consumed by dread, his body began to quake. He couldn't control the shaking. It would have felt like some type of out-of-body experience had his mind not been harpooned by the disquieting certainty that he was about to suffer. Again.

The shuffling steps were only interrupted by the chattering of his teeth. He'd once seen a coworker break down and have a seizure right before his eyes. It had freaked him out. But that's what he felt like he was experiencing now. It was as though his entire nervous system had been fried, and each circuit was exploding inside his body.

And then the shuffling stopped. He clamped his mouth shut and listened. The person was nearby, but in a different part of the room than Aquaman. Metal banged a few times, and then there was a pause. And then more metal banged. Was his captor hammering something into the concrete floor, possibly setting up a new torture station?

He couldn't imagine what would be worse than burning an appendage or waterboarding. What was left?

The hammering stopped, and then there were more shuffles. Was the captor going back up the steps? Maybe. Hopefully. The door creaked open.

Relief. The captor had left. For now.

Before he could start counting heartbeats or drift into another illusion, a series of staccato grunts echoed throughout the chamber. He scrambled to figure out what was going on. It only took a few more jabbing yelps. Someone was falling down the steps, creating a pained grunt with each drop. It finally ceased. And then there was silence.

A thought cracked his frontal lobe: maybe his captor had suffered a heart attack and fallen down the steps. He might be dead, or close to it. Hope… No, it was more than hope. Elation coursed through his veins. Maybe there was a way that Aquaman could free himself, and then they'd both be able to escape!

Cops would show up, and so would the paramedics. He was in dire shape. But he was still breathing. He could finally have the chance to redirect the course of his life, starting with his attitude. He'd hold his wife, his son, his daughter, and they would feel his love more than they ever had before. His love couldn't be contained. He would celebrate all the little things in life. He would see light when everyone saw darkness. He would be the pillar of strength when others were down and saw no hope. He would fill his heart with love, and it would manifest itself in every relationship, in how he acted, in what he thought of himself. He would not run. He would not hide. Shame would have nothing to cling to, and it would evaporate into nothing.

A slow groan. It was a man's voice, for certain. His captor was a man. That wasn't a big surprise. But then he heard a shuffling sound and what sounded like someone being dragged across the floor.

"What are you going to do to me?"

A new voice. Could it be a new prisoner had joined them?

"You will soon learn the root cause of hate."

His captor was alive, and those were the first words he'd spoken.

His heart plummeted. All hope was lost.

Twenty-One

Willow

I woke up with a crick in my neck. The kind that felt like a two-foot splinter had been driven through my shoulder blade.

"You awake?" It was Cooper. I opened my eyes and saw the glow of the car dash and darkness all around us.

"Where are we?" I asked, pushing myself up in my seat.

"Just south of Waco."

Waco. I took a breath, then recalled our conversation after dealing with Captain Jack Sparrow. Cooper had asked if I was up for a late-night road trip to Round Rock. We'd fondly recalled a couple of similar spontaneous excursions during our time together in college, once to Austin to party with friends who attended the University of Texas, and another trip all the way down to the coast. That was the trip where our sparks had turned into a full-blown fireworks show.

"How much longer until we get to Round Rock?"

"As long as there's no overnight construction on I-35, then probably about an hour. When you have a moment, though, we still need to find a specific address for our hang-him-by-the-tree buddy, Albert Mashburn."

"Right." I found an open bottled water sitting in the cup holder. "Is this mine?'

"We're sharing it. Feel free," Cooper said, shifting in his seat, his eyes still staring straight into the night.

I paused a second as the dashboard light framed his profile and straw-colored hair. A few weeks ago, when I'd first reconnected with Cooper after eighteen-plus years, I surmised over a period of time that he was a complete mess. I probably would have come to that conclusion even sooner if he hadn't played a game of delay-and-avoidance. He was a pro at that game. But maybe that quick realization would have led me to dismissing him and any friendship in short order, and without another thought.

So, what was the theme of what we'd experienced during our period of reconnection? Patience, maybe. And a bit of acceptance for being imperfect—as individuals and as a pair. What we had was a friendship, that much I was certain. The kind of friend who you enjoy throwing some shade at, just because you know it brings some pain, but you share some good-hearted laughs as well.

I had to admit it was possible that Cooper had a little more substance than I'd given him credit for, especially after he'd basically given me the Heisman in college. He still had his issues, those that went beyond the day-to-day difficulty of trying to escape from under the thumbs of Dr. V and the Sack Brothers. But who in this world didn't have issues?

Right, Willow. Who sitting in the passenger's seat of this BMW doesn't have issues? And most of that points right to your so-called relationship with Harvey. Plan on telling the truth anytime soon?

I was getting a headache in addition to the spiking pain in my neck and shoulder. I chugged more water. "Where's your phone so I can find Mashburn's address?" I asked, searching the front cabin.

He lifted the front console lid.

"Hey, my phone's being charged." I pulled it out and saw the charge at one hundred percent.

"You don't recall me stopping at 7-Eleven to fill up on gas and grab a charger, do you?"

"Well…"

"That's what I thought. You were sleeping off your two shots and The Bomb."

"Could be." I opened a browser and began my search for Albert Mashburn. "Found two people with that name living in Round Rock."

"That was quick."

"I'm using a phone made in the twenty-first century."

"You just don't appreciate classics."

"Classic movies, yes. Classic songs, definitely. Classic cell phones? That's like relying on a classic rocket—like, one that's fifty years old—to take you to the moon."

He gave me a side glance. "Kind of surprising, but your explanation makes sense."

"It does?"

"Doesn't mean I'm getting a new phone. Technology is overrated, anyway."

"Maybe. Although I'm probably as guilty as anyone for jumping whenever I see that shiny new object that someone else is carrying around."

"What-about-isms."

"You're speaking in tongues."

"People fall into the trap of thinking, 'What about Miss Molly who has the latest car, coolest phone, trendy dress?'"

"Or laptop computer," I said.

"I know. Mine's sucking wind."

"I think you're giving it too much credit. I heard some funky noises coming from it earlier."

"At least the keys work. I just have to press extra hard on the E and the H. Oh, and the comma button."

I just shook my head.

"What now?"

"You've got a lot to figure out."

"Already did. Push the E and H and comma buttons extra hard. It's easy."

I told him what exit he needed to take once we entered the northern edge of Round Rock, and then gave him the basic directions to the first Albert Mashburn house from my search results. "Have you thought about what we're going to say when we show up…if this is the Albert Mashburn who visited The Dive?"

"Not really." He scratched his stubble. Sounded like sandpaper.

"Oh."

"Did you think I was spending all my time coming up with a grand plan?"

"That would be logical."

"Am I logical?" he said with a smirk. "I'm probably more comfortable when I'm wingin' it. And no, I didn't say swinging it." He cracked up laughing and banged his hand off the steering wheel.

"Notice I'm not laughing?"

He shut it down. We rode in silence for a few minutes. More lights along the frontage road broke through the dark canvas than what we'd seen during the previous twenty miles.

"I read part of your story."

"Do what?" he shot back.

"On your computer. I got a little peek."

"You broke the rule."

"And what rule is that?"

"No peeking until I say you can peek."

"And you think *I'm* a control freak."

"Artistic control is different," he said, lifting a finger as if that made it more legitimate.

"I don't want to inflate your ego, but what I read was pretty good."

"Just pretty good?"

"Okay, it was really good. But, remember, I only got a quick peek."

"Which part did you read?"

"It was at the end of the page, midsentence. '*…they latch on to the kid with their meat hooks and don't let go until it rips flesh from bone. All in the name of money.*'"

"I like it even more when you say it out loud."

"Why do you think?"

"Honestly, because I think that every writer out there goes through a stage where they truly believe what they wrote is shit. And, even worse than that, irrelevant and meaningless."

"You've got nothing to worry about. Just don't get a big head."

"Who am I to say I've got a big head?" He gave me the typical Cooper shit-eating grin.

"You're a bad boy. But I kind of walked right into that one, didn't I?"

"This morning you did," he said with a wink.

"You and your gutter humor. Give me a minute to catch up. I'm still waking up." I couldn't help but smile, but I still reached over and pinched his neck. We drove in silence for a few seconds. I wondered if he might talk more about our momentary period of losing our minds this morning, but he didn't. And I wasn't going to address the topic.

I stared at the white lines along the middle of the road for a while, which helped me relax some. I could feel the pain in my neck and shoulder subsiding a bit.

"All in the name of money," I said, going back to his article. "You got me curious. Actually, if I were to speak in your terms, you got me hooked. And this story is about Rashad, right?"

"Yep." He released a sigh and looked at me for a moment.

"What was that all about?"

"What?"

I let my hand drop to my pants. "Seriously, we're going to play the dodge-and-deflect game? I know you, Cooper Chain."

He rubbed a hand across his face. "There's something I've been meaning to bring up to you."

"Since…"

"Technically, since your wedding rehearsal. Although, in my defense, there was no way to tell you anything because we were stumbling over dead bodies and chasing a serial killer before I had to run off to meet Dr. V and his cronies."

"And why haven't you told me since then?"

"First, you disappeared for a few days. Remember that? Then, when you showed up and told me how you and Harvey broke off the marriage but decided to still date…well, you've been busy."

"But you and I have still seen each other since that time."

"I guess I've been busy too."

That made no sense. I lifted my arm to gently grip his shoulder, and he flinched.

"Thought you were going to pinch my neck. It already looks like I have a hickey," he said.

"Do you finally have the testicles to tell me?"

"Not sure." He gave me an uncertain glance.

"It can't be that bad. We've already unloaded our life stories to each other."

He nodded while moving his jaw around.

"You look like a cow. You know that, right?"

He released a sigh. Something was weighing on him, something I wasn't aware of. "You're making me nervous. Just spit it out, will ya?"

"Okay, okay." He squeezed the leather steering wheel as if he were looking for a source of power.

"I'm waiting."

Another sigh. "Before everything went down at your wedding rehearsal—well, at least the part about me stumbling over the dead priest—your dad came up and spoke to me for a moment."

"Dear God, tell me he didn't ask you to step in and convince me to forgive him and jump-start a new father/daughter relationship?"

Cooper stiffly tilted his head to the right. "Crap. I think I gave myself a crick." He tried pulling his cast arm around to rub his shoulder, but he couldn't bend his forearm.

"Hold on…" I moved his hand away and pressed two fingers into the area just above his shoulder blade.

"Oh, yes…" he said.

"Feel better?"

"Oh yeah, baby. Don't stop, don't stop."

"Jesus, I'm glad no one is recording our conversation." I rubbed a few more seconds, then stopped.

"I said, 'Don't stop.'"

"You're good for now. You have more to tell me, don't you?"

"Eh. Kind of."

"Just rip off the bandage, please."

"So, to be perfectly honest, he did emphasize his desire to reboot his relationship with you, and he thought I could help."

"Did you tell him to go to hell?"

"Not in those terms, but I was rather direct."

"Good boy." I leaned over and scratched the back of his head like he was a puppy. When I sat back, I noticed a sign for Round Rock. It was ten miles away.

"But there's more," Cooper said.

"What do you mean?" I shifted in my seat so I wouldn't have to turn my neck.

"Your father said…"

For a moment, he looked like he had indigestion.

"You okay? Maybe too many Orange Crushes?"

"I'm fine. Your father told me that he was the one who put that money in the back of my car." He spoke as fast as an auctioneer. So fast, that I blinked a few times to process what he'd said.

"The fifty K you paid to Dr. V for your gambling debt—"

"Don't forget that included twenty grand in interest."

My chest burned. Was it my lungs? I had no idea, but my body was having some type of response to this information. I took three breaths.

"You okay?" Cooper touched my knee, and I promptly swatted it off. "I guess not," he said.

"So he was trying to pay you off so you'd help mend my relationship with him. Where did he get the fifty grand from?"

"I never got a chance to ask him."

"Why not? Wouldn't that be a logical question to ask, Mr. Investigative Sports Journalist?"

"That's not all," he said.

"What are you talking about?" I spread my arms until one hit the window next to me. My sense of space was off.

"There's more?"

"Of what?" My voice had some steel behind it.

He glanced at me while pressing his lips together. "When I told him I wasn't going to be his PR agency, he threatened to take the money back, and then he said, 'I'm not sure Dr. V and the Sack Brothers would appreciate that.'"

My body turned cold. It was all I could do to breathe, and even that was a struggle.

"Dammit, Will, I knew this would hurt you. That's why I was hesitant to share it with you."

I fumbled with the water bottle, but finally grabbed hold of it and chugged the rest of the water.

"Will?"

I wasn't sure what to think. Before I realized what I'd done, the plastic water bottle had been screwed into a tiny ball. I threw it to the floorboard. I clenched my jaw until my ears started ringing. “All the fucking men in my life are just…”

“All the men?” He kept glancing at me.

“Keep your eyes on the road.”

“Will, tell me what you’re thinking.”

“It’s not your fault, Cooper. I’m not putting any blame on you.”

“I don’t really care about that. Well, I do, actually. But if you need to work someone over, you can pinch my neck or punch me on the shoulder.”

I was about to put my fist through the window; tears pooled in the corners of my eyes. I was seething with anger, but it also felt like my heart had been skewered. How was that possible? I’d hardly seen my father in three decades. Then more questions started pinging my brain. “What else did he say after he threatened you?”

“Nothing. Well, he did tell me to enjoy the night and that we’d talk soon.”

“Jesus. Fucking. Christ.” I shook my head in disbelief. “Have you talked to him since then?”

He shrugged. “We haven’t talked. He’s yet to contact me. Honestly, I’ve wanted to talk to him, but I really wasn’t sure how to approach it. Is he really in bed with Dr. V and the Sack Brothers? If not, how the hell does he know who they are?”

“Those are some of my questions.”

“They probably connect to whatever the hell he’s been doing the last thirty years. Where did he get all of that money from?”

“Fifty thousand dollars in cash,” I said, looking out the window, searching for some type of answer that I knew didn’t exist. At least not at the moment.

A few minutes passed, and Cooper exited off the interstate then took a right at the light. “Just let me know when you want to talk to your dad, and I’ll be there for you. If you want me to say nothing, I can just stand there for moral support. Or would you rather have Harvey serve in that role?"

"No offense, but I don't need any guy to fight my battles, especially with my own father. He's got a lot to answer for. And he better be ready to tell me the whole fucking truth."

Cooper didn't respond. Probably wise. I knew I'd rip apart anyone who dared to challenge me right now.

He traveled west about a mile, then turned into a neighborhood where all the address numbers were painted along the curb in front of each home. He pulled to a stop.

"Did you see the address? This is 1736. Two houses down is 1740," I said, pointing straight ahead.

He slipped the gearshift into park. "Don't you think I know that?"

Twenty-Two

Cooper

A Camaro with purple lights rimming the frame rolled by us. A thumping bass sound rattled some loose metal in Willow's car.

"Those kids have no idea that they won't be able to hear a damn thing by the time they're forty." Willow peered out the back window, then flipped around and put her hands on various internal parts of the car, hoping to find the one piece that was rattling. There was way more than just one rattling piece.

I didn't want to be the one to break the news to her that her precious BMW was now closing in on the piece-of-shit category. It was a gift from Harvey and, when I first reconnected with her, was considered one of those head-turning vehicles. Or, in her most recent vernacular, a shiny new object. But that shiny object now had suffered mightily. She'd run into a sign at Books and Spirits, crunching the front end. Not long thereafter, the back end took a hit when the Sack Brothers plowed their steroid-induced pickup into us while we sat and talked in an alley. And just this evening, of course, the dents and deep scars from Captain Jack Sparrow's hook had now added "character" to the hood of the car. I get that term from my mom. A sweet lady who can drive you nuts with the near-constant blathering of how lovely and wonderful and perfect things are, from the way I might make a sandwich—"the best ever"—to the landscaping of an old home—"God's perfect frame of a classic."

But I digress.

"Isn't that kind of like our parents telling us not to sit too close to the TV screen when we were young?" I asked. "Or, even better, to wait twenty minutes after we ate before we jumped in the pool?"

"This is different. It's based upon medical science."

I wasn't going to poke a hole in her position. The news I'd shared with her about her father had shaken her to the core. Now wasn't the time to point out any faults, even if it was an inanimate (former) shiny new object.

I slipped out of the car and looked up and down the street. It was quiet and void of people.

"Why did you park two doors down?" Willow asked as I joined her on the sidewalk.

"Because." I started walking, but she quickly caught up.

"Because why?"

"Nothing specific. There's no handbook on this stuff. Just a gut feeling, I suppose."

"Is your gut saying that we might want to call the cops?"

I stopped for a second. "And tell them what, the story Rocky gave us?"

"That's a start. Tell them the truth."

"But that happened seven days ago in another city two hundred miles away. They won't do squat. This," I said, pointing at the home, "you know, will probably turn out to be nothing."

"Nothing." She put her hands on her hips. I tried not to think about my hand touching that hip earlier, which, of course, only flashed a set of sensual images in front of my eyes.

"If it's probably going to be nothing, then why did you park two doors down? Got you on that one," she said, tapping my cheek with an open hand.

"Just goin' with my gut."

Her eyes narrowed, and then her lips turned upward at the corners. "I think I just heard a hint of a country accent from Cooper Chain."

"Do what? I'm no Southern Belle."

"Dork, that's usually designated for women."

"Exactly." I moved on before she could counter my illogical comment and waved her on to follow me. We reached the front door of a one-story brick structure, and I put my finger on the doorbell.

"You might wake him up and piss him off," Willow said.

"Then we might see the real Albert Mashburn." I pushed the button, then took one step back and waited.

A minute passed. I heard nothing from inside.

"What are you hoping this guy will tell us?" Willow asked. "I doubt he's going to confess to kidnapping or assaulting or killing anyone."

"I know that. I just want to ask a few questions. If he gives us anything, then we chase it down to see if what he says is valid."

"What about your gut feeling?"

"That definitely plays a role."

"What kind of role? I mean, how did you go about doing your other investigative reporting stuff?"

I paused, thinking I'd heard something inside. But I hadn't. "I don't know, Will. I guess it's a combination of digging until I get the truth and following my gut. The first thing is trying to get people to talk. Whether they tell me the truth—the complete truth—is another thing. And then I try to get their version of the truth corroborated. You'd be amazed to hear people tell the most authentic stories, and then later, you learn that one small detail is off. It might be the time that something occurred, or how they forgot to mention another person was or was not in the car with them. Yep, at times, the big-picture story is framed so nicely it's easy to gloss over that one flaw. But if you look close enough, if you ask enough questions to the right people, you realize the big-picture story isn't feasible. And then sometimes, I end up chasing down a branch based upon my gut. Sometimes it pays off, sometimes I fall off the branch and land on my head."

"You're always getting injured. Your chipped tooth, your broken arm. You complain about a bum knee."

"I don't complain."

"Okay, but you still have a bum knee."

"Overuse injury."

"Kind of like your mouth," she said with a snarky smile.

"Funny." I held up a finger and put my ear closer to the door. Then I looked at Willow and shook my head. "Nothing."

"Anyway, it sounds like you have some decent experience."

"I'm no pro. Just doing what I can."

She nodded. "I'll ring it this time," she said, pushing the button.

Another minute passed. Still nothing.

I stepped off the porch and looked both ways. No lights on in the front windows.

"You smell something?" I asked.

"Maybe," she said, joining me on the sidewalk.

I walked around the side, crossed over a dark driveway, and ran right into a row of hedges that towered so high I couldn't see the sky. "What the hell is this?" I asked, suddenly tangled in the branches.

"Red-tipped photinias. Not surprising to see a hedge this big. The house is maybe thirty years old."

Falling deeper into the cocoon of the hedge, I extended a hand. She yanked me out of there like I weighed thirty pounds. "Damn, you're strong."

"Just trying to flatter."

"But you know it."

"Maybe." She turned her head, then went still.

"What is it, the smell? I think someone's having a cookout, although it's pretty late for a cookout."

"No, it's not just that. It's…" She walked along the wall of the bushes.

"What are you doing?" I asked.

"Looking for an opening. There's got to be a gate along here somewhere."

I hustled to catch up to her while at the same time looking behind me for any sign of an opening. "Maybe Albert Mashburn doesn't want to let anyone on his property."

I heard a shoe stop on the concrete. I whipped my head around just as I ran into Willow. Trying to avoid major damage, I spun off her, but then tripped and fell into the bushes.

"You're a piece of work," she said, arms folded.

I saw my shoe was untied, and I held it up. "It was his fault." I quickly tied the shoe, and she pulled me back up. No sooner had I reached my feet than she'd brushed right by me toward the hole I'd created in the hedge.

"Do you see an opening?"

No response.

I followed her into the thicket. She dropped to her knees, and so did I.

She glanced over her shoulder at me and blurted a loud whisper.

"Huh?"

She turned back around and said it again.

"I can't hear you if you're not facing me."

She turned, looked at me, pointed a finger in front of her, but by the time she spoke, she was facing forward again.

"I still can't hear you."

She continued on her knees, veering to the right. I thought she muttered something else, so I crawled faster and finally caught up next to her. "What did you—"

My head rammed straight into a wooden post. I saw lights for a second and teetered over like a drunken bull.

I blinked a few times. Willow was inches from my face, wiping my hair off my face. "I said there's a fence just ahead. But I guess you figured that out now."

"Uh, yeah." I rubbed the top of my head. It felt like an egg was sprouting from my scalp. Willow was peeling back more branches.

"Is that a lattice fence?" I asked, moving up to my knees.

"Shh!" She put a finger to her mouth.

I stopped moving. She moved her face closer to the fence. Yep, the fence was lattice.

"Is that lattice wiring, too?"

She didn't respond, so I moved up next to her and tried peeking through the same hole.

"Shh!"

"Do you hear something?"

"People."

I looked across a dark yard up to a raised deck that had privacy bushes surrounding it. I could see lights flickering off the side of the house. "Think there's a fire pit. Do you see how many people?"

She turned to me. "You're looking at what I'm looking at."

I guess not.

"Need to get closer." She started to climb the fence while swatting away branches.

"What if he has a dog?" I asked.

She ignored me and pulled herself up, anchoring her arms on the top beam. She didn't move. She needed a boost, so I used both hands to push her butt from behind. She kicked her foot, which clocked my jaw. She dropped to the grass on the other side of the fence. "Why did you poke my ass?"

"I thought you needed help," I said, working my jaw.

"Did I hurt you?"

"Not really."

"Damn." She snorted a soft giggle. "Just kidding. Get your butt over here."

I followed her. I wasn't nearly as graceful, but at least I didn't harm myself again.

She was already on her knees, crawling toward the deck. Now I heard voices. "How many?" I whispered to Willow.

She held up three fingers, then switched to four fingers and flicked her hand.

"Thirty-four?"

"No, stupid. Three or four."

"Just give me the dunce cap."

She stared at me.

"You've never heard of a dunce cap?"

She ignored me and kept crawling. We both reached the dense row of bushes rimming the bottom of the deck.

"Hold on. I gotta play this one song from the concert."

It was a male voice from above us on the deck. A few seconds later, we heard a song.

"Country," I whispered to Willow.

"Kenny Chesney."

"Impressive. Been hitting the honky-tonks lately?"

She smirked.

The song mercifully ended.

"See what I'm saying?" the man said. "It's got that perfect rhythm. You just can't help but dance." The man's chuckle was a rapid-fire "yuck-yuck-yuck."

I heard hard soles clopping off the deck. He must have been dancing.

A second later, a skin-peeling cackle skewered my brain. Willow grabbed my arm so hard I thought she'd cut off my blood flow. "Holy shit. It's Ma."

Twenty-Three

Willow

I lost my balance and fell from my knees to my butt.

"Just breathe," Cooper said, touching my arm.

"Don't. Touch."

"Sorry."

I shook my head, then I grabbed Cooper's arm—I guess I needed to be in control. "How the hell is my mother wrapped up in this? Are they holding her hostage maybe?"

Cooper cringed as he tilted his head up to try to see through the shrubs.

"See anything?" I asked.

A single shake of his head. "This is some crazy-ass shit, I'll tell you that much."

"But do you think she's in trouble, that she's being held against her will?"

Almost on cue, Ma laughed again. This one went longer and changed octaves, and then finished with an "Oh, gawd!"…and then more crazy laughter.

"That doesn't sound like your mom is being held hostage. Hell, let's be honest, Will. Would *you* hold your mom hostage?"

I wished I could have lashed out at Cooper, but he was right on so many levels, "Good point." I started chewing at a nail, unsure what to think.

"How do you want to play this?" Cooper asked.

"I don't know, dammit." I buried my head in my hands. "How is it that I have the most fucked-up parents in the world? How, how, how?"

I felt a gentle hand touch my elbow. I looked up to see Cooper holding a finger to his lips. I listened for voices. It was quiet. Too quiet if my mother was around. I shrugged and shook my head, not sure what to make of it. Cooper moved to his feet but stayed hunched over as he searched for a place to get a view of the deck. He moved from one spot to the next.

"See anything?"

He opened his arms and gave me a shrug that said, *I can't see shit.*

And then I heard a sound that sent the remnants from my stomach into the back of my throat. It was a groan. Not just any groan. The kind of sultry sound one might use if they'd lost all semblance of control.

"My mother is having sex?" I could barely get the words out before I launched myself upward.

"Wait, what are you doing?" Cooper said, pawing at me.

I couldn't take it anymore. I marched around the corner and up the stairs. "That's it, Ma. You're not going to have sex with me sitting twenty feet—"

"Ohhh!" she moaned, halfway standing up as a man was down on his knees….rubbing the back of her thigh.

The moment she recognized me, she fell back in her chair, nearly sitting on the man's head. I saw another woman next to them, her eyes swinging between Ma and me.

"Who are you?" she asked.

I opened my mouth.

"And who are you?" she asked as Cooper came up beside me and gave a round wave.

"That's my daughter," Ma said, huffing out breaths as though she'd been having… I tried to block the word and the visual.

"No worries, darlin'," the man said, standing and then cinching his pants up.

I gave him the eye. "I'm not talking to you." I pointed at Ma. "What are you doing here?"

"Not having sex," the other woman said while holding up a can of beer, then tipping her head back and drinking.

She was most certainly drunk. I tried to ignore her.

"Me? Ha-ha! What are you doing here, Willow?"

Ma was also drunk.

"I'm not the one who needs to answer questions. You're at the home of this bigot…and what in the world was he doing to you?"

"Bigot? Me? I ain't no bigot." The man brushed his bushy mustache like it was a pet guinea pig.

"I got a Charlie horse. I couldn't stand, and I couldn't sit. Good thing Charlie here was able to rub it down."

Cooper adjusted his stance. "His name is Charlie, and you have a Charlie horse?"

"The loser speaks," Ma said, slapping the arm of her plastic chair. "My daughter could have the most eligible bachelor in Dallas-Fort Worth, and she chooses to hang around this pathetic piece of crap."

"Nice to see you too, Florence."

She rolled her eyes. *God, I hope I don't look like that when I do the same.*

"Don't talk to me, mister. Look what you've done to my daughter. She's now spying on me?" She shook her head, shaking the loose skin on her face and jowls. Ma never put much effort into herself, her body. Cheap clothes, cheap hairdo—a matted beehive, circa 1970—and a cheap outlook. It was about the money. Always.

"Ma, I'm not spying on you. Do you know who you're hanging out with? This man isn't just a bigot, he's someone who threatened to lynch a black man up in Dallas."

I heard something behind me.

Then, Cooper nudged forward. I looked over and saw the barrel of a shotgun pressed against his back.

"You move or scream and your Bradley Cooper boyfriend here will be eating a 12-gauge."

Twenty-Four

Cooper

As I half-turned my head and my throat clamped shut, two things got my immediate attention, beyond the shotgun poking my back. The man's accent could have been pulled from the original *Rocky* movie. He was all Philly. Secondly, and much more disturbing, was Willow's response. I'd never seen those maple-syrup eyes any larger. And they screamed one thing: unmitigated fear.

"What's going on, dude? We're just here to see Willow's mom." I tried to sound casual, but even I could hear the quiver in my voice.

I shifted my eyes to the others and saw the tongues of the orange flames from the small fire pit flickering off three faces: Florence, the man with the squirrel on his upper lip, and another woman holding a can of beer—she looked like she might fall over in her chair. But that's when I noticed a fourth chair. I should have spotted it the moment I'd chased Willow up the steps. Three people, four chairs. The missing person behind me? It had to be Albert Mashburn.

"Albert, what the hell are you doing?" Florence said.

I knew the earth had stopped rotating if Willow's mother was coming to my rescue. Then again, I was one flinch of a finger away from having my guts douse her face.

"Stay out of this, Florence. These two show up and start accusing me of doing something that's not true."

"We're not accusing you of anything," Willow said.

"That's my daughter, Albert! Jesus H. Christ, put that fucking gun down."

I tried to turn my neck, but that crick had returned with a vengeance, and I must have flinched. Albert quickly shifted his feet. "You making a move on me, sucker?"

"No, it's just my neck and shoulder. It doesn't matter. But we're not here to harm you or—"

"Why did you crawl over my fence? Why did you run up on the deck and surprise us in the middle of the night, then? Hold on. Is this some type of diversion?"

I could feel the gun moving across my back. I guessed he was looking around the area.

"We're alone. This is no raid on your home," I said.

"I swear. We're just here to see Ma," Willow said.

"Ma, my ass. I heard you through the glass door. You started calling Charlie a bigot. You said he lynched a black man up in Dallas."

I replayed what Willow had said. Albert was wrong. She'd said that he'd *threatened* to lynch a black man in Dallas. Had Albert just misspoken, or had he actually just implicated himself in killing Rashad Hatley? Or maybe he'd carried out some violent act against Rashad and had him hidden away or left him in the middle of nowhere.

"I said no such thing," Willow said through clenched teeth.

Great, now she was pissed. The last thing I could deal with was Albert turning his gun on her. And then a thought hit me. Maybe that's exactly what we needed, or something like that.

Albert chuckled. Not only could I feel his spittle on the back of my neck, I caught a whiff of his beer breath. The cheap kind of beer. I tried not to make a face.

"Listen, missy, I don't care if you're related to the Queen of England, you step on my property, you pay the fucking price." He paused just a second. "Hmm. Now that I think about it, the old Queen herself might have to do some ethnic cleansing in house after that Hollywood actress weaseled her way into that redhead's life. But they all got their ways."

"Albert Mashburn, I've known you for thirty years. We go way back, but this…this here," Florence said, rising to her feet while swinging her finger at him. "It's fucking ridiculous. Put that gun down right this second."

"Shut the hell up, Florence! You got no business in this."

He began to shift his gun, but he brought it back down and thumped my back.

"Are you losing your fucking hearing, Albert?" she barked while tapping her ear. "That's my daughter. Now, the other guy, Cooper…I don't give two shits about. You and Charlie can take him out back and beat the crap out of him. But the gun? Really? That's taking it a little too far."

Now Florence had backtracked on her defense of me. If this went on much longer, she might offer to dig my grave.

"Ma, I have no idea how you know this guy, but just listen to him. He's a fucking racist!" Willow screamed.

Oh crap.

Willow's face glowed red like an old-fashioned thermometer about to blow. "He might have killed a man in Dallas. Did you hear me? Killed a man! I know it's hard to fathom in this day and age, but this man you say you've known for thirty years said he was going to hang a man. And as you can hear, he sounds like he's the head of the KKK."

"You shut your fucking mouth, you little tramp." Albert shifted his gun off my back and turned toward Willow. Now was my chance.

"Ohhh!"

I jerked my head over to see Florence two steps closer, moaning like she was having the big O while grabbing at the back of her leg. Charlie, who hadn't said a word since his buddy pulled a gun on us, quickly dropped to the deck and started kneading Florence's thigh—very high on her thigh. The whole scene turned my stomach.

I spoke—rather, *thought*—too soon. The beer woman instantly became the vomit rocket. Her gut exploded at a volume and speed I hadn't seen since the aftermath of the infamous Trash Can Punch Party of my freshman year. All of us felt the spray, but she soaked Florence. Her groans and moans turned into shrieks like something you'd hear in a horror movie. On the visual side, the puke dripped off her hair, hands, and face, which could only be described in one word: repulsive.

Willow lunged for her mother. I would have done the opposite, but they were, after all, blood relatives. I'd never understand the mystery of how DNA worked.

Mayhem had broken out. I called that "opportunity."

Albert had started cussing while wiping puke off himself. He'd moved around me, the gun now at his side. I rammed my foot into the side of his knee so that it buckled, then I grabbed the gun, but his hand was still on it. Bad idea. The gun went off.

Every person, including me, screamed. The bullet sounded like it had hit a tree in the back yard. Birds scattered.

"You crazy sonofabitch!" Albert shouted, now wrestling with me to take control of the gun. He moved within inches of my face.

"Not gonna happen," I said, pulling with everything I had.

A second later, my pull was used against me. The butt of the gun slammed into my forehead. I saw stars for the second time that night. I staggered a bit, but I didn't let go.

Willow turned and came after Albert. *Dammit!*

He jabbed the gun at her. She dodged the damn thing. It was like watching one of those superhero movies where they show Wonder Woman or Captain Marvel torquing their bodies to miss an incoming bullet. Except this wasn't quite as dramatic or as quick. Still, it took Albert's attention off the tug-of-war with me. With a firm grip on the gun, I pushed him away, then whipped him back toward me. I released my broken arm, and as he came back at me, his head popped against the hardened cast. It stunned him, and he stumbled back a few steps, but the gun had slipped out of my hand.

"Albert!" Charlie yelled, rushing at us.

Double crap.

Just then, I saw a shiny metal object sticking out of Willow's jeans. The switchblade. I snatched it from her pocket and tried to open it up. I failed. "Fuck!"

Willow grabbed it, flicked her wrist like some type of ninja, and the blade opened up. My eyes got wide. "You're a badass!" I took the switchblade by the handle and then used my cast to clothesline Charlie. He hit the deck and flailed like a fish out of water. I got to my knees, wrapped my arm around his neck, and put the blade right in front of his eye.

"Everyone freeze!" I screamed.

No one moved. Not until beer woman launched another round of puke.

"Sorry," she said in a nasally tone as she wiped stringy goo off her mouth.

"Disgusting!" Florence said.

Willow ignored the puke machine and snagged the gun out of Albert's hands.

"What did you do with Rashad?" she asked him.

He was on his hands and knees now. "Nothing. It was all bluster. I swear."

She looked at me. "You said you were going to hang Rashad. Where did you and Charlie go after the Uber picked you up?"

Charlie moaned, but didn't answer. His brain was probably still reeling from hitting the deck so hard.

No response from Albert.

"Start talking, or your buddy here is going to get a nice close shave."

Albert's eyes found me. "I didn't give two shits about your friend, Rashad. I found me a lady friend and spent the night with her. Then Charlie and I took the six a.m. flight back to Austin."

"You cheated on me?" Beer Woman said.

"I can do any damn thing I want to do, bitch."

What an ass. "What's her name, Albert?"

"Who?"

"The person who does your nails." I paused for dramatic effect, and he gave me a confused look. "Who do you think, dumbass? The name of the woman you spent the night with."

"Vivian Baker."

"How can I reach her?"

He chuckled. "Florence's daughter isn't good enough for you?"

"Shut the hell up, Albert!" Florence yelled.

"I'm going to track her down and verify your alibi, asswipe. How can I reach her?"

"She works at the No Touch Men's Club. You can have my sloppy seconds," he said with a chuckle.

Willow turned and kicked Albert in the face.

"Damn!" I said.

Blood spewed out of his nose. "Oh, bitch, you're going to pay for that."

"Don't threaten me, fuckwad! And you better start treating women better, or I'm going to come back here and stuff Charlie's head down your throat."

"Eewww!" Charlie said, now coming back to life.

Willow whirled around and tossed the gun over the bushes.

"Why'd you do that?" I asked.

"Uh…" She put a nail to her mouth.

"Let's get out of here. Grab your mom."

She took her mother's hand, but her mom groaned on her first attempted step. "I can't fucking move," she said.

I tried closing the switchblade. I couldn't figure it out, so I handed it to Willow, who flicked her wrist twice and slid it into her pocket. I rolled my eyes, then picked up her mother. She started slapping me, "Let go of me!"

Her slaps were harmless, and I hauled ass down the steps with a firm grip on her arm. "How do we get out of here?" I asked.

She stopped slapping me long enough to point me toward the gate hidden by the row of bushes. Willow opened it, and we jogged to Willow's car. I tossed her mom in the back seat. Five minutes into our trip, I'd wished I'd tossed her into the trunk.

Twenty-Five

Willow

We made a quick stop at a cheap motel, grabbed Mom's stuff, and headed toward my car. Ma stopped at the sidewalk and handed Cooper two plastic bags and a suitcase.

"Make yourself useful," she said, sounding like a drill sergeant. She started walking away from us.

"Where are you going?"

"To get my money back. I'm not letting these corporate windbags take my money. I paid for two more nights. They owe me!" she defiantly said, jabbing her finger toward the front of the motel.

Everyone owed Ma something. Or you didn't. That was how she divided up people in the world.

"Jesus, Florence, you think you can sacrifice a hundred bucks so we can get out of here before your gun-toting friend shows up?"

She moved to within a foot of Cooper's face. "It's one hundred fifteen dollars plus tax. You would think that someone like you—someone who doesn't have two nickels to rub together—would understand the value of money. But I should have known. That's probably why you're a permanent resident of Loserville. You have no concept of money."

"Ma, please just drop it," I said.

She kept her death glare on Cooper. "So, you get the car ready, and I'll be there in a second." She poked his chest and then walked off.

"I think I might walk back to Dallas," Cooper said as he placed her things in the trunk.

"Funny."

He put the keys in my hand. "You can't be serious," I said.

"As a heart attack. Hmm." He swung both hands up and down like two sides of a scale. "Having a heart attack might put me in a hospital, but I'd have some peace and quiet, and I might be left with an ounce of dignity."

I gave him the keys back. "Sorry she's such a bitch. But you can't leave me alone in a car with her. I can't take it."

He growled. We turned and saw Ma walking toward us.

"You owe me," he said with one foot in the driver's side.

Our eyes stayed connected an extra second as his words hung in the air. I'd normally snap off a sassy comeback, one that might have a playful, but harmless sexual innuendo attached to it. But after our little hook-up earlier, our play space had shrunken. At least for now. I was certain that after a little time and a brief discussion, we'd once again be razzing each other like brother and sister. We kind of already were. Maybe a discussion wasn't required.

"I appreciate your help, Cooper. Really, I do." I huffed out a tired breath.

He only gave me a single nod. I considered that a victory. As we got into the car, he bumped the top of his head.

"Fuuuudge," he said as Ma approached the car and slipped into the back. He gently touched the top of his head. I noticed the visible bruise on his forehead.

"That gun did some damage. Let's stop and get you an ice pack. Actually, two," I said.

"I'll be okay." He gave me a side glance.

"Ha!" Ma snapped from the back seat. "I can see Cooper now with a bag of ice on his head. The ultimate dunce cap."

Cooper and I stared at each other for a moment. Even she knew about the dunce cap. Then he pulled out of the parking lot and headed toward I-35.

"Ma, will you please give it a rest for this trip? Cooper doesn't deserve your insults. He just helped save you from those men."

"Cooper save me? What a joke. You don't give yourself enough credit, Willow. Never have. You're the one who knew how to work that switchblade and grabbed the gun from Albert."

"Ma, do you have selective vision? Cooper had the gun—"

Cooper put a gentle hand on my knee.

I heard a hand smack the back seat. "Holy shit. Are you screwing my daughter?"

Cooper and I both rolled our eyes on that one.

She sat forward in the seat. "You better not be. She put off her wedding to Harvey for some unknown reason. I guess that's her prerogative. But you're trying to get your fishhooks into her, using your blue-eyed charm like you're some kind of Paul Newman."

Paul Newman. At least she didn't say Bradley Cooper.

"Ma, please. Give it a rest."

Cooper cracked all four windows at once.

"Kind of cold back here," Ma blurted.

"Kind of smelly up here," Cooper said.

The putrid smell of Beer Woman's vomit was horrific, but given my nursing background, I was used to dealing with horrific smells. If I had a choice, though, I'd rather be in a warm tub of lavender-scented bubbles.

"You two ever going to tell me how you found me?" Ma asked.

I gave her the skinny version of the story, then said, "You see why we were worried about your pal, Albert?"

She looked pensive, which was a remarkable feat. "I've known Albert since I last lived in Philadelphia, and I've never heard or seen him do such nonsense."

I didn't want to debate Albert's character, or lack thereof, with Ma. Cooper and I would see if his alibi checked out.

"I never thought the weekend would turn out this way. When I told Albert I was having my house painted on the inside, he offered for me to come visit. Of course, I'm not loose like other women, so that's why I had the motel room."

This wasn't an area of her life in which I desired more information. Actually, less. Far less.

"All I know, Willow, is that you're too good of a person…trying to help this poor woman find her loser husband. Boy, we could compare notes. But you're always caring about other people." She patted my shoulder. "You make me proud to be your mother." She glanced at Cooper, and a look of repulsion washed across her face.

"Ma…" I said with a warning tone.

She sat back and crossed her arms. We rode in dark silence, and my thoughts couldn't help but go back to Jada. Even with her most likely having the flu herself while taking care of her sick mother, she'd tried to show courage in dealing with her husband's disappearance. But the body, the mind can take only so much pressure before breaking down. Stress can send a person to the sick bed even without the flu going around. I got the feeling her stress had become her shadow over the years, with relief only coming in small doses. As long as the drug demons haunted her husband, any long-term internal peace for Jada was probably more of a fading dream than any type of attainable goal. And that made me feel a lot of empathy for her. I also wondered how it impacted the kids and how she and Rashad—or maybe just she—raised them.

Cooper tapped the top of my hand. He had a wry smile on his face. "You hear that?" He used his thumb to point to the back. That's when I heard Ma's snore.

"As long as she's not moaning like she's…." I stopped myself short.

"Bumping and grinding the Charlie guy," he said, holding a fist to his mouth so he didn't break out in laughter.

"Oy. She's too much."

Her snore flipped into sounding like a clogged muffler. She started to wake up and smacked her lips.

"Shh," I said to Cooper.

A few seconds later, her snore was back to a whale mating sound.

I pretended to turn a key in front of my face—my way of showing Cooper we shouldn't speak if we wanted to maintain our sanity.

We did just that for most of the trip. Once in Dallas, I softly whispered to Cooper to first drive to my apartment. I said Ma would have to stay at my place until the painting was done at her house. Then I'd have a good reason to leave, telling Ma that I would need to drive Cooper back to his place.

A question interrupted my thoughts as Cooper rolled into the parking lot: was I looking for a reason to get Cooper alone again, possibly to finish what we'd started earlier?

No way. Not happening. Not part of my plan.

Didn't you just throw your plan on its head a few weeks ago when you called off the wedding?

I started pulling my stuff together and then nudged Ma's knee. "Time to wake up. We're at my place."

She snorted like a walrus a few times, then began her lip-smacking routine.

"Did you send Harvey a text to meet us here?" Cooper asked.

“Huh?” I said, lifting my head. “I haven’t looked at my phone in…” And that’s when I saw Harvey leaning against his Tesla.

I wasn’t sure I was ready for this conversation. Here goes everything.

Twenty-Six

Cooper

The first hug between Willow and Harvey seemed cautious and stiff. But that could just be me.

"Keep dreaming, Mr. Loser."

"Did you sleep well, Florence?" I looked in the rearview and gave her a toothy grin.

"Oh, brother. You think you can charm me like you charm my daughter? I was born before today, but not yesterday."

She'd perfectly read my thoughts: I, Cooper Chain, had wanted to charm Florence Ball while her daughter, my close friend who sometimes acted like a nagging sister, conversed with her fiancé about twenty feet from where I was sitting.

I ignored her. My mom would call that some type of Divine intervention. I'd call it self-preservation. "Can I help you get your things?" I asked with a cheery voice.

"I just want to take a shower. I smell like a sewer!"

She got that right. Then again, we all smelled.

I took my time grabbing Florence's things from the trunk. I peeked around the corner and saw Willow and Harvey still talking. Harvey was nodding some, looking off every once in a while. He looked uncomfortable. But there was something else quite strange about the scene. He was wearing jeans. I'd never seen the guy in anything but a suit. However, his idea of casual still included a starched button-down with cufflinks that glimmered off the BMW's headlights. And, despite it being well after midnight, his hair still resembled black plaster.

Florence came around the corner. She smacked my hand. "Jesus H. Christ, what was I thinking?"

"What did I do now?"

"You had your hands in my purse. You were trying to steal my cash."

"What? I was only grabbing the purse strap to give it to you."

"You always have an excuse, Cooper." She raised her finger, pointed it at me, and lowered her tone an octave. "I know your type. You don't have an ounce of the fortitude and character that my Willow has. You always try to take the shortcut, for money and to get your hands on my daughter. But I have faith in her, even if I have to nudge her a little to wake up and see what's going on."

"Tell me, Florence. What's going on that's so nefarious? How am I hurting your daughter? I care about Willow and her wellbeing."

"Don't act like you give two shits about anyone but yourself. Like I said, I know your type. Now do something helpful for a change and get my stuff in her apartment."

Why had I even tried? I needed a shower and a few hours of sleep. I shut the trunk and followed Florence toward the apartment. As we passed Willow and Harvey, they stopped midsentence.

"Hey, Harvey," I said.

He gave me a single nod of the head. It was the first time I'd seen the guy since the wedding-rehearsal fiasco. Part of me wanted to pull him aside and start drilling him on the details of his relationship with Dr. V. It was Harvey who'd asked Dr. V to intervene to help stop a madman from harming Willow or anyone else. I had a lot of questions for Harvey: how did he know Dr. V would have the resources (the Sack Brothers) to take care of such a request? Had he essentially ordered a hit, or was it a much more benign request? And, most importantly, was Harvey something other than the clean-cut, nerdy (albeit rich) accountant that he showed to the world? I knew that Dr. V's empire reached far and wide. He had his claws in a lot of people, and they couldn't all be like me (no money). On top of everything else, I was curious as to how Dr. V expected Harvey to return the "favor" of killing Ronnie Gutierrez.

I thought about the so-called favors I owed Dr. V as I took the staircase up to Willow's second-floor apartment. Each step felt as though an additional fifty-pound weight was being dropped on my head.

"What are you huffing about?" Florence opened the door and flipped on the lights.

"Nothing. Where do you want your things?"

She pointed a straight arm down a hallway. As I walked toward what I assumed was a second bedroom, I noticed framed pictures lining the walls. Every one was of Willow and Harvey, all smiles, in various locations. One picture showed them leaning their heads together at a dinner table on some type of deck with a brilliant orange sun setting on the horizon of an ocean. Other pictures were in mountains, overlooking rocky cliffs, of waterfalls in a jungle setting, and then I saw the Eiffel Tower and some other notable places in France and England. It was like an envy montage, one you might see on Facebook when a friend from your past shows how perfect their life is. Whose life is that perfect?

Willow and Harvey didn't have the perfect relationship, that much I knew. But I wondered what had been the catalyst for her making her move on me almost twenty-four hours ago. Then again, she probably thought I'd made the first move. Just saying.

I dropped the bags in the bedroom and walked through the living room.

"See ya," I said to Florence.

"Cooper, perhaps you want to stay up here until Willow and Harvey are done with their conversation. That would be the considerate thing to do."

I almost did a double take. Did Florence just use the word "considerate"? I thought about the idea of hanging out with her. No way. I'd rather sit on the curb, even if it was cold outside.

"I'm good."

"Selfish bastard," she muttered as I walked out the door.

I stopped, put my hands on the rail. Damn, that woman needed to be put in her place. I chuckled out loud. Did I actually think I could change Florence Ball? "What a joke," I said, skipping down the steps.

I saw Willow walking toward me. "I'm ready to be dropped off when you are," I said, purposely avoiding the topic of Harvey.

"Oh, uh…" She turned and looked over her shoulder. I followed her gaze to the parking lot. Harvey was reaching into the back seat of his Tesla.

"I thought you were taking me back to my place," I said.

"Harvey's going to stick around a while."

I knew what that meant: make-up sex. Might be uncomfortable with her mother there, but I knew once Willow had conviction behind something, nothing stood in her way, not even Cruella de Vil.

"Why don't you take my car?"

"No, I'll just get an Uber or something."

"That's a waste of money. Take my car. Please."

"But then you won't have your car."

"I'll drop by and pick it up tomorrow. Maybe we can figure out if there's anything left for us to do to help Jada find Rashad."

I thought about arguing with her about who would take an Uber, but it was late, and I had no pushback left in me.

"Okay."

As I started to walk off, she reached out and touched my arm. “Thanks for being my wingman tonight.”

“I was your wingman? I thought you were my wingwoman.”

She smirked while giving me a head shake. “You see, that just doesn’t sound right. You were my wingman.”

“Okay. Whatever. Later, Maverick.” I winked at her and took off.

Twenty-Seven

Cooper

On the drive back to my garage apartment, I kept the car steady, even through a couple of black ice patches, but my thoughts were all over the proverbial map.

I saw flashes of all the strange folks Willow and I had come across during the previous night. Bella and her blue hair at The Place. Actually, she wasn't strange, just unique in her own way. Captain Jack Sparrow (or should it be Hook?), on the other hand, was clearly troubled, and probably in multiple ways. I wondered if Jack's moniker for Rashad—Lando Calrissian—was something that he came up with, or if Rashad was really into that make-believe shit.

And then there was Rocky, the curmudgeon bartender at The Dive. After several shots, he'd given us the skinny on the argument between Rashad and Albert. And he'd witnessed Albert's disturbing last vengeful words. "Said they were going to get a rope and find a tree with his (Rashad's) name on it."

Even though I wasn't oblivious to news reports about racist acts across the country—hell, all over the world—to hear it up close was still jarring. I just didn't understand why people went there. Hadn't we evolved as a society?

For some unknown reason (insert internal sarcasm that realizes at least part of the world had *de*volved), my mind went to Florence and the mess we found her in down in Round Rock. Her cackle could peel bark off a tree. And then there were those moans. The chorus of disturbing sounds had been too much for Willow to take. I felt certain she'd have nightmares. Of course, I couldn't forget the Vomit Comet. How could I? She'd given all of us something to remember her by. Which is why I smelled…"like a sewa!" I said, using my best Philly Florence impression.

I laughed out loud. And then I felt guilty. Rashad was still missing. He might even be dead at this very moment from some type of drug overdose. I'd seen it happen way too many times in the sports world, or with people who used to be associated with that life. The crazy part about it was seeing friends and family try to cover it up or act like it was some type of unfortunate accident. But my mind always wanted to know more. What had led that person to start using? Was it about finding a vice to mask the pressure of trying to live up to someone else's expectations? Or was it tied to the invincibility factor…when athletes are put on this pedestal where nothing can take them down?

I knew that some young people liked to party. When I went through that phase, the partying was usually contained to alcohol. I smoked a few joints in my life, but booze and parties were woven into the fabric of the modern-day college experience. Rightly or wrongly. And I played that game as well as anyone. I wasn't proud of it. I guess I was just lucky it was simply a phase and didn't expose an addictive gene in my DNA.

Lucky me.

I pulled into the driveway alongside Mrs. Kowalski's house and saw that no lights were on in the big house. She was probably partying like it was 1899 at her new boyfriend's lake house.

A second later, I punched the brake and stared straight ahead. With the engine still purring, I leaned forward and blinked a few times, wondering if my tired eyes were deceiving me. Then I flicked on the brights. It was no mirage.

The garage had swastikas painted all over it.

Twenty-Eight

Cooper

Every minute or so, I'd hear a gasp above the buzz of law enforcement activity. I couldn't see much beyond the daze of lights—a combination of white with red and blue flashes—but it told me another neighbor had just walked up to the police tape and eyeballed the Nazi symbols.

The scene was beyond surreal. It was akin to being a kid and standing on stage, the lights both blinding and hot, with hundreds of unseen onlookers watching as teachers ridiculed the project you'd worked on. It was personal and distressing. And there wasn't a damn thing you could do about it.

I took another quick glance at the symbols that were spray-painted in black on the white-painted wood, then pulled out my phone. I was debating whether to call Mrs. Kowalski or wait until we knew more information. Preferably, they'd catch the asshole who did this in the next few hours, and then I could paint over the symbols before she got home. She was a sweet woman, and she didn't need to see her house soiled by such hate.

"This shit is going to be all over the news."

I turned to see an officer stick his thumbs inside his considerable DPD-issued belt that looked like something Batman might wear.

"Why do you think?" I asked.

"Just saw a freelancer drive up in a van, then jump out with his fancy camera. Seen it before. Networks pay money to whoever can bring in the most salacious footage."

Coming from the newspaper world, I wasn't unfamiliar with the concept. But I never expected to be part of the story associated with the pictures, even if I wasn't the one who'd committed the crime. "You've probably heard the phrase, 'If it bleeds, it leads,' right?"

"Not really." He adjusted his hat.

Now I could see he was probably no more than twenty-five years old.

"But I get it." He turned and released a piercing whistle, then made a hand signal.

"Can I ask what that was for?"

"Just telling my guys to make sure the perimeter is secure. Don't want media or anyone else messing with the crime scene."

"Makes sense." I heard another gasp. I cupped my hands over my eyes and looked beyond the sea of lights. All I could make out were moving silhouettes, although the number seemed to have increased.

"You've been formally interviewed, right?" the officer asked.

I held up two fingers. "Twice."

"There will be more, I'm sure. I don't mean to pry, but are you Jewish?"

"I was asked that already. I'm not."

"I'm sure you understand why I went there."

I nodded. "I just want to know how you're going to find out who did this."

"The paint's almost dry, so it wasn't done real recently. I understand that you've been gone all day and just showed up here at two a.m.?"

I'd already shared the bare minimum about where I was and whom I was with. They didn't seem too interested in learning more. Which was good. I didn't want them to focus on my itinerary while the trail to find the real vandals grew colder.

"Yep."

He looked at the house. "And the owner?"

"She's been gone for a couple of days. And before you ask, she's not Jewish."

"Have you seen anyone in the neighborhood who doesn't belong? Maybe a group of people?"

Before I could respond, I heard dogs barking in the back yard. Angry dogs. The kind that could take off your leg. "What the hell…?"

"Canine unit must have spotted something," he said, marching toward the back yard, which wasn't bathed in light like the area around the garage. He got on his shoulder radio and barked out some orders. I started moving in that direction but stayed within the lighted area.

Then I heard a man's a voice and officers yelling at him.

A different uniformed officer walked past me. I asked, "Did you catch the guy who did this?"

He looked left and right, and then met my eye. "We won't know until we interview the suspect, but if I had to make a guess, I'd say yes. He was up in one of the trees back there."

I made a small fist pump, as if I'd just thrown the game-winning pass in the Super Bowl. Maybe Willow was right, that I should get a gig working for the police. Of course, I'd have to change my name, create a new identity, one that didn't have a felony on it. Perhaps I could roam the local cemeteries and look for recent graves of men near my age.

Was I just thinking that? Wow. I was actually using brain cells to think of a felonious way to get a job working for the police. Did Mom drop me on my head as a baby? I rubbed the top of my head. Still sore. I really needed the ice dunce cap.

"Swear to God on my wife's grave, he'll vouch for me."

I looked up and saw a man in handcuffs being escorted out of the darkness toward me. It was one of those moments where only three words could be used. "What. The. Fuck?"

He chuckled. "Hey, Cooper. Glad you could make the cop party."

"Ben Dover. Were you in Mrs. Kowalski's back yard?" I asked, moving to within a few feet of his face.

"His name is Ben Dover?" The officer who flanked him looked both horrified and amused at the same time.

"Yes."

"No," Ben quickly retorted. "I already told you my name is Benjamin."

"Okay. Sure. I tried to find an ID on you, and you said you lost your wallet," the officer said.

"Actually, I think I lost it when those damn dogs were chasing me."

"From the canine unit?" I asked.

"No. It was these crazy dogs a couple of blocks over. Huge beasts. You should have seen them. I was lucky to escape with my own life."

"Why were you a couple of blocks over?" I asked.

"Good question," the officer said, turning back to Ben.

"The Uber driver dropped me off at the wrong house. Can you believe some of those drivers? Never pay attention, but they'll talk your head off. Then again, that must be a lonely job. Can you imagine being cooped up in a car all day taking strangers around town?"

The cop said, “This isn’t the time for idle chitchat. Sir, Mr. Chain, you know this individual and you’ll vouch for him?”

I released a long sigh.

“Come on, Coop,” Ben said with a forced chortle. “They’ve got me in handcuffs. Not a time to screw around.

“I guess I know him,” I said grudgingly.

“But will you vouch for him? I’m only asking because, well, besides him hiding up in the tree, we found black paint on his hands.”

“Ben? It was you?”

“What? I don’t have a racist bone in my body. That’s ridiculous.”

“How’d you get the black paint on your hands?”

“I touched it, like an idiot. I couldn’t believe my eyes, honestly. I thought you were upstairs because your car is here. Actually, go check it out. I bet you’ll find black paint on his doorknob.”

An officer broke off from the pack and walked up the staircase, leaned over, and eyed the doorknob. Then he turned and yelled over the side. “Looks like black paint to me.”

Ben tilted his head. “You see?”

The officer looked at me.

“I know him.”

“And…?” Ben said.

“And I’ll vouch for him.”

As they removed the handcuffs, I asked him why he’d dropped by so late in the night.

“Same chapter, different verse,” he said, rubbing his wrists.

“Do what?”

He leaned closer to me. “You know, my version of the ball and chain.”

“Reva.”

“Precisely. Well, that and her mini-me triplets.”

I'd met Reva, and she was a piece of work. Not exactly in the same way as Florence. Actually, in the opposite way. Silver-spooned and demanding. Not quite rude, but definitely direct. And she had a leash on Ben that didn't extend very far.

"Why are you still putting up with that, Ben? You're usually all about freedom and—"

"Rock and roll. Well, this isn't college anymore, is it?" He thumped me on the arm.

"Can I ask what you were doing in the tree?"

The officer from before shuffled closer and rested his hand on his holster. Ben stared at the pistol. "You're not going to use that on me, are you, sir?"

"It's just a prop for my hand. Can you answer the question?"

"I was scared, all right?" He spreads his arms, then let them drop to the side of his khakis.

"About…?"

"All of this."

"What is this?"

"Okay. I was behind your garage taking a piss, and all of a sudden a SWAT team descends on the scene like they're hunting El Gapo."

A SWAT team? And I thought I could win any embellishment contest. "It's El Chapo," I corrected him.

"Gapo, Chapo…same thing."

Ben wasn't a details guy. "Why didn't you just walk out from behind the garage? Actually, why do you keep using the area behind the garage as your latrine?"

"When I've got to go….well, I've really got to go."

Twenty-Nine

Cooper

I shook my head.

"You don't believe me?" he said.

"Cooper!"

I heard a woman's voice from the crowd. I turned and saw Courtney slide under the yellow tape and walk toward us.

"Hey." My eyes couldn't help but follow the curves of her denim leggings and fashionable boots. Meeting my eye, she touched my elbow. It was subtle, but still the kind of touch that said she was more than just a casual friend. Was she, though?

"I heard on the scanner there was a possible hate crime at this address, and I…" Her sights shifted to the garage. "Wow. Someone was trying to make a statement." She looked at the officer. "Any suspects?"

He turned to look at Ben. "We found him in the tree."

Ben smirked and shrugged his shoulders. "I've always liked to climb trees, what can I say?"

Courtney started to point at him, but slowly turned to look at me, her sculpted eyebrows inching higher. "Surely…"

I shook my head. "He's having girlfriend issues."

"Girlfriend issues?" Ben snapped back. "Come on, Cooper. You're making me look bad, dude."

"Okay, you were just dropping by to talk about your new awesome sneaker company, GOAT."

"Now you're talking." A grin cracked his face as he put his hands in his pockets and rocked from heel to toe as if he were a real high-roller.

"What's GOAT?" The officer looked at me, then his nose twitched.

"Don't ask. I've had a long night. As for anything related to GOAT, Ben's your man. He's the CEO or founder or whatever."

They started a discussion as I turned to Courtney. "It's the middle of the night. What are you doing listening to your police scanner?"

She motioned with her head, and I followed her, moving a few steps away from Ben and the officer, where the glare of the lights wasn't as severe. "Ever have one of those nights where your brain just won't shut down because you want to accomplish something, but it's just out of your reach?"

This sounded very specific. I stared into her dark eyes. She looked tired, but even more like she was gripped with stress. "Plenty, but what has you so anxious?"

Her eyes found the ground for a moment. She clasped her hands in front of her and then lifted her head. "It's Dante." She swallowed. Was she holding back tears?

"The boy who was so brutally murdered."

Her eyes shut for more than a second. "I can't stop thinking about what I saw."

"Nightmares?"

"Only when I sleep."

Damn. "I'm really sorry, Courtney. I know that doesn't mean shit, and I understand that you're no rookie, but you can't be so hard on yourself. The person who murdered Dante is a fucking animal. Unfortunately, society has a few of those roaming around." A quick reel of Dr. V's hiss-laughter played out in my head, and then his muscle, the Sack Brothers, grunting in support of their demented boss. They probably had nothing to do with this crime, but they'd done much worse.

She sighed. "Thank you for the words, Cooper. No offense, but I'm not sure how much they help. I want to catch the bastard who did this, and when I do, I might figure out a way to have five minutes alone with him."

I was shocked. Courtney always came across as someone who did everything by the letter of the law. But I could see her emotions were fully invested in what had happened to Dante. "I get it." I reached out and touched her elbow.

"It's kind of weird, though. I can almost predict how that might play out. I arrest the killer, I take him behind the station and beat the crap out of him, and then what?"

"Well, won't your Internal Affairs folks investigate you, possibly take your badge away? Hell, you could be charged with a crime."

She shifted a foot. She seemed annoyed at my feedback. "I'm just talking hypothetically."

"Right, hypothetically," I said, trying to find my way back to the same wavelength.

"I'm just saying even if I did something that extreme, I realize that working over the killer won't give me any long-lasting vindication. If anything, the whole violent-response thing seems hollow. But then, what am I left with? The killer goes to jail? I don't know. I'm just not sure how to deal with any of this."

The tension was coming off her in waves, but it was her tender vulnerability that tugged at my heart. "I wish there was something I could do."

"You're already doing it. You're listening to me. You're not running away."

Willow used to call me "cut-and-run Cooper," for taking off at the peak of our college relationship. We've since talked it through, but I knew there might be some merit in that moniker. Admittedly, it was a blind spot for me, at least until I looked in my rearview mirror. By then, though, it was usually too late, or maybe too painful, to undo certain things.

"Do you think you need to speak to a counselor?" I asked as gingerly as possible.

"If you'd asked me that six months ago, I might have bitten your head off."

I poked a finger against the side of my head. "I wouldn't be very compassionate if my head wasn't attached."

She was about to smile, but then she reached for my forehead. I flinched. "How did you do that? And if you don't mind me asking, what's that cologne you're using?" She scrunched up her nose.

I let loose a long sigh. "Yeah…a long story and a long night. Save it for another time?"

"Even your new cologne?" She crinkled her nose again. It was kind of cute.

Sharing all the gory details of what Willow and I were working on might send Courtney over the edge right now. I could procrastinate with the best of them, especially if it avoided a confrontation. "If I told you a snippet, it would open the floodgates and take an hour."

She shrugged a *whatever*, and we discussed the current situation with the Nazi symbols on Mrs. Kowalski's garage.

"Any idea on when I can paint over those symbols?"

"Not sure. But you could probably cover it in the short-term, maybe with some sheets."

She walked off and spoke to the detective in charge while Ben hit me up again about joining GOAT. For about the fifth time, I told him it wasn't a good fit for me, and again, he refused to take no for an answer. I was too tired to push it. I turned away and met up with Courtney at the base of my staircase.

"His team needs another hour or so," she said. "But he's fine with you putting sheets over the symbols after that."

I told her I thought I had some old sheets in my closet, and I started up the steps. She cleared her throat. I stopped at the landing and turned around. "Yeah?"

"You going to invite me up?"

"Sure. You've seen my place before. Willow thinks it's a pigsty. She's probably right."

"Willow," she said, almost under her breath.

Was that now a taboo subject?

I walked inside and flipped on the lights. "Want anything to drink?"

She walked timidly into my kitchen, her eyes growing wider by the second. She apparently hadn't fully appreciated my pigsty when she'd dropped by a few weeks earlier. She'd been in full-on detective mode—all business. The dynamics of our relationship had changed since then. Our attempt at a casual date never really played out, first with Willow interrupting us, and then Courtney being called out to investigate another homicide…the child, Dante. Had we hit the end of the relationship road?

My head turned to the area by the card table, and, involuntarily, I started to replay the mug-down scene with Willow. It was like going back in time two decades to our college days.

"You have anything besides Orange Crush?"

The question popped my memory bubble. "Uh, yeah…" I walked into the kitchen while chiding myself for my brief moment of fantasy. Well, Willow and I had kissed—that was no fantasy—but she and Harvey were still an item. It was complicated, yet I could see that she wanted to make it work with him.

You think? By inviting the guy to spend the night, Willow was essentially lowering the drawbridge so Harvey could skip across the shark-infested moat (another term for Willow's doghouse) and delight her in bed in ways that I'd rather not think about. Which, of course, I just did. Idiot!

As I opened the fridge, I realized it would be a worthless effort. Since when did I have anything other than the greatness of Orange Crush in there? I moved an old bottle of ketchup and found a pink surprise. I plucked out a can of soda.

"Tab?" She put a hand to her face and tried to suppress a giggle.

"I think Mrs. Kowalski might have left it in there a while back."

"Oh, is Mrs. Kowalski making late-night booty calls?" she asked with a full-on laugh.

Thirty

Cooper

I forced out a chuckle—I call it my best-effort laugh—as my face began to feel warm.

She popped the top and sipped the drink. "Haven't had one of these in about twenty years."

I put my arm around her and guided her to the lone closet in the living room. "If I have old sheets, they'd be in here," I said, opening the door. A pile of boxes, pictures, and assorted shit fell to my feet. I looked at her. "I'm pretty anal about staying organized."

"Uh-huh. I can see that."

We dropped to the floor and sifted through my crap. At the bottom of a box I found a dust-covered set of gold sheets.

"Gold? Really?"

"I think those are from college."

"TCU, right?"

"That's where I started."

"Where you met Willow, right?"

The question had a hint of jealousy. That was a path I hoped we could avoid. "Until I got the best offer of my young life and transferred to Canisius in Buffalo."

"Why there?" she said while looking through my box. She was probably just curious, but it felt slightly invasive.

I kept it short. "Basketball."

"That's all you're going to share?"

"Where did you go to school?"

She put her hands in her lap. "This is the kind of stuff you're supposed to talk about on a date."

"True. Want to give it another try?"

She leaned forward and kissed me…on the lips. It was quick, but it sent a quick jolt up my spine.

"Wow," I said, wiping my mouth. Then I realized I probably shouldn't have done that. "Thank you."

She shook her head and grinned. "That's kind of a weird response."

"Oh, sorry. I just, uh…"

She touched my shoulder. "What you've done for me, listening and supporting me, it's just what I needed. I should be the one saying 'thank you.'"

"You're welcome." I sounded like I was talking to a retail clerk. Hell, I was a retail clerk!

"By the way, no offense, but you really do smell like puke."

I opened my mouth, but she spoke before I could get words out.

"I know, I know, that's not something you want to get into right now. I respect that. Probably just some bachelor party. I've seen all *The Hangover* movies, so nothing would shock me."

She hadn't met Captain Jack Sparrow or, for that matter, Willow's evil mother. I was just glad that she knew me well enough not to keep pushing me. It took me time to open up.

Right—about the same time it takes for the sun to burn out.

I escaped to the bathroom long enough to wash off some of the grime from the road trip, and we walked out of the apartment with the sheets in hand. At the bottom of the steps, Courtney stopped and tapped a finger to her chin.

"Mrs. Kowalksi. You told me earlier she's not home."

"Right. She's off at some lake house with her new male friend."

"Is she Jewish?"

"Nope."

"Are you certain?"

"We've never discussed religion, but I've never seen any symbols of Judaism in her house, like a Star of David or a menorah."

Her eyes were scanning the swastikas on the front of the garage.

"You're falling into detective mode again." I tried the singsong voice, but I couldn't hold a note.

"Just looking," she said.

"And thinking, which means you're stressing. You need to find ways to de-stress yourself, not add more to the pile."

Her eyes shifted to me, one eyebrow arched.

Hold the phone! I think she might have taken my words as some type of sexual suggestion. "I forgot to grab the thumbtacks. Let me run upstairs," I said, turning away from her.

"They better be big thumbtacks. I'm not sure I can do much with anything little."

I stopped on the first step. She sidled up next to me. "What are you thinking?" she asked playfully.

I popped my forehead, and then quickly regretted it. "Crap!"

"You okay?"

"I'm fine." I hopped off the step to the driveway and pointed at one of the swastikas. "I should have thought about this earlier. I'd bet a case of Orange Crush that Myron Little did this."

"That man I found you throwing out of your apartment a few days ago?"

"That's the one. He can't stand that my classic LeBaron is viewable from the street. He acts like he's the great protector of this neighborhood when in reality he's just a bitter, hateful person."

"Wait a second. If he's so concerned about keeping the neighborhood perfect, then why would he spray-paint the garage…and with swastikas, no less?"

I spread my arms and shook my head. "The guy has a screw loose. Probably several. Maybe he thinks that he'll scare me enough to move out. Or somehow this proves that I might be a magnet for racist bigots, or at the least a bunch of vandals. I don't know his exact angle. How could I? But I'm telling you, he's the guy. Probably."

"Let me talk to the detective in charge and see if we can get a squad car to drop by his house. You know where he lives?"

"No, but I know how to use Google."

She tapped my cheek. "Thanks, smartass."

She walked off and spoke to the detective. I saw two black-and-whites leave shortly thereafter. She rejoined me and watched me pace. "Who needs a little stress reduction now?"

"Hey, I'm just hoping we can crack this case before Mrs. Kowalski gets home."

"Crack this case? Cooper, I think I might need to take away your TV."

I stopped pacing for a second. "Oh, that dusty thing? Not sure you noticed, but it's not even plugged in. The cable and satellite packages are too damn expensive."

"I hear ya. Cop pay sucks too, just so you know."

I went back to pacing and thinking about how sweet it would be to witness the expression on Myron Little's face as officers pinned him against the wall with questions.

"Why are you smiling?" Courtney asked.

"I smell retribution in the air."

She waved a hand in front of her face. "You sure it's not the puke bath you took?" She sidled up next to me and whispered in my ear. "Once this place clears, I think you need a shower. A real shower."

My tongue froze for a moment, although my mind raced (and tripped) over countless and conflicting thoughts.

They ranged from *Holy shit!* to *What are you thinking?*

That thought expanded into *You've already kissed two women in a twenty-four-hour period. And if you stepped back from your eighteen-year-old one-track mind for a second, you'd recognize something, or someone, is pulling at your heartstrings.*

And then finally my mind went to *But she's probably doing the sexy shower scene with her fiancé-in-waiting as you stand here and load yourself with guilt.*

Still tongue-twisted, I simply lifted my casted arm. "I can't take a shower," I lied.

Her eyebrows bounced, and I broke out in a sweat.

"Did I ever tell you that I've used these hands to mold pottery?"

"Like on one of those spinning wheels?"

She nodded as those eyebrows did some type of roll.

I heard a car pull up, and I turned to see a pair of officers jogging toward us. "Did you speak to Myron Little?" Courtney asked.

The officer was panting. "Couldn't. He's not home."

"He probably uses earplugs," I said. "Or he's so paranoid he might think that when you guys knocked on his door, you were fake cops trying to pull off a home invasion. That guy is too much."

"None of the above, sir. His back door was cracked open, so we walked in. Even though his car is in the garage, he's not in the house. Looks like there was an altercation, some type of struggle. Broken glass is all over the kitchen floor."

Courtney swung her head to look at me. "You might be right about the home invasion."

Thirty-One

Willow

I was counting down the minutes. Less than an hour until the end of my shift at the Community Health Clinic. Normally, I cherished my time at the clinic. Helping others, even in a small way, was my oxygen. Today, though, was a struggle from the lack of sleep and wondering if I'd done the right thing with Harvey.

During my nursing hiatus, my thoughts had turned sour on society, although I'd never really noticed. I was too busy feeling sorry for myself while working as a waitress, first at Waffle House and later at the Old Warsaw, a fancy five-star restaurant. I lived in the moment only because I didn't want to think about spending the next thirty years doing the same thing.

It was survival mode. That was my daily existence. Scrounging for tips, putting up with unwanted harassment, sexual and otherwise. Shame was this invisible lead weight strapped to my shoulders. Some days it felt like it was three hundred pounds, weakening not just my body but my spirit on a daily basis. The cumulative effect was utter exhaustion. The harder I tried, the more it seemed like some entity was adding another five pounds to the bag of weights. I'd escaped that life, thanks in part to

Harvey. But I'd always kind of felt like I'd taken the cheap way out. I just never wanted to admit it.

My mind, as structured as it needs to be, can, at times, play tricks better than a Vegas card dealer.

I squinted at the patient's chart I was updating. I could barely keep my eyelids open. I'd downed more coffee than ten nurses on an overnight shift. I'd used up my second wind, third wind, and every other wind I could manufacture. My body was starting to slowly shut down, and I knew I needed sleep soon.

But my need was nothing compared to what I saw around me. The clinic had been full most of the day. A lot of flu cases and two more drug addicts going through some type of forced detox. Heroin was their vice, the same we'd seen with so many others recently. Fortunately, the two, a couple who'd come in together, weren't violent and didn't lash out. They trembled as though they were encased in ice, and their eyes were hauntingly dark and hollow.

Dr. Mulligan had given them each a methadone pill and recommended a detox facility near the clinic east of 75.

"One more addict in the waiting room," Stacy said, walking by me in the hallway.

"Thanks. Just give me another second to finish this paperwork," I said, rubbing an eye.

Dr. Mulligan had just walked out of his office, stethoscope draped around his neck. His eyes were cast downward, a grimace on his face. Perhaps he'd received some bad news? Frankly, his scowl and outright poor attitude was the norm. Part of me wanted to ask why he worked at the clinic. When he wasn't around, the vibe of the place was upbeat. You could just feel the helpful energy. We were all in sync with the mission of the clinic, supportive of the patients and each other. Joan had done a masterful job in staffing the clinic on a shoestring budget, mostly from donations and a few small grants. But I just didn't understand her hiring Dr. Mulligan.

"Doctor," I said as he walked past me. Nurses were almost trained to bow down to the doctors. I'd tried to remove it from my way of operating, but I couldn't help myself, even with him. Perhaps I was trying to appeal to some type of kindness that might be buried inside the man.

"Did I just hear we have another goddamn heroin addict in the waiting room?" He stopped, set his hands at his waist. Out of the corner of my eye, I could see Stacy stop at the doorway leading to her workstation. She was wondering how I'd respond. So was I. A flare of heat shot up my neck. Knowing my temperament was borderline nasty, I paused just a second and took in a deep breath.

"Are you going to answer me?" he barked before I could respond.

"I only know what you heard, what Stacy told me. So, yes, Dr. Mulligan, we have another person who's suffering and needs our help. We can't do much for them, but we can see them, talk to them about getting help, and give them a single pill."

His eyes narrowed. Perhaps he didn't care for my blunt tone. Too damn bad. I didn't turn away or lower my eyes back to my paperwork. I didn't even blink. That fourth wind, one that I knew had developed out of the need to protect and stand up for the downtrodden, had just given me a spike of energy.

"I might be too busy to fit this patient in my schedule," he said.

I turned to Stacy. "How bad is he?"

"It's a woman. She's trying to be courteous and patient, but she's in a lot of pain. She doesn't look good. And she's mentally losing it, saying all sorts of things that make no sense."

I turned back to Dr. Mulligan. "You heard her. She's suffering."

He shook his head as a smirk cracked his face. "You of all people, Willow. I thought you would have learned by now after that lunatic attacked you. He could have killed you. And you still give a damn about people who make the choice to throw their lives away? I just don't get it."

"It's obvious that you don't get it." I looked over at Stacy. "I think room 3 is open. Can you bring her back?" I took two steps, then stopped and eyed Dr. Mulligan. "If you won't help her, then I'll ask Stacy to call in Dr. Alvarez. I think he might be working a double shift at Baylor Medical, but I bet he'd break away for a few minutes to come over and help."

He opened his mouth as though he were about to put me in my place. But I turned on my heel and walked off.

After taking a moment to wash cool water across my face, I walked into room 3 with the patient's chart in my hand.

"Hi, there…uh, Briana," I said, finding her name before looking up.

She was sitting meekly in a chair, wringing her hands, chanting something under her breath. She wore cotton sweats. They were gray, which blended with her skin tone.

I walked in front of her and set the chart on the counter. "I first need to check your vitals, and then we can—"

She lunged out of her chair. I hopped back and reflexively raised my arms, my heart nearly exploding through my chest.

"Sorry, sorry. I didn't mean to scare you." She practically fell against the wall and extended a hand that had puncture marks all over it.

"It's okay," I said, regaining my composure. "Why don't you have a—"

"I can't sit still. I'm just… I'm just…" Her red-rimmed eyes darted about like a bird's, and then she began to chew a nail, although all I saw were bloodied stubs at the end of her fingers.

Her anxiety was off the charts. I took a breath and momentarily considered walking out to find someone to join me.

"They're out to get me, they're out to get me," she rattled off. The tendons in her thin neck protruded like cables holding up a bridge.

"Briana, I'm here to help you," I said in the calmest voice I could muster. "So, to start off, we need—"

"You don't get it. No one does." She started pacing between the exam table and wall, only about a five-foot space. It was like watching some type of kids' video game.

I eyed the door, again wondering if she was about to lose it. For her own safety, she might need to be restrained. During my hospital days, I'd seen orderlies have to physically restrain some patients. The patients' wails still echoed in my head.

Her breath began to stutter. "I…I…I know I won't live long enough to…"

"Briana, have a seat and talk to me about it. I'm here to help."

Her arms flailed, moving from her face to smacking her legs. Her sweats were so baggy they looked like they might drop to the floor. Her fingers pushed her stringy hair out of her face, but they were caught in a knot. She started tugging like a little kid who couldn't deal with the frustration. She pulled harder and harder, her face turning red. "Fuck!" she yelled out.

I approached her slowly. "Will you let me help you?"

She flinched. "Don't hit me!"

Was she hallucinating? "My name is Willow."

Her eyes stayed on me as she took in a shaky breath.

"Let me help you with your hair." I reached for her hand.

She moved back a few inches.

"I won't hurt you, Briana. You're safe, and you're going to start feeling better." I gently untangled the knot in her hair, and her fingers became free. I noticed tan lines around her ring finger. Was she married? Had she sold her rings to pay for her habit?

I stepped back and leaned against the exam table. Casual and calm.

"What's your favorite thing to do in the world?"

"Besides shooting up?"

"Is it hiking in the woods, or running on a beach, or reading a good book? Because you can do those things, Briana. You just need a little help."

"My kids. I love doing things with my kids. But I don't have them anymore." Her chin bounced off her chest as tears rolled down her cheek.

I felt like I'd been kicked in the chest. Had she sold her kids to fund her drug habit? *Dear God, tell me no.*

"How old are they?"

She sniffled and lifted her eyes. I handed her a tissue.

"They're six and four. The most adorable, cuddly, perfect things in this world."

I was hoping Dr. Mulligan wasn't about to walk in. Given his views about those who suffered from addiction, he'd probably berate her right about now. Still, I was curious and concerned about her children.

"Briana, what's your favorite thing to do with your kids?"

"They love the playground and the park. They run around with this reckless abandon, and I pretend to chase after them." Her tears stopped for a moment, and her lips pulled up at the edges. I saw a glimmer of hope. But was it false hope?

"I love kids. Once you feel better, it would be cool to meet you and your kids at the park so we can—"

"They live at their grandmother's house. I haven't seen them in a month. I've been drugged up for weeks, living on the street, doing about anything to get my next fix. God, I'm a fucking mess." She teared up, covering her face with her hands. I walked over and put an arm around her shoulder. "Your kids are safe, though, right?"

She nodded. I pulled away and handed her the full box of tissues. "So we just need to get you healthy and feeling positive, and I'm sure you can…"

Before I finished my thought, she started shaking her head. "You don't understand. I'm not going to live long enough."

"Briana, you came into this clinic to get help. That's a courageous first step. I'm really proud of you. Once I get your vitals—"

"Are you fucking hearing me? They'll grab me off the street. That's really why I'm here. Just last night, they tried again, but I somehow got away."

There was something authentic about her words and the way she looked at me. "Can you give me some specifics?"

She took hold of my arm. I resisted the urge to pull away. "You don't believe me, do you?"

"I just don't know exactly what you're talking about."

She stretched the collar of her sweatshirt until it exposed her shoulder. "You see that?"

I saw a three-inch scratch, and it looked fresh.

"That's from the needle he tried to stick in my arm."

A heroin addict with needle scratches. Not uncommon. "Tell me more, Briana."

She released her collar then grabbed my shoulders and looked me in the eye. "A man tried to kidnap me last night." She started panting. "He was trying to drug me with something. I'm guessing it wasn't heroin. He either wanted to rape me or kill me." She gulped in some air. "All I could think about were my kids. I kicked and punched and fought for my life. Somehow, I got away and just ran. I found a spot to hide. I must have fallen asleep. When I woke up, I saw this clinic. I thought this might be my safe haven."

Her story sounded plausible. But I also knew that a mind so full of drugs could warp like old, weathered wood.

"You don't believe me, do you?" Her fingers dug into my shoulders.

"Briana, you've obviously been through hell. I want to help."

"You've got to believe me! There's a man who is trying to get me, maybe kill me."

I didn't respond immediately.

"You say you want to help. But right now, I just want one person in this fucked-up world to believe me. To believe *in* me."

"Okay, Briana. I believe you." I was only halfway there, but she needed to feel some hope.

She let go of me, and a tear rolled down her cheek, her chin quivering. "I only want to be a mom to my kids again. But I'm afraid that if I'm alone on the street, he'll find me and he'll kill me. I swear to God, I'm telling you the truth. Can you help me?"

I had to try.

Thirty-Two

Cooper

I'd never felt so refreshed after only three hours of sleep and working a good half-day at Books and Spirits. I'd wormed my way out of Courtney sticking around because I said I was just too damn tired. That was the truth. Partly anyway. As she helped me cover the swastikas with the sheets, my mind couldn't decide the best way to deal with her overture. So, I played the delay game. It came naturally to me. Later, after the place cleared, I took a long, warm shower…alone. I then somehow zoned out all the crap swirling in my head and crashed.

I was working the front counter at the bookstore, and the line of customers had been slow but steady. Not a lot of idle time to delve into deep thoughts about next steps on multiple fronts. I peeked at my phone to see if I'd received any text messages. The screen was blank.

"Looking to hook up with your lady friend after work?"

Slash was working the register next to me. He offered a gnarly smile, which made his oversized glasses fall down his nose. He pushed them up and kept smiling.

He had this fascination with Willow. "*Hook up* is the wrong phrase, man," I said. "Maybe *meet up*. But she's got a lot going on in her life."

I saw a customer approach the checkout line, and I raised a hand. "I can help you down here."

A woman with gray streaks of hair walked up. She didn't appear to be wearing any makeup. A few wrinkles tugged at her eyes and lips, but her natural look worked for her. She looked healthy and vibrant.

She set the book on the counter. *A Potter's Story: How to Mold Your Life and Your Craft*. Was some higher power trying to send me a message? I actually looked around the store for any sign of Courtney. Maybe she'd paid this woman to bring this book to the counter. Or maybe I was nuts for even thinking that.

"Looking for someone?" the woman asked.

"Oh, just my boss."

"I thought you were the boss."

That had to be related to my age. Most every other employee at Books and Spirit either was in school or had recently graduated, including my manager, Brandy. Boy, she was a piece of work.

"Nope, this is just a side gig." I realized I sounded like I was puffing out my chest. But this Rashad Hatley story had gotten new legs now that he'd disappeared, his wife worried that he might have fallen off the wagon. I could only hope we could find him alive, and I'd get one of the biggest scoops of my professional career. I might receive a bevy of new writing offers just from posting this story on *The Wire*.

"So, what's your main gig, if you don't mind me asking?" she said.

"I'm a writer."

She gave me a long nod. She was probably thinking what most people thought: how many wannabe writers worked at bookstores? Probably a lot. But I was different. At least I hoped I was.

I scanned the book, tapped the screen a few times, and told her she could insert her credit card.

My phone buzzed, and I picked it up. It was a text from Ishaan, whom I'd texted earlier this morning asking for an update on how much progress he'd made on establishing a connection with a star player at SMU. Of course, he thought it was all about the Rashad Hatley story. It wasn't. It was to get him in the position of leading the point-shaving scam. I read his text to myself.

Making good progress. Will try to set up a meet-and-greet with you and my new friend in the next day or so.

I didn't want to meet his new friend. But I guess it might be necessary if I wanted to keep Ishaan on the end of the hook for now. I thumbed a quick response.

Nice work. Let me know.

"What genre do you write in?" the customer asked as she slid her credit card into her wallet.

"Genre?" My mind was doing cartwheels as I thought more about how I could pull off this stunt with Ishaan, somehow take down Dr. V, and come out of it all without implicating myself and still be breathing.

"You're not really a writer, are you?"

"I'm an investigative sports journalist. Working for a new operation that's just getting off the ground. But to be honest, I have a few ideas for a book, maybe more than one book."

She gave me a knowing nod. "Well, good luck with your writing endeavors."

"Thanks."

The door dinged as she walked out. A second later, two hands smacked off the counter. I flinched, but then I saw Willow's warm eyes. While they were still knee-buckling inviting, they were red and puffy.

"You okay?"

"Didn't sleep a fucking wink."

She looked on edge.

"Need something to help you sleep? I'm sure Slash can hook you up."

"Oh yeah," he said. "I can definitely hook you up, Ms. Ball."

She looked at him with contempt. "It's Willow."

"Oh. Sorry."

I asked Slash to cover for me, and I walked Willow over to the lounge. "Have a long night with Harvey?" I asked once I'd sat down in a large chair. She didn't sit.

"Will you stop it with the Harvey questions?" she snapped.

Yep. "On edge" was putting it mildly. Something had gone wrong. Or possibly way right. They could have had an all-nighter in the shower and everywhere her mother wasn't. Maybe they'd kicked her mom out. I could almost feel a smile coming to my face.

"You're smirking. Why are you smirking when I asked you not to razz me about Harvey?"

"I thought I was hiding it."

"Just as bad. Actually, even worse," she said, rubbing her temples.

"Can I get you a drink?" I turned toward the bar and saw a couple cozying up to each other while sitting on two barstools.

"No. Well, I am a little thirsty. Just water. And I don't care if it's tap."

Just a few weeks ago, she was into checking alkaline levels of her bottled water. Now she didn't care if it was tap water. The Harvey silver spoon had fallen to the floor, it appeared. As I poured two waters, she sat down and continued kneading her temples. She was stressed about something.

"Here you go." I handed her a glass, and she gulped for a ten straight seconds.

"Thanks. I had too much wine last night."

Wine. Hmm. "Did you win or lose playing spin the bottle?"

Her eyes shot darts at me.

"Oops. Pretend I didn't say that."

"Do you care about me?"

That had to be a loaded question. "Of course."

"I know you think you're so damn funny with all your comebacks, but now is not the time."

I sat down, put my hand on her knee. She stared at it, so I quickly removed my hand. "What's going on, Will?"

"I really don't want to get into all my personal crap."

Oookay. "I've been told I'm a good listener, so I can just sit here and nod."

"Who?"

"Who what?"

"Who said you're a good listener?"

"I need to tell you about last night."

"About last night…" We looked at each other. "Don't say it. I know you're thinking about the Demi Moore and Rob Lowe flick and how we'd watched it four or five times over one weekend."

"That's not all we did," I said.

She couldn't help but crack a grin. "Anyway, what about last night?"

I told her everything. Well, I left out certain parts that didn't deal with the main theme, like Courtney kissing me, or Courtney wanting to lather me up…or was it down? *Mind out of gutter, Cooper.*

"You still think Myron Little painted the swastikas, even though he might have been kidnapped from his home?" she asked.

"I'm guessing ninety percent of the people in the neighborhood hate that man."

"At least he has a few people who like him."

"That was a joke. I'm sure the remaining ten percent have yet to meet him. You're always thinking the best of people."

She shrugged and asked if I was worried about being the target of some type of skinhead gang.

"I'm telling you, Myron Little did it."

"But, Cooper, it doesn't make sense why the neighborhood watchdog would want to defile the homes he wants to look pristine."

"Courtney believed me," I shot back.

Willow had her glass at her lips, but she paused. "You didn't tell me Courtney came over."

"Uh, yeah. She showed up," I said, rocking my head, wishing I'd thought before speaking.

"Was there a murder I'm not aware of?"

"Nope. Said she was listening to her police scanner and heard the call."

"In the middle of the night?"

"She has sleeping issues, apparently."

"Apparently," she repeated. She sipped her water, then carefully set it down on a coaster. "I guess I shouldn't be surprised. You guys are still officially dating, right?"

"You and Harvey are still doing the big nasty, right?"

"You're so crude."

"Am I wrong?"

She released a guttural sigh. I silently responded by crossing my leg onto my opposite knee. Mr. Defiant.

We sat in silence until the couple at the bar giggled and then kissed, their hands pawing each other like hormonal teenagers. Like Willow and me yesterday. That seemed like a lifetime ago at this point. What the hell had we been thinking?

Without looking at her, I said, "I just want to see Myron Little in jail. He deserves a little retribution."

"If they find him."

I turned to look at her. "The guy's such a pain in the ass, who would want to keep him?"

She just stared at me.

"Okay, okay. I shouldn't be so flippant about the guy if he's been hurt or kidnapped…or whatever."

She drank more of her water, then sat on the edge of her seat. She motioned for me to move closer, so I leaned forward on my knees. "Yep?"

"You haven't asked me how my day has been."

Following this woman sometimes was more perplexing than the history of the universe. "Okay, dear, how's your day been?" I said in monotone.

She reached over and punched my shoulder socket. It hurt like hell, and she smiled.

"Feel better now?" I asked, rubbing my shoulder.

"Much, thank you." She rubbed her hands together. "Two big items. First, I talked to Jada and—"

"Rashad came back home? Cool, when can I interview him?"

"Can I finish? He's not at home. She's still not even heard from him."

"Damn. I was just hoping."

"She was asking if we'd learned anything. The good news is she's feeling a little better. So is her mom."

"So, she knows I'm helping?"

"I told her you were, mostly to make her feel like it's not just one person out there."

I shook my head. "I think we need to bring in law enforcement, Will. I mean, what else can we do at this point?"

"You don't think I suggested that?"

I held up my hands.

She blew a loose curl flapping over her eyes. "She suggested we talk to her kids. Well, at least her daughter. She said Rashad and Kina are pretty close."

"She thinks Rashad might have been in touch with his daughter and not his wife?"

"She didn't break it down for me. I mean, she's still sick, doesn't have much energy. I think she's grasping at straws right now."

"How much did you tell her about our escapade to Round Rock or, for that matter, all the unique people we came across along the way?"

"I kept it high level. Said we're working a couple of leads, but nothing solid yet." She stood up. "When do you get off?"

"About thirty minutes. Want to go visit Kina? Does she go to school around here?"

"University of North Texas up in Denton."

"Not too long of a trip. And we get to avoid Albert Mashburn and your mother."

"Ah, Ma." She sighed while trying to move locks of curls into place.

There was a story there, but I didn't want to open the door. It would invariably lead back to Harvey and last night, and then I was sure it would volley back to Courtney. "You can hang out here, read a book or something, and hope that Brandy will let me out of the dungeon on time."

She clapped her hands. "Kiss her ass, and maybe she'll let you go early. We have one other stop to make before we go to Denton. And I'm sure you'll think you've died and gone to heaven."

I was curious.

"Got your attention?"

"Can I get a clue?"

"I know you don't have any money, so you can ask Slash if he has any one-dollar bills."

I jumped up and down, looking for a mullet, then turned back to her. "What about the second big item you wanted to tell me about?"

"I'll tell you in the car."

Thirty-Three

Willow

I glanced in my blind spot, then punched the gas, sliding just in front of an eighteen-wheeler whose driver quickly laid on the horn.

"Trying to get us killed?" Cooper said with one hand planted against the roof.

"Don't have time to waste."

"You're usually all about hands at ten and two and driving under the speed limit, you know, like your great-aunt Daisy."

"You know I don't have a great-aunt Daisy."

"They're going to be putting daisies on our grave unless you… Watch out!"

I turned my head to see an SUV's brake lights almost in my lap. I stabbed at the brake, realized we couldn't stop without a collision, checked my blind spot, then jerked the car left, clearing the potential debacle. I floored the gas pedal.

"You can breathe now," I said, trying to hold back a smile.

I could feel Cooper's eyes on me.

"What?"

"First you won't let me drive; now you drive like you have a death wish. Are you taking any psychedelic drugs?"

"I have to be taking drugs because I want to drive my own car? It's not 1950, Mr. Pig."

"I'm just kidding. I kind of like you embracing your wild side."

Out of the corner of my eye, I saw him wrap his hand around the grab handle. "I'm guessing your crazy-ass driving has something to do with the second big item you wanted to talk to me about," he said with his eyes looking straight ahead.

We hit a red light at Northwest Highway and Harry Hines, and I glanced at my phone.

"Good news or bad news?"

I gave him a thumbs-up sign.

"Good news from Jada?"

"It was Ma giving me the thumbs-up sign."

"Oh," he said, like he'd been punched in the stomach.

"I'd texted Ma while I was waiting on you to clock out from your bookstore gig. I was wondering if everything was okay with her and Briana."

Cooper swung his head in my direction, and then the light turned green. I squealed rubber, and then he squealed like a prepubescent boy. "Ho-ly shiiiit!" he said as I zigged and zagged around cars.

"I'm not trying to show off my mad driving skills. Well, maybe I am a little bit. But by the time I get home, I want to make sure that Briana is still there and hasn't been freaked out by Ma."

"Who is Briana?"

I told him the story about her showing up at the clinic and how someone tried to steal her right off the street.

"You put an addict going through detox with your mother in an apartment? Someone's not going to make it out alive."

"Don't be so morbid," I said. "Plus, I really had no other option."

"A detox center, perhaps?"

"She wouldn't go. Initially, she said she'd let me take her. But once we got in the car, she swore she saw the same van and asked me to try to lose them. So I did."

A long nod. "That's when your mad driving skills blossomed. Did you get a license plate number so you can give it to the cops?"

I sighed.

"You never saw the van, did you?"

I pointed a finger at him. "Her paranoia level is over the top."

"You're admitting that she made it up. She could have made up the whole attempted kidnapping thing too."

"I thought about it. She didn't want to be alone at the detox center. So, as a backup plan, I offered up my apartment, since I knew Ma would still be there."

"What happens later, even if the two of them don't bite each other's head off?"

"I don't know. I'm still hoping I can convince her to go to the detox facility. But I do believe someone tried to grab her. Mostly."

"Mostly. Willow, you can't be everyone's angel. I admire you for trying, but I think you're setting yourself up for some major disappointment."

"Eh. We'll see. Have some hope, will ya?"

He balled up a fist and mumbled something.

"What were you doing?"

"Making a wish, like it's my birthday."

"Does that wish have anything to do with my mother?"

"If I tell you, it won't come true."

I pulled into the parking lot at No Touch Men's Club and spotted a busty woman walking hand in hand with a guy who could be Santa Claus.

"It's nice to see that true love does exist," Cooper said. "Do you know if Albert's date is working right now?"

"I put in a call, yes."

We slipped out of the car, and he just stared at me. "A renaissance woman."

"That's an archaic term. And I have no idea what you're talking about." I grabbed his arm and walked to the front door. I opened it.

"You see? Something's changed with you, Willow. Not that you were old-fashioned before, but the way you're driving, the fact you stashed an addict at your apartment with your mother—your *mother*, for chrissakes—calling up a strip club…"

"I made a phone call. What's the big deal?" I rolled my eyes while suppressing a smile.

He turned and looked inside. "True. I think I see the real big deal. Actually, two of them."

Thirty-Four

Cooper

I punched the ignition button and revved the engine. "Thanks for letting me drive this time, Mom." I winked at Willow and backed out of our space, then pulled to a stop at the end of the strip-club parking lot. "Now, remind me why I'm driving again?"

She turned and let me witness the lunar eclipse of her eye-roll. "You won the bet, dipshit. Don't gloat; it's not sexy. Just go."

I gave her a mock salute and pulled onto Northwest Highway while laughing to myself. Well, I might have laughed out loud just a bit.

"Humiliating," she said.

"Which part? You mean when you said you'd get on the stage and do your own topless act if Vivian Baker could identify Albert Mashburn?"

"Funny. You know that was when I thought she was an older woman wearing coke-bottle glasses."

"So, if I can just sum it all up, you're saying that the leading private eye in the great Southwest—"

"Never said that," she said in a loud monotone.

"I did. It helps paint the picture." I stopped at a red light and turned in my seat toward her. "So, the leading private eye in the

Southwest made an assumption before ensuring she knew the identity of the real Vivian Baker. You're just lucky that I gave you the fallback of allowing me to drive your car versus making you hold up your end of the bet."

"Whatever. I'll get you back, mark my word. But I doubt that's her real name, anyway. You saw that whole redhead *Pretty Woman* act, didn't you?"

"Missed that. I was busy studying Vivian's face to determine if she was the lying type."

"Oh, given what she told us about her and Albert, I think she's the laid type."

"Weak, but I'll give it to you." She leaned over and pinched my neck. "Ow, ow, ow!"

A car horn honked from behind us. "Go," she said.

I hit the gas and headed for I-35, then took the interstate going north. "So, we can cross Albert off the list," I said.

"Unless she's lying."

"Didn't she say something like, 'I could give you a description of every one of his eight moles on his ass if that will help you believe me that we spent the night together.'"

"It could just be bravado," she said.

"Could be. A great private eye might ask for visual evidence."

She turned and smirked at me. "Actually, that's the type of thing the Great American Sports Investigative Journalist should do since 'investigate' is part of your title."

"Not my title," I said.

"It's not a title; it's a way of life. I'm surprised you don't carry a red, white, and blue shield and wear one of those blow-up shirts to make your muscles look big."

I might have rolled my eyes.

We reached the UNT campus and Willow guided us to the correct dorm. We parked along the road and headed for the front door. She stopped at the steps, staring at her phone. "Dear God, Ma is teaching Briana how to cook."

"But your mother doesn't really know how to cook, does she?"

"Only if you count bland mashed potatoes with about ten sticks of butter in it as cooking."

I cracked up, and we walked inside. "Did you give Kina a heads-up?" I asked, pointing toward the staircase.

"I considered the idea. But just in case she's covering for her dad, I didn't want to give her time to think about her answers."

I played with the back of her hair. "Underneath that thick bed of curls is a brain that never stops."

She smacked my hand away. As we made our way up the staircase to the third floor, a mixed bag of music grew louder: classical, punk rock, even a twang of a country guitar. Lots of voices were singing. A few could really carry a tune—not surprising, given the university's emphasis on music. Their One O'Clock Lab Band was legendary. "Seven Grammy nominations," I said at the top of the steps.

"Huh?" Willow was distracted by two boys running down the hallway with their chests covered in green and white paint.

"I was saying that the—"

"I know all about them. Seven Grammy nominations. They've been around for seventy years, Cooper." She flicked her hand against my chest and led us down a corridor. Half the doors were open as kids walked in and out like it was one big home. Nearly everyone was holding a cup of something. The smell of beer wafted across the hallway, but it was the euphoric and drunken screams that pinged my senses.

"I don't remember it being this bad," Willow said, wide-eyed and leering into each room we passed.

"Letting loose wasn't considered bad. The more excess the better," I recalled. I saw lots of couples, or maybe couples for the night, chasing each other around—all in fun, from what I could see.

"Her room's at the end of the hallway," Willow said.

We got halfway there, and a girl ran out of the room in just a sports bra and shorts. She was scream-laughing and stumbled a couple of times. A guy wearing only boxers ran after her. "You can't have my bra, Danny! Not until you take off your shorts." She ran into another room and slammed the door shut. He fell against the door and was asleep in seconds.

Willow pointed. "Were we that bad?"

"God, I hope not. But we might have been."

I realized we were both talking twice as loud as normal in order to hear ourselves above the party chaos. The drone of a thumping bass jarred my rib cage. We walked as though we were moving through a minefield, which we kind of were. We tried hard to avoid stepping in the many remnants of food scattered across the floor—crushed apples and pears, French fries, hamburger wrappers, packets of ketchup. "Your home away from home," Willow said with a smirk.

"Funny. My place is just a little disorganized."

"Right." We finally got to Kina's room, and Willow leaned inside the partially open door. People were screaming in exaltation.

"He said, 'Joey,' and you know it! Drink up, bitch!" That was a girl's voice from inside the room.

I put my hand on Willow's shoulder. "Drinking game."

"Really, Sherlock?"

She loved to mock me. Admittedly, the sentiment toward her was mutual.

A girl wearing a UNT T-shirt and shorts came to the door, stopping so fast she almost stumbled back into a boy who was cupping his hands around her waist. "What's up? Are we in trouble? My mom can't handle it. She thinks I'm the good one."

She cracked up, then turned around, and he planted a kiss on her. She wiped it off. "Jason, do you think I'm the good one?"

My body tensed as the boy pawed at her. She flipped back around to face us. "You're still here. I thought you left hours ago," she said with a drunken snort. She nearly toppled over.

"Kina?" Willow said.

"Who wants to know?"

"Your mom sent us."

"Look out, Mom's on the fucking warpath again." She pushed the door all the way open. I saw two other couples. "Hey, let's all drink to my mom!" Her boy toy poured beer into red plastic cups, and Kina downed hers in one gulp. Then she burped. "Oops." She snorted out another laugh. Jason came up and started kissing on her neck, and his hands ran up under her shirt. She pushed his hand away. "You know I don't go there, Jason."

"Maybe if you're drunk enough, you will."

"You can always try." She giggled and then grabbed a beer from a girlfriend, chugged until the cup was empty, and tossed it to the floor.

Willow gave me a worrisome glance, then said, "Kina, can you give us a minute? It's important." I was glad she was taking the lead. I wasn't sure how to handle this interaction.

"Just one minute. *Friends* will be back on, and the drinking game will commence once again."

"Wonderful," I said under my breath.

Kina stepped into the hallway and leaned against the wall. The door was still open, and the noise was nearly deafening.

"Can we go someplace that's not as loud?" I asked.

"I told you I'd give you *a minute*. I meant it. So, what's so important?" She'd started to slur her words.

"It's your father. He hasn't been seen in a week," Willow started. "Your mom is really worried."

"That old bag gets her panties in a wad about everything."

Jason popped his head out the door and put a cup of a clear liquid in front of Kina's face. "Did someone say 'panties'?"

She grabbed the drink. "Get your mind out of the gutter, Jason. You're probably wearing panties yourself."

"Only yours!" He howled like a wolf—a very drunk and sexually charged wolf—and then ran back into the room.

Kina gulped the liquid like it was water. Maybe it was, but I doubted it.

"Have you seen or talked to your dad?" I asked.

She looked at me like I had three eyes. "Why the hell would Dad talk to me?"

"Your mom said you guys were pretty close."

She shook her head and rolled her eyes. "Not really anymore. I think he knew I was more like him than Mom, and that scared him."

"How so?"

"He knew that I like to par-ty! Woo-hoo!" She twirled around and shouted into the room. "Is *Friends* back on yet?"

No one answered. Looked like all the couples were all drinking or mugging down or some combination of the two.

"When's the last time you spoke to your dad?" Willow asked.

"I don't know. I'm not his damn keeper." She set her hands at her waist and cocked her neck with more attitude than almost any athlete I'd run across. "If Mom can't keep her man in the house, I guess that's her issue."

I was floored. A family therapist could have a field day with the Hatley family.

Willow touched Kina's arm. "This is serious. Your mom is really upset and worried."

Kina pulled her arm away. "You don't get it. It's time for me to live my life without having to worry about all their damn drama. I'm in college, and when you're in college, you can do any damn thing you want to do."

Jason popped out into the hall again. He waggled his eyebrows and smiled at Kina. He was almost twice her size. "Did you say 'any damn thing'?"

She smacked him on the arm. "Jason, you just never give up, do you?"

"The show's back on, and Rachel and Ross are kissing. You know what that means, right?"

She playfully rolled her eyes at him.

Willow and I looked at each other. We had to be thinking the same thing. They were too young to be doing this, and they weren't even trying to hide it. Still, I knew what was at the root of my unease.

Willow pulled out a pen and an old receipt from her purse and wrote her phone number on it. She handed it to Kina, taking her focus off Jason, who seemed annoyed with the interruption. "Can you call me or your mother if you hear from your dad?"

"Yeah, okay. Whatever." She stuffed the receipt into her shorts, and we started to walk off. I peeked over my shoulder and saw Jason getting handsy with her in the hallway. I stopped at the top of the steps, hoping one of them would look in my direction.

Willow put her hand on my shoulder. "Okay, Dad, you've got to cut the strings and walk away."

I growled to myself, and we walked out of the building. My ears instantly appreciated the reprieve.

"Can't believe we were that over the top in college," I said, padding down the concrete steps.

"We had our moments. But whenever we were together, we were usually much more chill," Willow said. "Now, when it was just you, Benjamin, and the boys, I'm not sure what went on."

"You don't want to know."

We stopped at the car. I glanced back at the dorm, found the third floor, and then identified which one I thought was Kina's dorm room. The lights were still on. I was sure all the couples were drunker than hell from playing their *Friends* drinking game.

"Did you ever cheat on me?" Willow asked.

"Seriously?"

"Well, just being back on a campus makes me remember how there weren't really any rules back then."

"Never. Not even close."

"Come on. Not even close? Even I came close."

"Really?"

"I'm a girl. Guys hit on anything with two legs."

"You've got great legs."

"So you say."

"You do."

"Stop. You know you shouldn't go there. We shouldn't go there. Not after…"

She didn't finish. There had been a lot of afters. After our little dalliance. After her night of make-up sex with Harvey. And, even if she didn't know it, after I'd been on the receiving end of some aggressive overtures from Courtney.

"You ready to go talk to her brother?" she asked, noticeably switching gears.

"Didn't know that was on the docket this evening. I thought you were worried about keeping the peace between your mom and Briana."

"Got another selfie. They're baking something. Looks like brownies."

I could feel my brow inch upward.

"No, they won't be hashish brownies like the ones we had in school. I'm just glad Ma's helping out. It's a frickin' miracle. But I'll take it."

I opened the car door and took a final glance up to the third floor of the dorm. The light in Kina's room flicked off.

"What are you waiting on?" Willow said from inside the car.

I didn't respond right away. My mind was envisioning what my daughter might be experiencing in her life right now, or maybe at some point in her future. And where was I?

Willow's hand touched my back. "Cooper, what are you staring at?"

"Give me a second." I retraced my steps toward the front door of the dorm.

"You think of more questions for Kina?" she called out.

I did a quick three-sixty. "Only for her boyfriend."

Thirty-Five

Cooper

I plowed through the door and took the steps two at a time until I hit the third floor. I wasn't winded a bit. My adrenaline had kicked in. It was almost like a drug, masking some feelings while fueling a state of mind that was getting hotter by the second. I marched down the hall, bumped into a college boy fifty pounds bigger than I was.

"Hey, dude. Watch where you're going!"

I ignored him. I had rarely established those red lines in my life, the kind that forced me to take a side. I typically kept to myself and rolled with the punches. But this was different. I couldn't allow this to go unchecked. It hit too close to home for me. I couldn't allow any girl to be taken advantage of. Ever. I could feel a swell of emotion rising inside me, and I knew I was on a collision course with taking a stand.

If it's needed, Cooper. You might be overreacting.

My sights zeroed in on the closed door at the end of the hall ten paces before I reached it. I glanced around, looking for familiar faces. Most of the adult-sized kids were stowed away in their rooms, or someone's room, the loud clatter now muffled behind walls.

I stopped at Kina's door and raised my hand to knock, but I paused. I turned to put my ear to the door. At the exact moment I spotted Willow rushing down the hall, I heard what sounded like a pinched squeal.

It was a girl, and it sounded like Kina. Whatever was going on, I couldn't say exactly. But one question raced to the front of my mind: was it consensual or not? If she were my daughter, I'd either be on the verge of embarrassing her—to the point where she would want to transfer to another school—or saving her life.

I held my breath and didn't budge. I'd give myself to a count of five. One. Two. Three. Four. Another high-pitched grunt. This one chiseled a piece out of my heart. My mind flashed to memories and lost chances of another little girl who wasn't little any longer.

I wrapped the door with three hard knocks. No response. I knocked again just as Willow walked up.

"What do you think you are doing?" She had this look of horror on her face.

I hit the door three more times.

"Go away." It was Jason, his voice raspy.

"I want to talk to Kina." My voice sounded nice, but my emotions were like a tornado.

"She doesn't want to talk to you, old man. Get the fuck out of here."

Willow touched my shoulder and met my eye. "Do you think…?"

I nodded. "Kina, can I talk to you for a second?" I attempted the calm voice, but this time I heard a quiver, one filled with a boiling rage.

Willow and I locked eyes on each other. A few seconds passed.

"Are you going to kick it down?" she asked as if she already knew the answer.

I backed up a few steps. I'd never kicked in a door. I wasn't sure what would break first, the door or my body. I turned to look up the hallway, searching for someone a little older, a resident assistant who could open the door with a key. No sign of anyone other than a couple of boys stumbling and laughing by their door.

I took in a full breath, rocked backward a step—but I stopped in my tracks when I heard a metal latch move. The door cracked open two inches.

"I'm fine." Kina tried to sound casual, but I wasn't buying it.

The room behind her was dark. I could only make out an eye and part of her face.

"Can you come out here so we can talk to you?" I asked. Willow moved in front of me; she was always thinking. Let Kina feel more comfortable to see a woman.

"I'm okay. We're just chilling out." She paused, her eye disappearing into the darkness for a split second. When it returned to the crack in the door, she said, "Just need some privacy."

She sniffled, and the door shut.

"Did you hear that?" I asked.

"The sniffle? Yep," Willow said.

I put my hand on the doorknob, turned it quietly, and inched the door open. Just then I heard a grunt. I swung open the door and saw the silhouette of Jason's hand swinging into Kina's face.

I launched myself forward as I heard the smack of his hand against her skin. I yelled as I rammed into his back, sending us tumbling over a side table, knocking a lamp and clock radio to the floor. He was quick and tried to slither away, flinging loose paper and clothes into the air. I rolled to all fours and grabbed him by the shoe. As I yanked him back toward me, I threw a straight punch that clocked his chin. He grunted as he dropped to the floor. I could see Willow running behind him to get to Kina, who was standing on her bed, yelling and crying.

"Watch out!" Kina yelled and pointed.

I turned just as a dark object was inches from my head. The clock radio. I wasn't quick enough to move, and it clanged off my forehead—the same spot where I'd been hit with Albert Mashburn's gun. It stunned me, and I flopped against the side of the bed on the opposite side of the room. I heard a smattering of quick footsteps, and I looked up to see Jason running out of the room. By the time I got to my feet and looked out the door, Jason wasn't in sight, but I did see a girl and a very large boy walking my way. They looked perplexed.

"Who are you?" the guy said.

I ignored him and turned back into the room.

"Did you see him?" Willow asked me.

Kina got off the bed. She was shaking. Willow put her arm around her, and she started to sob.

"He was nowhere in sight. Just some girl and a tall lumberjack-looking guy."

Kina looked up. It was still dark, so I couldn't determine if she was injured. A second later, the overhead light flipped on.

"I asked who you are." It was Lumberjack.

"Misty!" Kina ran over and hugged the girl.

Misty looked over Kina's shoulder. "I'm her roommate."

Willow and I both nodded. Lumberjack pointed a finger at the two of us.

"We're friends of Kina's mother," Willow said.

"Oh," he said, clearly unimpressed.

Lumberjack set his feet shoulder-width apart and folded his arms across his chest, which was the size of Mount McKinley.

"You play football?" I asked.

He nodded as he stared at me blankly. His neck was more like a tree stump.

"O-line or D-line?"

"The O-line is for wimps."

Kina turned around and put a hand on Lumberjack. "This is Misty's boyfriend. He's kind of our protector."

"Have you seen this guy Jason around here before?" I asked.

Misty looked to Kina, who gave her friends the details of what had happened. I stepped closer and could see bruising around her eye. "Did he do that?"

She scoffed. "It's nothing. You look worse than me."

Willow walked up and started to reach for my forehead. "Don't touch."

"You're going to laugh at yourself when you look in the mirror," she whispered with a snicker.

"Kina," Misty said, "I told you that boy was a tool. I'd heard stories, and you didn't listen to me."

"I know, I know. I should have listened. He just happened to come over when we were playing our drinking game, and I kind of got caught up in it."

Misty moved some hair out of Kina's face. "Girl, you're scaring me with all your drinking."

Kina held up a hand. "Please don't act like my mom. I can't deal with it right now." She put her hands over her face. Misty glanced at Willow and me.

There was some awkward silence, so I introduced us, and we all shook hands. Lumberjack's name was Tony. But "Lumberjack" was a better fit.

"You can tell her mom that I got this," he said.

Misty put a hand on his shoulder. "We're calling the campus police. This is ridiculous. That motherfucker—excuse my language—but that punk is going to jail."

I liked her attitude. I looked over to Kina, who'd grabbed a tissue and was dotting her eyes. "You're right, Misty. About Jason, about my drinking. I think I need some help." Misty went over and gave her another hug.

We stayed long enough to talk to campus police. As we started to leave, Lumberjack pulled me aside. "Coop. I can call you Coop, can't I?"

Who was I to argue with a lumberjack? "Sure. What's up?"

"Just to let you know, Jason is a complete prick. He and two of his rich buddies once keyed my truck, but the cops couldn't prove it. Misty made me promise not to pound the guy." He shifted his eyes over to Misty and Kina. "But after what he did to Kina…well, he's going to pay. I promise you. And I won't let any guy hurt Kina again. Can you tell that to Kina's mom?"

Interesting that he didn't mention her father. "Just don't kill the guy," I said, thumping his shoulder. It was like hitting skin-covered granite.

Kina caught up to Willow and me in the hallway. She hugged both of us. "If you hadn't come back, I might have been…"

Raped. She couldn't say it. I didn't even want to think it. "Just get the help that Misty suggested," Willow said.

"I will. I just don't want to end up like my dad," she said as tears pooled in her eyes.

"You really haven't seen him in a while?"

She shook her head. "The last time I saw him, he was all angry about something. We didn't say much. I really hope he's okay, but my family's kind of a mess. Mom's not exactly easy to get along with, and that doesn't help Dad's anxiety."

Like I noted before. Family therapy sounded like a requirement. But first we had to find Rashad.

"If he contacts you, please have him call your mom or us at the number I gave you," Willow said.

Kina pulled out the slip of paper. "I'll do that. Thanks, Miss…"

"Just call me Willow."

"Willow. And—"

"Just call me Cooper."

"Thank you for not listening to me and following your gut. You saved me from being…hurt."

I gave her a wink. "Take care of yourself."

"Just find my father. Please."

"We'll do everything we can."

Thirty-Six

Willow

After insisting on stopping at a drugstore so I could pick up some supplies, we were back on I-35 heading south in light traffic. Cooper had one arm draped over the steering wheel. The opposite hand, which held a small ice pack, was resting in his lap. I leaned over and started raising it to his forehead.

"But it's cold," he whined.

"You are a master of the obvious."

He started to lower it.

"You want me to pinch your neck for the entire drive to Dallas?"

"Okay." He grudgingly put the ice on his forehead. "Satisfied?"

"Only once you tell me how you knew."

"Knew what?"

"Oh, is Mr. Evasive making an appearance? Haven't seen him since you played dodge ball with my questions leading up to my wedding."

He glanced at me, and his hand holding the ice dropped back to his lap. "You think I can read your mind?" he asked.

I pointed at the ice pack. He sighed and brought it back up to his head.

"I'm asking how you knew that Jason was trouble? Well, not just trouble, but *that* kind of trouble."

He shrugged a shoulder.

"That's it?"

"Call it my intuition."

"Intuition. Sounds like something a woman would say."

"You're being sexist."

I ran my eyes up and down him at the same time my brain processed everything that had happened. This wasn't the same Cooper. Something was different. "I'm not sure I recall you being so quick to lose your cool."

"You sound like I was some maniac who'd put a gun to his head. I was in complete control of my actions."

"Feelings."

He blinked and snagged a glance at me. "Huh?"

"Feelings. Emotion. Something was tugging at your emotions."

He dropped the ice on the center console, then wiped his hand across his face. I chose not to badger him about the ice. We drove past two exits, but he remained mute.

"Cooper…" I put my hand on his thigh until he looked at me for a second. "What's going on?"

He swallowed once, then grabbed my hand. Tight. From the glow of the dashboard, it looked like his eyes were glassy. But I didn't say anything. I waited for when he was ready. He veered off the interstate in Carrollton, at least ten miles away from where we should be exiting. But I still didn't say anything. He pulled into a gas station and stopped the car.

After another full minute, he turned and looked me in the eye. "I have a fourteen-year-old daughter. Her name is Lauren."

The engine purred, and the lights from a truck turning into the gas station flashed through our cabin. I was still replaying what he'd just said.

"Your mouth is hanging open," he said.

"Where is she?" was the first question that came to mind.

"In Miami. I think."

"You don't even know?" I bounced a hand off my head. "Sorry. That was rude. I don't know anything, so I'm just not sure what to think."

"I get it." He was quiet, subdued. His eyes started sinking. I didn't want to lose him, so I hit him with another question.

"From your ex-wife?"

He nodded.

"But I thought you guys lived in New York."

"The Jersey suburbs, but that's close enough. We were there for many years." He paused, rubbed the back of his neck. He was in pain, but I wasn't sure any massage would help. "It all changed once I was set up on that drug charge."

That part I knew about. He'd been set up by an athlete about whom he was writing one of his feature stories. Well, the blame game was executed by the athlete—a New York Yankee who'd yet to live up to lofty expectations—and his posse during a party that Cooper had interrupted to ask the guy some questions about his drug use. Ironically, at that party was a mound of cocaine. The athlete and his posse gave the cops the same story, claiming the large amount of coke was Cooper's. He didn't serve time, but he lost his job, and apparently a lot more.

"Did your wife not believe you?"

He cleared his throat. "It was an easy out. She hadn't believed *in* me for a long time."

His eyes shifted away, perhaps recalling a fond memory or maybe reliving a painful moment. I couldn't quite tell. But having this glimpse beneath Cooper's sarcastic layers was beyond surreal, something I hadn't ever been sure was possible. I felt honored, yet anxious. Maybe like a surgeon who had this power to heal, but with one little twitch, I could take out a major organ.

I heard laughter to my right. I turned to see a man bent over at the knee, chuckling, as a young girl stood next to an ice cream cone turned upside down on the grimy concrete. Her grimace turned into a smile, which then morphed into a full-on belly laugh. Father and daughter were having a moment. Normally, my gaze might cast itself inward as I contemplated if I was meant to have children, if it was part of the plan. But my introspection wasn't important right now.

I swept my sights back to Cooper. His eyes were trained on the same scene, and my heart sank.

"How long has it been?"

"Since?"

"Since we were last on the moon. You know, since you last saw Lauren?"

"Over seven months. Even before then, though, her mom had trashed me. I wasn't a real dad in her eyes." He took in a full breath and appeared to hold it for a moment, just as he held his gaze on the girl and father. Then, he turned to look out the front window and slowly emptied his lungs. "Because Lauren followed her mom's lead on just about everything, she didn't think I was much of a dad, either."

His usual energy had evaporated, as though he'd been temporarily drained of the desire to live.

"I might be out of line here, but what a bitch!"

He tried to muster up a laugh, but it never got there.

"Did I cross a line? If I did, I'm sorry."

"Nah. I can see why you'd think that. It's just …" He ran his fingers along the dash.

"I know I need to dust my car, thank you."

"Or have someone do it for you."

"Those days are over."

"Over?" he said, turning his head my way.

I motioned with my hand. "You were saying something a moment ago."

"Right."

But he didn't continue. Not right then. An old Chrysler pulled into the gas station, spewing exhaust while backfiring every couple of seconds. It lurched to a stop next to a gas pump. I wasn't sure it would be moving from that spot anytime soon.

"It's hard for me to go there," Cooper said.

"Go where?"

"You probably know that I'm rather profuse in my ability to share my opinions."

"*Profuse.* You're such a writer. But, yes, you can be a smartass on just about every topic and every person."

"I just can't bring myself to say that about Carmona."

"Carmona is your wife?"

"Ex-wife."

"You're saying you can't call her a bitch, even though she turned your daughter against you?" I sounded bitter, and I was, even though I knew firsthand that the complications of relationships were like a tangled ball of twine and never one-sided. "Sorry if I crossed the line."

He shook his head. "You can have your own opinion. I guess I just can't go there because I love Lauren like nothing else in this world. And I guess I feel that her mom is an extension of her. Sounds kind of crazy to say it out loud."

I reached out and touched Cooper's shoulder. "It's not crazy, Cooper. It just shows…" I took in a breath, and he turned to look at me. "I might regret saying this, but it shows your maturity."

"Ha! Maturity." He chuckled.

It was good to see him smile, if only for a few seconds.

"Are you going to try to reach out to Lauren?"

"I did," he said with a heavy sigh. "Right around the time of your wedding, or I guess after you showed up at the bookstore."

"And?"

"It was brief. I could tell she didn't want to talk. Or maybe her mother was standing nearby."

"Well, which one was it?" I put a hand to my head. "I'm grilling you like we're sitting in an interrogation room."

"I don't mind, at least from you. I haven't really told anyone about this."

I had more questions about so many things, but I tried to keep the focus on him regaining some type of relationship with his daughter. "So…"

"I didn't know what to say. I'm not great with conversations over the phone where I can't see what people are thinking."

"So you just said hi, and there was silence?"

"You really want to know all the details?"

"Only if it's helpful."

"It's a little painful. But I can't keep everything buried forever. I already carry a fair amount of guilt. Probably for a good reason."

This wasn't Cooper. Not the Cooper I knew from twenty years ago, or even now.

"Cooper, there is no good reason for a mother to turn her child against her father." I paused as I replayed the scene with Kina and thought about the pain that family had suffered from her father's apparent multitude of issues. "Actually, I shouldn't be so black-and-white about it. I know there are situations where one parent is so negligent or harmful that the other parent has no other choice. But I know that's not the case with you."

"You sure about that?"

"Hell yes, I'm sure. Aren't you?" I popped his shoulder with my fist—lightly, for a change.

"Okay. You're right." His voice had regained some life. "I wasn't perfect, but dammit, Carmona was difficult and demanding. She never thought I made enough money."

"This is about money?"

His hand dropped to the bottom curve of the steering wheel. "That was the main theme until the end. Then, after the arrest, the floodgates opened up. And in her eyes, I was right on par with a crime boss."

Our eyes met for a second. I wondered if he'd drawn the connection of "crime boss" to Dr. V, the man who actually behaved like one. But I didn't want to dredge up even more shit to wade through right now.

"Look, Cooper, I know I'm only hearing one side of the story, but I think I know you pretty well. Crime boss isn't exactly your game…on many levels."

"You don't think I carry myself like John Gotti?"

"I was thinking about John Travolta."

"I know you're not talking about the *Saturday Night Fever* Travolta. He had too much swagger."

"And he could dance like no one else. And definitely not the *Grease* Travolta. He not only shook his booty, but he also sang. Not your thing."

He snapped off a brief chuckle. It lightened the air in the car.

"I was thinking about Travolta in that Gotti movie."

"Never saw it," he said.

"Harvey wanted to, but I actually put my foot down on that one. Turns out it was named one of the worst movies of the year."

He wrinkled his eyebrows. Probably had something to do with Harvey, but I chose not to lay into him again. I'd save it for later.

"Funny thing…" He was talking to me, but I got the feeling he was trying to admit something to himself.

"Yeah?"

"Those illegal bets I made? I knew that Dr. V was a bad dude. But you know, I think, subconsciously, I made those bets hoping that I could really hit it big. Almost like winning the lottery or something. Then, I could show Carmona that I was a high-roller, like some of the athletes I covered. Didn't quite work out, though."

My heart ached for him. "Cooper, you're being too hard—"

"Hey, I didn't tell you all this for you to feel sorry for me. I made my own decisions. Some were pretty damn stupid."

"Like when that baseball player set you up on the drug charge? That wasn't your call. It was his."

"I could have walked out of his house the moment I saw the drugs."

"Stop being so hard on yourself."

"Stop trying to be my defender."

"Dammit, you're so fucking hard-headed!" I huffed out a breath, then I realized his blue eyes were staring right at me. Without thinking, I twisted my torso over the console, where he met me halfway, and we embraced. An embrace like welded metal. For a moment, I wondered what I was doing, breaking the rule that I'd set up for myself to not engage in this type of physical intimacy with Cooper. Then the next moment, I wondered if he or I would tilt our head toward the other. If that happened, we might never stop.

I thumped his back, and he returned the thump. I was relieved.

We finally unlocked our hug and found our seats again.

"If you want to talk to me about how to win over Lauren, I'm available whenever," I said.

"Eh."

"Noncommittal. But that's fine. No pressure. Just know you're not alone on this."

He slid the gear shift into drive and gave me another glance. "Thanks. Now tell me where I need to go."

Thirty-Seven

The tortuous screams had finally ceased, but he could still feel the reverberation inside his chest wall. A chest wall that seemed as though it were collapsing into itself. Cratering, just like his mental faculties.

He had tried to beg his captor to stop hurting the new prisoner, but his voice simply could not produce anything more than a pinched wheeze. Even then, it felt like his eyeballs were about to pop out of their sockets.

Oh God, when will this nightmare end?

He shifted his body slightly on the concrete floor. The jolt of pain that shot up his spine exploded at the base of his skull. He should be numb to the pain by now. But he certainly didn't feel numb. The sound of bone skidding off the concrete made his dulled senses spark back to life—it was bone from his lower back.

He started counting his heartbeats once again. While mentally exhausting, it momentarily allowed a brief respite from the sole focus of his own misery. Now calmer, he listened for any type of sound from the newest member of their torture club, Electric Man. That was his nickname for the man who'd endured endless electrical shocks.

The captor had attached electrodes to the new victim's body and then used some type of metal clamps—they looked like the ends of jumper cables—to fry his victim. Electric Man had pleaded for mercy. And after his first shock session, his pleas turned so desperate that he offered to do anything for his captor. From robbing banks to killing any other person on the planet. Anything.

He could recall doing the same thing when his captor had burned off his first finger. In some respects, it seemed like so long ago. And the response to Electric Man had been met in the same manner: more torture, which led to cries that didn't sound human.

"You will soon learn the root cause of hate." Those had been the only words his captor had spoken to anyone in the dungeon.

He hadn't been able to stop repeating that phrase in his mind, hoping that it would somehow make sense. He broke down the words individually, even rearranged their order. But none of it made a whole lot of sense. Not surprising, since he was barely able to put two thoughts together. And then he considered that his captor was simply certifiably crazy. Wouldn't he have to be to carry out these brutal acts?

Learn. He blinked twice, and his mind translated that as his captor being some type of teacher. He considered himself to be some type of expert on…what exactly? Torture? Could you get an advanced degree in torture? He knew that idea was as insane as this whole event.

Mumbles broke the silence in the chamber. His breath hitched as he strained to pick up the location and words being spoken. He waited a few seconds, maybe a few minutes. It was hard to tell.

A new wave of mumbles surged into the damp air. He turned his head—it had come from the direction of Aquaman. What the hell was he trying to say?

Once again, he tried to will his body to produce words, to ask Aquaman a question. Nothing came out. *Fuck!*

"Dead." Aquaman had finally uttered something he could understand.

He went still. Was Aquaman saying he was about to die? That could be it. In fact, they were all very close to death. Hell, after his initial cries, Electric Man hadn't made a peep since his most recent shock session. He knew that Electric Man's heart could only take so much. It was very possible he was dead.

A babble of words echoed in the chamber. He arched his neck, somehow believing that would allow him the ability to decipher what Aquaman was saying. But this could be the end of the show for Aquaman. His brain was probably nothing more than mush after being waterboarded countless times. He had empathy for Aquaman and for Electric Man. Once they were gone, he would have no other real human close by. There would be no power in numbers, because there would no longer be any numbers. There would be one. Himself. Alone.

A sob erupted into the darkness. "I'm sorry, God. Sorry for…"

It was as though Aquaman had been blessed with a burst of clairvoyant energy. Would that be all, or would he convey more to this story? The man listened intently while counting his heartbeats silently.

One. Two. Three. Four…

Thirty-Eight

Cooper

I stopped in my tracks and crinkled my nose. "I smell weed."

Willow grabbed my casted arm. "Don't tell me…"

She didn't want to say it much less think it. Neither did I. Could it be that both of Rashad Hatley's kids had addiction issues?

"Maybe we got the wrong room number." We were standing on the second floor of Julius Irving Hall. Every dorm on this campus was named after a famous basketball player. Not surprising, given the university's name: Sports University. It was a new concept, created in the last three years. The Dallas campus was the university's third satellite campus across the States. The other two were in Chicago and LA. SU was not a part of the NCAA like most other accredited colleges or universities, and they didn't hide their mission: to mold young men and women athlete-students (*notice the flip of the term from student-athletes*) in a way that will allow them the best opportunity to play professional sports. Secondarily, SU also provided a comprehensive set of courses to prepare the athlete-student for real life.

Willow quickly checked her phone and shook her head. "Nope," she said dejectedly. "This is the room number that Jamaal's mom texted me."

We walked a few more steps in the direction of the only room remaining on the second floor. "If this were Colorado or some other state where weed was legal, we wouldn't be worrying about it. Or maybe he has a prescription for medicinal marijuana," I said, trying to find something positive to say.

"If that were the case, he'd most likely be taking a pill or using as an oil, not smoking it," she said.

We reached the door, and she blocked me before I knocked. "Let's try to make it out of this conversation without a fight breaking out."

"You call what happened at Kina's dorm a fight?"

"True. Sorry I said that. Hope for the best," she said.

"Prepare for the worst," I said, inching a brow upward as I rapped on his door.

Almost instantly, we heard a string of cuss words. Two voices, both male and quite deep. "Not a good sign," I said, looking at Willow.

"Should we just turn around right now and save ourselves from the confrontation?"

Her question had merit. I didn't need or want anything physical to go down, certainly not with two young athletes who could probably break me into many pieces. But my curiosity buzz had kicked in. The same one that drove me to dig deeper on every investigative story I'd been assigned. While I knew Rashad's life was potentially on the line, someone had to write the narrative of his life and of those in his orbit. The complete unfiltered story. I was invested in this story—like many others before it. Maybe more so, considering the beating I'd taken.

The door opened before I could answer Willow or walk away. A guy standing about six-seven with a pick sticking out of his profound afro gave me the once-over. "You ain't no RA."

"Nope. I'm—"

"You one of those PI's the coaching staff hired to spy on us?"

I patted my front pockets. "Sorry, I don't have the credentials, and I don't have the Magnum mustache."

I could see he had no idea whom I was referencing. "Why is some old-ass fart knocking on our door?"

"Jamaal?"

He smacked his lips. "Don't tell me you're another agent."

"Hey, Trae, don't be a dick. Let the man in." A smaller guy ducked under the armpit of Trae and stuck out his hand. "Yo, I'm Jamaal. How's it going?"

I shook it and introduced Willow.

"You even brought your assistant," Jamaal said.

"Must be big-time," Trae said, stepping back into the room.

Without the tree standing over him, Jamaal's physique became more evident. Probably a shade under six feet, he wore a Dri-FIT red tank top with "Cougars" written on the front—SU's mascot. Jamaal looked like he had the body of a twenty-five-year-old. I wondered how much was due to DNA and how much to hard work.

"Just to be up front, Jamaal, we're not agents, although I'm pretty familiar with the sports world."

He squinted his large, round eyes, but he didn't speak. He immediately didn't trust us. But I was focused on the whites of his eyes. His pupils were normal-sized, and there were no red lines.

"Your mom asked us to reach out to you," Willow said.

"Mom," he said with a heavy sigh as he turned and walked back into his room. "You can come on in." He plopped on his bed, then grabbed a basketball and started spinning it on his finger. "What does Mom want, and why did she send you to talk to me?" His eyes were trained on the spinning ball, occasionally popping the fingers from his opposite hand off the ball to keep it spinning. Didn't look like he was trying to show off, though. It was probably more about keeping himself occupied.

The scent of weed was partially masked by one of those fruity sprays. It was a poor attempt at covering their tracks.

"She's really worried about your dad, Jamaal. Has she already told you that?" Willow asked.

His eyes momentarily shifted off the spinning basketball over to Willow. "She doesn't tell me shit. She knows better."

Was he threatening his mom? Wow, this guy was something else. Might be a carbon copy of his father.

"Dude," I said, snagging his attention in a direct way. "Your dad has disappeared. I'm sure you understand how dangerous it is for him, given his, uh, situation. She's just worried. Show her some respect."

He snatched the ball off his finger and gave me a frozen glare.

I wasn't going to give in to his intimidation attempt. "Have you seen your father, or has he contacted you?"

His gaze stayed on me, and I didn't turn away. Finally, he reached over, grabbed a cup from a small table, and took a drink. I wondered if it was alcohol. Anything to escape reality. Meanwhile, Trae was digging under some clothes on the floor. He found two barbells, and he started doing curls.

"Are you going to answer Cooper's question?" Willow asked.

"Cooper. Some kind of name," Jamaal said, setting the cup down. "What's your name again?"

"Willow."

"Like a tree."

"I guess. Are you going to answer us or not?"

"Nah, I haven't seen him or talked to him. We don't really get along much. But I kinda understand why. He's got his demons and all, and he can't really focus on acting like a real dad."

That took the air out of the room. Trae paused his curl routine for a couple of seconds, then started back up without saying a word.

"When's the last time you talked to him?"

He shook his head. "Not sure. I sent him a text on his birthday a few weeks back."

"Did he reply?"

"Just with a thanks." He looked to the floor for a moment. "I keep hoping he'll break out of it. I try to encourage him sometimes, but it just doesn't stick. He's always got something eating away at him. It's more sad than anything. Deep down, I think he's a good person. It's those fucking demons. They just won't let go of him."

Trae started grunting out each rep. Veins were popping out all over his arms and shoulders, which looked cartoonish huge. Think Popeye.

"Trae, man, you don't need to show off your muscles."

"What you talking about Jamaal," he said in a pinched voice. "Just part of my normal routine."

"Yeah, after you smoke one out."

Trae growled as he lifted the weights—they looked to be fifty-pound dumbbells—twice more and then set them on the floor. He found a towel, wiped the sheen of sweat off his face. "You know, Jamaal, not all of us can fall back to our bloodlines. Some of us gotta work at it." He grabbed an empty cup. "Going to get a cup of ice." And then he walked out of the room.

"Damn, that musclehead is clueless." Jamaal opened a drawer from his side table, pulled out a can of Glade, and sprayed it across Trae's side of the room.

"What kind is that?" Willow asked.

Jamaal chuckled. "Red Honeysuckle Nectar. It was on sale. What can I say?"

She looked to me, and her eyebrow inched upward. "Maybe you need to make the same three-dollar investment."

"Funny."

"I got it for two bucks at Walmart. It was the only kind on sale." Jamaal put up the air freshener, then started spinning the ball again. Before he could react, I tipped the ball off his finger, then rotated it until it started spinning off my forefinger.

"Showoff," Willow said.

"Basketball is my drug. What's your drug, Jamaal?"

"What?"

"You're not smoking weed, are you?"

"Hell no."

"Booze?"

"I'm not going to say I haven't had a drink here or there, but I don't live for it. I got much bigger goals in mind."

I flicked my fingers off the side of the ball, speeding up the rotation. "Coke, heroin more your game?"

"I don't do any of that shit. You can drug test me or do whatever. I ain't gonna mess up my chance at playing in the Association."

Willow plucked the ball off my finger and put it under her arm. "So, you're saying your roommate is the druggie?"

"That's such an old-person term. I wouldn't call Trae a druggie. He likes his weed, but he doesn't go hardcore. I thought you guys weren't spies for the coaching staff," Jamaal said, setting his feet shoulder-width apart. He had the kind of legs that looked like they could jump out of a gymnasium.

"Can you dunk?"

He made a scoffing noise. "Can I dunk? You mean, can I go between my legs in midair and bring it down with my left hand? Hell yes. But that doesn't make a player. That's just a highlight reel. Like I said, I got bigger plans."

"Your dad had big plans."

"Don't be dissing my dad," he said, puffing out his chest.

He was taking up for him. Odd, but cool to see. "Addiction is tough, Jamaal. It's a never-ending battle, both for the person fighting the battle and his family."

He nodded.

"Your mom. She's been through a lot."

"Yeah. Whatever."

"Why are you so dismissive of your mom?" Willow moved the basketball under her opposite arm. "She's got a bad case of the flu, and she's trying to take care of your grandmother, who's also sick."

"I love Granny."

"Glad to hear it. But your mom is a mess because your dad hasn't been seen in a week. She's thinking he might have fallen off the wagon and something bad might have happened to him."

Jamaal stared at Willow for a second. Then he wiped a hand across his face. His eyes became glassy. "I love Dad. Damn. I just don't know what to do." His chin bounced off his chest.

"Do you have any idea about who he might turn to if he was enticed to start using again?"

"He never opened up to me like that. The only thing we ever did was practice hoops at a park in South Dallas."

"Which one?"

"Called Opportunity Park. Kind of funny. My old man thought he could beat me in one-on-one, even this last summer."

"And did he?"

A grin cracked his face. "He doesn't know it, but I let him beat me."

I found a pen and paper on his desk. "Here's my phone number. Call me if your dad reaches out to you."

Willow and I started walking to the door, but she stopped and turned around. "You might want to call your mom. She could use your support."

"Eh."

"What's with the attitude with your mom?"

He drew his lips into a straight line and took in a heavy breath through his nostrils. "She gave up on Dad a long time ago."

"What do you mean?"

"She said things like how he embarrassed her and our family, and that with all his addiction issues, eventually he'll get what he deserves."

Sounded a tad menacing, but relationships weren't all about Facebook selfies full of perfect meals, perfect smiles, and around-the-clock, breathtaking joy.

"Were they fighting when she said that?" Willow's voice was calm yet measured, as if she'd flipped the switch to turn into a shrink. A hot shrink at that.

"Yeah, sure they were. But Dad never said mean personal things to her. He'd get mad at the world, but I never heard him attack her character."

"Did you ever see him be abusive with her?" I asked.

He ran his eyes up and down me. "Hell no. Mom would have gone ballistic if he'd done that shit. And I wouldn't have just stood there watching, I'll tell you that much."

The Hatley family might need a psychologist *on retainer* from what I knew so far.

Willow kindly pointed out my phone number again, and we said our goodbyes. We passed Trae on our way out. He gave us a "later" nod as his biceps twitched. Was that involuntary, or was he just showing off for Willow?

The street was dark, although the white BMW was easy to spot amongst the long row of parked cars. I stopped and opened the door for Willow.

"What's this all about?"

"What do you mean?"

"You opening the door. You never do that."

"I've done it before."

"With me or your ex-wife?"

"Actually, both. Are you going to get in?"

"Twenty years ago. That's the last time you opened the door for me." She looked inside the car for a second. "Just saying that makes me feel old. I'm hanging out with a guy I dated twenty years ago."

"It sounds like you're yelling to the world that you have hives."

"Do you see me scratching?"

"Maybe not visibly, but you seem like you're distraught after your sudden reflection on life."

She put her hand on the roof of the car and looked back to the dorm. "Maybe it's being at these college campuses. Lots of memories."

"I get it. I mostly see a lot of young people who have too much time, too much energy, and hormones raging."

"That was us," she said.

"Not really. We weren't that immature. At least I don't think we were."

She turned and gazed into my eyes. I felt a flutter in my heart. "I was talking about when we had our impromptu kiss."

"That was a lot more than a kiss. And what about it?"

"Our hormones were raging."

Was she trying to say we'd acted like a couple of horny teenagers? Following her mental and emotional state of mind felt like running through a maze in the dark.

"At this age, I'm glad I have hormones to rage," I said. "Better than hemorrhoids." I snorted out a laugh. It took a few seconds, but she finally smiled, although it came with a head shake.

"You've changed, Cooper. But there are some things about you that will never grow up." She reached up and touched my cheek. She rubbed the stubble for a second as we held our gaze.

That magnetic pull returned, the same one that had drawn us into our impromptu mug-down session. She lowered her hand to my chest.

"Yes, I have a heart," I said. "I'd put my hand on your chest, but I don't want to be out of line or anything."

"You're so gallant," she joked.

"I just happened to leave my armor at home." I tried flexing my pecs.

"Nice try." She nodded her head while kneading my chest. "Have you been doing push-ups?"

"Not really. I'm just naturally buff."

"Uh-huh. I don't think your blood is reaching your brain."

"Actually, I'm in pretty good shape for someone my age."

She slid her hand down my torso, but stopped at the top of my jeans. "Buff in some places, probably just hard in one place. I think your blood is flowing to the wrong head."

"And that's my fault?"

She took hold of my chin, then pulled her hand back. "Ouch! Your gray whiskers are like the quills of a porcupine."

"But my blood flow is like I'm twenty-one," I said with a toothy grin.

She ran her hand across my chest, and then she leaned in closer. Her warm breath brushed against my neck, and goose bumps formed on my body. I gently put my hand on her hips and closed my eyes, tilting my head and beginning to move my mouth to hers.

She stiffened her arms. "I can't. You can't. You're with Courtney, and—" She stopped short and dropped her butt into the passenger seat, her eyes sifting through her purse as though she were trying to look occupied. "Let's get going. Need to make sure Ma and Briana are still being friendly."

I didn't know how to respond to her hot/cold actions. "Okay." I shut the door and turned right into two man-boobs made of concrete. I looked up and saw the crooked smile of Milo Sachen. Or was it Elan?

"How's it going, dickwad?"

The blood flow just came to a screeching halt.

Thirty-Nine

Willow

The mountain of a man scared me. His hand had Cooper's neck in a vice grip. While I'd had the same desire a time or two in my life, I knew this guy wasn't being playful. And then a second man appeared on the other side of Cooper. A carbon copy of the other, outside of the color of the muscle bodysuits. His was red. The guy who was holding Cooper like a puppet wore blue.

I knew they were the Sack Brothers. I'd met them once. The pair had cornered us in an alley, threatened us. This was before I knew about all of Cooper's checkered history. Does anyone ever know all of Cooper's checkered history? Still, the Sack Brothers were bad news. And they worked for a guy who was even worse news.

The Blue Sack rapped a knuckle on my window. Without taking my eyes off him, my hand found my phone in my purse. I moved my thumb over the ID imprint, hoping that it unlocked. I tried to tap where I thought the phone app button was, then blindly attempted to dial 9-1-1.

I heard a loud beep, followed by an electronic voice saying, "I'm sorry. You've dialed an incorrect number. Please hang up and try again."

Blue Sack put his face right up against the window. While his eyes almost disappeared under his Cro-Magnon forehead, his nostrils began to flare. Damn, he was ugly. And pissed. I lifted both hands up to show I had no phone.

"Open the door," he ordered. His breath left a dollop of fog on my window.

I shook my head like a petulant ten-year-old. The door was the only leverage I had. Maybe if I waited long enough a cop would drive by.

My eyes shifted to Red Sack, who used his opposite hand to grab something from behind his back.

"A gun!" I yelled, putting a hand on the window.

He chuckled as he dangled the gun like it was a toy before resting the barrel against Cooper's ribs.

I had no choice. I pulled the latch on the door. Blue Sack opened it.

"Glad you came to your senses, dickwad," he said.

"You can't call her dickwad," his brother said. "That's my name for Cooper. And she's a lady. It's just not right."

"Okay, what should we call her, then?"

"How about biyaatch?"

"Makes sense to me." Blue Sack offered his hand. "Can I help you out of the car, biyaatch?"

I smacked his hand away and got out of the car. "What do you guys want?" I asked.

"You're coming with us." Blue Sack grabbed my upper arm and took a step. I planted my foot and jerked my arm backward.

"Shouldn't have done that," Cooper said under his breath.

"Milo, what did we do to the last person who disrespected us?" Blue Sack asked as he breathed down on me. He smelled like cheap aftershave and a boys' locker room.

"We cut him up, and someone we know had a little snack," Milo said as he licked his lips. The lighting wasn't good, but that tongue did not look human.

They were probably talking about their dismemberment murder of Ronnie Gutierrez, although it's entirely possible they could have cut up someone since Ronnie. And from what Cooper had shared, Dr. V had similar qualities to Hannibal Lecter in terms of his diet.

"Okay, fine. I'll come with you. Just don't touch me," I declared.

"Whatever, biyaatch."

I walked alongside Blue Sack, also known as Elan. Milo and Cooper were in front of us. Milo had his arm around Cooper as if they were a couple strolling down the street, although I spotted the gun still poking into Cooper's side. Whatever their intentions, or wherever they were taking us, I didn't like our chances.

For a few seconds, I pondered my options. I might be able to kick Milo's hand away, allowing Cooper to jump him, and then I would swing my leg back and crack Elan between the legs. Or maybe I could leap on top of Milo's back, wrap my legs around his waist, and bite into the back of his neck until he dropped the gun.

What was I thinking? Did I think I was Lucy Liu?

We cut through a parking lot and walked another half a block. I figured someone would see us and call the cops. But the night was still, and a fog had dropped on top of us like a ghostly blanket. It was as though the Sack Brothers had already threatened the people in the neighborhood to stay inside or they, too, would suffer the same fate as Ronnie Gutierrez. Just as I started studying the buildings around us, Milo stopped.

"Don't move," he said to Cooper.

"I'm not going anywhere." Cooper lifted his hands in the air, but his eyes were on the gun that was pointed at his chest.

Milo pulled out two long strips of plastic. “Turn around, both of youse.”

“Youse?” I questioned.

“You making fun of us?” Elan grabbed a fistful of my hair and yanked my head back so fast I thought a vertebra in my neck might crack.

“Nope,” I said.

“Glad you said that, because I don’t want to have to deliver broken goods.”

“Goods?” Confused, I looked at Cooper

Cooper shook his head. “Just turn around, please?”

I ended my questions and complied.

“Hands behind your back,” Milo said.

I followed Cooper’s lead and did the same. I felt plastic wrap around my wrists. With a quick zipping sound, they were locked in place. Cooper’s were too.

“In the car.”

I turned and saw Elan holding open the back door of a large SUV with windows tinted nearly black.

Cooper paused. “Is Dr. V in the back with his fork and knife and drool bib?”

“You wish,” Elan said.

Cooper’s brow became furrowed. “Actually, that’s the last thing I’d ever wish for, just in case you’re making a Christmas list for me.”

“Shut up and get in, dickwad.”

Cooper slowly crawled in.

“You too, biyaatch.”

I almost took offense to the name, but my hands were tied behind my back and Milo was holding a gun three feet from me, so I crawled inside. Actually, without my hands to brace me, my face fell onto Cooper’s lap as the door shut behind me. I looked up, and he popped his eyebrows. I said, "Really? You think that's the right thing to do at this time?"

"I was going for levity."

As I pulled myself upright, Milo got into the front passenger seat and pointed the gun at Cooper. Elan slid behind the wheel and pulled the SUV away from the curb.

"Where are you taking us?" Cooper asked.

Milo started chuckling, although it sounded more like a hog in heat. I picked up another waft of his combo aftershave/body odor.

The SUV jerked to a stop, and Elan turned to his brother. "You forgot to put the blindfolds over their eyes."

"I got the gun. That was your job."

"I'm driving."

"But you weren't when they got in the car, fucktard."

Sibling squabbles. I would have laughed had one of the fucktard brothers not been pointing a gun at Cooper.

"I've got to do everything in this operation." Elan slid the gearshift into park and got out of the car. He opened the back door and pulled a black knit cap all the way over Cooper's face. He put a knee in Cooper's groin—Cooper yelped and flailed his torso—and then Elan reached over and pulled a knit cap over my face too.

As Elan got back behind the wheel, I could hear Cooper wincing and Elan chuckling. "Serves him right."

"For what?" I asked, not really thinking it through.

"For being a dickwad, that's what. You got anything else to say, biyaatch?"

The pair grunt-snorted, and the SUV took off. We didn't drive for very long, but we must have made two dozen turns. Ten minutes later, we were ushered out of the car. Each step echoed as though we were in a chamber. And then I was told to sit. The chair was made of metal. The masks were pulled off our heads, and a spotlight immediately blinded me.

"Jesus H. Christ," one of the ogres said with an ear-splitting laugh. "Check out biyaatch's hair. Looks like someone stuck her finger in an electrical socket."

My curls had morphed into a mess of frizz. What can a lady do?

"Where are we? What are you doing to us?" Cooper asked as we turned our heads away from the spotlight. From what I could see behind us, it appeared we were in a warehouse. I saw wooden pallets stacked against the wall and rolls of plastic piled next to them. Other than that, the place was empty, at least the part I could make out.

A second later, I heard the pull of a rotary engine. After three attempts, the engine turned over, and someone revved the engine until it whined.

Without even seeing it, I knew it was a buzz saw. My whole body broke out in a sweat at the same time my skin turned ice cold. My body, like my mind, was freaking out. Tears started to pool in my eyes as I wondered which one of us would be dismembered first? And would they go after my foot or start with a finger?

But why? What exactly was precipitating this level of violence?

"What the fuck are you doing?" Cooper yelled.

The saw whirred louder and louder. The echo only made it that much worse. The sound was deafening and ate a hole in my gut. "Stop!" I yelled. "Don't kill us! Please! Don't—"

The engine rumbled to a stop.

Maybe they'd listened to my pleas. A second later, the lights dimmed, and a round man with thinning hair and yellow, jagged teeth plodded in front of us. "Cooper, Willow…so nice to see the two of you again." It was Dr. Vijayakumar Khatri, one of Harvey's former clients—at least I assumed he was now classified as "former." Harvey had tried to convince me as much the other night. He tried to convince me of a lot of things.

"I'm not sick. No need for me to see a doctor," Cooper said, still panting from the saw scare tactic. I then realized I was breathing like I was climbing a mountain.

"That's what I like about you, Cooper. You can crack a joke even in the face of sure death."

I snagged a glance at Cooper.

"That's right, I said *sure* death. Let that sink in a bit." Dr. V walked over to Milo, grabbed the saw from his hands, and brought it over to about two feet in front of Cooper and me.

"This is one of my favorite tools, although sometimes I like to use smaller tools, similar to what an archaeologist might use."

"Thanks for the tip," Cooper said.

Always a wiseass.

Dr. V rested the idle blade of the saw just above Cooper's knee. "Do you own a pair of crutches?"

Cooper turned to look out across the warehouse. But I couldn't take my eyes off Dr. V and the crooked smile that had formed on his face. He enjoyed toying with us. Was it nothing more than a threat, or were we about to see blood and body chunks sprayed through the air?

"Cooper Chain does not answer the question," Dr. V said, as though he were holding court. He turned and handed the saw to Milo, then pulled a metal object from his front coat pocket. He pushed a button, and a carving spoon popped out.

He then walked to me and rested the cool metal against my cheek. He looked at Cooper. "How do you think Willow would look with no eyeballs? I could season and roast them. My own version of Swedish meatballs." He laughed. It sounded like a panting snake. Every time he hissed, spittle sprayed on my face. I cringed, closed my eyes, and tried not to vomit all over him.

Cooper jostled in his chair, scraping the metal across the concrete. Elan rushed toward him, grabbed him by the throat.

"Stop. Not yet," Dr. V said.

"I just want to watch him take his final breath. I want to see his face turn blue," Elan said.

"Maybe your dreams will come true," Dr. V said. He put a hand on Elan's arm, and the thug carefully peeled his mitt off Cooper's neck. Cooper gasped and coughed.

Dr. V leaned in closer and studied Cooper's forehead. "Has someone already taught Cooper another lesson?"

No response from either of us.

Dr. V said, "Cooper, you don't exactly know how to make friends, do you? And here I was thinking you had such great connections."

Cooper coughed twice as his eyes darted along the floor.

"Here's my quandary, Cooper." He turned to look at me. "And Willow."

"Leave her out of this."

Dr. V paced back and forth in front of us, his hands clasped behind him, although they could barely reach. He paused and looked at Cooper.

"I can't afford to do that. You owe me two favors. Two. And have you delivered on either one?"

Cooper lifted his head. "Of course I have."

"You sound so certain."

"As you know, it's not a one-time exercise. I'm working with your nephew, Ishaan. You can ask him for yourself."

"Your contact with him has been minimal at best."

"I've been busy. But I'm meeting with him tomorrow. It's in my daily planner."

"Daily planner. You think you're in a position to joke?"

"Just giving you the straight shit."

Dr. V stopped right in front of me and stared me down. "How's Harvey doing, Willow?"

I didn't know how to respond, but his creepy gaze made my face go flush. It felt like every artery above my neck was about to explode.

"He's fine," I finally said.

"Leave her out of this, dammit!" Cooper yelled.

Dr. V quickly shuffled to his left as though he were a blitzing linebacker. He jabbed his finger into Cooper's neck. "Listen to me, Cooper. You need to adjust your priorities. Where are you on making progress in setting up our point-shaving operation? Why is this not moving? We have money to make. And every day you waste is money I'm not making. Do you hear me?"

Cooper swallowed. A trickle of blood snaked down his neck. That's when I noticed Dr. V's nails—they looked like old-fashioned letter openers. I shuddered at how this monster's body and mind were put together.

"I fucking hear you!" Cooper grunted, then shook off Dr. V's finger.

"Want me to hold him in place, Dr. V?" Elan ran up and placed his paws on Cooper's head.

"Not necessary. I think he got the point." The monster held up his crimson-covered nail and licked it.

Just when I thought the creep factor couldn't get any higher, Dr. V had topped it. And then some.

"Just tell me what the fuck you want out of me!" Cooper yelled.

I saw Elan rear back his arm.

"Look out!"

Cooper turned in my direction just as Elan's punch connected with his head. I heard a crack as Cooper tumbled off his chair, falling to the dusty concrete, writhing in pain.

Elan started jumping up and down shaking his hand. "Motherfucker, motherfucker!"

"Way to go, dumbass," his brother said. "You're about as smart as a tree stump." He chuckled at his brother, whose cussing storm morphed into something resembling the growl of a caged animal.

Cooper moaned and turned over just underneath me. "Can you see okay?" I asked.

"You're upside down," he said.

"Because I am."

His eyes went all googly.

The snake-hissing laugh of Dr. V jerked my attention in front of me. "You and Cooper are such a cute couple. It's so…adorable."

The sound of his voice, especially when using endearing words, made the hair on my arms stand up.

"Does Harvey know that you and Cooper are screwing each other?"

"Shut up!" I immediately regretted saying that.

"So protective," he said, sucking in an elongated breath. "But the question is…for whom? Harvey or Cooper?"

"Do you like soap operas, Dr. V?" Milo asked.

Dr. V's eyes shifted off me for a second, but only a second. He scanned my face. Actually, he appeared to be studying every last pore. It was beyond invasive. Then he moved his dagger finger up to my cheek. I flinched, and my breath hitched.

"Cooper Chain, look at me."

"Huh?" he said from the floor.

"Look. At. Me."

With his hands tied behind his back, Cooper had little leverage. He jostled on the floor like a fish on a dock, banging his legs off the metal chair. "What?" Cooper asked, his head and shoulders partially propped against the leg of the chair.

Dr. V started to press his nail into my skin. I moved my head back, but he grabbed my hair and continued pushing.

"Stop it, you fucking beast!"

Dr. V chuckled. "Do. Your. Job."

"I told you I would. I can't get much done, though, if you guys keep going with this little chat."

Dr. V's eyes focused on my mouth. No, it was above my mouth.

"How would you like your girlfriend here to not have a nose?"

"What the fuck are you saying?"

"I've taken a fancy to Willow's nose. It's so…perfect, even if it's larger than your average nose. Listen closely, Cooper. Neither you nor Willow can hide behind Harvey any longer. You have two days to set up our point-shaving operation, or I'm going to bite her nose off her face, sprinkle a little powdered sugar on top, and eat it for dessert."

I lurched, trying to escape the grip of his hand. He finally let go and took a step back, but his eyes practically melted my skin.

"Did you hear me, Cooper?"

"Yes. Now leave us alone, dammit!"

Dr. V flicked his wrist toward his two ogres. The spotlights flicked off, and then I saw the inside light of the SUV go on as the three men slipped into their seats. They drove off, and we were left tied up in the dark warehouse.

Forty

Cooper

Lifting my body off the concrete floor without the use of my arms was difficult enough. But once I got to my feet, it felt like I was on a surfboard.

"Earthquake?" I asked as I wobbled from side to side. My brain felt like a coin in a tin can.

"Afraid not."

I could see the dark outline of Willow from a crack of light splintering through a small window at the top of the open warehouse space. She moved to her feet. "I think you suffered a concussion from Elan's punch."

"Yeah, well, I think he broke his hand." I shuffled my feet to make sure I wouldn't fall to the ground. "And no reason to insert jokes about me being hard-headed."

She didn't respond. It was too dark to see her expression. And then I heard a sniffle. "Willow, are you okay?"

"I'm fine."

She didn't sound fine. "It will be okay. I'll figure out—"

"Cooper Chain, stop putting up the walls. You can't just say you'll protect me like I'm some butterfly."

"You're no butterfly. I'd never use that analogy. Bulldog is more like it."

"Ha-ha. Do you see me laughing?"

"Actually, I only see the outline of your body. And Cooper likes what he sees."

"You're referring to yourself in the third person. Are you punch drunk from the concussion?"

I replayed what I'd just said. "Ignore my other personality that made a brief cameo. He's gone now. Say goodbye."

She moved closer to me, accidentally kicking a metal chair.

"That was loud. Oh my."

"What is it?"

"My head hurts."

"Which part?"

"All of it. Feels like a baseball bat was fired out of a howitzer and put a hole right through my skull."

"Need to get you to an ER."

"Did I tell you I'm a little short on health insurance?"

She ignored my inane, albeit true, comment. Probably for the better. She started gyrating her shoulders and arms. "Damn ties. I can't slip my hands out."

"We need a knife or something."

"Won't find it in here. No light. Follow me," she said.

I started walking. "Who moved the floor?"

"You're a mess," she declared.

"Say what you want now while I'm down for the count. Just wait, though, and I'll fire back with plenty of zingers when I'm not scooping up my brains."

She moved to my side. "Lean against me as we walk. I'm headed for the garage down where they left."

"Roger that."

We began to walk. Well, she walked and I wobbled, but at least I didn't fall down.

"What are you doing?" she asked as we made it up the ramp and onto a sidewalk.

"Smelling you."

"Why?"

"Because under the layer of vomit, I smell you."

"Don't say another word."

"Who, me?"

"Ugggh." She started walking up the sidewalk.

"Don't leave me here," I called out.

She came back and scooted up next to me. "No comments about how I smell."

"It was a compliment."

She turned and looked at me. "That's what I was afraid of."

We went two blocks, and I asked if she knew where we were going. She ignored me again. It must have been two hours before we finally got back to her car.

"Got scissors?" I asked.

"In my purse." She dumped all the contents of her purse on the sidewalk as I leaned against the BMW in amazement—the purse wasn't organized like everything else in her life.

"No comments from the peanut gallery," she said, sifting through the mess on the sidewalk. "Could have sworn I had a pair of sewing scissors in my purse." This exercise continued for a good ten minutes. I was thirsty and could use some ibuprofen, but what could I say as the spectator?

I heard footfalls, and I peered over my shoulder to see a very tall man crossing the street. When he got closer, I could see it was Trae. We asked for his help. He obliged with a shrug of his shoulders. He found the scissors and cut off the ties and didn't even ask any questions about how we'd ended up in this situation.

"Thank you," I said.

He touched his neck. "You know you got a little blood…"

"I'm fully aware. I'm all over it."

Then he turned to Willow. "Something definitely happened since you left our room. Your hair kind of has that—"

"Thanks, Trae," I said, jumping in before he uttered anything that might get him in trouble.

"No prob."

He walked off, and we got into the BMW. "Organize my purse while I drive." Willow plopped her purse in my lap. The mess of stuff was brimming over the edges.

"You're the anal one. This isn't my sweet spot."

"I'm driving."

"Okay. I guess I'll try." I pored through the hair clips and chewing gum and lipstick and three different sizes and four different colors of paperclips. I had no idea how to untangle everything, let alone organize it. Then, for no particular reason, I had a flashback of her falling into my lap in the back of the SUV.

"Are you laughing?"

Didn't know I was. "Just thinking about what happened?"

"You find any of this funny? It's disturbing and macabre."

"Ooh, good word."

She draped an arm over the steering wheel while trying to corral her hair.

"Can you find me the blue hair clip?"

I glanced in the purse and then looked at her. I tried not to laugh; I didn't want to rattle my brain. But I was smiling.

"What's so funny?"

"I think I have a better chance at finding your G-spot than finding your blue hair clip."

"Oh, God. Did you just say that?"

Before I could respond, she started reaching for my neck, but she stopped. "There's hardly a place on your body that's not injured. I'll wait until you heal, then I'll pinch you until you scream like you're losing your left nut."

"You sure you don't want to use the word 'ball'?"

She glanced at me, and I snickered. A jolt of pain splintered through my head, and I winced.

"We're going to the ER first," she said.

"Whose body are we talking about? Actually, whose wallet are we talking about?"

After a five-minute debate on the worthless exercise of dropping by an ER, she gave up—a victory for me—and we drove to her apartment.

"Looking forward to checking in on Ma and Briana," she said, steering the BMW through the winding parking lot of her massive apartment complex. "Did I mention that I told Briana I'd help her find this person who tried to kidnap her?"

I pinched the corner of my eyes. "I know my brain's not operating like it should, but I thought we agreed that Briana was most likely making it all up."

"I have my doubts."

"About what part?"

She shook her head and moved her shoulders in different directions. "I just said I'd help her. You don't have to lend a hand. No worries."

The closest parking spot to Willow's apartment was two buildings over. Feeling a little more lucid, I was able to walk without assistance. We marched across the grass to the next area of concrete until we could see the second-floor landing of her apartment. I put my hand out, stopping Willow in her tracks.

"What's that for?" she asked.

I pointed up to her apartment, where a man was peering into one of her windows.

"Is that…?" she asked.

"I think Briana might have been telling the truth."

A second later, Willow took off in a sprint.

"Crap."

Forty-One

Willow

Cutting between two pickups, I shot out from under the covered parking area, but I didn't see the garage creeper until my foot touched down on the wheeled unit. Completely off balance, I rode the garage creeper with one foot like a skateboard until it rammed into the curb, which launched me forward into the grass. *Damn Mr. Hopper and his car-repair side business,* I thought as I sailed through the air.

I hit the wet grass and kept sliding. When I finally stopped, I had a mouthful of dormant grass. I opened my eyes and saw Cooper standing over me. "Now look who's injured."

He extended his hand, and I pulled myself up. A quick body check, and I was all in one piece—no major injuries. I twisted my torso to get my bearings and saw the man racing down my staircase. He must have heard the clatter and spotted us rushing toward him. He took off running in the opposite direction.

"Call the cops," I said to Cooper over my shoulder as I darted out of my stance.

The man had a good fifty-yard head start on me, but I pumped my arms harder. I was gaining ground quickly—either I'd gone back in time fifteen years to my peak sprinter speed or this guy was dragging extra weight. Just when I thought I had him dead in my sights, he cut around a dumpster behind a row of apartments. *Isn't that a dead end?* Halfway to that mark, I heard a cat's screech pierce the air. My breath hitched, which made me swallow saliva. I slowed down, breaking out in a coughing fit. Had this maniac just killed a cat? If so, I'd rip him to shreds before the cops showed up.

As I rounded the corner, I heard Cooper call out from behind me. No idea what he said. I was too focused on the darkness in front of me. There were a few lights from apartments up high, but on ground level, it was like all light had evaporated into a black hole. I put on the brakes, now moving at Cooper's pace from earlier, minus the drunk wobble. But another feeling consumed me. It was as though I were being watched. And even worse, I had no weapon. I had no sidekick so I could at least feel protected by outnumbering this guy. And if this was the same person who'd tried to kidnap Briana with some type of injection, he probably was prepared for a confrontation. Gun, knife, needle, I wasn't sure.

My eyes didn't blink as I scanned the area. Walls, clusters of bushes, tree trunks. He could be hiding behind any of these, but for some reason I kept moving, my heel-to-toe steps almost completely quiet.

There were no sounds of a cat or any other animal, only gusts of wind that fluttered my hair into something that might scare little kids. But it was the flutter of my heart that made me realize the potential danger I was in. Still, I couldn't help but ask myself *why*. Why had this man attempted to kidnap—and maybe even kill—Briana? She was an addict, that much was obvious. Maybe she hadn't told me the complete story. Could she have stolen drugs from this guy?

Just then, I heard what I guessed were shoes crunching against small pebbles. But with tall buildings on three sides of me and sounds bouncing all around, I couldn't tell their origin or in which direction they were moving. I hunkered lower, bracing myself for someone to tackle me.

And then the crunching-pebble sound stopped. I flipped my head around. Had the man circled behind me in the darkness and jumped onto the grassy area by the end of the building? It had to be.

Crap.

I took off in a sprint, jumped onto the grassy area, and rounded the corner. I saw a flash of someone disappearing around the next cove between apartment buildings. *Dammit!* Then I started questioning that quick image. Was it really the same man, or could it be any other resident in the complex? I jogged ahead, realizing I was essentially heading back in the same direction from where I'd started this chase. I slowed for a moment and did a quick three-sixty. Maybe I was mistaken. Maybe he'd gone toward the back of the complex, not the front.

I slowed for a second and swiped hair out of my face, three times. It was useless. I was basically eating wild strands of hair as the wind kicked up even more. I peered over my shoulder again, out of self-preservation and questioning if I should reverse course again. I was questioning just about everything at the moment.

A scream cracked through the wind, followed by another loud grunt. It was in the direction of my apartment, and my heart bounced. I couldn't predict what had gone down. I bolted out of my stance, raced across the grass, and whipped around the corner. I slipped on the grass the moment I saw Cooper—my hand braced myself, keeping me from falling. He was leaning against the wrought-iron railing of the staircase leading up to my apartment.

"What the hell is going on?" I could barely get the words out, hands on my knees, pumping out breaths.

"Someone you know got tripped up." He casually folded his arms across his chest as though he were working the front counter at Books and Spirits.

"Huh?" I pushed more hair out of my face and mouth.

"Take a look-see down there." He pointed off to his left at a bed of bushes. That's when I saw the man dressed in black rolling over, releasing a soft groan.

That groan sounded familiar. I cautiously moved closer to him.

"Who is that?" I asked Cooper. "And what's he doing in the bushes?"

"He ran by, and I stuck out my foot. He didn't see me or the foot, and he crashed and burned. Simple as that. But it's *who* that person is that might get your attention."

I turned my sights from Cooper to the man, who sat up and tried to move his arm.

"Hi, little Willy. It's Dad."

I almost keeled over right there.

Forty-Two

Cooper

Watching family squabbles is best done from afar. There can be some humor involved as long as you stay far enough away so you don't get hit with shrapnel.

I was about to start the interrogation of Raymond, but Willow ordered me to stand where I was, huddled next to a support beam on the covered garage. She stepped over to her father, and *her* interrogation began. Arms moving wildly. Cursing. Talking so fast Raymond never really got a word in. He just nodded as she went on and on. He'd apparently resigned himself to taking the punishment.

I just wasn't sure how he thought he could weasel his way out of this one—whatever *this* was. If there was any silver lining to this situation, it was that Florence had no idea we were right under her nose. A Florence/Raymond interaction never went well, not for them or anyone in the vicinity. I had personal experience: I had been at Harvey's house when Raymond made his grand reentrance into Willow's life three days prior to her wedding. Florence was also there and…well, she left a handprint on the side of his face. Willow almost passed out from the emotional shock—and then she made it a point to declare to everyone at the party that she was *not* pregnant.

Of course, Raymond was on my shit list for other reasons as well. I wasn't about to let him leave this apartment complex until I had my own turn talking to him.

My phone buzzed, and I pulled my eyes off the family drama to see if it was Ishaan. I'd texted him a while ago asking for an update on making friends with the SMU star basketball player—a key priority if Willow and I wanted to avoid a date with Dr. V's buzz saw.

It was Ishaan.

Dude ur hurting my game.

I waited for more, but a few seconds passed, and I saw nothing. He was blowing me off. For his so-called game? Wait a second. He wasn't talking about a video game. I quickly typed in a reply.

Your game = girls. If ur serious about ur career, u will take my direction.

I waited a moment and then looked up to see Willow waving me over.

I held up my phone as I walked, hoping to receive an Ishaan text with a detailed update. My phone stayed silent.

"How's it going?" I asked.

Willow gave me a stressed stare. I knew her emotions were churning like a stormy sea.

"Cooper, nice to see you. I think," Raymond said with a hearty chuckle.

I didn't laugh in response. I just stared at the guy. It must have lasted a good minute.

"Are you suffering from something related to your concussion?" Willow asked me.

"Cooper hit his head?" Raymond said. "Ah, he'll be okay. He's got nothing but rocks up there anyway, right?" He laughed some more.

"Dad!"

"It's okay," I said.

"Sorry, sorry. It was just the perfect setup, Willy. No harm, no foul, right, Coop?"

"Sure, Raymond. Whatever you say." I slid over next to Willow. "Making any progress?"

"Hell no. He's saying he just dropped by to see me."

"I miss you, Willy. You're the main reason I came back to town. Your brother and sister aren't ignoring me like you are."

"And so you show up at her apartment at one in the morning?" I asked.

For a split second, Raymond's *aw-shucks* expression showed a crack.

"You could wake up Ma. Do you want that?"

"Actually, I just happened to see her when I looked in the window. She's up awfully late, but when I saw her, I thought it was prudent that I go ahead and leave. I don't want to upset her unnecessarily."

"How kind of you. It's so nice of you to think of someone else for the first time in your fucking life!"

It was pretty dark, but I was certain that vein on her forehead had just grown to the size of a worm.

"Willy, come on now," Raymond said, spreading his arms. "Let's hug it out like a normal father and daughter."

"Normal father and daughter? You've got to be joking. What is normal about a dad leaving his family for thirty years, then just showing up before my wedding to…I guess take credit for raising me?"

Raymond glanced at the ground. Maybe he felt a little guilt. Or maybe he was trying to conjure up another excuse. I was betting on the latter.

"Hey, do you want me to take over?" I asked Willow.

"Did you call the cops?"

"Never got around to it."

She growled.

"Sorry, I was too busy watching you act like one of Charlie's Angels." I smiled.

She didn't. Bad timing. I should have known that.

"I can call the cops now if you want me to," I said.

"Cops. Why the cops?" Raymond's arms dropped against his thighs.

Willow chimed in. "Oh, maybe because you tried to kidnap a girl."

I watched Raymond very carefully. His eyes bugged out, probably like mine would have if someone accused me of kidnapping a girl.

"Willy, I may not have been a great father—and for that, I have many regrets—but do you really think I could kidnap anyone?"

He sounded sincere. He looked sincere. But I still doubted his honesty. Call me a cynic. Willow tried to use her fingers as a pick to pull her hair back. It didn't work, and she grimaced. I stayed quiet for the moment. But only a moment.

"We could always get Briana down here and see if she recognizes him." I could feel the heat of Raymond's eyes on me, but I kept my gaze on Willow.

"Who's Briana?" he asked, a little too innocently for my liking.

"She's a very troubled girl who's going through a lot of issues with her addiction," Willow said.

My jaw tightened, wishing she hadn't shared that much information.

"Wait a second. Is this some druggie you met at the health clinic?"

Willow lifted her chin, but she didn't say anything.

"Wow, Willy, it's like I'm guilty before I have a chance to defend myself."

Willow shuffled her feet. She should have been untying her knotted tongue. He was throwing all sorts of shade in her direction.

She finally caught my eye. I said, "Hey, I can still call Courtney and keep this investigation low-key, or I can go up and get Briana."

"If anyone goes up, it would need to be me. She trusts me. Well, I guess she trusts Ma too."

Raymond belted out a chuckle. "You're kidding, right? Your mother bonding with this druggie? I could only see that if Florence has some type of skin in the game."

Willow's eyes narrowed. "Skin in the game?"

"You know, a vested interest. Maybe she's making some extra money on the side by dealing."

I couldn't believe what I was hearing. Willow shook her head, closed her eyes, then extended a flat hand toward Raymond's face. "Stop. Just stop right there, Dad. Ma is a lot of things, but drug dealer isn't one of them. And for you to suggest that… You've got to be fucking insane!" she yelled.

A few seconds later, a light flipped on and a door opened from above us, as in Willow's second-floor apartment. *Ohhh. Craaaap.*

"Who is that down there?" Florence shouted.

I didn't even look up. I was hoping we were far enough under the stairs and blocked by a nearby tree.

The three of us—Willow, Raymond, and I—were like squirrels blending into the background. We went still. None of us wanted to stick a finger in the Florence garbage disposal.

"Helloooo! I'm not blind. Cooper, is that you?"

I sighed. "Yes, Florence, it's me. How are you doing this evening?"

"That's a stupid question. Wait… Willow is that you? Are the two of you trying to hide your little tryst from me? I don't think that's very wise. A mother always knows."

"Ma, can you get your mind out of the gutter? It's nothing like that. I'll be upstairs in a minute. We're just having a discussion."

And then I heard slippers tapping the stairs. I looked at Willow, who in turn glared at her father. He looked over his shoulder as if he were contemplating running. I couldn't blame him, even if I didn't trust him.

Florence came around the staircase and cupped a hand over her eyes to block the light from above. "Jesus H. Christ. Raymond, is that you?"

"Hi, Florence." He gave a round wave.

"What the hell are you doing here at this hour, and why are you wearing all black?"

Willow turned back to her dad. "Yeah, why are you wearing all black?"

"I'm a trendy guy in my old age, what can I say?"

"You're a fucking scoundrel, that's what you are." Florence charged in his direction. I moved in front of her like I was setting a pick (it's a basketball thing). This was all for Willow.

"Get out of my way, Cooper."

I looked at Willow.

"Ma."

Her mother ignored her. "Cooper!"

"Ma, Ma, listen to me." She took her mother by the shoulders. "Go upstairs, please. This is a personal matter between Dad and me. Oh, and Cooper too."

The last thing I wanted was to be locked in another closed space with Florence. I appreciated the reprieve.

Florence calmed down a bit and smoothed some stray hairs in her 1970s beehive hairdo. She appeared to be mulling over her next move.

Just then, my phone buzzed again, and I snuck a quick glance. Ishaan had sent another text:

I set up meet-and-greet with u and my new contact. Tomorrow at noon.

Uggh. He'd actually followed through with setting it up. But I still hoped to get Ishaan to be the conduit for this scam. That way I could stay clean and figure out how to gather some type of evidence against his psycho uncle. I knew that would take a serious conversation with Ishaan. And maybe a little luck. Hell, maybe a lot of luck. I couldn't delay it any longer, though. Dr. V's threats were the main catalyst to get this point-shaving operation set up.

I replied with: *Where?*

As I watched three dots blink across the bottom of my screen, Willow walked her mom up the stairs, talking quietly to her along the way. Damn, that woman had patience and kindness that just wasn't normal. Not normal for me, anyway. My eyes caught some movement on the landing area. A woman with her arms folded against her chest was shifting like a little kid who had to pee. That had to be Briana. And she appeared to be frazzled. I was no expert, but it had to be part of her detox reaction, right?

I glanced at my phone—Ishaan was apparently typing up a novel-sized text—then I looked at Raymond. He had his head buried in his phone, but his position had changed. He was tucked closer against the apartment building under the stairs.

I felt a prick at the base of my skull. Was he trying to hide from Briana?

The patter of Willow's footfalls made my breath hitch. She was hopping down the staircase. Florence and Briana, I assumed, were in the apartment.

I approached Willow as she came around the corner. "Hey, I think we might need to—"

"There's my little girl," Raymond belted out, oblivious that he was interrupting me. Or maybe not. "Everything calm on the western front?" He followed up with a deep chuckle.

Willow had a confused look on her face. Well, confused, annoyed, stressed, and even tired. No way I was going to tell her she looked tired, though. That would derail any conversation.

"Dad, I'm not a little girl any longer. I'm a grown woman who can think on her own and not be swept up by all of your laughter and acting like you're so perfect and innocent."

Raymond looked at me for a moment. Was he expecting me to bail him out? He was fucking nuts if he thought that. He rubbed the back of his neck, then walked over and took hold of Willow's hands. "I remember dancing with you, Willow. One of those cartoon shows had some theme song that you loved."

"It was a movie, *The Little Mermaid*. I dreamed of being a mermaid after watching that movie."

"Ha! You must have watched that video a hundred times. And every time I was around, you grabbed my hands just like this and wouldn't let go until I danced with you."

They were having a moment. And I was about to heave. I couldn't believe Willow was falling for his bullshit ride down memory lane. I literally bit into my tongue to stop myself from blurting out something bordering on rude.

Willow let go of his hands, took a single step backward, and lifted her arms. "Dad, you're trying to distract me or maybe even brainwash me into focusing on a handful of times when I was a kid. This has to stop."

That's the Will I know! I tried not to pump my fist in jubilation.

"Stop what?" he said with such innocence it again activated my gag reflex.

"Dad, stop. You're not listening. You have questions you need to answer or Cooper is going to call the cops. Do you understand?"

He paused, staring at her face. Was he trying to put her under his spell? Damn, he was starting to not only piss me off, but also creep me out.

"Okay, Willow. The only thing I want is to rebuild our relationship. I'll take on any questions you have."

"Where did you get the fifty K that you put in the back of my trunk?" I blurted.

He snapped his head at me like a snake about ready to pounce.

Willow raised a finger. "And while you're pondering that question, can you explain why you thought you could pay off Cooper to convince me to give you a second chance?" Even in our reduced lighting, I could see her neck and face turning as red as a tomato.

"Willow, I…" He spread his arms and took a step forward. She countered that with another step back.

"I thought you were going to answer our questions." Willow set her hands on her waist. She looked defiant, but she also looked strong. It's like she'd morphed from the Little Mermaid into the Lion King—if I stayed gender neutral.

Raymond went back to rubbing his neck, then he snagged a glance at me. "You told her. I can't believe you betrayed my trust."

"Trust!" Willow screamed. "You tried to pay off my friend to get me to like you. How fucked up is that?"

"Pretty fucked up, if you ask me," I said.

She gave me a blank stare.

"Sorry, I guess you didn't ask me."

Her eyes went back to Raymond. "And I know you brought up the names of Dr. V and the Sack Brothers. How do you know them?"

"Darlin', I meant no harm to you. I only wanted to rekindle our special relationship."

A gun fired, and I literally jumped two feet off the ground. I looked up and saw Florence holding a pistol into the sky. "Raymond Ball, you stop harassing and brainwashing my daughter, or this next bullet is going for your ass."

Raymond jumped out of his stance, running in a zigzag pattern across the grassy area. I guess he thought he was making it more difficult for Florence to shoot him. Who knew? Willow flipped around on her heels and raced up the staircase. "Ma, you can't do that. Put that gun away right now!"

I wanted no part of that scene, so I moved as fast as I could to follow Raymond into the parking lot. But when I reached the covered area and gazed across the sea of cars and buildings, I saw no one.

Then I heard tires screeching. I thought the sound came from the parking area behind the next building over. I lumbered over to the adjoining street and saw the back lights of a vehicle leaving the complex.

It was a van.

Forty-Three

Cooper

There are yawns, and then there are bone-tired yawns. I'd just released the granddaddy of bone-tired yawns.

Slash snickered from across the table where we were both reassembling the books on display. "Dude, my uncle has a dog, and that mutt once yawned so wide that he got his jaw locked."

I grimaced.

"Sucks balls, right?"

"And then some. How did he get it unlocked?"

"My uncle used to work in the circus… You know, before they shut the thing down because it was too inhumane on the animals. Anyway, he grabbed both sides of the dog's mouth and pulled it open another inch. It unlocked, and the dog was able to close it. It was badass, I'm telling you."

"Badass." My mind went back in time when my saintly mother took me to the circus as a kid. I watched with utter amazement as the lion tamer stuck his head inside the mouth of the enormous lion as the white fangs glistened off the spotlights—not unlike how I'd felt when Willow and I were kidnapped and threatened by Dr. V. As much as I tried to veer my thoughts elsewhere, I couldn't help but flash on the visual of his jagged teeth, his dagger-like fingernails, his round, grizzled face with those demon-like eyes.

It sent a shiver up my spine.

I released a deep breath and flipped my head around to look outside. No sign of Ishaan. He was supposed to pick me up shortly. Not sure where this meet-and-greet would be with his new basketball connection—the punk never replied to my text—but the conversation with his hoops contact would be the second most important of the day. First, I had to convince Ishaan it would be in his best interest to run this operation.

I could take a hundred deep breaths and it wouldn't reduce my anxiety. I was taking a huge risk by going down this path with Ishaan. If he told his uncle of my plans to make him the big man for the point-shaving scheme, the payback would likely redefine the word "painful" for Willow and me. He might even kill one of us—just for fun. But if I didn't take this route with Ishaan, I wasn't sure I had it in me to continue living with this sword hanging over my head. Every time I walked out of a coffee shop, or strolled down the street, or even slept in my own bed, I wondered if the Sack Brothers would be right there. They, or their boss, could find a hundred reasons to justify breaking a bone, cutting off an appendage, or simply beating my ass into the ground.

Ah, the good old days, when fights ended with nothing more than a black eye or a bruised rib.

"Dude, you hear me?" Slash was snapping his fingers.

I'd zoned out. "What?"

He nudged his head to the side. "Hot babe alert."

I flipped my head around, hoping to see Willow. It wasn't her, just some young coed wearing an SMU T-shirt. "Go for it, Slash."

"Maybe I will, but I first need to check out the goods from afar, if you know what I mean," he said with a chuckle. All of a sudden, I connected his laugh to something from my past. He sounded just like Beavis from the *Beavis and Butt-Head* cartoons. Those cartoons were a top draw when I was in college. I probably wasn't as mature as I thought I was back in those days. Some might say I haven't changed much. Florence would undoubtedly lead the charge.

Florence. That crazy woman could have killed someone with her gun early this morning. If there were a list of people who should never be allowed to own a gun, she should be on it. Willow had done a decent job of calming her down. Essentially, she'd given her a large shot of whiskey in the bathroom, away from Briana, whose nerves were still jangled when I'd entered the apartment.

After Willow and I took a moment to ourselves to trade thoughts on the whole experience with Raymond, we asked her mother to stay in the bedroom while we sat in the living room with Briana. Willow asked Briana if she was freaked out by seeing or hearing her potential kidnapper outside the apartment—we didn't want to lead her too much by identifying Raymond specifically.

She went mute on us. And then, as she rocked back and forth in her seat, she started muttering phrases, something about wondering if she'd ever see her kids again. Willow and I were perplexed, so Willow went into the bedroom to ask Florence for some guidance on how to calm Briana down. Cooking, apparently, was the trick. Not that Florence knew how to cook, but somehow the two of them had bonded over the experience.

By the time Willow got back, however, Briana had lost all energy and said she only wanted to sleep. We didn't push it, and Willow covered her with a blanket on the couch. In just minutes, the girl was snoring lightly.

After everyone was settled, Willow and I stepped outside on the landing. I asked if she knew what kind of van her dad drove, although I admitted that when I spotted the van driving out of the apartment complex, the lighting was so poor I had no idea what the make or model was.

"I thought he drove a sedan, not a van," she said. "But I'll talk to my brother and sister and see if they know for certain."

"Any way he could have been the person in the van who tried to kidnap Briana?"

We spent no more than five minutes brainstorming on why Raymond would want or need to kidnap Briana. We came up with zilch. Briana's behavior, for obvious reasons, was difficult to corral. Willow said she'd talk to Briana again when they woke up to see if she would share more about what had happened to her, as well as try to convince her to go to a detox facility. Willow admitted that when she invited Briana to stay at her place, she'd made the decision more out of empathy than logic. And now she wasn't sure how she could just let Briana back on the streets. Willow felt like she had no way out.

No way out. The story of my life.

"Va-va-voom."

I looked over at Slash, who was popping his eyebrows. I glanced around, searching for the girl in the SMU T-shirt. "Where's your hot babe?"

"She's in the Romance section, probably trying to find an image of me on one of the covers."

"I'm sure that's what she's doing," I said, tongue firmly in cheek. But I wasn't sure he noticed.

"Yeah, I'll make my move in just a minute. But I was talking about the Raven Goddess walking in the door."

I turned to see Courtney opening the door and removing her sunglasses. The tight jeans, ribbed turtleneck, and silky, straight hair would turn the head of any guy—or even girl. The glow had returned to her face.

"Cooper, there you are," she said, walking in my direction. She didn't stop until she planted a soft kiss on my cheek. It was unexpected, and it gave me a jolt. But was the jolt from the shock of her doing it or the resulting feeling I had inside? Too much to parse through right now.

"Hey, what's going on?" I found myself inching back a bit. Slash walked away, probably heading to Romance.

"I've got some news on the Myron Little disappearance. I dropped by your apartment since I was in the neighborhood, but you weren't there."

I held up a book. "Early shift."

"Right."

"Did you guys find the old Grinch?"

"Nothing that meaty, but one of the detectives made another round in the neighborhood to talk to people. Apparently, a neighbor who lives two streets over was walking her dog late that night and saw a van pulling out of Myron's driveway."

It felt like hardened concrete had just been poured into my body cavity. "A van," I said, trying to expand my tight chest.

"That's what I said."

"Did she get the license plate number?"

"Not surprisingly, no. But the witness said what stood out for her was the fact that the van had lettering on the side."

"For a business?"

She nodded. "She couldn't recall the exact name, but believes she saw the word 'plumbing' on the side."

"Wow. That's huge." I raked my fingers through my hair as my gaze shifted to the table of books. I was questioning whether I should share with Courtney the whole saga with Briana and her possible attempted kidnapping. Of course, that would open the door to Raymond—if I were to be completely transparent with my thoughts about the guy—which would definitely complicate matters. It would likely force me to tell another partial story because of his possible association with Dr. V and the Sack Brothers. And if Raymond was somehow involved in both crimes—kidnapping Myron and attempting to do the same with Briana—then the floodgates would surely open.

Would that be a bad thing, though? As much as I tried, I couldn't picture a scenario where Dr. V wouldn't inflict some type of horrific retribution on Willow and me. Someone needed solid evidence to tie that maggot to a crime he couldn't slither away from. I remembered the story about Capone. He'd killed or ordered the killing of dozens of people, but the Feds ultimately got him for tax evasion.

Hmmm. That made me think about Harvey, since he had been Dr. V's CPA for a brief period of time. Maybe he even still was—we didn't really know for sure.

"Cooper, you look like you're in a daze." Courtney put a gentle hand on my back.

I tried to breathe in, but an invisible steel cable must have been wrapped around my chest. I coughed, then said, "I'm just trying to think all this through."

"Are you wondering when you can paint over the swastikas?"

"Uh, yeah. It would be nice to get that done before Mrs. Kowalski gets back. Any ideas?"

"I don't, but I can check with the lead detective right now, if you like."

"Sure. That would be cool."

As she brought the phone to her ear, she winked and took hold of my arm. "Maybe we can see each other tonight. I'm open. How about you?"

I wasn't sure how to answer that question. I wanted to see her. I think. But with so much chaos, violence, and uncertainty in my life—and in Willow's life—swirling around, I just couldn't see myself taking a break, chilling with Courtney on my couch while watching an inane romantic comedy. And then what would happen? A little smoochie, maybe a nice back massage, and then hands might start to wander. Hers or mine, though? Hers for sure. But why not mine?

"It's not a multiple choice question, you know."

I looked into her eyes, so dark and mysterious, though at the moment, I clearly saw desire. "Well, I—"

She pointed at the phone. "Detective. Hi, this is Detective Bouchard. Need to bounce something off you on the swastikas investigation and…" Her voice faded as she turned away from me.

A second later, the door dinged open.

"Cooper, hey."

Ishaan was sticking his head in the door, waving me toward him.

"Hey, Ishaan. I, uh…" I swiveled my head to Courtney, who was still talking on the phone. My anxiety spiked as I thought about the potential of my two worlds colliding.

"Dude, we need to run. Let's go," he said.

"Yeah, I'm almost ready." I moved a few books around, unsure how to handle this exit with Courtney.

"Cooper, we're going to be late. And I don't think you or I want to be late for this meeting."

I flipped and glared at the kid. It was as though he knew what this was really about—setting up the point-shaving scheme. But there was no way he could know about it. So, what was really going on?

"Hey, I need a second, okay? It's just about a profile story," I said, trying to downplay the importance.

"Yeah, well, maybe you haven't heard, but I saw on Twitter that Rashad Hatley hasn't been seen or heard from in over a week."

"What the fuck?"

"You didn't know?"

"No," I said unconvincingly.

"Well, I think this contact of mine can help on two fronts, but we can't be late."

"What two fronts?"

"I can explain it in the car. Let's go."

I looked to Courtney, who was still on the phone. Slash walked back up to the front, alone. "Hey, Slash, can you tell my friend that I had to run?"

His eyes shifted to Ishaan at the door, then back to me. "Why?"

"Why what?"

"She's going to ask why you had to run."

"Tell her it was a personal emergency."

"Okay. I'll tell her just that."

I wasn't sure how well that would go over, but I couldn't think of another option. "Thanks, dude."

"No prob."

Forty-Four

Cooper

As much as I loathed the fact that I was feeling up Ishaan's car like I'd done to Jennifer Lopez in my teenage dreams, my hands couldn't stop touching every sensual curve of the leather and walnut interior.

"Nice ride." I went for casual admiration.

"Eh. I wrecked my Porsche. This is nice if you're old."

He equated owning a Tesla to being old. Interesting.

Ishaan cut through the streets of Dallas as though he were racing through the streets of Monaco. Horns blared every few seconds. He dismissed them with a lighthearted chuckle.

Through the maze of new buildings, I spotted the brick façade of American Airlines Arena, the home of the Dallas Mavericks. I thought about Rashad Hatley and how he could have been the type of player to lead a young franchise to the promised land of a championship. When he went pro, he seemed destined to have his jersey hanging from the rafters. Now at a legitimate retirement age, he should be basking in the glow of an amazing career. Instead, he'd seemingly disappeared into thin air. Where the hell had he gone?

I swung my sights from the arena over to Ishaan. "Any idea how Rashad's disappearance made it to Twitter?"

He gave me a quick glance as he turned right onto Field Street. "Sounds like you knew about it."

"I haven't been able to reach him," I said, telling a partial truth, something I was apparently pretty good at. Not a trait you want to pass on to the next generation.

Lauren. A sudden pain throbbed through my chest wall, as if someone were beating me with a sledgehammer. But I knew it was self-inflicted.

Compartmentalize, Cooper. Your go-to strategy for self-preservation.

We zoomed through a yellow light and crossed over Woodall Rogers. "So," he said, shaking a finger in the air. "I think it might have been a story by this news outlet called *BuzzFeed* that kicked off the whole viral wave on Twitter. But that name sounds bogus, so who knows how much of this is true? Lots of bullshit to wade through on the Internet."

"Can't disagree with you on that. But *BuzzFeed* is a legitimate company. Based out of New York."

"Hmm. What's it like working in our field in the biggest market in the US?"

Our field? Ishaan had already made the mental leap into considering himself a veteran reporter with a thousand articles under his belt. He probably thought he could fool the journalism world into thinking as much.

"It's cold," I said.

His thick brow responded with a confused twitch. "Huh?"

"Cold. The weather, the cutthroat nature of working in New York City, especially when people know you're trying to hunt down the truth on a story that might make them look pretty shitty."

"How do you think Rashad will respond when he finds out you want to expose him as a loser drug addict?"

I turned to look at him. "I admit that a lot of my stories go where people aren't comfortable. And that can expose some baggage. But my hope is that I'll also find a silver lining, maybe something people can learn from, or how the person I'm profiling has begun to turn his or her life around." I thought about what he'd said for a moment. "Why would you put it that way, calling him a loser drug addict?"

"Just going by what that article said. You should be proud of me. I actually read a story, hoping I'd learn a few things."

"Proud" wasn't the word that came to mind, but I kept that to myself. "How the hell would a *BuzzFeed* reporter know about Rashad Hatley's disappearance? Rashad has been off the radar of the sports world for a good decade. Who did they use as a source, do you recall?"

"Anonymous source."

Anonymous on a missing person that hadn't been reported to the police. Hmm. I suddenly felt very antsy. I wanted to call Willow to bounce an idea off her, but I knew I couldn't get into it in front of Ishaan.

The tall, glass buildings of downtown Dallas vanished the moment we crossed I-30 into South Dallas. I could see Fair Park and the Cotton Bowl off to the east as we motored down Highway 352. We hit Pennsylvania, then turned south again on Trunk.

"You ever going to tell me where we're going?"

He smirked. "If I did, I might have to put a hood over your head." I didn't move for a second. Was he making a reference to the kidnapping his uncle had ordered on Willow and me?

"Have you gone catatonic on me?" he asked

"Uh, no."

"I was just joking. I'm a big fan of the Batman movies. No one could know the location of the Bat Cave."

"What's going on, Ishaan? Why all the cloak-and-dagger shit?"

"Dude, chill. Didn't you hear the part about me joking? Besides…" He motioned with his head. "It's right up here. And I didn't even need to put a hood over your head," he said with a chuckle. He was enjoying this little game. I tried to ignore everything that was Ishaan and look for a person standing on the side of the road. The Tesla pulled up to a curb, and Ishaan got out. I chastised myself for not discussing the whole point-shaving idea and how I needed Ishaan to run it before we got here. Now I'd have to wing it. At least I had practice at that.

"I don't see anyone," I said.

"Just follow me." He shut the door and started walking. My gut heard all sorts of warning bells going off, but I followed him toward a park. Just before the entrance, I stopped in front of a sign.

"This is Opportunity Park?" I'd heard that name recently, or maybe I'd read it in a story somewhere, but I couldn't place it. Either I was getting old or the near-constant drama had dramatically impaired my memory.

"You can read! No wonder you're such a good writer." He never slowed down. If he wasn't such a petulant ass, I might bond with him over his sarcasm. Not in my lifetime, though.

I caught up to him as he rounded a cluster of trees. I stopped in my tracks as my sights zeroed in on the person standing under the nearest rim on the basketball court.

"Yo, Cooper, long time no see."

"Hey, Jamaal. What are you doing here?"

Forty-Five

Willow

The words on the patient's medical chart started to blur. I pinched the corners of my eyes.

"Nurse Willow, do I need to prescribe a methadone pill for you too?"

My brain had been stuck in the mud after a night of little sleep on the couch. But as I turned to face Dr. Mulligan, a laser of heat seared the cobwebs from my mind. "Excuse me…doctor?"

"It was just a joke," he said, motioning with his palms turned downward, as if he could sense my annoyance. My eyes caught sight of his bandaged hand. *And what the hell is that all about?*

He pressed his lips together, but there was no hiding his smug grin.

I wanted to smack that grin right off his face. "A joke about what? About who? About these poor addicts who are coming in faster than we can keep up? A joke about me suffering from heroin addiction myself? Tell me what exactly is so fucking funny, Dr. Mulligan. And what's up with your hand? Slip up in surgery?"

His face went slack. I'd poked the bear. Right now, I wasn't in the mood to bow down to his majesty.

"You do remember who you're speaking to, do you not, Nurse Willow?" His nostrils flared. The guy looked like he wanted to rip my neck off. The feeling was mutual. "For your information, not that I need to explain anything to you, but I spilled boiling water on my hand. I was in a hurry, trying to make my rounds, trying to help these...*patients*." He said the last word with a snarl.

"You are nothing more than a—"

A hand gently touched my shoulder. It was Stacy.

"Hey, Willow, I have a question about a patient you saw earlier. Can you take a look at my computer?"

I released a slow breath as my eyes stayed on Dr. Asshole. "Sure, Stacy. I enjoy helping people who are nice and here for the right reasons." I twirled around and left, leaving the doctor with his mouth open.

When I joined Stacy in her office niche, she sat in her rolling chair and put her hands in her lap.

"What did you want me to review with you?" I asked.

"Nothing. I just wanted to save you from further humiliation. I know Dr. Mulligan can be difficult."

"I was getting ready to rip that guy a new one."

"And then what would have happened?"

I looked off for a second. "I would have felt better?" I said it as more of a question. I tried to smile, but I didn't have it in me.

She tilted her head.

"Okay, I get the point. But still, he made it personal. I don't understand why he does...this." I spread my arms, then let them drop to my sides.

"This, as in work at the clinic?"

"The profession of being a doctor. The guy doesn't seem to have an ounce of compassion for anyone. He just sits on his perch and judges people. I really think he's better suited to be a mortician."

She covered a light giggle. "You're a hoot." She turned in her chair and shuffled through some files as I turned to walk out the door.

"Oh, I've been meaning to ask if you've heard how that one patient, Briana Varney, is doing? I know you dropped her off at the detox facility the other day. That was such a nice thing to do for her. I could tell she was in a mess of trouble."

My phone buzzed in the front pocket of my scrubs. I pulled out my phone and said to Stacy, "Did I forget to tell you that Briana didn't want to go to the detox facility?"

She twirled her chair to face me. "Most patients don't, right?"

I shrugged, not sure what to say.

"Are you saying you didn't drop her off at the facility?"

I bit the inside of my cheek. "She was very emotional. I thought she might jump out of my car if I approached the facility. So I let her stay at my apartment."

"Willow…"

"I know, I know. That's not something we're supposed to do."

"It puts you in the position of caregiver. And you know that could be dangerous—for you and for her."

My phone buzzed three times in rapid succession. Someone must have an urgent message for me. Maybe it was Jennie or Kyle. I'd sent them an early-morning text asking if they knew what kind of car Dad drove. "You're right, Stacy. But I tried to get her to go, and she wouldn't."

"Was she mumbling more about being kidnapped?"

"You heard her say that when she was here at the clinic?"

"In the middle of everything else she was saying, and none of it made a lot of sense."

I paused a second, thinking through my interaction with Briana before I'd left for work. When I'd brought up the previous night, to get a sense if she'd heard or seen her kidnapper—essentially, implicating my father—she tried to change the topic. I pressed her a bit, but she wouldn't listen to me. Instead, she went into the kitchen and started cooking pancakes.

"She's just freaked out, Stacy. Probably for a lot of reasons. But one thing I'm pretty sure about is that she has kids who she misses terribly. I need to figure out a way to get her to the detox facility."

"Is she still at your apartment?"

I nodded while trying to peek at my phone screen, but my eyes never made it.

She threw up her hands. "Willow, she could be hurting herself or damaging your apartment right now!"

"It's not that bad. My mother is there."

"Well, if your mom is anything like you, she's probably okay."

I bit the inside of my cheek again, hard. "My mom isn't exactly like me."

"No?"

I went with an excuse I'd used with my friends when I was in high school. "She had a rougher upbringing."

Stacy gave me a long nod. Maybe she got it. Maybe not. I finally stole a glance at my phone. When I first saw a bunch of demon emojis, I knew this wasn't a positive message. And then I read out loud who'd sent the texts. "Kina."

"Who's Kina?" Stacy asked.

I read the messages to myself.

Such a bitch!

Can't believe her.

It's all about her. Always has been.

I looked up, first noticing the white on my knuckles—I had the phone in a vice grip. Then I saw that Stacy was staring right at me. "Everything okay?"

"Uh, yeah." Worried about Kina's mental state, wondering if she was drunk again, I went back to the messages.

This is bullshit.

I fucking hate her!

"Who, Kina? Who?" I said out loud as I scrolled down the screen and kept reading.

Doesn't care if he lives or dies.

Going back to work? It's hard for me to comprehend.

Said she's moving on with her life.

Just talked to Mom. Said she can't keep waiting for Dad.

"Willow, do you need some water? Your coloring is a little off," Stacy said, now standing beside me.

"No, I'm good, thanks. I need to reach out to a friend."

"About what? Did you receive bad news?"

She started to peek over my shoulder, but I headed toward the doorway. Without turning around, I said, "It's going to be okay. I think."

I took another step and ran nose-first into an immovable chest. I bounced off and saw Dr. Mulligan with his hands at his waist, arrogantly shaking his head. "Has Nurse Willow been a bad girl?" He started wagging his finger at me.

A ball of fire rushed up my gut, but alarms had already sounded off in my head. This guy was a psycho—and not in a medically-correct way. "I have things I need to do." I started to walk past him, but he moved to block my path.

"Excuse me," I said, somehow holding back a string of four-letter words.

"I think I might have a little leverage on you, Willow. It's just a matter of how I want to use it." He scratched at his chin and held that smug smile.

"Leverage. You think you have leverage on me?" I said, poking my chest harder with each word. "What kind of sick, twisted person are you?"

He moved his jaw like he was grinding his teeth. "You think you can talk to me like that and not suffer the consequences?

Maybe you think you should get a second or third chance like all the other losers who walk into this clinic."

I could feel my insides trembling, not from fear. Well, maybe the fear of losing control on this asshole.

"Cat got your tongue, Nurse Willow?"

My phone vibrated again. It jarred me back into focusing on more important things than office politics, or the twisted Dr. Mulligan version of it.

"I can't deal with your shit right now. But know this: you will not intimidate me or coerce me into doing anything for you…or especially with you."

I tried to walk past him again, but he grabbed my arm and didn't let go. "You think you get to dictate things? You're just a lowly nurse."

I drove my elbow down, ramming his wrist.

"Ow!" he yelled.

"You fucking touch me one more time, or say another word that's out of line, and I'll call the cops. Dictate that!" I turned and walked down the hall.

"I think you hurt my wrists. I'll sue you if this impacts my career."

Without turning around, I held up my middle finger and walked out the back door.

Forty-Six

Cooper

I watched Ishaan and Jamaal share an awkward handshake, a series of hand slaps ending with a quick thump on the back. It seemed like Ishaan was trying to act like he was a regular kid with a little bit of street in him. Just like I was next in line to take the throne in England. *Damn.*

While my radar was still picking up weird signals about this meet-and-greet, on the surface Ishaan appeared to have done the right thing journalistically. He'd actually hunted down Rashad's son. But was it really that innocent?

"You look surprised to see me, Cooper." Jamaal, in his SU silver-and-black sweats, lowered himself and began stretching his hamstrings and groin muscles. Despite being ripped, he was as limber as any athlete I'd seen. I'd been around some talented players during my time at Canisius, especially when we made our brief run in the NCAA tournament, but seeing Jamaal warm up was another reminder of how the basketball DNA appeared to have been passed down from his father.

"Not all that surprised, I guess." I swung my sights over to Ishaan, whose mouth started to turn up at the corners. "Did I miss the joke?"

"Nope. No joke." He pressed his lips together, rocking from side to side. As Jamaal moved to a standing position, the pair took a knowing glance at each other. Now I knew the weird signals on my personal radar weren't imaginary. Something was up. Big time.

Jamaal lowered himself, and then without taking a single running step, leaped straight up in the air and grabbed the rim with both hands. His vertical had to be close to forty inches. He was nearing the Michael Jordan range.

"If you're trying to impress me with your athletic prowess, Jamaal, it's not necessary. I can see that you're talented."

He did three quick pull-ups, then let go of the rim and dropped to the ground with the sleekness of a panther hunting its prey.

"Talented enough to go number one overall, like my dad?" he asked.

"I haven't seen you play, but it appears you have a pretty serious attitude. I wouldn't bet against you."

He smirked. "That's the problem, though. I finish out this season and probably need one more under my belt to hone my skills before I declare for the draft. That's my plan, anyway. But a lot can happen in a year. A person's stock can rise or fall based upon factors they can't control."

"Like injury," I said.

"Or playing with teammates who bring you down. If guys miss shots when I feed them the ball, then that's one less assist. But the injury thing, that's the big one. If I do a crossover on that one slick spot on a court, my knee could be shredded. With modern medicine being as it is, I'm sure I'd be able to make a comeback."

"Especially with your work ethic."

"Damn straight. But I don't want to be a comeback player who gets invited to an NBA summer league camp. I'm not stupid. Even with my name, they're not going to reserve my seat in one of the first five slots of the NBA draft."

"Good to see that you have perspective. Your studies are important, even if you feel like you could conquer the world. What's your interest?"

"Basketball."

"I get that, but beyond basketball."

He paused, glancing up at the rim for a second. "The finances of basketball."

"That's cool. I've heard of several retired athletes who got into financial planning, helping other athletes manage their money. You can get certified while you're still playing."

"You think I don't know that?"

He was showing some attitude. I could roll with it. "You're a smart kid, Jamaal." I looked to Ishaan, wondering where this was going.

"I don't want to be my dad," Jamaal said, snagging my attention once again.

"I can understand why you'd say that."

"It's not just the drugs. I've never done drugs, and I never will. I'll never piss away all my earnings, either."

This was building up to something. But the dots weren't connecting for me. "Sometimes we learn what not to do from our parents. I'm guessing you've had to grow up a lot faster because of the troubles your father has experienced."

He shrugged. "Got to own my life. Can't run from it, you know what I'm saying?"

I nodded while shifting my eyes to Ishaan. He was quiet. Too quiet.

"But here's the deal, Cooper. I can't guarantee anything in the future. I can only control my earning potential right now. So, it's time for me to cash in on some of my talent. You know, a little bit on the side until I deposit that first NBA check."

A dotted line had just grown into a solid one, but I wasn't going to relay my thoughts out loud, just in case there was that one-percent chance that Jamaal was really one of the good kids.

"You're not saying anything, Cooper," Ishaan said.

"I'm letting the game come to me, so to speak." I looked at Jamaal. "What are you really trying to say, Jamaal?"

"I'm your man. That's what I'm saying." He casually popped a fist into the palm of his other hand.

"*My* man?" I was playing the stupid guy. I couldn't pinpoint exactly why, though. Maybe I just didn't want to believe we were really going down this path, both Jamaal and me. I knew Ishaan had no ethics.

"Listen to him…" Jamaal grinned at Ishaan, and then looked at me. "You want me to spell it out for you?"

"Sure, Jamaal."

"I don't need to pat you down like this is *Hawaii Five-O*, do I?"

"For a wire? You're safe."

"So, here's the deal. I'll be your boy on this point-shaving deal. But I want a decent cut. Not just a hundred bucks here or there. I'm talking serious cash."

He'd actually said it. I felt my heart sink. I rubbed a hand across my face as my stomach did backflips. I wanted to say how wrong this was, yet I knew if we didn't go down this path, Willow and I might end up dead.

I looked at Ishaan. "You knew."

"I had my suspicions," he said, holding up a finger. "And then I found out the real scoop."

Vomit shot into the back of my throat. "You told your uncle about this?"

"Chill, chill. I found out what I needed to know without making you look bad. Nothing to worry about, bro."

Bro. Again, he's Mr. Street. I tried not to roll my eyes.

"So, we gonna formalize this arrangement?" Jamaal asked, eyeing both Ishaan and me.

"Look, Jamaal, this isn't just breaking the speed limit. Once you go down this path, things can get…complicated." My phone rang. I pulled it from my pocket and saw Willow's name. I punched the side button to forward her to voicemail.

"Why are you doing this?" Ishaan asked, shaking his head. "I got the perfect guy. We've already looked at the Cougars' schedule to identify the games where it makes the most sense to throw the games."

Now I was the one shaking my head. "And I actually thought you wanted to become a sports journalist."

"I do. But I can't ignore the family business. It's really more about having options. My own way of setting up a diverse portfolio."

"Yo, Cooper," Jamaal said with a smile on his face. "Looks like we're all into finance. You joining our team? I mean, Ishaan tells me that this is your business. You call all the shots. Am I right?"

My head was spinning. All of this was hitting me in a way I'd never expected. Probably because I'd gotten to know Jamaal and knew his backstory, and how his dad was missing because of some drug habit he couldn't kick. Add in the angle of Ishaan basically playing me, and I wasn't sure I could keep my breakfast down.

"If it helps at all, once I make it in the NBA, I won't blow you off, Cooper. I'll get you tickets to my games, introduce you to my teammates. You're a sportswriter, right? So, you'd have all those contacts. Another win for you."

He thought life was so black-and-white and full of easy choices with no repercussions. "Jamaal, have you been watching how college basketball is being torn apart by investigations by local district attorneys and the Feds? They've charged coaches and others in the industry. It has more to do with player payoffs, but still, there are people who are watching this game right now. Lots of risk. You want to take that chance?"

"SU is not in the NCAA."

"You're splitting hairs."

"You're taking the risk, and I doubt you want to go to jail."

My mind was spinning. I didn't know what I was trying to accomplish with this back-and-forth with Jamaal. I could feel Ishaan's eyes on me.

My phone rang. It was Willow again. "I need to take this."

"No prob. I got my ball over here. Take all the time you need, Cooper. I'll teach Ishaan how to shoot a layup," Jamaal said then burst out laughing.

I turned and punched up the call.

Forty-Seven

Willow

The sound of heavy breathing came through my phone. I looked at the screen to make sure I'd tapped the right contact.

"Cooper, are you there?"

"Yeah, give me one second."

"One. Where are you?"

"Busy."

"What are you talking about? 'Busy' isn't a location."

More heavy breathing.

"Don't tell me you went back to that strip joint."

"How'd you guess?"

"So I'm right."

"Well, they told me that you're going on in about twenty minutes. There's a line out the door. Everyone's chanting your name."

"Funny. Not. Look, no one here at Books and Spirits knows where you are—"

"You didn't talk to Brandy, did you?"

"Give me some credit. I know she's your arch nemesis."

"Who still happens to be my boss."

"You still haven't said where you are. Actually, it doesn't matter. Just get back here now. We need to run back up to Denton."

"I'm kind of in the middle of something."

"'Something.' Is that a code word because you're being held hostage?"

"Wow. We just had the Dr. V incident, and you're making jokes about me being kidnapped? Breaking news: Willow has officially gone to the dark side."

I heard laughter. "What's so funny?"

"Oh, it's just Jamaal cracking up because Ishaan can't shoot a layup."

I replayed what he'd just said. "You're with Jamaal? Why is Ishaan there with the two of you?"

"Remember that side project I had in mind for Ishaan that would save our lives? Well, it turns out he knows about it, and he's found our point-shaving mole."

"Jamaal. Not Jamaal."

"That's what I thought. I'm still trying to make sense of it. But you called just as they were pushing me to bless our new arrangement."

I tried to make sense of what I'd just heard. I couldn't. Just then, I heard screaming laughter. "What's going on now?" I said, irritated.

"Pretty funny, actually. Jamaal kicked the ball just as Ishaan was about to pick it up. Now he's running out into the street."

Sounded like a bunch of elementary school kids messing around. "Cooper, we need to get to Denton."

"You never said why."

"Oh. Well, just a little while ago, I got a series of text messages from Kina and—"

"What did they say?" he asked.

I read the whole string verbatim.

"Holy shit. Why don't you just call Kina?"

"I tried six times, and she's not picking up. I'm worried that because of this news from her mother, she might have done something to herself. And frankly, I can't be certain everything she said, or hinted at, is even true. I just want to make sure she's okay, then get the full story from her own mouth."

"You want to make sure *everyone's* okay," Cooper said.

"You were the one who rushed back up to Kina's dorm room to beat up that boy."

"He deserved it. I hope Lumberjack has paid him a visit."

"Okay, so do I need to come get you, wherever you are?"

"I'm at Opportunity Park."

"Wait—didn't Jamaal mention that to us? It's where he and his dad used to practice basketball."

"You have a better memory than me."

"I don't want to believe he's involved in this, uh…"

"Cluster fuck?"

A blur of motion snagged my attention. Cooper's work pal, Slash, was walking toward me. His eyebrows were doing some type of worm-like dance. "Again, are you coming back here soon? If not, I'll just leave without you."

I heard Cooper grunt as if he'd been hit.

"Cooper, are you okay?"

Loud voices blared through the phone. One became higher pitched, if not frantic. "Cooper?"

No response, but I heard heavy breathing again, then, "Where's the car?"

"Just across the street." That was Jamaal. I could feel my throat tighten.

A few seconds passed, then Cooper said, "Holy shit."

"What is it?" I asked.

"Jamaal just found his father's car. Jamaal," he shouted, "don't touch the car. I'm calling the cops."

"Courtney?" I asked.

"Yeah. I don't think we can wait any longer, Willow. This is proof that he's missing. Who knows how long his car has been here?"

Forty-Eight

Cooper

Ishaan wanted nothing to do with the cops. After I did a quick check of the area with Jamaal to make sure we didn't see his father anywhere around, I called Courtney from Ishaan's car.

She was just about to speak to another detective working the Dante Chilton murder, so she only had a couple of minutes. She asked me a few quick questions and said she'd make sure a team of her DPD colleagues was sent to the location by Opportunity Park. She said she'd call me later with an update.

Ishaan pulled into the parking lot at Books and Spirits as he received a call from a female friend. It took about ten seconds for him to drop me off and speed away for his next conquest. What a tool.

Willow honked her horn to get my attention. I slid into the passenger seat, and she punched the gas before I could latch my seatbelt.

"Did you share what I found out from Kina with her brother?" Willow asked as she took the north ramp to I-35.

"No way. He's pretty upset about finding his father's car. I think it made the whole thing much more real for him. For me too, actually. Plus, you said you have your doubts about what Kina said is really true."

Willow kept her eyes on the road and didn't respond.

"Are you changing your assessment?" I asked.

"I've had a hundred different thoughts, and they're all over the place. I'm worried about Kina not picking up her phone."

"She could be in class or studying."

Willow's eyes met mine for a second, but it was long enough to feel that extra flutter in my chest.

"So, you don't think she's in class or studying," I said.

"I know she told us she'd get help with her drinking problem, but if she had this emotional interaction with her mom, then it might send her on a downward spiral."

As much as I didn't want to go there, my mind veered down the path of my daughter, Lauren. Snapshots of her childhood flashed before my eyes. Her fourth birthday when she was giggling uncontrollably after dumping a bowl of flour on her head. Her snaggletooth smile and snarled hair at age seven. Chewing a huge wad of gum while she attempted to do the hula hoop at age ten, but she had no hips on her stick-like little body and the hoop kept falling to the ground. Still, she persisted at the exercise for nearly an hour.

She was fourteen now, still more into sports than boys—or so I hoped—and her tangled hair, a shade darker than mine, was now usually brushed out, although it took some work. I remembered just a year ago finding lice in her hair after a sleepover at a friend's house. She was emotional about it initially, saying it made her feel dirty. I calmed her down, and for the next five hours, I methodically combed her scalp, picking out lice and their eggs. But what I most recalled was our conversation. It was casual, easy. For a girl who didn't normally open up to me since she'd turned into a teenager, she couldn't stop talking back then. She would even ask about my work and offer up supportive comments. It was the coolest thing.

Willow reached over and put her hand on mine. "You thinking about Lauren?"

"Yeah."

"It will work out, Cooper. After all this, you can fly down and see her."

I snorted out a laugh.

"What's so funny?"

"I don't have money for a ticket. I'd have to stow away in the luggage compartment."

She tapped the steering wheel as if she had a thought.

"What?"

"That money you found in your trunk—which we now know was put there by my loser dad… After you paid Dr. V the fifty K in gambling debt, wasn't there some money left over?"

I went still for a second. "Damn, I forgot all about it. I stuffed it in the back of my closet, thinking I'd use it as an emergency fund."

"You didn't put it in the bank?"

"I'd thought about it. But walking into a bank with five grand in cash from a questionable source made me nervous."

She sighed. "That's the perfect description of my dad: questionable source."

"Did you ever hear back from your brother or sister about what kind of vehicle he drives?"

"Not yet. Need to follow up on that and try to…" She trailed off, shaking her head.

"Sift everything through the bullshit filter and see what sticks?"

"Yeah, that." She took the exit at North Texas Boulevard and headed for the UNT campus.

As we walked through the entrance of Kina's dorm, Willow put a hand on my shoulder. "After all this is behind us, you're going to use the money to fly to Miami to see Lauren, right?"

I paused a second.

"I'll go with you if you need support."

"It's more like needing a bulldozer. Carmona is obstinate and may not let me see her." She opened her mouth, but I held up a hand. "It's complicated and messy. Maybe we can talk through some options."

"Yeah. Let's do that."

We hustled up the steps, dodging young people who didn't see us. It was nice to see kids walking around holding books and not drunk out of their minds.

While some of the doors on Kina's floor were open, hers was shut. Willow knocked three times. We waited at least a minute, and then she knocked again. Another minute passed.

"She may not be here," I said, looking down the hallway for any sign of her or her roommate.

Willow took out her phone, tapped the screen twice, and put it on speaker. It rang five times, then Kina's voice came alive and said we could leave a message. Willow ended the call. "I've already left two voicemails. Not sure what we can do. Maybe just sit here and wait."

Two girls walked past us, talking and laughing about something. "Excuse me," I said. "Do either of you know Kina, the girl who lives in this room?"

They both shook their heads, and the tall one said, "Sorry," before they walked off.

I then put my ear up against the door.

"Hear anything?" Willow asked.

"Only you talking."

She pinched the side of my neck. "I don't need another hickey."

"I didn't know you had a first one."

I thought I heard something from inside, and I got very still.

"You don't think that Jason kid showed back up, do you?" she asked.

My pulse surged to another gear. I then gave the door four hard pops with my knuckles and put my ear to it again.

"Anything?"

I pulled back from the door and frowned. "Maybe I didn't hear anything."

"Willow?" We both turned to see Misty walking up with a backpack slung over her shoulder.

We gave her a quick explanation as to why we were there. She said she'd been in class and at the library all day. She unlocked the door, and my eyes went straight to the open bottle of vodka next to Kina's bed, where there was a mountain of pillows and blankets.

I stopped two steps into the room. "She's been drinking. Any idea where Kina could be, Misty?"

Willow walked over to the bed and pulled back a comforter to reveal Kina's arm. We both quickly threw off the other pillows and blankets. "I think she's passed out," I said.

"Dammit," Misty said. "She promised she'd stop."

Kina was lying face down. Willow shook her back. "Kina, come on, wake up and talk to me."

A few seconds later, Kina turned over, slid off a sleep mask, and then pulled plugs out of her ears. "What the fuck is going on?"

Forty-Nine

Willow

Cooper brought Kina a cup of water. She was sitting on the edge of her bed, wiping the corners of her eyes.

"Thanks." She gulped the water, then looked at each of us. "I only had one shot of vodka. I was going to drink more, but I put in my earplugs and fell asleep."

Misty sat on the bed and put her head on Kina's shoulder. "Proud of you for stopping at one."

"I'll get help, though."

Misty smiled, then realized she was late for her science lab. She gave Kina a quick hug of encouragement and hurried out of the room.

"Maybe I'll make school a priority…someday." Kina set the cup on her side table, then picked up her phone and looked at the screen. "You were trying to reach me, Willow. Sorry I didn't answer. Hell, I'm sorry to pull you into all this family drama."

I pulled a chair from a desk and sat in front of Kina's bed. Cooper stood next to me. "Kina, the text messages you sent me… Were you telling me the truth?"

"Unfortunately," she said as her eyes dropped to the floor.

"When did you talk to your mom?"

"Early this morning. I called to see if she'd heard from Dad and, to be honest, to also ask her for some extra money."

"So, she's feeling better?"

"She was heading to work."

"Where does she work?" It seemed strange not knowing that, even though we knew so much about the Hatley family.

"She's a therapist, a counselor, or whatever you call it."

Neither Cooper nor I said anything for a second.

"I know you're shocked to hear that. I would be too."

I could hear Cooper scratching the stubble on his face. "It's not what I expected," I said.

"You don't have to be so politically correct. It's fucked up. She gives people guidance on how to live their lives, and look at what a bitch she is."

I cringed hearing her say that about her mom, the woman I'd seen so devastated at the clinic. "Your mom seemed pretty torn up by your father's disappearance, Kina."

She looked me straight in the eye. "How do you know what she was really upset about?"

"What do you mean?" Cooper asked.

"She's always resented Dad, thrown shit back in his face. Hell, how would any recovering addict not start using again when you're constantly shamed by the person you're married to?"

"Why did he stay with her, then?" Cooper followed up.

She shrugged. "He never confided in me, but I think he carries a lot of guilt. And sometimes that builds into a lot of anger."

Her eyes became glassy as she released a slow, jittery breath. "I just hope he's okay, you know? I mean, I didn't help. I didn't make his life any easier."

I reached out and touched her knee. "Kina, you can't accept responsibility for the actions of others, especially adults. Stay positive, and we can work together to figure this out." Just as I wondered how the hell I could say that, I felt Cooper's hand on my back. My wingman.

I took in a fortifying breath and asked her to replay the conversation she had with her mom. Kina spent five minutes doing just that. I maintained eye contact and gave her supportive nods every few seconds.

"Mom said she didn't care if he lives or dies. She actually said that. She fucking doesn't care if he dies!"

Kina calmed herself and finished without completely breaking down, and then I gave her a long hug.

My main takeaway from what I'd heard: Jada's attitude toward her missing husband was cavalier at best. A cynical person might say her callous response to her worried daughter wasn't just irresponsible but also sounded like she'd found some joy in his apparent demise.

Cooper caught my eye as I stood up. I sensed he was in the same place as I was. Had Jada been completely honest with me the day I met her?

Cooper refilled Kina's cup with water, and we watched her drink all of it. I studied her for a moment, knowing I needed to ask her another question. I hoped she could handle it without losing it.

"Kina, I don't want to make you upset, but I have a question that I—"

"Go ahead. If it will help figure out what happened to my dad, you can ask me anything," she said with hopeful eyes.

I paused a second, forcing my lungs to expand for a breath against a chest that felt like cinderblocks were sitting on it. "Have you seen any signs that your mom might be having an affair?"

Cooper's ringing phone made my breath hitch.

"Sorry." He quickly pulled out his phone. "It's Courtney. I think I need to take this."

He walked into the corner, while Kina and I continued to chat. Just moments later, I couldn't believe what she was suggesting.

Fifty

Cooper

When I turned around, Kina was pulling her laptop out of her backpack. She opened it up on the bed as Willow started to look over her shoulder.

"What did Courtney want?" Willow asked without looking at me.

"Some new evidence on the Dante Chilton situation came in." I'd avoided using the term "murder," so Kina wouldn't be alarmed. Willow gave me a quick glance, but she looked confused. Had I not told her about Dante's murder?

"I'll give you the details later. But she also had an update on Rashad's car down at Opportunity Park."

Kina stopped typing. "They found my dad's car?"

I explained how his car had been found by her brother. I told her that he and I had met up to talk about the article I was going to write. There was no way I could mention the point-shaving arrangement. Damn, the whole scheme smelled even funkier since Jamaal had become associated with it.

"The detective, who's a friend of mine, just related to me that your father wasn't in the car, and, so far, the crime scene team has only picked up one set of prints. So, they believe those will likely prove to be Rashad's."

"Okay. It's good that the cops are involved, right?"

"Definitely. They might be reaching out to talk to you," I said.

"That's fine. I should share everything I told you guys?" she asked, turning to Willow.

"Of course." Willow motioned at the laptop screen with her hand. "You sure you're comfortable in doing this? I don't want you to feel like you're betraying any trust you have with your mother."

I edged closer, curious as to what they were talking about.

"What trust? I don't trust her; that's the problem." Kina went back to typing.

I looked at Willow, wondering if I should ask or just let the game come to me.

"Since you were on the phone," Kina said with her eyes still on the laptop screen, "I told Willow that I have access to my mom's email account. And we're about to go in and see if we find any evidence of her cheating on my dad."

"Uh, thanks for sharing. Can I ask how you have access?"

She stopped for a second and glanced at Willow and then me. "I knew school officials were emailing Mom about a couple of drunken incidents I had here on campus. So I logged into her account, found the emails, and deleted them."

"Resourceful," I said, choosing my word carefully.

"I know it was wrong, but I've also never admitted to having a drinking problem. I'm going to get help, because I don't want to live this way any longer."

Willow gave her a comforting pat on the back. As for me, I couldn't help but ask another question.

"How did you know her password?"

"Found it on a slip of paper next to her computer at home. I knew there might be a reason it would come in handy someday. And this might be another one. Maybe the biggest one."

I walked over and stood behind Willow as the glowing screen showed a long list of emails.

"There are over five thousand emails in her inbox," Willow said. "This will take a very long time."

"Maybe. Does she have any folders set up in addition to her regular inbox?"

Kina looked closer. "Nope."

"Okay, if she's anything like me, she deals with the important stuff and lets all the other emails just bake. So, I'd check to see where that magic date is when the emails suddenly jump back a few weeks or months."

"So that's how your mind works?" Willow asked.

Not wanting to get into it in front of Kina, I took the high road and didn't respond. I wasn't very familiar with this road, though.

"Hey, I think your theory might be right," Kina said after a couple of clicks. "After about the first fifty or sixty emails, the date on the emails is from almost two months earlier."

"So let's start by reviewing those fifty emails, each of which can have their own thread."

Kina methodically reviewed each one. Some were easy to eliminate. An order update from Amazon for office supplies, a blog post from a doctor in her field about some type of white paper on new therapy techniques, a recipe for cheesecake, and many more just like those. It took us a good thirty minutes to review them all.

"Fuck." Kina banged her hand on the computer in frustration. "I would say I'm sorry for cussing like that, but right now, I don't give a shit."

Willow spoke up. "This is good news, Kina. We don't know anything more about your father, but maybe this shows your mom doesn't have any big secret. She could just be fed up with life. It happens."

Kina nodded. "Yeah. Maybe."

She didn't sound convinced. I wasn't, either.

"We haven't checked the trash folder. When you delete an email, it's not deleted for thirty days," I said.

Kina grinned. "You're a genius."

I looked at Willow and popped my eyebrows. She shook it off.

Kina started to review each deleted email. She made it two weeks back when she came across an email thread with a professor.

"Isn't that the guy who wrote the white-paper email that's in her inbox?"

"I think you're right," Willow said.

A minute later, Kina's finger nearly punched a hole in the screen.

I'd just read the same paragraph in an email from Jada. Kina read it out loud. "Go ahead and start the experiment on Rashad. While you're testing him, I hope he feels every bit of the pain I have for the last twenty years."

Kina put her hands to her face. "Holy crap. Mom and this guy were working together to do some type of experiment on Dad? This professor might have kidnapped my dad!"

We found his name and home address at the same time Misty came back from class. We told Kina we'd let her know what we learned and raced out the door.

Fifty-One

The brakes squeaked as the man turned into the parking lot at the Frank Crowley Courts Building off North Riverfront Boulevard just west of downtown. He found an empty spot that gave him a perfect view of the exit of the courthouse and parked his service van.

Someday, people would learn that the service he was providing to society would capture the attention of not only academic institutions, but every hard-working person who just went about their business. It was that important.

He wasn't naïve. He knew his methods for proving out this theory might get the initial headlines, but once people in his field read his white paper that he was almost finished writing, his legacy would be forever solidified. While he couldn't help but feel a sense of pride in having the guts to carry out this experiment, it wasn't about him or his ego. Ultimately, he hoped people would become enlightened and change their perspective on the root cause of the most fundamental emotion in the human psyche: hate.

As he gazed across the sea of cars to watch people walk in and out of the courthouse, he rested his hand on his medical bag next to his seat. It gave him a sense of power that he couldn't deny, but more importantly, it gave him the confidence he needed to apprehend his latest subject.

He readjusted his cap, then opened his photo app on his phone and scrolled through pictures he'd taken two days prior. He stopped on the best one, the one that captured the true essence of Billy Ray Dalton. He zoomed in on the man's face. He had a scar under his left eye—a result of a knifing during his last stint in prison. But it was the subject's offensive tattoos that made you know what Billy Ray Dalton truly stood for. Racial epithets were in plain sight, as well as the one global symbol of hate: a swastika.

The man felt his pulse quicken as he stared at Billy Ray Dalton. It was someone just like Billy Ray who'd left an indelible mark on his life at a very young age.

As a gangly, awkward twelve-year-old, he didn't have much confidence. He wore thick-rimmed glasses, his pants were always too short, and he wasn't popular amongst his classmates. Anxiety was an extra fifty-pound weight loaded into his backpack every day he went to school.

One day while walking home from school, an older kid—one he later learned was temporarily on leave from juvenile detention—caught up to him at the edge of the woods near his house in Nacogdoches. The teen started razzing him, shoving him around. He could take it only because he'd been treated that way on countless occasions in school, right under the noses of teachers and administrators who probably deemed it as "kids horsing around."

But this confrontation had been different. The stillness of the woods only added to his discomfort. Pine trees that appeared to touch the sky were silent witnesses to the harassment that grew more physical with every passing second.

And then the burly teen took out a knife. What little light that peeked through the woods flickered off that blade. The man could still recall the unmistakable dread that coursed through his body. The anxiety weight had instantly tripled in size, and it felt as though roots from underground had wrapped their tentacles around his ankles and were pulling him down. A second later, the teen rushed at him, screaming wildly like the savage that he was, slashing him with the knife, punching him in the torso and face until he was almost unrecognizable.

Stop!

A bird landed on the hood of the man's van. A cardinal. He took in three purposeful breaths. The bird pranced curiously on the hood. It reminded the man that life of any kind on this planet was precious, yet sometimes there had to be sacrifices if society had any hope of changing its path toward extinction.

Involuntarily, the man touched his chest. The scars were still there from that afternoon three decades earlier. He could have had surgery to cover them up, but he chose not to. He looked in the mirror every morning to see the word etched into his body, into his soul: COON. It was a racial slur that was used primarily in the south. Many people thought it was born out of hate. In fact, a whole new category of crimes had been created to highlight their importance: hate crimes. But he'd never seen empirical evidence to prove that creating a new classification of crimes would change people or, more importantly, identify the root cause of the hate.

How can you fix something if you don't understand the root cause?

The man was lucky to have survived the assault that spring day as a twelve-year-old. But he knew it was meant to be, allowing him to focus his mind on learning everything he could about the human psyche and all the variables that shaped people's opinions and actions. Ultimately, he created his own hypothesis. It was simple, yet foundational to the problem. But a hypothesis with no test data was no more valuable than the ink on the paper. He was lucky to seemingly stumble into his first subject. A gift from the universe, perhaps?

The man's eyes spotted Billy Ray Dalton walking out of the courthouse. Dalton was, once again, a free man. His latest assault had been thrown out after a judge ruled that the search of his home was executed without the proper warrant. And now he could walk the streets like anyone else.

That would soon change.

Billy Ray got into his rusty, blue pickup and drove out of the parking lot. The man's service van was right behind him. Billy Ray drove to his home at the end of a dirt road in east Dallas. The man waited a few minutes, then walked up and knocked on the door. A few minutes later, after injecting Billy Ray with a dose of propofol, he dragged him into his van and started the trek back to his test facility.

Billy Ray would soon learn what the man had already proven three times before now: the root cause of hate was fear.

Fifty-Two

Cooper

I drove the BMW this time, so I gave my phone to Willow and asked if she could call Courtney.

"No answer," Willow said.

"Leave a message," I said. "Tell her where we're going and why."

After she left the voicemail, I said, "She could be wrapped up in the Dante Chilton murder investigation."

"You might think you told me something about that, but you didn't."

"I didn't?" So, I began to tell her everything I knew about Dante Chilton's murder.

"Damn," she said with a sigh. "I hope they find the bastard who did it."

"Maybe. But they might have found something else that connects to our world, or at least your world."

She gestured with her hand to keep talking, so I did.

"Courtney said a fellow detective found video footage of a man in a leather coat walking down a sidewalk the night Dante was killed. Another man—shorter, but you can't see his face—brushes up against the man in the leather coat. Within seconds, he's falling over. And then the shorter man tosses him into a van. They didn't get the full plates on the van, but they did see the word 'plumbing' on the side."

Her eyes got wider than normal. "You think this is the guy who could have tried to kidnap Briana?"

"The MO is similar. I mean, how many people are driving around town in a van pulling off a kidnapping? What's even crazier is that Courtney said a witness saw a van with 'plumbing' on the side leaving Myron Little's house in my neighborhood."

"Maybe my dad was telling the truth."

"I know you're hopeful, but it's hard to trust your dad right now. Have you heard back from Jennie or Kyle?"

"Nope. They must be ignoring me. I'm going to send them another text right now."

She used her thumbs to type a quick text and then tapped send. "This shouldn't take long. I threatened to send Ma to live with them if they didn't reply in an hour."

"The great motivator."

We passed under the LBJ overpass and continued moving south into Dallas. "One more thing on the Dante murder investigation. Courtney said they captured the picture of the man in the leather jacket, and she said she was going to personally walk it around Deep Ellum to see if anyone recognized him."

"Is she thinking the kidnapper in the van killed Dante, or this man in the leather jacket?"

"She didn't say, and I didn't ask. She was in one of those intense moods, where you just go along with it and get out of the way."

"Hmm. I guess I don't know her well enough to know all of her moods."

Speaking of moods... But I stayed silent. Bickering wasn't allowed right now if we hoped to work together and find Rashad Hatley.

The BMW navigation system was broken, so Willow found our destination—just east of 75 off Walnut—the old-fashioned way, using Google maps. Of course, my parents used actual paper maps, the *true* old-fashioned method.

The brakes squealed as I turned down the side street and stopped two doors down from the one-story home of Professor Marcus Becnel. Gray brick with blue shutters and lots of clean lines, it was vintage 1970s. The neighborhood was older, so the landscaping was mature but still neatly kept.

"Any idea on our plan once we get to the door?" Willow asked.

"Courtney didn't text back, did she?"

Willow handed me my phone back. "Nope."

"Okay, we wing it. This guy is a professor, not one of the Sack Brothers."

The blue front door swung open just a few seconds after Willow pushed the doorbell. A matronly woman wearing a pink apron pushed the screen door open. "Are you the new neighbors who just moved in down the street? Dear me, I'm so embarrassed that I haven't dropped by yet. I'm actually right in the middle of making you an apple pie."

She said all that in about two seconds.

"It's okay, Mrs.—"

"Just call me Nancy. And what are your names?"

"I'm Cooper and this is …" I'd almost said "my wife." The thought made me break out in a sweat. "Willow."

"Did you forget your wife's name, silly?" Nancy giggled and wiped her hands on her apron.

I sensed that Willow was about to make a wisecrack, so I nudged her with my knee. I just laughed, and Willow joined in.

"I love apple pie," I said, rubbing my belly.

"So, is your husband home? We'd love to meet him as well," Willow said.

"I'm afraid Marcus is working late again. He so enjoys sharing our home with our friends and neighbors. We both do, really. He'll probably be home in an hour or so. We can drop by your home then, and I can give you the apple pie, if you like?"

"You know, we have to run some errands. Maybe another day," I said.

She started wagging her finger at me. "This pie will knock your socks off, so you'll be seeing me no later than tomorrow. In fact, Marcus and I might just surprise you later tonight," she said with a playful wink and good-natured smile. She looked down the street to her left.

Was she glancing at the home she thought Willow and I had just moved into? I followed her gaze and said, "Yep, the good old homestead." Did I just say that? How lame.

Willow hooked her arm inside mine. "We have to run, but it was nice meeting you, Nancy."

"You all take care, and I can't wait for you to taste my apple pie." She waved goodbye, and we walked to the car, got in, and drove off.

"Good old homestead?" Willow said, shaking her head. "Who talks that way?"

"Cooper Chain, MD."

"Just what I need in my life, another crazy doctor."

"I didn't know you had even one crazy doctor in your life." I took a left and started to loop around the neighborhood. "But you can tell me all about it during our first stakeout together."

Fifty-Three

Willow

Cooper continued circling the neighborhood until we turned down the far end of the Becnels' street. He parked along the curb behind an SUV, where we still had a line of sight of their home and the driveway that ran alongside it.

"Tell me about this crazy doctor in your life," Cooper, slouching in his seat.

I gave him the nuts and bolts of my interactions with Dr. Mulligan.

"Yep, 'crazy' is the right word. Maybe Lumberjack can pay him a visit too," he said.

I sighed. "You talk as if Lumberjack is our muscle, like how Dr. V uses the Sack Brothers."

"He's not a thug. He's a D-lineman for the Mean Green."

"The North Texas nickname," I said.

"Technically, they're the Eagles, but they're also called the Mean Green because Mean Joe Greene went there back in the day."

"Way back."

Cooper scratched his scruff.

"You obviously just had a thought."

"Oh, I was just thinking how we could use our Mean Green to rid ourselves of the gangrene. Get it?"

I rolled my eyes.

"You're not falling out of your seat in laughter? I thought medical humor would do something for you."

"Maybe I should laugh. Dr. Mulligan is a joke of a doctor, that's for certain."

The conversation went quiet, and we did a lot of glancing down the street at the Becnel home. Time seemed to move at a snail's pace. After a while, without the purr of the engine, the silence in the car was like a third person sitting there.

Cooper couldn't let it rest, though. He cupped his hands over his mouth and blew air into them. "Little chilly this evening," he said. He glanced out his window, then turned to me. Was he giving me some kind of look?

I tried to ignore him and instead looked at my phone. "Nothing back from Jennie or Kyle yet. Those little shits have thirty minutes. I might even have Ma call them personally. I'd rather not bother her, though, since she's being so helpful with Briana." I shifted my eyes down the street—no activity at the Becnel home—then turned back to Cooper.

He nodded. Some of his hair fell into his eyes, and he did that finger-rake thing.

"You could cut your hair, you know."

His nod turned into more of a head-bobble.

"You're truly strange, Cooper."

No verbal response, but his eyes shifted ever so quickly to the back seat. Was that a purposeful eye-shift or just a normal glance because he was bored?

Then his straight face became strained, as if he couldn't contain himself.

"Clearly, I'm missing the joke." I took another quick glance at the Becnel home. Still quiet.

He spread his lips into a wide smile. "I was just thinking back to one time in college. I was just lost in a nostalgic moment. I guess that happens when you get old."

His eyes were like blue crystals. They always had that piercing shine. But they were telling me something. Maybe something I didn't want to hear.

"What are you doing?"

He glanced at the back seat again. Like a bolt of lightning, I finally pieced together his nonverbal clues.

"Do you think the two of us are going to jump in the back seat and go after each other like a couple of rabbits?"

"I'm not saying we should. But you remember that time in the winter…"

"The heater went out in your car. You said the only way we could survive was if we were skin to skin. Can't believe I fell for that trick."

"Did you really fall for the trick, or just use it as a good reason to… What did you just call it? Ah, yes. 'Jump in the back seat and go after each other like a couple of rabbits.'"

I laughed but still punched him in the shoulder socket. "Let's keep our focus on the Becnel house."

Another moment passed, but only one before Cooper offered his opinion.

"I don't think Rashad is at the professor's house."

"Because he has a wife who seems nice and normal?"

"Maybe it's that. He might be hiding his other life from her. He could have some lab at another location that's hidden from his wife and the free world."

I tapped my chin a few times.

"You have a different theory?" he asked.

"Mmm. I'm thinking about the words in the email, how Jada gave him the go-ahead to test Rashad, like he was some type of lab rat. And then her saying that she hopes he feels every bit of pain she had from the last twenty years."

Cooper trembled as if he had a chill rush through his body. "Kina's right. Her mother is wicked."

"But what if his little experiment of pain went too far? Rashad might be dead right now."

Cooper rested his head against the steering wheel. "Ow."

He pulled back, and I could still see the bruising on his forehead from getting hit by the gun and the clock radio.

"Don't say anything about ice. I'm fine." He grabbed his phone.

"Any word from your girlfriend?" I asked with a smile.

He kept his eyes on the phone. "Courtney is not my girlfriend. We went on one date and had one kiss. That doesn't constitute a girlfriend."

"You kissed her?" I'd spoken without running my thoughts through a filter. Big regret.

"Should it matter? At least she didn't spend the night rocking my world. Not yet."

A surge of emotion rushed up my chest, and I tucked a foot under my bottom, ready to say something. Was he implying that Harvey and I had…? My phone buzzed. "Hey, Jennie just replied to my text. Dad drives a Lexus sports car." I dropped the phone on my lap. "It figures. He's going through his second midlife crisis."

"But he doesn't own a van." He thrummed his fingers on the dash. "That van I saw at your apartment complex. I wonder if there's any way it could be the same person in that video Courtney told me about."

"The plumber," I said.

He nodded. I could see his tongue pushing the inside of his mouth. I tried not to think about the kiss we'd shared. But, of course, I did.

"I just texted Courtney again," he said. "If the professor doesn't show up soon, we're going to need the full DPD cavalry on this one to find Rashad and to question Jada. She could be in a lot of trouble for accessory to…"

"I hope it's not murder. God, those kids—Kina and Jamaal—they've been put through hell."

A flash of headlight snagged my attention. I peered down the street and saw a Honda Accord turn into the Becnel home.

I looked at Cooper, who said, "You hungry for Nancy's apple pie?"

Fifty-Four

Cooper

I forked the last bit of crust and ate it. “Wow. That might be the best apple pie I’ve ever had.”

“I think you might be telling the truth, Cooper. You had two pieces.” Nancy smiled ear to ear as Willow and Marcus chuckled. “I’m so glad you came back around tonight. I knew you couldn’t resist the apple pie. Plus, Marcus was anxious to meet you.”

We sat around their red Formica table. The kitchen was a flashback to the 1950s. Black-and-white checkered linoleum—not tile, though the countertops were covered with small, yellow square tiles. The cabinets were white and the pulls red. It was like walking into one of those old TV shows my parents used to watch, *Happy Days* or *Laverne & Shirley*.

“You have a lovely home,” Willow said, running her gaze across the kitchen.

“We remodeled it a couple years ago.” Marcus sat back, put his napkin on the table, and crossed his leg over his knee. He was on the short side, probably three inches or so shorter than Willow. He wore metal glasses that gave him an academic look, but I could see the veins in his forearms.

"The place was a mess for…what, Nancy…?" He gently rubbed her shoulder. She rested her head on his hand for a second.

"It was a big dust pile for almost six months. But we figured it out. It was like living out an adventure without leaving home."

A little poodle ran into the kitchen. "Oh, and Barney survived the great house makeover along with us." Marcus leaned over and gave Barney some of the crust from his pie.

His wife playfully smacked his arm. "You know you shouldn't be feeding Barney from the table."

"But he's hungry."

"You're teaching him bad habits," she said. She got to her feet and took our plates to the sink.

"Hey, if you have a few minutes, let me show you around," Marcus said, lifting to his feet.

"Sounds good," I said.

"Nancy, you going to join us?"

"I'm busy cleaning up, plus I have another pie in the oven for our new friends."

"Okay, well, I guess Barney will lead the way."

We covered every room in the house, with Barney in front the whole time. During the home tour, Willow made the appropriate "oohs" and "aahs" while I stomped my feet in each room and looked for any signs of a struggle or that any other person might be in the house. Nothing seemed out of place. Marcus even opened his closets to show how they'd doubled in size.

I wondered how I could approach the email we'd read from Jada's account. I considered simply taking the direct approach. But I couldn't envision this simple, good-hearted man doing anything wrong, or admitting it if he had. In fact, even though I'd read the email with my own eyes, I wondered if somehow we had the wrong guy.

Nancy met us in the foyer with a covered baked pie.

"You're so kind," Willow said, giving her a half-hug.

"It's nice to make new friends in the neighborhood," Nancy said, glancing at her husband.

He adjusted his glasses, then rocked back and forth. "A while back, we had some real rabble-rousers who rented a home not too far from your house." He eyed both Willow and me, but we stayed quiet.

"Yeah, they were nothing but trash. I was walking Barney one afternoon and heard some horrible whines of a dog. I looked through the slats of their fence and saw this poor dog on the ground, bleeding from wounds. I also saw the owners and friends jumping around holding up this other dog with bite wounds in his side."

"Dog fighting?" Willow asked, a hand to her chest.

He nodded.

"What did you do?"

"I got my gun out of my safe and—"

Nancy smacked his arm. "Don't say that. You don't want to even pretend you're like them."

"Well, I wanted to. But I called the cops, and they arrested them. Never saw them again. I just hope they learned their lesson. Too often people never really learn from their mistakes. How can society evolve like that?"

A heady question.

Everyone said their goodbyes, and we left.

Once in our car, I looked at Willow. "You believe their act?"

"I want to," she said, gazing back at the house.

"Me too." I started the car and drove up to the stop sign.

"Why did you stomp your feet in every room we entered?" she asked.

"Well, I knew they had a slab foundation, but when they said they did a remodel, I wondered if they might have created a pocket under a room that was pier and beam."

"Hold on. You were thinking he might have some room hidden underground?"

I shrugged. "Basements aren't common in Texas, but up north, they're everywhere."

"Did you guys have one in your house?" She reached over gripped my arm before I could respond. "Sorry, Cooper. That was pretty insensitive of me. Forget I said it."

"You're just curious. Like me." I glanced over my shoulder and caught one more look at the Becnel house.

"You're thinking something," Willow said, following my gaze.

"It's nothing from back there." I pulled out my phone, opened the Safari browser, and did a quick search.

She repeated the words I'd just typed. "Dallas County home records." Looking up at me, she asked, "What are you looking for?"

I held up my finger and clicked on the first link for the Dallas Central Appraisal District. She moved her face right next to mine as I typed in the last name of "Becnel," checked the boxes for Residential, Commercial, and BPP, and tapped the search button.

"Are you checking to see if they have a portfolio of properties?"

"I once knew a football player who kept a separate home from his wife for all of his—and this is what he called them—bitches and hoes."

"You think Professor Becnel has, uh…bitches and hoes?"

The results screen came back with two links. "Nope. But Marcus does have one other home."

"What are we waiting on? Let's get over there."

Fifty-Five

Willow

As luck would have it, the second Becnel home was on the street behind the first Becnel home. The brakes on my BMW squeaked loudly as we stopped in front of a house that looked abandoned.

"What a piece of shit!" Cooper exclaimed.

"I know. Boards over some of the windows, weeds everywhere."

"I was talking about your car. It's getting close to reaching the level of my car."

"Your car has about fifteen years of age on mine. Let's go." I shut the car door and stopped on the cracked sidewalk leading up to the front door. "You think he rents it out?"

"Not if he has bitches and hoes dropping by," he said, walking past me toward the front door.

I joined him on the small front porch. He rang the doorbell, and we waited. No response. He put his ear to the door, listened for a moment, then shook his head.

With me right on his heels, Cooper walked next to a lone leafless shrub and cupped his hands against a front window that wasn't boarded.

"See anything?"

"Just a dusty shade." He stepped back, and we both ran our eyes up and down the front of the house.

"I'm not sure anyone is home. Or maybe no one can get to the door."

"Solid point. It could be like Hotel California."

"What? Ohhh…"

Then together we said, "You can check out, but you can never leave."

He tapped me on the butt, then walked toward the garage.

I tried swatting his hand, but he was too quick for me. I caught up as he tried to look through the one garage door window that didn't have a board covering it. "Hmm."

"Hmm what?" I asked.

"I see what looks like a vehicle covered with some type of canvas."

"What kind of vehicle?"

"If I had to guess, a van."

I grabbed his shoulder, and he turned around to look at me, but we didn't say anything. He went back to looking inside the window.

"Something else in there?"

"Some gardening tools."

"Like shovels and hoes?"

He flipped his head to glance at me over his shoulder. His teeth glowed in the dark.

"I can be funny too," I said.

I saw the handle for the garage, so I took hold and pulled up. It hardly budged. "Locked."

"Hold on." He jogged toward the front of the house. While he did that, I spotted a window next to the garage door and tried to pull up on it. It was also locked. He came back around a few seconds later.

"Every window along the front and the front door are locked."

"That's not strange. If no one lives here, you don't want anyone breaking in and pretending they're living here."

"Hotel California."

I waited for more, but that's all he said. "Are you trying to suggest someone is trapped inside?"

"Hotel California."

"You're starting to sound like a robot."

"Ho—"

"I get it."

He patted my upper arm. "He could have used special locks where it's not possible to unlock them from the inside."

I tilted my head left and then right. "Where did you come up with that? Did some athlete do that too?"

"I've read Stephen King, where every fucking thing happens."

We walked around back and found more of the same. Boarded windows. No visuals to the inside, and everything locked down.

He stepped back from the porch and peered upward along the roofline. "Tree's in the damn way."

"Of what?"

He kept moving back, and I followed him. "There it is," he said, pointing to the roof.

"You wanted to see if there was a chimney?"

"I guess it could be a faux chimney."

"Not on a house this old." I felt something tickling my ankles. I moved my feet around and realized I was standing in the middle of some longer grass. I took out my phone and flipped on my flashlight, shining the beam in a ten-foot circle around us.

"What do you see?" he asked.

"Green grass," I said.

He took hold of my wrist and aimed the light to the other part of the yard, and then we looked at each other and said in unison, "Brown grass."

"That's odd, but what does that really tell us?" I started wading through the grass, not sure what I was looking for.

"Maybe he had a cow grazing back here for a while."

I knew he was joking.

"The question is, why is it green just in this area?" I crouched down, plucked a few blades, and eyed them.

"Hold on. Is that winter rye?"

"You're right." I shined the light back on the brown grass. "Everything else is Bermuda, which, of course, goes dormant in the winter. So why would he plant winter rye in this one area?" I held the edge of the phone in my mouth and started crawling around on my hands and knees.

Cooper dropped down and mimicked my movements. "Ohh," he moaned.

"Your knees?"

"Maybe." He stopped moving.

"Did you pull a muscle or something?"

He stayed still.

"Earth to Cooper."

"Shine the light where my left hand is."

I did as he said. And then I felt the grass by his hand.

"It's fake." My pulse did double time as we felt around the artificial grass.

"I've got to stand up a second," he said, lifting to his feet as if he were twice his age of thirty-nine.

A few seconds later, I found a latch that had artificial grass glued to the top of it. I pulled up on it, then twisted it. A metal cover opened like a lid, which exposed a larger latch, like one you might see on a porthole. "Ho-ly crap."

He tapped my shoulder and pointed. "Is that the Becnels' home over there?" I started to shine the phone toward the scraggly trees in the back. He plucked the phone out of my hand. "Don't do that. They might see you."

"You sure it's their home?" I squinted.

"Yep, I can see the color of their cabinets through the kitchen window. And wait, there's Nancy in her pink apron."

"Okay. Fine. But look what I found down here."

He flipped around and put his hands on knees. "Ho-ly crap." He grabbed the latch with both hands, tugged on it a few seconds, and then it unlocked. He pulled open a large metal door. I could see only a few steps leading into a pit of darkness.

"Ladies first?"

Fifty-Six

Cooper

Just as the light of my phone found the last two steps, I heard the rattle of metal on concrete. I stopped dead cold. Willow didn't. She plowed into me, and we both clumsily tumbled until we landed on a damp concrete floor.

"You okay?" I whispered, reaching for my phone that had slid slightly out of reach.

"Fine. Shine the—"

A moan interrupted her. Then, "You gonna rescue me from that maggot?" The voice had a southern twang.

I got to my knees and pointed the light of the phone off to the left. A man with tattoos covering his torso was chained to the side of a wall. We walked closer.

"Damn," he said, glancing at Willow. "Prayers have been answered. A hot piece of ass has come to rescue me." His face was bruised, but it was the two carved letters on his chest that snagged my attention. The bloody letters were R and A.

"Did Professor Becnel do that to you?"

"Is that his name? Don't know the fucker, but fuck yeah, he did it. He thinks I'm a goddamn racist just because I like some creative ink. Or maybe it's because my case was thrown out of court. It was all made up, anyway. They're all out to get me. I hate every last one of them. And once you free me, I'm going to hunt down that bastard and slash his throat."

I took a dry gulp. This guy was a victim, but he was also dangerous. He started licking his lips as he ran his lustful eyes up and down Willow. She nudged up against me.

Another groan, but this one came from across the room. I quickly turned around and held up my phone light, which didn't have the greatest power.

"Hey, what are you doing?" Hick Man said from behind me. "Get me out of these damn shackles before you work on the others. I think most are dead anyway."

Willow and I padded across the concrete toward the person on the ground who I thought had groaned.

"What's that?" She dug her nails into my arm and swung the cone of light to the left.

"Oh my God. Is that…?" I rushed over to a table and saw a man with cathodes attached to his body, which had burn marks all over it. The man wasn't moving. His blue, thick tongue stuck out of an open mouth that looked like a frozen picture of his last scream.

"Who…who is it?"

"Myron Little."

"The guy who painted the swastikas on your garage?"

"I'm pretty sure it was him. Look, see the black paint on his hands?" I wiped sweat from my brow, then added in a near whisper. "He was one of the biggest jerks I'd ever met, but he didn't deserve this."

She started to touch his neck, but stopped short. "He's dead, Cooper."

I swung around and pointed my light back to the man on the ground. He shifted ever so slightly, and I didn't waste any time rushing to his side.

"It's Rashad!"

Willow gasped. "Are you kidding me?".

Rashad's eyes were nothing more than tiny slits. His lips, cracked and coated in dried blood, were moving. He was alive.

"Arms and legs are all bolted to the floor with these metal cuffs." Willow covered her mouth for a second, then said, "Oh my God. His hands."

I moved the cone of light down by his side. Most of his fingers looked like burned candle stubs.

"Need to get him to the hospital." I handed Willow my phone and started kicking at the metal cuff holding his left wrist. "Fucking thing won't budge. "We need tools or... Call Courtney, then dial 9-1-1."

I used the butt of my shoe to kick the metal cuff from a different angle.

"Crap. Can't get a signal down here. Back in a second." She ran across the room and up the steps, leaving me in near darkness.

"That shriveled-up man is all but dead," Hick Man said. "Get me out of here. I'm the only one of us four worth saving."

Four?

Just then, Rashad uttered words, although I couldn't understand them. I leaned closer. "We'll get you out of here, Rashad. Just hang on a few more minutes." I turned and hollered toward the opening. "Willow, do you have an ETA on the first responders?"

She didn't reply. Probably couldn't hear me from this bunker.

Rashad mumbled again.

"Are you trying to say something to me?"

"A-qua-man."

I blinked and replayed what he'd said. He had to be delusional by now. "Rashad, please stay with me. It'll be okay. Just hang on. I won't leave you."

"A-qua-man." He nudged his head to the left. Was he pointing at something? I turned and followed the direction of his gesture. I saw the outline of some type of structure.

Four. Hick Man had said there were four people in this room. "Hold on a second, Rashad."

With my hands out in front of me, I walked toward the faint structure. My feet ran into a large bucket, and then I saw a man lying on a table angled so that his head was lower than the rest of his body. He wasn't moving. I reached out and felt a wet towel. It was covering his face. Then I glanced up to see a spout attached to a hose that snaked into the dark ceiling.

Was this some type of waterboarding gizmo?

I quickly pulled off the towel, tossing it to the side. Not able to see his eyes, I nudged his shoulder. "Can you hear me?"

"Don't you fucking listen?" Hick Man snapped. "I tried telling you, they're all dead. Well, everyone except that one guy on the ground. But he might as well be. Now get your ass over here and free me from these shackles."

I ignored the asshole and went back to Rashad's side. "Rashad, are you still with me?"

I shifted to within inches of his face. Nothing moved. I put my fingers on the side of his neck. It was scaly, but I thought I felt a weak pulse.

"Willow!" I shouted over my shoulder.

No response. I considered quickly running upstairs, but Rashad groaned again. "Hey, I've talked to Kina and Jamaal. They love you and can't wait to see you." I prayed he could hear me, even if I was fudging the truth a bit. His kids hadn't actually said that, but it was the feeling I ultimately got from them.

"Rashad?" I nudged his arm.

He mumbled again.

"What is it, Rashad?"

I heard footfalls on the steps behind me, but I stayed close to his ear. He uttered five words. It took me a frozen second to connect the dots. But when I did, those five words made my heart leap into the back of my throat.

"Cooper." It was a meek Willow from behind me.

I turned around, and my throat clamped shut. The beam of light from Willow's phone shined upward, providing an ominous picture of Professor Becnel holding a pistol to the side of her head.

"Why did you do this, Cooper…if that's really your name?" Becnel asked.

Willow's whole body was clenched so hard I thought she might burst. Her eyes darted around like a bird's. Becnel was trembling, including his gun hand, but I couldn't pin down what emotion was driving it.

"Marcus, we just want to help our friend Rashad."

He snapped off a laugh that bounced off the walls of this dungeon-like room. "Friends?" he exclaimed, smiling so widely his glasses slid down his nose. He pushed them up with his gun hand and continued. "Rashad Hatley has no friends. He's a bitter, angry, mean person who's filled with nothing but hate. Just like the other subjects in this room and, unfortunately, far too many people in our society."

I was trying to assess this guy's sanity. His thoughts made sense, so why wasn't he writing books and appearing on talk shows and podcasts instead of kidnapping and killing people? "Marcus, no one is perfect. We all—"

"Are you fucking kidding me? That's like saying a pool of water is the same size as the Gulf of Mexico."

I'd started to inch toward him and Willow, but I stopped. Clearly, I'd pissed him off. *Stupid move, Cooper.*

"Quit offering excuses for the most egregious offenders against society. They hate people for one reason. You want to know why?"

"Why, Marcus?" I dialed back my intensity as much as possible, even as my heart did a drum roll against my chest.

"F-E-A-R. Fear. That's why most people hate. They're full of fear. No one likes to admit they're fearful, and they sure as hell don't have the mental capacity or emotional maturity to work through those thoughts to understand that their hate, their fear, is usually baseless. Everyone is just too fucking consumed with one-upping the next person. They're a bunch of frightened sheep. I used to think it was sad. But I had to learn more. I had to dig deeper. I had to find the right set of subjects in order to perform the proper tests on them."

"Tests? To test what?" My tone was one of annoyance. My patience with crazy people had reached its limit.

Willow's eyes darted from me to the doctor.

"To push them beyond what they can comprehend. To make them see what true fear is all about. And if any one of them should survive, to see if it would truly change their outlook going forward."

"That's not a test; that's a punishment. You were the fucking judge, jury, and executioner. What gives you that right?"

He shook Willow's shoulder while pressing the barrel of the gun even harder into her head. The cone of light flickered across their faces and the ceiling. It was like watching a black-and-white film with spasms of jump cuts.

"Stop, stop, stop!" I pleaded.

Willow screamed. Hick Man hollered some nonsense. And then Becnel shouted above all of us. "Quiet! You will not sit there and be the arbiter of my character. I don't give you that power."

"But why Rashad? And how do you know Jada?" I asked.

"Jada." He wiped his brow and considered the name. "We met at a conference. She was a troubled woman who, amazingly, didn't have the personal tools to see her own troubles, let alone know how to deal with those in her family. I could see that Rashad was a perfect subject. So, I was patient with Jada, shared my thoughts and theories with her. Eventually, she came around, just like I knew she would. But you know what's funny? I thought Rashad would give up and just die. But he's held out the longest. Kudos to him. Maybe he does have a future."

"Then you'll let him go?"

"Not right now. He'll first need to watch you and Willow suffer until you feel the greatest fear of your lives. It will be enjoyable to try out my methods on a nice, loving couple."

"We're not married," Willow said with some attitude. "We only said that to fool you."

He shrugged. "It matters not. You've given me something very exciting to execute."

I saw a shadow from the top of the steps. "Are you looking forward to going to jail?" I motioned with my head, and he turned around. That's when I rushed him. I grabbed his gun hand, but I stepped on Willow's foot and turned my ankle. I lost my grip, but not my willpower. I lifted up just as he rammed the butt of the gun into the back of my head. I wasn't sure if I saw the flickering phone light or stars. Still, I kept myself from dropping to the floor.

I let out a roar, twirled around him, stuck my arm under his shoulder, and tried to reach his gun with my free hand.

"Hey!" Willow shouted.

Marcus looked right at her, and she fired a straight punch heading right for his nose. He ducked, and she clocked my jaw.

"Ah, crap!" She shook her hand as I felt something metallic floating in my mouth, my head throbbing like a strobe light.

A bullet fired—I must have jumped ten feet in the air, then landed unforgivingly on the concrete floor on my hands and knees. Willow was right next to me. I looked toward the steps.

"You two misfits need to back the fuck away from my husband." Nancy was standing at the bottom of the staircase, aiming a rifle at us.

"Dear, be careful with the weapon." Marcus picked up his glasses.

"Shut up, Marcus. You're too damn gullible. I knew these two were no good. We should just put a bullet in their heads and be done with it."

"What are you talking about? We've stumbled into a plethora of riches. More test cases, and I didn't even have to go out in my van."

The van. Based upon that and the witness who saw a plumbing van pull out of Myron Little's driveway, Marcus had to be the plumber. He must have used a similar MO to kidnap all of his so-called subjects. But my thoughts went to Rashad. I hoped he was still clinging to life. I knew Kina and Jamaal would be devastated if he died. Would they even know? The Becnels could kill us, lock us in their dungeon, and the world would never know after they ditched Willow's car.

"I told you to shut up!" Nancy said.

He practically shriveled into a standing fetal position.

She lifted the rifle to her eye.

Marcus raised a hand toward her.

"Don't touch me, and don't say a word. Do you understand?"

"Yes, Nancy." He lowered his head like a little kid who'd just been denied his dessert.

"Hey, you might want to look over your shoulder," Willow said.

"Ha! I'm not my naïve husband. Get ready to meet your maker, Willow."

"You mean her money-maker?" I went with a joke—I'd tracked Willow's eyes, and I needed to waste more time.

Not surprisingly, Nancy didn't smile. But her brow furrowed like cooked bacon.

"I realize now's not the perfect moment to profess my love of Willow's ass, but sometimes a man gets certain urges. Impossible to predict," I said with my palms turned to the ceiling.

Nancy shook her head while glancing at Willow. "Is he for real?"

"Actually, he forgot take his meds. Multiple personalities. Which one you get, no one knows."

"He's crazy, and I think you're missing a couple of screws yourself."

"Can I fix you a screwdriver?" I asked.

"Huh?" She cocked her head back in disbelief.

Willow said, "Sometimes he thinks he's a bartender. Just roll with it."

"You're both fucking crazy. The world will be a better place once the two of you are dead. And best of all, no one will ever find you." Her throaty laugh shook my chest. It was bone-chilling.

Marcus started to turn his head toward the stairs. Crap!

"Hey, Marcus…" I snapped my fingers.

He did a quick double-take on me.

"Did I tell you that I once was beaten up as a kid?"

"What…?"

There was a creak from the staircase. Marcus jerked his head around and yelled, "Look out!" He jumped behind his wife as a bullet was fired from the staircase. He fell to the ground, grabbing at his shoulder where blood spurted like an oil blowout.

I heard a cackle, and I looked to my right. Nancy was aiming her gun at my chest. Out of nowhere, Willow's foot kicked the barrel of the gun, ricocheting the butt off of Nancy's head.

"I hated your fucking apple pie!" Willow screamed as she kicked the rifle away.

A second later, Courtney made it to the bottom of the steps, followed by two DPD officers. They grabbed the weapons, and she jumped into my arms.

"Thank God you're okay."

Fifty-Seven

Cooper

I handed Courtney a tissue, and she dotted her moist eyes.

"Thank you, Cooper. You're really one of the good guys."

I knew that was still up for debate, but it was nice to feel appreciated. Courtney and I were on our second official date. Subway sandwiches. She'd picked the place because she knew they carried Orange Crush.

She had me at hello, or at least *hello, Orange Crush*.

"Is that the only reason you're upset?"

She'd just told me about her experience at the funeral service for Dante Chilton. His mother and other family members had broken down in the church. Paramedics were called because they couldn't calm Dante's mother down. She would be okay, but the incident had only added to the gut-wrenching anxiety.

She sighed and looked me in the eye. "Did I tell you we ID'd Aquaman?"

She'd actually told me over the phone the previous day at the same time she'd asked me out on this lunch date. But I could sense she was carrying a heavy heart, so I just rolled with it.

"I don't think so. What's his name?"

"Edwardo Delatorre. It was his face on that video in Deep Ellum. He was the one who was injected with a sedative by Becnel and tossed into the plumbing van to become Becnel's second so-called subject."

I nodded.

"I already told you this, didn't I?"

I gave her a half-shrug. "Maybe."

"But I do have more, and it started with those five words that Rashad told you?"

"'Aquaman said boy's a snitch,'" I repeated.

"Well, as you now know, we found DNA that connects Delatorre to the murder of Dante." She took a hard swallow, but kept going. "But we kept digging on Delatorre. Turns out he was wanted by Interpol. He's carried out several hits across the globe."

"For whom?"

"Ever the writer," she said, sipping from her can of Diet Coke. "To answer your question, it's whoever pays the most. Drug lords, shadow governments in small countries, rich people who have a vendetta. So far, they've connected him to ten assassinations, using various aliases. There could be more."

"I don't get it. Why a thirteen-year-old boy in Dallas?"

"It connects to the word that Delatorre had begun to carve into Dante's chest. The S and N are the first two letters of 'snitch'—we figured that out when you told us what Rashad had said. We learned that Dante had been running drugs on the street when he became alarmed at what was going on, so he apparently told a beat cop. The cop got busy or didn't take the kid seriously. Either way, he never followed up on it."

More tears pooled.

"You can wait and tell me another day."

"No. No, I need…I want to share everything. Just get it all out." She blotted her eyes and continued. "Delattore was most likely hired by the people who are running this new heroin operation that's hit the Dallas area."

"A professional to take out a kid?"

"The investigation is ongoing. FBI and DEA are both heavily involved, putting me on the outside looking in. But they believe Delatorre was brought in for another job. They just don't know what. Not yet, anyway."

I tried to veer the subject away from Dante. "Rashad is still in the hospital after a week, but he's getting better every day. He loves having his kids around him."

"I'm really happy for him and his kids. Jada won't be so lucky. She'll probably serve time on a kidnapping conspiracy charge. She's been very remorseful, but they all are once they're caught."

I could understand her skepticism.

We talked about the latest movies that we each wanted to see but never had time for and even the weather. Then the conversation burned out. We got up to leave. Once we reached our cars, I was ready for a quick goodbye hug, but Courtney's embrace was not short or subtle. I didn't pull back—I wasn't sure I had the strength to pull her off. Then I heard a sniffle.

"What's wrong?" I moved the hair out of her face.

"It's more than Dante," she said tearfully.

"What do you mean?"

She rested her forehead on my chest for a second, then looked up at me. "My sister was fourteen—just a year older than Dante—when she was kidnapped."

She'd told me about this a few weeks ago. But I thought her sister had been murdered. Or was this another sister? I didn't pry. I just waited and listened.

Her eyes stared at nothing for a second. "They found her body in a shallow grave weeks later. ME's believed she was buried alive."

"Jesus."

"I prayed a lot for those three weeks. And then I cursed the universe after they found her body. I couldn't understand why. I still don't, but I've learned how to deal with it. This Dante Chilton murder brought back those memories for some reason. The age, maybe. Her death is why I got into this business. I guess I secretly keep hoping there's some magical way I can bring her back to life."

I took her in my arms and held her. We rocked back and forth for what seemed like ten minutes. She patted my back. "Gotta run. And I know you do too."

I'd told her I was going out of town, that I needed to visit family. Another partial truth. *Damn, I have issues.*

She gave me a quick kiss on the lips, and I said I'd call her once I was back in town.

I drove off with my nerves already jangled, and my plane wasn't even supposed to depart for another three hours.

Fifty-Eight

Willow

Ma gave Briana a hug before she left. I thanked Ma at the door.

"No big deal. It was nice not talking to a blank wall for a change."

"Maybe you can come over and visit soon," I said for some unknown reason.

"Yep. Sure. I'll call you," she said with a wave over her shoulder.

She was as warm as ever.

I shut the door and Briana brought in a bag of personal items she could take with her to the detox facility. She asked if I could brush her hair before we left.

"My mom used to brush my hair when I was younger. It helped calm me."

"Glad to do it," I said.

She didn't talk much at first, but I could feel her shoulders relax.

"Thank you for letting me stay here with you."

"You're welcome."

"You didn't have to do that. I'm already feeling better, but I know I need tools for dealing with my addiction."

"I'm proud of you, Briana."

"Let's wait for a month before you give me an award. But I really just want to see my kids, to raise them myself, and to love on them every day."

She really seemed determined. I was hopeful.

I counted out one hundred strokes and then started to put her hair into a ponytail. My eyes snagged something odd, and I held up her hair. I saw what looked like a recent incision on the back of her neck. Had she harmed herself? I had to ask.

"Briana…"

"You saw it, didn't you?"

I reached for the wound, but my finger stopped before I touched the skin. "How did this happen?" I tried to keep my voice calm and casual. I didn't want her to get upset moments before I was supposed to drop her off at the detox facility.

She released a sigh. "If I tell you, you can't tell anyone, okay?"

I paused a moment.

"You have to tell me you won't tell anyone." She already sounded agitated.

"Okay, sure, Briana. Just between you and me."

"The man who I said tried to kidnap me is…well, was kind of my boyfriend." Her head dipped for a moment. "Actually, I hate using that term. He used me for sex because he knew I needed his drugs."

She reached a hand toward her eye, but she kept her emotions at bay. For now.

"He was your dealer?"

"Yes and no. I met him through my regular dealer."

I was confused. "Was he a user, another customer of your dealer?"

"Oh, no. He never used. Said he had to keep a clear mind."

"How did he have access to the heroin?"

She wiped a hand across her face. "I think he pretty much runs the whole operation. Can't say for sure. He wouldn't talk about it much. And I was so out of it most of the time I didn't care to know."

Briana had valuable information to share with the police, who I knew were desperate to find the people behind this new heroin operation. But I'd promised her I would keep it between us. I glanced at the wound again.

"What about this cut?"

"Actually, I'm not entirely sure. That last night with him was kind of a blur. When I try to recall it, I only remember flashes, and it's…" Her voice faded with a weak quiver.

I could sense fatigue and stress setting in, the kind that goes with sharing parts of your life that are painful and uncomfortable. She would undoubtedly go through this process a lot over the next several weeks. I had to remember that getting her into rehab and getting her healthy were the most important things right now.

"You don't have to tell me, Briana." I used a rubber band to tie her hair back, then stood. "You want any water to drink before we go?"

She shook her head and then lifted to her feet, wrapping her arms around my neck. "I won't forget what you've done for me, for my kids. I won't fuck this up. I'll stay in rehab and get clean."

I dropped her off at the facility and felt something I hadn't felt in a while: hope.

Fifty-Nine

Willow

I ran my eyes across Cooper's bed where a tangled mountain of clothes waited to be stuffed into his backpack.

"Is that the same backpack from college?" I asked.

"Maybe."

Mr. Elusive. Or was it Mr. Cheapo?

"I pack light. Low maintenance is my theme."

"You don't own any luggage. That's what you're saying."

He went into the bathroom to grab his toiletry bag.

I started to fold his clothes. "Are you going to take your swimsuit?" I came across a pair of his boxers.

"Why would I need a suit?" He snatched the boxers out of my hand and tossed them on the bed. Then, in the most unorderly way imaginable, he began to shove his clothes into his backpack.

"Hello? You're going to Miami. You might want to take Lauren to the beach."

He lifted up and gave me a vacant stare. "That's what normal families do. I'm just trying to get her to talk to me…hoping she'll let me in her life again." He swallowed hard and then went back to stuffing his bag.

I spotted white paint on his fingertips. “I didn’t even notice, but I guess you painted over the swastikas on the garage?”

“Sure did. Mrs. Kowalski got back a couple days ago, and she was pretty upset by everything that had happened, including Becnel killing Myron Little. She offered to pay me for the work, but I couldn’t take the money. Painting over those hate-filled symbols was the least I could do.”

I sighed. “Yeah, I wish it was that easy to cover up all the hate out there. Becnel had the right idea about fear being the root cause of hate.”

“Somewhere along the way, though, he went off the deep end. Way off.”

“And so did his wife.”

“Maybe they can have connecting cells in prison,” he said.

“I don’t think they allow that, and something tells me they’re not eager to reconnect their marriage.”

“Speaking of reconnecting, have you seen your dad recently?” he asked.

“Got a text from him last night. Said he was leaving town on business, but that he looked forward to doing fun things together when he got back.”

“Fun things?”

I shook my head and wiped an eye. “He’s acting like everything is normal.”

“Maybe the new normal.”

“He’s oblivious, Cooper. Seriously, he mentioned going to a museum or a musical. Said he could get us great seats.”

“Wish I had that kind of money to help me win over Lauren.”

“You know it’s not about money.”

“Wouldn’t hurt, though.”

I recalled our last group conversation under the steps by my apartment. “Dad still hasn’t told us about his connection to Dr. V and the Sack Brothers. Until he does that, I'm not even going to consider trying to make this father/daughter thing work."

"I couldn't agree more."

"I was just waiting for your endorsement." I gave him a wry grin and then punched his shoulder. Softly. My knuckles even lingered there an extra moment, as if they had a mind of their own.

"You're full of sass today. Even more than usual."

"What can I say, you're rubbing off on me."

He leaned over and grabbed his Kindle off his side table, then turned right into me. We were face to face. Actually, body to body. We gazed into each other's eyes long enough for my heart to release a thump so prominent I thought he might feel it in his chest. Just as quickly, we both turned away, and he stuffed his Kindle in the front pocket of his backpack.

Part of me wanted to address "us." I'd been wanting to share some things about Harvey and me, and I felt compelled to tell Cooper before he ran off to Miami. Why the urgency? I couldn't pinpoint it. Still, I knew he'd just gotten back from his second date with Courtney. He hadn't said a negative word about her or the date, so maybe it was best to leave it alone and move on.

He glanced at his phone. "We still have a few minutes. Want a drink?" he asked on his way to the kitchen.

"Don't tell me…it's either water or Orange Crush." I walked into the kitchen, and he gave me a little-boy grin.

"Only the best, baby."

"Don't baby me," I said with a smirk. "Just give me a water."

"Please?"

"Please."

We sat on his couch, and he propped his feet on an old chest, his makeshift coffee table.

"I dropped by the hospital and talked to Rashad yesterday. Said he wants to tell me his whole story. He knows he needs a lot of therapy, but this would be a good start. Said he wouldn't hold anything back. He's eager to feel better, rebuild his life and his confidence, and start a new life with Kina and Jamaal."

"That's cool, Cooper. I look forward to reading your story."

He winked and tipped his head back to drink from his bottle of soda.

"Kina and Jamaal probably have a lot of mixed emotions right now, since their mother was involved in hurting their dad," I said, then sipped on my glass of water.

"Kina quit school and is going to rehab."

"Good for her. That addictive gene was apparently passed along from father to daughter."

"The other gene, the incredible athletic talent, went to Jamaal."

"Are you going to follow through with setting up this point-shaving deal with him and Ishaan?" I asked.

He sat on the edge of the couch, leaning on his knees. "I'm not sure I have much choice."

"You could tell Courtney."

"We've been down this path, Will. Dr. V could get to us and hurt you. I can't let that happen." He sounded protective, but also kind. "Speaking of evil doctors, how's it going with Dr. Mulligan?"

I could feel a grin coming to my face.

He tilted his head.

"Stacy apparently caught our last confrontation on her phone."

"Oh yeah?"

"Video and audio. He thought he had something on me because I took Briana home. I bent the rules, but I did so because I care. He cares about no one."

"Glad Stacy's working for the good guys, or gals, as the case may be."

"It gets better. She showed it to Joan, the director, and Joan fired Dr. Mulligan on the spot."

I gave her a wink. "That's one less bad person in your life. Things are looking up."

I reached over and squeezed his knee. He squirmed like a little boy.

"I bet you were antsy as a kid when sitting in church."

"I had a bony butt, what can I say? Damn church pews were wooden and had no cushion. So, yes, I was a little antsy."

"You just said 'damn' and 'church' in the same sentence. Not sure Doris would approve," I said.

"My mom is a saint, even if she does turn a blind eye on occasion."

"Continuing on the theme of blindness, has Benjamin given up nagging you about that job at GOAT?"

"He's given me another extension. I was thinking that maybe I should give it a shot. Making big money isn't a bad thing, even if I don't think I'm right for the job."

"So, you're going to take it?"

He twisted his lips. "I'll think about it more on the trip." He took our drinks into the kitchen, then turned and clapped his hands. "Okay, I think it's time."

"You sure you don't want me to go?" I asked.

He ran his fingers through his hair, then walked over and picked up his backpack. "I think I need to do this on my own. It's time I step up and not shy away from the tough stuff. Plus, I'm sure Harvey would get jealous."

We started walking toward his door.

"He's not allowed to get jealous," I said.

"Huh?"

He stopped the moment I put my hand on the doorknob.

I took a breath, unsure if I was ready to go down this path.

"You can tell me anything, Will. I won't judge. At least not to your face."

I smiled. He always made me laugh, even if I was, at times, laughing at him. "Oh, Cooper."

I peered into his eyes. Neither of us looked away. Our faces were blank, but the energy between us was enough to power a city. I put a hand on his chest and squeezed.

There was a knock on the door.

We both smiled and said in unison, "Mrs. Kowalksi."

Cooper opened the door. His backpack slid off his shoulder.

"Lauren," he said as if all air had been sucked from his lungs.

"Hi." She gave a round wave and tried to smile, but it wasn't really filled with joy. She looked awkward. Then her eyes found me.

"Hi there." I took a side glance at Cooper, and what I saw shocked me. His stubbly face had turned pink. I'd never seen him so emotionally vulnerable.

"I'm sorry. I think I interrupted something," Lauren said.

"Oh, no. It's fine. I'm happy you're here." Cooper reached a hand out to her, but he flinched when a woman jumped right behind Lauren.

"Hello, Cooper. Happy to see your ex-wife, too?"

Dear Reader,

Are you still feeling the internal reverberations? So much took place in that book...some of it painfully obvious, some of it lurking under the surface.

Willow and Cooper, though, clearly, have some unfinished business. Or, really is it their side business that will doom their fate?

Book 3 awakens demons from the past, sending our pair of unlikely crime fighters on this mission to find the truth. But will this kind of truth get them killed?

For reasons you'll soon learn, different people can't afford the truth to come out. Is there enough faith in each other for Willow and Cooper to turn over the right rocks and not get bitten?

While Willow and Cooper have their moments of wit and sarcasm, it's a fight for survival on so many levels.

Pick up *BURY* and enjoy the next Ball & Chain thriller!

Best,

John

John W. Mefford Bibliography

The Ball & Chain Thrillers

MERCY (Book 1)

FEAR (Book 2)

BURY (Book 3)

Redemption Thriller Series (24-book series)

The Alex Troutt Thrillers

AT Bay (RTS #1)

AT Large (RTS #2)

AT Once (RTS #3)

AT Dawn (RTS #4)

AT Dusk (RTS #5)

AT Last (RTS #6)

The Ivy Nash Thrillers

IN Defiance (RTS #7)

IN Pursuit (RTS #8)

IN Doubt (RTS #9)

Break IN (RTS #10)

IN Control (RTS #11)

IN The End (RTS #12)

The Ozzie Novak Thrillers

ON Edge (RTS #13)

Game ON (RTS #14)

ON The Rocks (RTS #15)

Shame ON You (RTS #16)

ON Fire (RTS #17)

ON The Run (RTS #18)

The Alex Troutt Thrillers

AT Stake (RTS #19)

AT Any Cost (RTS #20)

Back AT You (RTS #21)

AT Every Turn (RTS #22)

AT Death's Door (RTS #23)

AT Full Tilt (RTS #24)

Other Thriller Series

The Booker Series

BOOKER – Streets of Mayhem (Volume 1)

BOOKER – Tap That (Volume 2)

BOOKER – Hate City (Volume 3)

BOOKER – Blood Ring (Volume 4)

BOOKER – No Más (Volume 5)

BOOKER – Dead Heat (Volume 6)

The Greed Series

FATAL GREED (Greed Series #1)

LETHAL GREED (Greed Series #2)

WICKED GREED (Greed Series #3)

GREED MANIFESTO (Greed Series #4)

To stay updated on John's latest releases, visit:
JohnWMefford.com

Made in the USA
Columbia, SC
15 October 2020